. . . and for her previous Jackie Flowers novels

Extreme Indifference

"[It] will keep you turning the pages."
—*The Denver Post*

"A tight, well-written thriller with an ending that caught me completely off-balance."
—Les Roberts, *Cleveland Plain Dealer*

"[P]oses some intriguing legal questions and finds some surprising answers."
—Kathy Reichs, author of *Monday Morning*

Blind Spot

"In a land populated with disaffected lawyers who drink too much and fight with their ex-spouses, [Flowers] is a refreshing new hero."
—Stephen White, author of *The Best Revenge*

"Jackie Flowers [is] the law profession's answer to Kinsey Millhone."
—*Publishers Weekly*

"A new, exciting author has come on the scene with a fresh voice."
—*The Midwest Book Review*

SEEDS OF DOUBT

STEPHANIE KANE

POCKET BOOKS

NEW YORK   LONDON   TORONTO   SYDNEY

This book is a work of fiction. Names, characters, places and incidents are products of the author's imagination or are used fictitiously. Any resemblance to actual events or locales or persons, living or dead, is entirely coincidental.

 POCKET BOOKS, a division of Simon & Schuster, Inc.
1230 Avenue of the Americas, New York, NY 10020

Copyright © 2004 by Stephanie Kane

Previously published in hardcover in 2004 by Scribner

ISBN-13: 978-0-7434-6682-0
ISBN-10: 0-7434-6682-9

This Pocket Books paperback edition November 2005

10 9 8 7 6 5 4 3 2 1

POCKET and colophon are registered trademarks of Simon & Schuster, Inc.

Cover design by Jae Song
Cover photo by Lee Atherton/Superstock

Manufactured in the United States of America

For information regarding special discounts for bulk purchases, please contact Simon & Schuster Special Sales at 1-800-456-6798 or business@simonandschuster.com.

To the memory of Jed Mattes

ACKNOWLEDGMENTS

My thanks to Susanne Kirk, Jimmy Vines, Leslie Hoffman, Mary Ann Kane, Susan Brienza, Mike McPhee, Joe Saint Veltri, Dr. Jane Bock, Dr. David Norris, Colonel (Ret.) Billie E. Thornton, Barbara Gibson

And as always, John

"Our animals were more or less injured at first, and almost every steer gives them one trial, but hardly ever a second one; they remember the pain, and they keep at a safe distance thereafter."

—*American Agriculturist,* February 1880

SEEDS OF DOUBT

May 1973

"Y ou wanna see it, don't you?"

Gravel pierced his sandals as he struggled to keep up.
"Slowpoke."

A dusty wind fanned purple flowers in the field. They
passed a trailer with a chicken-wire hutch. He saw the
rabbits prick up their ears.

"Sissy."

The sun was hot and his mouth tasted like dirt. The
footsteps he was following got longer. They'd left the others in the shade of the park.

"Change your mind?"

He'd never go there alone, he'd get spanked if he got
caught. But he wasn't alone. So it was okay, wasn't it?

"Then hurry up!"

He stumbled but kept on his feet. Now they were
trotting, and the only sound was trucks whipping by on the
interstate past the railroad tracks. When the footsteps
came to a stop he almost fell. He looked up and saw twin
flashes of silver.

Arrows with gleaming tips pointed straight at the sky.

Rocket ships.

"Go on, you can touch them."

He took a step forward and ran his fingers over the
ribbed metal. Slowly he circled the huge bins that guarded
the windowless tower. It was cooler here in the shadows;
the highway was in another world and he stopped thinking
about what would happen if he got caught.

The tower was so tall he couldn't see the top. Braided wire thick as rope tied the ships to the ground. Ducts and chutes, an upside-down funnel big enough to swallow and spit him out whole—

He felt a warm breath at the back of his neck.

"Pretty neat, huh?"

From where he was standing, the highway and the railroad tracks were gone. Even the town had disappeared. How would they look from the tower? High above the bins stood a catwalk with a small platform.

"What are you waiting for?"

Metal bars hugged the wall with nails for handholds. The ladder was too steep, but he wanted to *see*—

"I knew you were too little."

He stepped onto the first rung, sandal slipping on the greasy metal.

"I'm right behind you."

He'd really catch it if his mom— A gentle push made him reach for the handhold.

Slowly he began to climb.

"Go on . . ."

Driven by soft grunts behind him and the creak of heavier feet on the rungs, he kept climbing. After five steps his arms were shaking and his fingers cramped. Halfway up the ladder his trousers caught something sharp. He heard them tear.

"Not gonna stop now, are you?"

He'd show *them*.

When he reached the catwalk his legs were jerking so badly he couldn't stand. Dropping to his knees at the platform's edge, he shut his eyes.

"Well, go ahead. Take a look."

The four-wheelers on the interstate were the size of his red truck, the railroad tracks no bigger than the ones in the train set his brother got for Christmas. On the other side the ground was patched like a quilt, one piece brown and flat and the next ribbons of green. A gust of wind parted the grass and ran through the field like a comb.

"Wanna see something else?"

A flash. Something flat and shiny, with a—

He grabbed, but it was snatched back.

"Come and get it!"

Now it was above his head. He reached up with both hands only to have it pulled away. He was hot and he was out of breath, and suddenly he was too tired to play.

"What do you think you're doing?"

"Wanna go home . . ." The whiny voice was his.

"I knew you were a baby."

He made himself stand.

"Pull them down."

The giggle added to his confusion.

"I said, take them off!"

A smile, but this was no longer fun.

"Do it *now*."

He stepped back and bumped the railing. He felt a warm surge.

"Don't be a baby. It's just a game."

Pee rolled down the inside of his leg.

"Not a fraidy-cat, are you?"

He could hear the trucks on the highway.

"Do it."

The eyes shined like black buttons. His heel touched the platform's edge.

"Do it *now*."

The voice was scarier than the eyes. Metal flashed. Then his sandal slipped. He tried to grab the railing. His feet went out from under him. It was too late.

All he could hear was his own scream.

One

You were the chief investigator at the scene of the accident?"

Seated at the defense table, Jackie Flowers kept her voice low. Courtroom 12 was as tight as a shoe box and the jurors were so close they could have heard Assistant District Attorney Tom Tuttle break wind.

"Objection!"

Tuttle sprang to his feet and two jurors winced.

"This is a manslaughter case," Tuttle said, oblivious to the judge's pained expression as his words echoed in the airless room. The walnut slats covering the wall behind the bench made Jackie feel as if she were trapped inside a pipe organ. "'Accident' is hardly appropriate in view of the fact that Ms. Flowers's client *decapitated*—"

"My client has already sworn under oath, and he intends to repeat that testimony in this court"—gracefully rising, Jackie caught the same two jurors, now joined by a third, gazing at her client with renewed interest—"that he secured his trailer to his pickup truck with a steel bolt and chains. It came unhitched and sailed across the median into oncoming traffic. That sounds like an accident to me."

"Overruled," the judge said. "If this were a murder case, Mr. Tuttle, you wouldn't be assigned to it."

Jackie strode to center stage.

Accident. Focus the jury on the accident, not her client. Or, God forbid, the victim. In her cobalt suit and two-inch alligator heels she stood eye to eye with the seated witness. Positioning herself directly between him and the jury box, she hooked a honey blond curl behind her ear and softly continued.

"What was the condition of the road?"

"Irregular."

"Help us out, Officer. Don't you mean washboard?"

"I guess."

"And you were able to ascertain the exact section of that washboard asphalt where my client's trailer came unhitched?"

Damned if he did, damned if he didn't. Admit Jackie's client hit a three-foot pothole, or pretend he didn't know where to look for that wire and bolt? The biggest mistake most cops made was getting in a pissing match with the lawyer instead of focusing on the jury. The witness looked helplessly at the DA and Jackie smiled. With every eye in the courtroom on her, she could afford to be generous.

"You told this jury your job was to examine the highway for evidence that the hitch was or wasn't bolted. What precisely were you looking for?"

"Metal bolt and piece of wire." Sweat prickled his upper lip.

"What did you find?"

"Bottles, cans, rubber. You name it." The officer gave a weak laugh and tried to look past Jackie at the jury. "Some people think I-25's their personal dump site."

"How high are the weeds at the side of the road? Eighteen inches?"

"Thereabouts."

"So you used a metal detector."

"Well, no."

She took a step closer. "Get your uniform dirty?"

"Beg pardon?"

Now she was leaning over the witness stand.

"When you got down on your hands and knees on

the shoulder of I-25 and dug through all those weeds and trash looking for a three-inch scrap of wire and a sheared-off steel bolt!"

"I—"

"No further questions, Your Honor."

Tuttle and his two assistants fled through the door behind the bench as soon as the gavel dropped. Jackie watched her client being manacled and led off by a deputy laden with chains, pepper spray, stun gun—enough junk to stock a militiaman's RadioShack. Until he hit that pothole, he'd been just another carpenter on his way to work. Albeit one with two previous DUIs to his credit. Shaking her head, she took her time packing her briefcase with the blank legal pads and unopened Rules of Criminal Procedure that were her stock-in-trade. When the courtroom finally cleared she left.

On this first Monday in April, the fourth-floor corridor of Denver's City and County Building was a cacophony of wailing babies, bleating walkie-talkies and screeching cell phones. The marble pillars and terrazzo floors made the clattering heels of hookers and their higher-priced attorneys audible from the far end of the hall, and a tide of shackled prisoners whose color-coded scrubs denoted their presumed level of culpability streamed from the sheriff's private elevator. Jackie stood aside for a trio of women in washed-out olive and pea-green jumpsuits destined for drug court.

"We'll knock it down from manslaughter to neg homicide."

It had taken ADA Tom Tuttle eight minutes to recognize his case was going down after his chief witness bailed out. Record time.

"The only negligence is your office going to trial with this case."

"Come on, Jackie." He was trying not to beg. "What choice did we have? Sixteen-year-old honor student driving down I-25 in a brand-new Mustang, minding his own business—"

"That cop never even looked for a bolt, and you know it."

"Your client's been busted twice for drunk driving."

"Not this time, he wasn't. The most we'll consider is careless."

"Careless driving?" A felon shuffling by in leg irons and Day-Glo orange turned to look, and Tuttle lowered his voice. "Duncan Pratt's not going to like that."

Since when did the Denver district attorney have to bless every plea?

"He'll like it more than an acquittal. When my guy takes the stand tomorrow all bets are off." Tired of waiting for the public elevator, Jackie started for the stairs.

"Hear about that six-year-old boy who's been reported missing out by the country club?" Tuttle was at her elbow. The marble staircase behind the elevator bank conferred an unwanted intimacy and she quickened her pace. "Another missing kid, right up your alley."

"Missing kid?"

"Didn't you defend that sleazebag accused in one case last year?"

Why did every DA take his brethren's defeats so personally?

"My client walked," she said. "And the alleged victim was a college coed, not a six-year-old boy."

"Maybe you'll be lucky enough to defend another innocent client."

"Keep filing on the wrong guys, and what do you expect?" She began counting the steps to the lobby. "So you've already made a bust?"

"He's only been missing since yesterday."

Not even long enough to file a missing person's report. DAs were all alike; they took it personally and they saw a pervert behind every bush.

"Maybe he ran away."

Tuttle's smile pitied her.

"How far can a six-year-old run?"

Jackie stepped through the City and County Building's majestic doors and into the sunlight. Standing with her adversary beneath the fifty-foot columns, she gazed down at beds of purple and yellow pansies whose festivity mocked the grim business within. Across Civic Center, the gold dome of the state capitol gleamed but clouds were massing to the north.

"You know how easy it is to lure a kid," Tuttle said before turning to go back in. "All it takes is something bright and shiny."

A little girl in a frilly dress. A man in a dark sedan easing to the curb and leaning out the window. A handsome man, with a snap-brim hat and an easy smile— Blinking away the memory of the public safety film shown so many years ago to her grade school class, Jackie started down the granite steps.

Since when did evil wear a snap-brim hat?

Two

Winter had given way to a streak of balmy days.

Crocuses had come and gone, crab apple blossoms were as dense as cotton bolls, and cherry trees had unsheathed their pink-tipped claws. But Denverites were not deceived. In true Front Range form, snow was forecast.

Rounding the corner onto her block after an early evening stroll to the nearby Botanic Gardens, Jackie waved absently at Einig. The papier-mâché Danish longshoreman camped on her neighbor's wooden swing seemed more stooped than usual. Permanently out of work, stranded in a landlocked state. Einig's slump seemed to mirror the postpartum depression that marked the end of every case for Jackie. Or was it the posture of her client's supposed victim, that headless kid in the shiny red Mustang convertible?

She showered while her soup was heating. Settling into a comfortable armchair, she wondered if she was at loose ends because the trial would end sooner than anticipated. Tuttle would undoubtedly cave the next morning, just before her client took the stand. She thought about calling her investigator, Pilar Perez, but Pilar would want to celebrate by barhopping with the sixty-year-old insurance adjuster she'd been dating.

It wasn't that she was *lonely*, Jackie told herself.

She hadn't had a roommate since college, and she loved the century-old Denver Square home in which she lived. The sturdy brick box with its hipped roof and dormers, the jutting front porch that spanned the facade, even the stupefied look created by the asymmetrical placement of the second-floor windows. Sitting in her den with its cream walls, oak molding and sumac rug, she reminded herself again that she enjoyed living alone, she enjoyed making her own decisions.

But tonight she was restless. Her eyes strayed to the window overlooking Lily's house next door.

Four years old when she was adopted from a Shanghai orphanage, and full of personality and complexity, Lily had been much more than Jackie's neighbors, Britt and Randy, had bargained for. *We didn't think she'd be so* old, Britt had confided to Jackie that first night. Having lost all her bottom teeth, Lily had already mastered the storm-cloud face that made you want to shoot her. She'd arrived in Denver fluent in Cantonese, the tongue of peasants. Had it been Mandarin, her new parents might even have encouraged her to speak it.

It was Jackie who'd straightened her bangs after Lily chopped them off to look like the American doll that Britt and Randy had given her on the plane. It was Jackie in whom she'd confided how it felt to be called Madame X, Jackie to whom she'd run after her classmates jeered when she ended the Pledge of Allegiance with "liberty and Jesus" for all. The tide had turned when she finally agreed to read English and Jackie helped her apply for her first library card. Now ten years old and going on thirty, and still too much for her parents to handle, Lily was half a continent away, at boarding school in Vermont. Jackie missed her terribly.

The phone rang as a spring storm's first fat flakes began to drift past Jackie's window.

"I hear you tore a cop a new one in court yesterday afternoon," a deep voice said.

Dennis Ross, her former lover. Pilar must have told him.

"Make you miss the old days?" Jackie said.

"Nothing like defending a pariah."

"Those three-button pirates you represent are no saints. How's life at Kippers & Hemp?"

"Kellogg & Kemp."

"You could go back to the public defender anytime you want."

They'd both cut their teeth there. And more. Why did hearing from Dennis always make her feel this way?

"On some things you can't turn back the clock," he said, and Jackie slammed the door on the memory of their last time in bed. Tried to slam it.

"How *is* life in the fast lane?" she said.

"Let me take you to dinner to celebrate, and you can find out."

Their unfinished business rankled, but Dennis had conveniently forgotten that. As of eight months earlier, when she'd last seen him, he'd worn the years well; his wavy hair had been threaded with silver and was still an inch too long for his hand-tailored suits, and his broad shoulders and trim physique gave no hint of his aversion to exercise in all but one form. Suddenly Jackie was hungry for more than soup.

"Still at the office? Don't tell me they make you earn those bucks."

"Give me ten minutes."

Dinner, and then what?

Misreading her hesitation, he pulled back. "I guess it is a little late."

"Actually, it's early. You're the one who never celebrates till the fat juror sings. Any fascinating con men wander into K&K today?"

"Matter of fact, an old client did stop by. Christopher Boyd." CEO of Frontier Banks, the largest bank holding company on the Front Range. "Since I walked that S&L

honcho a few years back, the executive committee thinks I'm an expert on banking law."

"Not your typical embezzler, then?"

Dennis didn't laugh. "Kellogg & Kemp prefers repeat business."

"Ah! Something else white-collar criminals and white-shoe firms have in common."

"Banks are far more civilized than Seventeenth Street lawyers, Jackie. Advancement's less cutthroat. It's a pyramid, not a ladder. You don't get to the top just by clawing over the back of the guy ahead of you."

Dennis's banter seemed mechanical. Now that he was head of litigation at Kellogg & Kemp, criminal defense was the smallest part of his practice. But a client was a client, and since when did Dennis Ross chitchat about any of his clients?

"So what was it today," she said, "a social call?"

"You heard about that missing six-year-old out by the country club?" The snow outside Jackie's window was swirling faster. "He's the son of Chris Boyd's gardener."

So this call wasn't entirely social. If and when the body was found, someone would need a first-rate defense lawyer.

"Boy's mom had a weekend shift," Dennis went on, "so his old man brought the kid to work. Boy was pissed because his folks wouldn't buy him a game. Pokémon, Nintendo, who the hell knows. Handsome little tyke."

"What's it got to do with your client?"

"The job where his old man brought him to work was at Chris Boyd's house."

Child molesters were nobody's favorite, but Dennis's former clients had done equal or worse. You didn't get to be the PD's top dog by being squeamish.

"It's early yet," she said. "And the country club is right

in town. Lots of places a kid could wander off. He'll show up." But she was thinking about that public safety flick they'd shown her third-grade class so long ago.

A girl in a frilly dress, a man in a dark sedan. *Wanna see a rabbit?*

The hat brim shaded the upper part of his face; you could see his mouth but not his eyes. The girl peered at him attentively—curious, like a rabbit herself. Uncertain whether to step closer or bolt. Would her curiosity overcome her? Jackie had wanted to shout *don't*, but she'd been riveted by the black-and-white images on the screen. The girl climbed into the car and it peeled off, tires squealing. Jackie had nightmares for weeks.

"Who's the last person the child was seen with?"

When Dennis answered, he sounded tired.

"Chris Boyd's sister."

A school yard ditty from decades past ran through Jackie's head.

Rachel Boyd took a knife . . .

With it came the image of another little girl. Not the one abducted by the man in the car. This one had bangs, cut straight across her forehead. She stared at Jackie with a chilling blankness in her round black eyes.

"Jackie, are you there?"

"I'll take a rain check on dinner, okay?" She hung up without waiting for Dennis's reply.

She would have that nightmare again tonight.

For the first time in thirty years.

Three

W ho's your exterminator?"
A bad way to start the day.

Pilar Perez cornered Jackie at the second-floor landing of her law office in the stone and brick Victorian on Denver's former Millionaire's Row. Jackie continued up the puckered Oriental runner, past the tiled terrarium in the window well and into her inner sanctum. Undaunted by her boss's grunt, her investigator followed with black coffee and the morning mail.

Just as Jackie had predicted, Tuttle had folded on the I-25 case first thing that morning, before her client took the stand. But Pilar's perkiness was particularly hard to take after a poor night of sleep, and reminding Jackie of her close encounter with yellow jackets three weeks earlier did little to endear Pilar to her boss that morning. The metallic pendant peeking from Pilar's scarlet blouse made her eyes gleam; her cropped salt-and-pepper hair belied her racehorse legs and zeal for ridding the universe of flying objects that stung. If Jackie had let her, she would have clambered onto the roof outside Jackie's bedroom window and sprayed poison into the cracks in the eaves herself. Fortunately, the exterminator had done the job. The next morning half a dozen fat yellow jackets had lain belly up six inches from the sill, the valiant ones who'd managed to stagger out as lethal dust floated into their nest.

"Do I want to know why you're asking about an exterminator?" Jackie said.

"Remember that client who said he heard buzzing whenever he came to the office?" They'd thought he was trying to fake an insanity plea. "Those jackasses who replaced the roof stirred up a hive in one of the chimneys. It sent scouts down Cliff's fireplace."

Jackie shuddered. First her home, now the office. Pilar had no compunction about using Jackie's fear of insects to try to convince her to lease space in more modern digs. Still, it was oddly fitting that the hive should dispatch an expeditionary force to the office of the Zoloft-popping estate planner down the hall.

"Are they dead?"

"I'm saving the corpses for Lily." Pilar tossed the mail on Jackie's immaculate desk and plopped into a chair. "When's she coming home? We had so little time last Christmas, before Britt and Randy took her on that cruise."

"Britt says she's made a new circle of friends."

"Could of done that here, if they let the poor kid stay put. Bouncing from school to ballet camp and then that Miss Sycophant—"

"Sullivant." Jackie skimmed the mail. Pilar had triaged the correspondence, tossing the junk and highlighting the rest with colored markers. "Miss Sullivant's Academy in Upper Brattleboro, Vermont. Lily will be receiving guests at home at the end of June."

"School lets out that late?"

"Britt and Randy have her scheduled to the max. Multicultural enrichment program on campus, then a pit stop in Denver—"

"Multicultural enrichment? You mean another way to squeeze a few grand from parents with more money than sense. She's too young for boarding school. If they had any brains, they'd let her come home and be with you."

Jackie turned from the familiar argument to her window.

Overnight it had gone from sixty degrees to ten inches

of snow. Not the powdery kind, but granulated sugar atop a slab of ice that made shoveling feel like hauling wet cement. Water streamed from the gutters of the apartment house across the street. The view of egg carton balconies with cement trim reminded her that this mansion had outlived its neighbors, most of which had been converted to boardinghouses or tuberculosis wards in the early part of the century.

Maybe it was time to move.

The silver baron who'd built the place had gone bust in the crash of 1893. There had been countless owners since. A recess in Jackie's office that used to be a double doorway now held floor-to-ceiling bookshelves, the plaster garland in her ceiling was truncated where the room had been cut in half, and there were three entrances to the lavatory she shared with Cliff. The investment company that now owned the building promised to do the first serious renovation in fifty years.

But nobody was fooled; improvements were always bad news for tenants. Replacing the slate roof with authentic-looking cement tiles had cost ten times the original construction. It was just a matter of time before rents would be raised, and the ragtag band of lawyers squatting in the silver baron's old digs would be forced out. And now killer bees . . . Returning to the stack of motions Pilar had typed, Jackie began scrawling her signature wherever there was an arrow. "Speaking of kids, what do you know about that six-year-old who went missing over the weekend?"

"Benjamin Sparks?" Pilar said. "Cute boy, his mug's been plastered all over the TV. I hear his dad's the gardener for some fat cat out by the country club. Why do you ask?"

"Dennis Ross called last night."

Pilar's eyes turned shrewd.

"Finally outta the doghouse you put him in, eh?"

"He never—"

"Guy makes one tiny mistake."

"It wasn't a mistake, Pilar. Dennis cost me my job at the PD's."

"Or is it the fact that he married a paralegal on the rebound?" Jackie slid the motions across the desk more forcefully than she'd intended, and Pilar caught them before they knocked over her cup. She wisely changed the subject. "What's Dennis got to do with Ben Sparks?"

"That fat cat's his client. Kid wandered off, he'll show up where they'd never think to look."

"You know how they'll find him, Jackie. And I hope whoever did it fries."

"Jesus! Is there something in the coffee this morning? Our job is to bring clients back to the campfire. Not cast them into the wilderness."

"There's folks out there with no conscience, and they're getting younger every day. Remember that kid who talked his pals into helping him kill his own mom? Beat her to death for money to buy a Sony PlayStation. Cops who busted him say he was real sweet till you crossed him. Even at the end his friends were willing to take the rap."

"The adolescent code of silence." Jackie wondered when Pilar's hormones were last checked. Was Walgreen's out of black cohosh and wild yam root? "Kids play at being outlaws, Pilar. They're more afraid of betraying a trust than getting caught."

"You make it sound like a game."

"To them, it is. They don't realize the effect of what they've done until—"

"What about that thirteen-year-old who killed his grandpa?"

"As I recall, he'd been abused by his mother's pimp."

"Out on the street in two years, and three days later he shoots a liquor store owner in a holdup."

"Why rag me about it? Dennis represented him."

"I don't work for Dennis. I mean it, Jackie. No one's safe."

"Because one six-year-old wanders off?"

"You know what I'm talking about! This isn't about a missing kid, it's about—"

Fear.

The pendulum had swung from rehabilitating youth offenders to warehousing them until they were too old to do more harm. But what juvenile psychopaths had to do with Benjamin Sparks, Jackie couldn't begin to guess. That her normally tolerant investigator could make a leap from a missing child to kids who killed and their inability to be redeemed said more about the social climate than any Gallup poll about the failures of the justice system.

"Don't you believe in evil?" Pilar said.

Hell of a question for a criminal defense lawyer.

"I'm more impressed with the power of individuals to change."

"You believe that crap, or is it because you have to?" Pilar rose, her coffee sloshing. "You look for good in your clients because if it ain't there, you don't have a prayer of selling them to a jury!"

Maybe it was a hot flash.

"Aging is the greatest cure," Jackie said.

"If you're born without a conscience, there's no way to grow one."

"How'd we get off on this, anyway?"

"Benjamin Sparks. The missing six-year-old. You brought him up."

And therein lay the return to sanity, or at least a distraction. She could appeal to Pilar's bottomless well of sources that made Pilar so superb at the work she did.

"What makes you think the Sparks kid has been molested?"

"He's a prime target."

"Oh, yeah?" Jackie's mind was turning to the day's work. Wrap up the plea on the I-25 case, meet with a date rapist she'd just as soon—

"His mom moved out."

What had Dennis said? The boy's father brought Ben with him to Christopher Boyd's house because his mother was working a weekend shift.

"In trouble at school," Pilar continued. "Suspended for smacking his playmates."

Jackie shook her head. "Hell of a way to get attention. Next you'll say he wore a sign around his neck."

"Didn't need to. That creep who snatched Ben Sparks just had to whistle."

Four

The snow was already a memory when Jackie left her office, but rush hour was still an ordeal. Flashing lights spelled more than flooded gutters, and her shortcut only brought her closer to whatever had caused the police to cordon off the intersection leading to the Botanic Gardens and Congress Park. Parking in the alley behind her house, she walked toward the commotion around the corner.

"What's going on?" she asked a neighbor.

"Something over at the gardens."

Whupwhupwhup.

"There's Channel 7!"

The Botanic Gardens' thumbprint of a lot was jammed with police cars. Live TV trucks had pulled up to the hillside below the soccer fields to the north of Congress Park. Marshy spots marked the turf's edge, where it sloped to a dense bramble leading down to Capitol Heights. In early spring the slope was a ruddy haze.

"Move along, miss."

With relief, Jackie turned away. She'd been to enough crime scenes to know that so many cops and reporters in one place meant only one thing.

A body.

Her phone was ringing as she unlocked her door.

"Quick, turn on the TV!"

It was Pilar. Jackie ran upstairs and hit the remote beside her bed.

". . . breaking story."

The camera panned over a squat building on the south side of the soccer fields, then to the two-hundred-foot transmission tower. It lingered before cutting to the bramble and a swarm of polo shirts and khaki trousers on the hillside. Without warning, it zoomed in on a small white body bag being loaded onto a gurney. The little boy had been found, not at the country club but here, two blocks from Jackie's house.

A face filled the screen and Jackie's breath caught.

Straight bangs and staring eyes. A child from the past.

Rachel Boyd took a knife,

Her little friend begged for his life . . .

How could she forget her fascination with the girl who had been just a year or two older than herself? And the awful thing Rachel had done.

"—sister of Christopher Boyd, president and CEO of Frontier Banks, the largest—"

They'd called her a bad seed, used the word "defective."

"—convicted of the notorious thrill murder of little Freddie Gant in the quiet agricultural community of Vivian, Colorado, on May 5, 1973."

And now little Benjamin Sparks was dead. Was it a coincidence that Rachel Boyd was staying at the home from which the child had disappeared? Or was it something more?

Five

Jackie poured herself stale coffee from the pot by the fax machine in her office pantry. It was Wednesday morning and she already regretted agreeing to this favor for a friend. Rather, for the sister of a client of a friend. Of course the client just happened to be the president of the largest bank holding company on the Front Range.

Dennis's second call had come Tuesday night, after Ben Sparks's body had been found. It was no surprise.

"No arrest yet," he'd said, but that was just a matter of time. "You'll like her, Jackie, you really will. Just meet her . . ."

His version of the story was compelling.

The Boyds had been a devoted family, the mother a homemaker and the father a prosperous businessman in the farming town of Vivian, 160 miles east of Denver. Three years older than her brother Christopher, Rachel Boyd had been a model child until the day she murdered a younger playmate. After thirty years in prison she'd recently been paroled. Her brother had invited her to stay at his home till she got back on her feet. Then came this ghastly coincidence with another boy, albeit one who was angry at his parents, disappearing from that very house after a trip to an ice cream shop, out from under Rachel's supposedly watchful eye.

The only questions Dennis couldn't answer were why Rachel Boyd would have thrown a four-year-old off a catwalk at a grain elevator in Vivian and how the press had tumbled so quickly to the connection between the notorious child-killer and her hotshot banker brother. Or, for that matter, why Dennis *himself* was unable—

Hearing Pilar in the foyer, Jackie rose.

"How kind of you to take the time to meet with us," Christopher Boyd said as he strode into the dining-cum-conference room. His blond hair was slicked back and his grip was firm, but his blue eyes held Jackie's a beat too long. Was there a hint of panic beneath that spit-polished exterior? Despite the snowy handkerchief in the pocket of his double-breasted pin-striped suit, he seemed too young to be heading a powerful bank. "Dennis speaks so highly of you."

But the woman behind him drew Jackie's attention.

Rachel Boyd was more arresting than beautiful. She had a strong chin and prominent nose, black hair that fell in a curtain to her jaw and the same brilliant eyes that had incited such revulsion in newspaper photos thirty years ago. As she stepped forward and extended a cool hand, Jackie caught a whiff of tobacco.

Dennis gave Jackie's arm a squeeze. "Thanks for fitting us in. It was hairy getting here. There must be a dozen reporters camped on Chris's lawn."

High-profile cases produced their own hydraulic pressure, and who knew what Rachel Boyd's arrest would drive to the surface? Media coverage the first time around had been vicious. Dennis had said one reporter in particular got in early and led the pack, a cub who'd used the tragedy to make a name for himself.

"How'd they make the connection between the Sparks boy and what happened thirty years ago?" Jackie said.

"Good question. We don't know. No one knew Rachel was staying with Chris."

"We'll have to talk about—"

"'No comment.'" The banker stepped to the head of the walnut table. "Dennis warned us."

Pilar brewed fresh coffee and Jackie took the opportunity to observe her visitors more closely. So much would turn on what happened in these next few minutes. First impressions were vital because juries operated that way. As the Boyds took their seats, Jackie tried to assess them through a juror's eyes.

Christopher Boyd was as fair as his sister was dark. As he held out the chair next to his for Rachel, Jackie registered his golfer's physique. Not beefy, but kinetic—a blond panther. His lower lip was fuller than the upper one, lending a vulnerability to his otherwise unremarkable features and subtracting at least a decade from his age. When Pilar passed the cream, the pitcher slipped and he caught it with a smooth motion. A man good at damage control?

As self-contained as her brother, Rachel seemed oblivious to the near miss with the pitcher. When she accepted a cup of coffee from Pilar, her bangs fell forward and Jackie saw a small white crescent-shaped scar above her temple. Her sand-colored silk jacket and tailored slacks were too fashionable and fit her slender frame too well for someone newly released on parole. Her only resemblance to her brother was in her sleek movements and her curiously round eyes. A certain unblinking focus.

Because the first moments with any prospective client were so crucial, Jackie would have preferred to meet with Rachel alone. At least not with her brother and his attorney. Aside from their ability to pay the freight, she had one ironclad criterion for taking on clients: she had to have a shot at convincing a jury of their innocence. To do that, Jackie had to believe in it herself. That meant striking a nerve, teasing out some kernel of warmth or wit or desperation that would enable jurors to relate.

She took the seat opposite Rachel.

"Let's start with Sunday, the day Benjamin Sparks disappeared."

Pilar began taking notes.

Christopher Boyd answered. "Shelly and I—" Catching Jackie's confusion, he smiled. "That's what we called her when we were kids. *Rachel* and I had breakfast and read the Sunday papers. We'd picked up a load of peat moss and mushroom compost from a garden center on Saturday to plant a rose bed in the backyard. Then I got the call from the bank."

Rachel had neither looked at Jackie nor spoken.

"Let's back up." Jackie directed her question to Rachel. "How long had you been staying with your brother?"

"Rachel was paroled four months ago," Christopher said. "Naturally, I was in close touch with the parole board, and as the date approached—"

The sheer force of Jackie's smile stopped him in mid-sentence.

"Mr. Boyd—"

"Chris."

"I really need your sister to answer."

"I was just—"

Again that hesitancy. As they locked eyes Jackie glimpsed a different man: one accustomed to control, one whose universe had precariously slipped. Now her sympathy was real.

"I know how difficult this is for you, Chris, but Rachel's words are the ones that count." Pilar refilled his cup and busied him with the sugar and cream. Rachel's coffee remained untouched, her hands folded in her lap. Jackie returned to her. "When did you move into your brother's home?"

Her voice was cultured, an unexpected contralto.

"December."

"Who else lives there?"

"What difference does that make?" Chris said.

Jackie wondered what Dennis had told him about her.

"If there are other witnesses to what happened that day, I need to know."

"A housekeeper who comes three days a week, and my groundsman, Harry Sparks." He winced. "Ben's father. He came over Sunday morning with the child to aerate the lawn."

"How did you come to be alone with the boy?" Jackie asked Rachel.

"As I started to say," Chris said, "after Harry arrived I got a call from the bank. The sprinklers outside the atrium had broken; they'd flooded the planters and were running into the street. Harry and I left right away. Shelly—"

"It was my idea," Rachel interrupted. As she met Jackie's gaze, her luminous eyes flickered.

"Which idea was that?"

"For Ben to stay with me. Chris and Harry had work to do."

"Had you met the boy before?"

"Harry had brought him over several times when he came to work," Chris said. "Shelly and Ben were—"

"—friends," Rachel finished, more sharply than she'd perhaps intended, and her brother recoiled as if he'd been slapped. Jackie wondered at the quicksilver dynamic between them.

"Whose idea was it for you to take him to the ice cream shop?" she asked Rachel.

"Why do you need to know that?" In a final attempt at control, Chris pushed back his chair. "What could it possibly—"

"Sit down and quit being an ass," Dennis said mildly. Jackie wondered again about his relationship with the banker. Since when did a Seventeenth Street lawyer address his most important client as if he were a habitual offender? "Jackie knows what she's doing."

"But—"

Rachel squeezed her brother's arm. It was an oddly maternal gesture, and the tension drained from Chris's face. Jackie picked up where she'd left off.

"Whose idea was it for you to go to the ice cream shop?"

"Ben wanted a treat," Rachel said. "I offered to take him to the park."

"What time did your brother and Mr. Sparks leave?"

"Around noon."

"What did you do after they left?"

"Walked to Toody-Froody."

The ice cream parlor was two miles from the country club. Quite a trek for a six-year-old on a warm day.

"Why didn't you drive?" Jackie kicked herself for asking. Rachel had been in prison since she was twelve. She didn't know how to drive. "Did you go straight there?"

"We stopped at the swings in the park. The ones near the ice cream store."

Cheesman. Two blocks from Jackie's house.

"Talk to anybody at the park?"

"No one I knew."

"And at Toody-Froody?"

Rachel blinked.

"I didn't know anyone there either."

"Can you describe the person who served you?"

"I—no."

"You don't remember?"

"He was a kid."

How impenetrable her eyes were! They registered all and gave nothing back.

"What time do you think that was?"

"Two o'clock."

"And after?"

Rachel shrugged as if it had been just another Sunday.

"We walked to the park on the other side of the Botanic Gardens. By the soccer fields." Congress Park, where the body was found. On the way back to Chris's house but still a mile from the country club. "We watched a game. Then we went home."

"When did you arrive?"

"Before three."

"And?"

"Ben looked tired, so I suggested we both take a nap."

"That's it?"

"The next thing I knew, Chris said Ben was missing."

Jackie never expected the truth from clients. At least not the first time around. The ones who'd been around the block quickly figured out what you knew, then gave you a sympathetic story. If they told the truth, they made every effort to ensure you understood; they'd jump on the table if they had to. Out-and-out liars were more interested in keeping their facts and their faces straight.

But Rachel Boyd was an enigma.

She'd answered each question precisely and without nuance, as if she'd learned her vocabulary from books. Which, given the thirty years she'd spent in penal institutions, she undoubtedly had. Yet there was a disturbing lack of detail and emotion in her account, particularly in contrast to her brother's recall.

Jackie laid it on the line.

"You're a suspect in Ben's murder because of what

happened in Vivian thirty years ago. To defend you now, I'll need to know everything about Freddie Gant's death."

"Shelly, we don't have to put up with this." Chris pushed back his chair. "This town's full of lawyers. We'll find—"

"No, Chris. It's okay." Rachel rose. Something inside her had shifted, and suddenly the indifference was replaced with an emotion so powerful it was as if she'd been stripped bare. "Do you know what it's like to be labeled a bad seed, Miss Flowers? To hear people call you evil?"

Re-tard, *re*-tard.

Jackie was seared by the childhood memory.

Re-tard, *re*-tard.

Give them what they want so they won't see what's there. Let them think they know the worst, so you can protect what you really want to hide. Was her own transformation a fraud, all the devices that made her successful in court a sham?

Even before Rachel continued, Jackie knew she had to represent her.

"I'm as innocent in Ben Sparks's death as I was responsible for the murder of Freddie Gant all those years ago. I won't let this case destroy my brother's reputation or all the things I've fought so hard to change in myself. If the only way to defend me now is to resurrect the child I was thirty years ago, they can lock me back up."

Six

Dear You,
    Today I waited & waited. Where were you?
    School was boring, boring, boring. Miss Robey thinks she knows everything. But we know about her. And Mrs Trent.
    Were in charge. Together were strong.

    Yesterday I cut my hand but it didnt hurt. I did it twice to make sure.
    Your turn.

                        Dear me!

DIARY OF RACHEL BOYD DATED APRIL 28, 1973

Dear You,
    When we get out well go. They cant do anything.
    Its our secret. They cant make us talk. Im not afraid.
    I count the days. You know what happens to rats.
    You wont chicken out will you?
    It wont be over til we say so.

                        Dear me!

Seven

J ackie, how lovely you look!"

Cal Doby had rusty hair, ruddy skin and piggish eyes. He was a font of boring and irrelevant anecdotes about his kids and referred to his wife as his better half. Jackie had never trusted his off-the-rack double-knit suits; as the oldest if not most senior trial lawyer in the Denver DA's office, he could have afforded better. The only honest thing about him was his dandruff.

"You're not looking too bad yourself," she said as she took her seat.

"Nice work on that I-25 case. You caught my young colleague with his pants down. I knew it would plead."

"Oh?"

"Got a live one this time, eh?" Doby's voice, normally too soft for his size, caromed off the gilded pilasters to the molded ceiling and down the well of Judge Greta Mueller's court. He shambled over to the defense table anyway. Re-arranging his features into a sincerity that would have done an undertaker proud, he leaned over the defense table. "Terrible thing."

"Hmm?" Jackie busied herself with the files Pilar had stuffed in her briefcase. Rachel had been arrested at Chris's home Friday evening, an old trick to ensure she spent the weekend in jail, and a phalanx of cameras lined the corridor outside Courtroom 16 in anticipation of the perp walk. Jackie'd wanted a moment alone with her client before the arraignment, but there wouldn't be time. Greta Mueller never started late.

Glancing over Jackie's shoulder, Doby smiled at the

AP stringer. If reporters expected to see Christopher Boyd in the gallery, they would be disappointed. Rachel had insisted her brother not attend and Jackie admired her the more for it. As Doby leaned into her ear, the smell of spearmint masked something rank.

"That little gal of yours is gonna fry."

"Beg pardon?"

"What nice shoes," he said a little louder. The pews in the gallery were filling with representatives of the media. Doby gazed mournfully from her lizard-skin pumps to the rubber-soled orthopedic oxfords he wore to draw attention to the fact that he was pigeon-toed. There was no one Cal Doby resented more than private attorneys, especially ones with the guts to wean themselves from the government tit. What was scary was how often he scored with juries. "Genuine croc, if I'm not mistaken."

Let him think they were real.

"You're the expert on crocks, Cal."

The doors swung open and Rachel entered in manacles and chains, escorted by two beefy male deputies and a female twice her size. Her neon orange scrubs were too large, but she'd rolled the sleeves in a way that made them almost stylish. With the docility and defiance of a lifer, she held out her wrists for a deputy to unshackle them. Jackie made a mental note to remind her client not to look as if she belonged in jailhouse garb.

"Are you okay?" Jackie whispered before a door behind the bench opened.

Greta Mueller strode to her chair in front of the gabled oak shrine flanked by Ionic columns with gilded scrolls. With her double chin, plastic-framed bifocals and the unflattering maroon silk blouse she wore with a floppy bow peeking out from under her robe, she looked as if she would have been more at home at a confab of sugar beet farmers on the Eastern Plains, where she'd been raised. Just two counties from Vivian. Not one to waste thirty seconds, she entered the lawyers' appearances for them.

"Ms. Flowers, how does your client plead?"

Jackie stepped to the lectern. "Not guilty, Your Honor."

"I suppose you want bail."

"As a matter of fact—"

"The People oppose any petition for bail." Doby could move surprisingly fast when he had to. "This little lady has committed the most *hen*ious crime in the history of—"

"Ms. Flowers?" The judge looked confused.

"Beg pardon, Your Honor?" Doby said.

"Is the little lady you're referring to defense counsel?" Mueller pushed her spectacles up on her nose and began thumbing through the motions the DA's office had filed that morning. "Because the only person referred to in your papers is a Miss Rachel Boyd."

"Yes, ma'am."

"And if *Miss Boyd* is the person to whom you are referring, for the sake of the record"—she gazed meaningfully at the reporters in the front rows—"you'd best refer to her by name and not label."

Doby shuffled. "Yes'm."

"Ms. Flowers, proceed."

"Miss Boyd is entitled to bail because the proof is not evident nor the presumption great that she had anything to do with the disappearance of Benjamin Sparks, much less the crime for which she's been charged. The DA has nothing but speculation—"

"Is it speculation that this boy's murder is almost an exact repetition of the depravity for which this defendant was convicted three decades ago?" Doby had dropped the country preacher routine. The courtroom was so quiet Jackie could hear the scratch of a pencil against a pad in the front row. "Hiding the body, letting it lie for days in the snow . . . Thirty years ago Rachel Boyd was able to lure little Freddie Gant to his death because she was an older child he trusted. As an adult in whose care Ben Sparks was placed, she abused an even greater position of trust vis-à-vis him."

Jackie was used to clients being punched up by the media to look like monsters before they even walked in her door, but she was damned if she'd let Doby do it in open court. He was pandering to the fears Pilar had expressed: not just of kids who killed, but worse, those who killed their most defenseless companions. Mueller was starting to look interested and she had to derail this fast.

"Your Honor, there's not a shred of evidence my client had anything to do with this child's death."

"Nothing to do with his death?" Doby turned to Rachel, his stubby forefinger wagging with rage. "She wasn't just the last person that poor kid was seen with, but Congress Park was the last place he was seen alive! A soccer player saw them. Sure, she reported him missing. But that was after she said she brought him home. Kinda strange, isn't it, that not a single person saw them together after Congress Park? Is it any coincidence that thirty years ago—"

With one smooth step, Jackie interposed herself between her client and Doby's accusatory finger. "She paid the price for what happened then—when she was herself still a child."

"Paid the price? She never provided a word of explanation for what she did, much less show remorse."

"Rachel Boyd is a convenient target, not some depraved—"

"She gloried in it!" Doby whirled again to Rachel, whose bored expression was not lost on the judge. "While Freddie Gant's body had not yet been found, she taunted the authorities by breaking into a grade school and leaving threats on the blackboard. The only reason more boys weren't tortured—"

"Tortured?" Jackie said.

"Didn't your client mention those wounds below the belt?" Doby shook his head and turned back to the judge. "She likes little boys, Your Honor. Not that you'd know it based on her behavior in Cañon City—"

Mueller's warning was as swift as her gavel.

"Mr. Doby, that's quite enough."

"Your Hon—"

Her steely gaze impaled them both.

"If you intend to try this case in the press, you're in for a rough ride. Contempt citations are just for starters. Ms. Flowers, I believe you were requesting bail before Mr. Doby attempted to prejudice this court with salacious tidbits. Having reviewed the district attorney's submissions and not being persuaded to the contrary by anything I've heard today, I'm inclined to release your client on a personal recog—"

"*PR?*" Doby was so rattled he committed the sole crime for which there was no pardon: interrupting a judge. But he wasn't the only one who was surprised. The moment Mueller had mentioned releasing her, Jackie had felt Rachel stiffen. "Are you aware of the recidivism—"

"—bond," Mueller finished.

"She can't go back to her brother's house! That's where the child was abducted. It's a crime scene, Your Honor, and it's an enormous estate. Evidence is still being collected. You absolutely can't—"

"On one condition," Mueller said. "That Miss Boyd

be released to the custody of someone other than her brother."

The words tumbled from Jackie's mouth.

"She can stay with me, Your Honor."

Even Doby was stunned.

"And she'll want a speedy trial?" Mueller squinted at her calendar. Having forced Jackie to put her money where her mouth was, she was inclined to be even more generous. "I'm sure Mr. Doby agrees it's in the People's interest to resolve this matter with dispatch. How does August third sound? Why, that gives you three whole months to prepare."

"But Your Honor—"

"Now, now, Mr. Doby. Justice may be blind, but is there any reason for her to be slow?"

Eight

NOTES FOUND ON MAY 7, 1973,
FOLLOWING BREAK-IN
AT VIVIAN ELEMENTARY SCHOOL

DeaR Me
WilL get You—yore Next!
Won't be the Last

Nine

Chin out, shoulders hunched, hips swaying with sensuous deliberation, and that look on her face that said screw you, you only *think* you know me, Rachel Boyd matched her pace to the camera crew shuffling backward as they filmed her promenade down the marble corridor. If not for her orange jumpsuit and the leg irons that shortened her stride, she might have been a supermodel strutting down a runway in Milan.

Curled up in her royal blue robe and sipping a mug of milky tea, Jackie tried to put herself in the mind of the viewing public as they watched her client's perp walk on Channel 9. Her own bedroom, with its yellow blinds, oak floors and the familiar glow of her bedside lamp, seemed far removed from the City and County Building and any life Rachel Boyd had ever known. That afternoon had passed in a blur of signing for Rachel's release, fetching her belongings from her brother's house and installing her in the guest room at the end of Jackie's hall. Now Jackie had her first moment to herself since her impulsive decision in Greta Mueller's court.

At the creak of a door, Jackie muted the TV with her remote. Through her transom she could see light at the end of the hallway. She'd been surprised at how little her guest brought with her, one small but expensive leather suitcase that looked new. When Rachel joked about Jackie being the only person in a five-state region not afraid to let her in her house, Jackie remembered Dennis saying Chris had wanted to be in court and stayed away only at his sister's insistence. He would have taken

Rachel, had he been allowed. Tired and pale, Rachel had politely refused Jackie's offer of dinner and said she was going to bed. Was it a mistake to bring her home? Pilar thought so.

Jackie flipped to Channel 7. All the networks carried Rachel's story on the ten o'clock news. Here the adult perp walk was replaced by a grainy precursor, black-and-white footage of two figures marching up the steps of a granite building with a domed roof. A slender woman clutched the hand of a girl who had a firm chin and straight bangs. The camera moved in as they entered the Seward County Courthouse and bustled down the corridor in matching heel-to-toe stride.

Maybe Pilar was right. But didn't everyone deserve a second chance? She thought of Lily, just two years younger than Rachel had been then. What if, two years from now, she were shut away for life?

The woman on the screen wore white gloves and a tightly belted floral frock, and her blond hair was freshly permed. The girl had on a party dress with a lace collar. As she stared into the camera with eyes as glassy as a doll's, Jackie thought she looked younger than twelve—closer to Jackie's own age at the time. Her blank expression changed to one of curiosity, as if the cameraman were the fish in the bowl and not her.

Rachel blinked and everything changed.

Now her face was suffused with a preternatural awareness.

That was the look Jackie remembered. And it summoned a tide of images she preferred to forget. Because Freddie Gant's murder had marked one of the darkest periods in her own life. As early as the first grade, she had discovered that she was different from her classmates. She couldn't read. Reading equals intelligence; every schoolchild knew that. But what if a short in the wiring of your brain made reading torture?

When letters squirmed and switched places on the page, the alphabet beyond ABC was a nightmare. And if Jackie couldn't read, how on earth could she spell? As she struggled to figure out how her classmates could tell the difference between "was" and "saw," she knew there was something she just wasn't getting. And when she couldn't connect what she saw to the words she said and heard, her priority became concealing her ignorance.

Being polite and cute helped girls survive, but that wasn't enough.

Grade school taught Jackie to be a first-class fraud.

When her classmates turned the pages of their readers, so did she. She became adept at guessing what a story meant by its illustrations. She made a myth out of literacy by memorizing, and when her memory ran out, she improvised. Given enough time, she could copy just about anything. Gradually her repertoire expanded.

Jackie got other children to do her homework or to let her copy theirs. She could pass any class by averaging: A on homework, flunk the test, C for her final grade. The social skills she developed in learning to bribe, lie and manipulate the school system ensured promotion year after year. They even laid the foundation for her success as a lawyer.

Jackie's charming habit of stumbling over longer words came in handy in cutting experts down to size and wooing jurors who awarded points for the common touch. Alertness to cues, split-second timing and hours of practice in front of the bathroom mirror sharpened her courtroom skills. But like all frauds, she lived on borrowed time. Even as she transformed what used to be a source of entertainment for her classmates into devastating effectiveness in court, she waited for the ax to drop. . . .

Her TV screen filled with the image of a small boy. Freddie Gant was round-faced and blond, the wave in his hair like a dip of custard. But his earnestness made him seem peculiarly mature, one of those kids you could imagine twenty years later in a coat and tie. His photo brought Jackie back to the first time she'd seen Rachel Boyd's face. The end of third grade, just before school let out.

With its emphasis on reading aloud, that academic year had been particularly grueling. As spring wore on, Jackie blundered more and more but was still managing to get away with it. Then her teacher had shown that film of the girl who jumped into the sedan with the man in the snap-brim hat and her nightmares began. Suddenly the picture of a glassy-eyed girl not much older than Jackie was on the front page of the *Post*.

"Who's that?" she'd asked.

"Never mind," her aunt said, and when it came on TV she switched stations.

"But what did she do?"

"Something terrible, don't talk about it."

"Bad seed" and "defective" were on everybody's lips. Sixth graders chased each other around the school yard chanting *Rachel's gonna getcha if-you-don't-watch-out*. The girls in Jackie's class even had a jingle for skipping rope:

> *Rachel Boyd took a knife,*
> *Her little friend begged for his life.*
> *When they asked what she had done,*
> *She said, "I did it all for fun!"*

The last day of third grade was celebrated with an oral spelling bee. Throughout the school year, Jackie could have set her calendar by the spelling test every Friday.

Monday the teacher handed out the list of new words. Tuesday Jackie ignored the list. Wednesday she gave it a glance. Thursday she frantically tried to memorize the words. On Friday, in a blind panic, she would develop a stomachache and stay home.

The weekly test's saving grace was that it was written. If there was no escape, at least her humiliation was private. But oral spelling bees were torture. And whoever heard of a stomachache on the last day of school?

Jackie's teacher divided the children into two teams and lined them up on opposite walls. The first child in each row was given a word and his opponent had the chance to correct him if he misspelled it. Jackie tried to jump to the head of the line so she could be eliminated at a stage when losing didn't count. But that morning she was slow and ended up second from the end. The teacher had brought a box of chocolate-covered cherries for the winning team.

The rounds were swift and the competition brutal. It wasn't until the best speller in the class, a girl four places up the line, was felled by "nickel" that Jackie began to panic. The teams had started out evenly matched but her side was going down. Suddenly everyone was looking at her.

"Well, Jackie?"

"Um . . ."

"Come on, now. It's an easy word." The teacher tapped her pencil. "Shall I use it in a sentence?"

Hope surged. She could tell which word it was by the emphasis, and if the sentence painted a picture she might even—

Tappety-tap.

"The farmer planted a *seed.*"

Flat and shiny, a hard black shell. But this time the picture was no help.

Taptaptap . . .

"Seeed," the teacher said.

"C—"

The boy opposite Jackie sniggered.

"C-e-" She didn't recognize her own voice.

Taptaptap . . . Tap-tappety-tap.

"Let's give her one more chance, children. Come on, Jackie."

"C-e-e-" She was squealing like a pig and the class erupted in laughter.

Losing wasn't nearly so bad as what happened later.

Jackie had never liked heights. It wasn't just clumsiness that made her run the wrong way when she finally connected with a ball, or her lack of depth perception that would later make driving impossible at night. Whatever had happened to the wiring in her brain had given her the terrible sense that she quite literally never knew where she stood. But the spelling debacle had left her with something to prove. When one of the sixth-grade boys pointed to the fire escape outside the school auditorium at lunchtime, she saw her opportunity.

The teachers' aides were smoking at the far end of the school yard. The fire escape was clearly off limits, but it was the last day of school. The aides were breaking the rules, weren't they? And the sixth grader had nothing to lose. Next year he'd be off to junior high.

"C'mon," he said. "Not afraid, are you?"

The girl who'd won the spelling bee looked over at the aides. Their backs were turned, and the student monitors were nowhere to be seen. But she was too smart to make a move. She wasn't the teacher's pet for nothing.

"What are you, chicken?" the boy said to the crowd. He dug his fingers into his armpits and started clucking.

Buck, buck, bu-uck. He turned to one of his buddies. "I told you they're babies."

A fifth grader stepped onto the fire escape and began to climb. Two of his classmates followed. Jackie watched her fellow third graders turn away.

"What about you, Jackie?" the spelling queen said. "Not scared, are you?"

Just stupid, she read in those blue eyes.

"Yeah, how 'bout it?" another classmate said. Everyone fell silent.

Jackie looked up. The school was only three stories tall, and the metal fire escape was sturdy and wide. It climbed up the outside of the auditorium, stopped at a landing, then turned and continued like a flight of stairs past the classrooms on the second and third floors. Just because she was stupid didn't mean she lacked guts.

"I'll go."

Even the sixth grader was impressed.

Not daring to look down, Jackie grabbed the railing and stepped onto the first tread. She scampered up on the heels of a fifth grader. Half a dozen others followed. At the top of the stairs she had to step over a little ledge before she reached the soft black surface. For the first time she turned and looked down.

The school yard seemed a universe away and the children were specks. Tar rose from the roof in the hot sun. The smell was overwhelming. Instead of being on top of the world, she was an ant about to be crushed. Her stomach heaved.

"What's wrong with her?"

Blindly she reached out for something to hold. Her knees buckled and she clutched her sides so she wouldn't fall.

"Oh, that's Jackie," said a boy from her class. "Look at her, she can't even stand."

"Jackie, spell 'seed'!"

Two others joined in, their voices blurring in a high-pitched hum.

"*Se*-ed, *se*-ed . . ."

"She can't spell because she's a retard," the sixth grader said.

"*Re*-tard, *re*-tard."

"She's a bad seed."

"Like Rachel Boyd!"

"Not a seed, a *bird*brain."

"Dodo bird!"

They were swarming her now and she could no longer recognize their faces. Just that nauseating smell of tar and voices buzzing around her head like bees.

"Can't spell."

"Maybe she can fly."

"Dodo birds can't fly."

"Chickens don't either!"

"Come on, Dumbo."

"Flap your wings, stupid."

"Are you a chicken, Jackie? Can you fly?"

Somehow she'd gotten turned around and they were pushing her back. Back to that ledge. She reached out again to grab something, anything, and her arms flapped.

"Look, the birdbrain's flying!"

Jackie's heel hit the edge of the roof, where the ledge met the tar. She froze.

"Jump, Jackie. Jump!"

She bit back hot tears. Should she admit to her terror and give in to their taunts? Suffer their ridicule, or defend herself?

"Dumbo!"

"Birdbrain!"

"Fly, Jackie. Fly!"

Or do what she always did when her back was to the wall?

Jackie made the only choice.

She reached out her arms and flapped. She opened her mouth and clucked. *Buck, buck, bu-uck.* Blinking away her tears, she joined her schoolmates in their laughter. And for one terrible moment became her own tormentor . . .

In the safety of her bedroom thirty years later, Jackie flipped the remote.

Channel 4 showed aerial footage of a grain elevator whose massive storage bins towered over a rural town. Vivian was laid out in a grid, with the elevator at one end of the main street next to the railroad tracks, and the opposite end anchored by a brick building that looked like a school. Neat blocks of Quonset huts and single-story homes lay in between. The dividing line between the edge of town and the surrounding farmland was so sharp it could have been drawn with a knife.

Jackie could only sense the fear and outrage that percolated through that placid agricultural community thirty years earlier. Colorado courts had never been particularly kind in their treatment of juveniles, not when their crimes were violent and especially not when they murdered other children. Freddie Gant's murder hadn't been the only notorious case back then; a boy not much older than Rachel had strangled a girl on the Western Slope and hidden her body under a shed on his parents' farm. The tabloids heralded an epidemic of brutality by angelic children transformed into monsters overnight. A bumper crop of bad seeds.

The camera pulled back and Jackie was struck by the geometric purity of the grain elevator. Not a building, but a colossus jutting from the plains flanked by massive steel cylinders that gleamed in the sun. As the camera drew closer the play of light on metal, the black crevasses between tower and bins, seemed sinister. Surrealistic. It panned from a tiny catwalk two-thirds of the way up the tower before jumping to shadows forty feet below. Had Rachel really pushed that little boy from the grain elevator so many years ago? Did Jackie have any idea who this woman staying in her guest room really was?

The toilet in the guest bathroom flushed and water ran in the sink. Jackie switched off the TV just before the soft knock at her door.

"Do you have any soap? I brought my own tooth-paste."

Rachel stood in the threshold in a worn terry-cloth wrapper.

"Didn't I leave you some?" While Rachel unpacked, Jackie had stocked the guest bath with the lavender soaps and body oil Pilar had given her for Christmas.

"They're too nice."

"Don't be silly. Want a cup of tea?"

"I know what this is costing you."

"Not a thing if you won't even use my soap."

"You were watching the news, weren't you?" Correctly interpreting Jackie's silence as an invitation, Rachel settled at the foot of the bed. Her teeth were white and very straight—courtesy of the state. *Rachel Boyd took a knife* . . . "I'll bet they showed that old footage from Vivian."

"Matter of fact, they did."

"Me in that silly dress with the lace collar. Mother must've thought we were going to a party."

When they asked what she had done, she said, "I did it all for fun!"

"Was that what it felt like?"

"God, no!" Rachel's anguish had to be real. "I was so scared. I had no idea what they would do to me. But I guess I deserved that question."

"No, I—"

"Because you deserved more of an answer when you asked about Freddie Gant."

"You said you were responsible for his death." And Jackie had a thousand questions more. Who, what, when, how . . . "Why?"

"It was my fault." Rachel spoke as if by rote, her slender fingers plucking at the bottom of her robe. The hem was almost completely unraveled. "I was weak when I should've been strong."

"What do you mean?"

"It got out of control. I'd do anything to take it back." It?

Was Rachel talking about losing her temper? An accident, something beyond her control? Or did her culpability lie in watching a boy plunge to his death? Jackie braced herself for the detail and emotion Rachel had withheld.

"You were a kid."

"I'm still responsible. But being strong can make things worse."

"Worse?"

"Like what happened with Chris."

"Chris?"

"Our dog. Didn't he tell you?"

Jackie leaned back against the headboard. "The only time I've spoken with your brother was that day in my office."

"I don't know why I thought he would've told you." Rachel shook her head. "It had nothing to do with what happened. Except it was earlier that spring."

"Before Freddie Gant?"

Rachel hesitated, then nodded. "Chris and I, we've always been close."

"He's made quite a success of himself."

"Because he left Vivian and never went back. I guess that's why I'm bringing it up. So you'll understand why sometimes he can be such an ass."

"He's trying to protect you."

"More than that. He feels he owes me."

And Rachel certainly owed him. Each day under her brother's roof the debt grew. Was that why she was so relieved when Jackie took her in? As Rachel drew up her knees and clasped them to her chest, Jackie sensed there was more.

"What happened that spring?"

"George—"

"George?"

"George Boyd. Our stepdad. He brought home a collie. It was supposed to stay in the yard but it kept getting out. So George wanted to fix it."

"Fix it?"

"Do the cutting on him so he wouldn't stray."

Jackie tried not to let the image form.

"Don't vets usually do that?"

"Not in Vivian. They're too busy with horses and cattle to tend to pets. And George grew up on a ranch. But the thing is, he wanted Chris to watch. 'That dog's your responsibility,' he told him, but I knew Chris couldn't handle it. He couldn't stand to see anything hurt."

"So what happened?"

Rachel's voice was calm, but an unguarded emotion crossed her face. A fierce protectiveness. "I begged George not to do it but that only made it worse. He said, 'What is he, a sissy?' He grabbed that dog, tied off his sack with a piece of wire, took out a knife—"

"I get the picture." Jackie was trying not to be sick. Instead of a collie, she imagined a nine-year-old boy. So sensitive his sister knew the scar from watching would be infinitely worse. "What happened to the dog?"

Rachel shrugged, and her features softened.

"When George was away, Chris cut his leash. That collie never did come back."

At least one of them got what he deserved.

"And Chris?"

"It—shredded him. All because of me." Rachel pulled her robe around her and her eyes welled with remorse. Jackie wanted to reach out but something warned her not to. "If I'd kept my mouth shut and let things go their way, George might not have made him watch. So it doesn't always pay to be strong. And if being strong can't save the ones you love . . ."

Rachel rose.

"You see how far he's come?" she said. "How much Chris has to lose by standing by me now? And you. You didn't have to take me in."

She stood there in her threadbare robe, backlit by the hall light. So utterly alone that there was only one thing Jackie could say.

"Yes, I did."

Ten

Every time Jackie climbed the stairs to her second-floor office she felt more grateful for the quiet harmony of her home. The sprigged wallpaper that began halfway up clashed with the walnut banister and the leaded glass in the window, and the wicker furniture in the landing had been spray-painted a chalky substance that would have made the silver baron cringe. Pilar ambushed her there the morning after Jackie brought Rachel home.

"I was about to call the cops."

"Sorry I'm late," Jackie said. "I should have house-guests more often. This one fixes breakfast. And not just eggs, but pancakes and—"

"Did you know she was on kitchen detail in Cañon City?"

"Rachel also worked at a French restaurant when she was at the halfway house. Tonight we're having chicken cordon bleu. Care to join us?"

"I prefer franks and beans. Gruel, for that matter."

Jackie ignored the mail Pilar handed her.

"Speaking of food, what's eating you?"

"Gee, I dunno. I was saying to myself just the other day, isn't it time Jackie brought a client home? After all, she can do only so much for them in court. It's been so long I can't *remember* the last—"

"Come on, Pilar. Give it a rest."

Pilar folded her arms across her formidable chest and planted her feet a marine's shoulder-width apart. "It's not like you don't know the risk of overidentifying with clients. You learned that day one at the PD's."

"As I recall, you were my first major felony."

The reminder that Jackie had walked her after she shot her husband only incensed Pilar more. "I plugged that bastard in self-defense!"

"Which is exactly why you needed a good lawyer. If Rachel had had one the first time around, maybe she wouldn't be facing another thirty years in prison now."

"Meaning?"

"There's two sides to every story. You know that better than most. Rachel never told hers and I'm damned if I'll let them railroad her twice."

"Railroad her? Jackie, she's a baby-killer!"

"Maybe you should call Cal Doby and see if there's an opening on his staff."

The shock on her friend's face made Jackie wish she could take that back.

"They were little boys, Jackie," Pilar said softly. "Not much younger than Lily. It's bad enough to defend her, but to bring her home?"

"If it's Lily you're worried about, she's two thousand miles away."

"Would it have made any difference if she was here?"

The intercom spared Jackie the need to answer.

"Chris Boyd to see you," the temp said.

Pilar's eyebrows shot up. "At least we know who to chase for the retainer," she said on her way out. Jackie heard her mumble a greeting on the stairs and a moment later Rachel's brother was at her door.

"I'm sorry to intrude without an appointment, Ms. Flowers. But I wanted to thank you in person."

Christopher Boyd's pin-striped suit was a carbon copy of the one he'd worn earlier, except it was gray instead of navy. Probably had a closetful, Jackie thought, along with a lifetime supply of snowy shirts and three-pointed hankies like the one in his breast pocket.

"No need for that, Mr. Boyd. I did what any defense—"

"Chris."

"Chris. I'm just doing my job."

His cologne seemed too woodsy for a banker. Had he stopped here on his way to work? Or given his secretary a story about a meeting outside the office? As he scribbled in an alligator portfolio with a gold pen, Jackie's resentment mounted. He'd done a lousy job watching over his sister. Was he trying to make up for it now by buying her lawyer?

"Perhaps this will make your job easier."

So long as the client was aware of it, there was no conflict in Rachel's brother paying Jackie's fee. But this check was twice the size of her normal retainer.

"Chris—"

He cut off her protest.

"I want you to hire any assistants you need. And expert witnesses. Whatever the cost."

At least he hadn't insisted on paying his sister's room and board.

"That's very generous. But Pilar Perez—"

"I'm sure she's the best in the business. If you need other help, money is no object. You needn't account to me for how you use it, and when you run out all you have to do is ask." End of subject. "I brought something else."

He handed Jackie a photo album. Its quilted cover was fastened by a cord.

"Open it."

The first six pages were filled with snapshots. Skipping ahead, she saw the rest were blank. She turned back to the beginning.

The first photograph was a studio portrait of a small boy who resembled Freddie Gant. But his cheeks were not so plump and his hair was a shade or two lighter, without the wave. It was Chris Boyd. In the next a black-haired toddler held a swaddled infant who was an even smaller version of the child on the previous page. An adult hand steadied the girl's shoulder. *My* baby, Jackie read in Rachel's glowing dark eyes.

The next showed Rachel at around five with Chris in denim overalls, his hand resting casually on her knee. Even at that age one could see the resemblance. Round eyes and high cheekbones, that secretive smile . . .

Looking up, Jackie saw Chris watching intently.

"Cute kids," she said.

"Yes."

School pictures followed, notable only for neatly combed hair and the queasy grin that came from being forced to smile for the camera. A yellowed scrap of newsprint showed two children in matching parkas on a sled, the girl hunched protectively over her brother as his chubby fists gripped the crossbar. Jackie tried not to think about that collie. She started to turn the page.

"See that one?" Chris pointed at the picture with the sled. "Right after it was snapped we went up the rise for a last run. Hit a rock and my chin went into that bar. I lost my bottom teeth."

The fullness to his lower lip was a scar.

"What happened to Rachel?"

"Shelly gashed her forehead." The pale crescent above her temple. "Blood all over the place, but she carried me home. In the car on the way to the hospital she locked me in her arms. No one but the doctor could touch me."

One final study of an older, unsmiling Rachel in a gingham dress with a bib collar and wide sash. Appliquéd to the bib was a small dark fruit, a strawberry, perhaps; it was as black as the girl's staring eyes. The next page had faded spots where other photos had been affixed. The rest were blank.

The scrapbook ended before Freddie Gant was killed. Except for that final picture of Rachel, none was taken after she was eight or nine. And why no adults? Closing the album, Jackie returned it to Chris. Dennis wouldn't like her talking to his client without him present, but she was never one to look a gift witness in the mouth.

"Tell me about your parents."

"What do you want to know?" The wariness was gone. Had the simple act of paying her to take care of his sister alleviated his guilt?

"What were they like, are they still alive?"

"Totally devoted to each other. And us. Dad—"

"Your stepfather?"

"George was the only father I knew, the one who gave Shelly and me his name. The other one ran off right after I was born." He seemed to bear no animosity toward either. "George was a real estate appraiser. In a town like Vivian, that's like running the local bank. Died three months after Shelly was sent away. It was very hard on my mother."

Was that why Chris had toughened, starting that long climb up the pyramid to head the region's largest bank? Or did he do that to prove he could go his stepdad one better? Unless success had been handed to Christopher Boyd.

"What happened to you?" she asked.

"I went to live with another family."

The man who never returned.

"You seem to have done okay. That must've been hard, after—"

"I owe my success to Shelly. You can see from the photographs. She was so good to me, like a little mother."

Better than his own? It was time to get real.

"I know you'll do everything you can to help her, Chris. And part of that is making Rachel come alive to the jury. So the more I know about what she was really like as a child—"

He nodded, acknowledging the stakes. "Maybe it's because she was older, but Shelly was the one who caught hell. I stayed out of the line of fire."

"Line of fire? Did your stepfather—"

"You've got it wrong. George was a cream puff. Give him a Mitch Miller album and a bottle of Schlitz and he was fine. Mom had the temper, that's why our real father walked out. She was harder on Shelly than on me. Maybe that's why . . ." He stopped. "Shelly had nothing to do with Ben Sparks's disappearance."

"How can you be sure?"

"Because it was my fault."

Jackie held her breath.

"He'd be alive today if Harry hadn't come over to work at the house. And when I got that call about the sprinklers, I didn't have to go."

Jackie had wondered about that herself. Traipsing to the bank on a Sunday for a broken sprinkler was hardly the CEO's job.

"Why *did* you go?"

"The manager was on vacation and his on-call guy was at a family reunion a hundred miles away. I said I'd go with Harry and handle it myself."

Chris had worked his way up.

"Why didn't you take Ben?"

"Ever been around a six-year-old boy? Harry couldn't watch him and fix the sprinkler at the same time. Shelly said they'd get ice cream."

So that was why Chris felt responsible.

For one fatal moment he'd placed the bank above his sister and now she was paying the price. No wonder he seemed relieved to whip out the checkbook. But something was missing.

"Did Rachel ever talk to you about Freddie Gant?"

"She didn't have to."

"Why's that?"

Leaving the album on her desk, he reached for his briefcase. Once again he was Christopher Boyd, CEO of Frontier Banks, down to the patronizing smile.

"There was nothing to say. I know my sister better than myself. Shelly never killed that boy."

He left before Jackie could reply.

Pilar showed up so fast she must have been at the landing.

"And . . . ?"

"Get me everything you can find on the murder of Freddie Gant."

Eleven

Received call 0655 from JACK TOBIN at VIVIAN MILLING & GRAIN, 10 CENTER STREET, VIVIAN. Did arrive 0725, proceeded to storage bins adjacent grain elevator. Found body of WYM, 3–5YO, blond/blue, cotton trousers, blue/white striped shirt, one sandal. Appeared to have fell from catwalk approx. 40 foot above bins. No sign foul play. Sheet tin approx. 2 by 3 foot and pine board 2 foot long partially covered body, lying face up in shaded area between bins. Flies and other insect activity immed. vic. alerted JACK TOBIN. JACK TOBIN did not touch or move body, other than look under tin. THIS OFFICER did radio HQ for backup.

Further inspection of site revealed no other sheet metal or lumber immed. vic. body but similar materials at trailer 15 yds. away. Misc. smaller sheet metal and steel, bolts, nails etc., incl. 4-inch cast iron scrap with blue paint under right hand. One child-size tan sandal found on catwalk, other on left foot. Visual inspection showed bruises right side face, back of right hand, forearm to wrist. Shirt pulled up, trousers tore at knee and bunched down around hips. Top button of fly missing, 3rd button in 2nd hole. 3 scratches approx. 3 inches in length across lower stomach, possible result of fall, no visible blood.

THIS OFFICER made no further inspection, awaited arrival of backup.

Twelve

Jackie left the City and County Building, where her client had just entered a no-contest plea to misdemeanor careless driving in the I-25 case. Community service, no jail time. ADA Tom Tuttle had accepted defeat with a curt nod to her after the judge left the bench, but he'd get over it by lunchtime.

At a quarter past eleven on a weekday morning, seats were already in demand at the Sixteenth Street Mall. As Jackie threaded her way through the businessmen, construction workers and tourists jamming the pedestrian corridor, she slowed her pace. This was one date she didn't want to be early for.

Once the location of Denver's first crosstown streetcars, department stores and banks, the mall had become a poster child for the excesses of urban blight. Food courts and schlock shops that muscled out the emporiums now cowered in the shadow of multimedia complexes and chain coffee bars. Like lemmings, the office workers came. They overflowed the microbreweries and pub-cafes gawking at tourists, lined up at the steam wagons for hot dogs, and tripped over hard hats who had the sense to eat their sack lunches on the sidewalk in the shade.

Jackie avoided the mall.

The state and federal courthouses were situated at either end, within a brisk walk of her office or an easy drive if she didn't mind paying a fortune to park. Masses of people weren't the problem. It was the commotion she couldn't stand, the rot from the Dumpsters behind the food courts, the shuttle buses that barreled down the pedestrian concourse with no warning but a flashing light. Strolling the pedestrian corridor was like walking into a swarm of fleas.

Jackie also avoided large social groups and cocktail parties. Back in the days when she'd let Pilar drag her to bars, it wasn't unusual for her to receive a call the next morning from a smitten stranger whom she'd engaged in a scintillating one-on-one simply to drown out the rest of the noise. Blocking out the world was more than a survival skill: it was one of the keys to her success in court. But it also wreaked havoc on her personal life. Which brought her to the man she was about to meet.

Dennis Ross.

He knew the focus it took to win, the adrenaline high that was a trial lawyer's best friend. Keeping secrets from him was the problem. Strange, because aside from their love of the courtroom they had so very little in common . . .

A clock chimed the half hour just as Jackie arrived at the Cambridge Grille. Dennis knew her well enough to have chosen the one downtown restaurant that served decent coleslaw and chowder. She was on time; by noon the line would stretch from the bar all the way past the canvas awning at the front door.

He'd asked her to lunch to thank her for taking Rachel's case, but she knew what he really wanted. To stay on top of the defense. Fine. There were certain things she wanted from him. Like his consent to her meeting with Chris Boyd again without his lawyer present. Which would drive Dennis nuts. And she would *not* let him get her loaded—

"Sorry I'm late." Dennis gave Jackie a brotherly peck on the cheek, and the roughness of his skin reminded her how heavy his beard used to be. As he drew away, she caught his familiar scent. "Been waiting long?"

"Just got here."

"Thanks for meeting me."

"I'm the one who should be thanking you," she said. "Especially for a case like this."

"Not every lawyer would jump at the chance."

"Oh?"

"Word's out: no deals. Duncan Pratt's got a hard-on for you a mile long."

"Then he should be trying it himself."

"Doby's his point man."

"Or fall guy."

"Watch your back, Jackie. And don't count on a plea."

"Who said anything about a plea?"

Dennis's smile said he knew damn well how much she relished a fight. Did he envy her this one? Or did he have yet another reason for inviting her to lunch? As they were led to a table for two, she vowed to make him work for whatever he wanted.

Dennis had been a brilliant student totally unsuited to academia. When he graduated from law school, he'd turned down offers from every Seventeenth Street firm for a slot at the Public Defender's Office. There his distaste for convention and contempt for known risks rocketed him to the top. By the time Jackie joined five years later, Dennis was decades more experienced. He took her to court with him that first day, but it wasn't until she won her first murder trial that they slept together. Right after the jury acquitted Pilar . . .

Jackie went through the charade of skimming her menu. When she looked up, Dennis was staring at her.

"Something wrong?" she said.

"You've cut it."

"My hair?" Rachel had trimmed it the day before, keeping the bangs and the fullness on top. But the sides were sleek—just long enough to run your fingers through. "What do you think?"

"I liked it long."

Their eyes met and Jackie was jolted by the memory of him wrapping his hands in it. Dennis looked away as the waiter returned for their orders.

"No Guinness?" she said. They had it on tap.

"I have a deposition this afternoon."

"So that's what you do when you aren't holding bankers' hands."

"Pays the bills."

"And now mine."

Dennis would have given his eyeteeth to have been able to keep this case, and Jackie wondered again why he didn't. The potential of a conflict with Rachel's brother, or because his firm wouldn't let him? He answered her unspoken question.

"I'll level with you, Jackie. Whatever damage this might cause Chris's career has already been done. He's a survivor; either way, he'll come out on top. What Kellogg & Kemp cares about is protecting Frontier Banks from the pounding they'll take if this case is tried in Denver." He shifted in his chair, for a moment looking as if he wanted to say more.

"I'm not at liberty to discuss defense strategy."

"Come on, Jackie. You really think I'd sell out my client's sister?"

"You sold *me*—"

"I shouldn't have gone off and left you like that. It was a selfish thing to do."

Men never apologized, least of all Dennis. The waiter came with her chowder and his hamburger, and Dennis transferred half of his julienne fries to Jackie's bread plate.

"You could have ratted me out whenever you liked," he said. "Of course, if you really believed I leaked that grand jury transcript to hurt you, you wouldn't be sitting across from me now."

"Hurt me? That stunt cost me my career at the PD!"

"And if you hadn't left you would never have known how good you really are." He picked up his burger and began eating it.

Had Dennis really thought he was helping her when he anonymously sent a sympathetic reporter a copy of a sealed transcript in a statewide vice case? Or did he do it because Jackie dumped him? Whatever the motive, his act had torpedoed a corrupt investigation and ended the political aspirations of an unethical prosecutor. But there'd been a price to pay, and having represented one of the witnesses in the grand jury, Jackie paid it. When the transcript hit the front page of the *Post*, Dennis had already resigned from the PD and was in Belize licking his wounds. By the time he returned she'd been booted. He'd tried to call but she refused to talk. Not even Pilar could intercede. And then he married that damn paralegal . . .

"What's he like?" she said.

"Funny, I thought you were going to say 'she.'"

"She?"

"My ex-wife."

"Fine." Ignoring the fries on her plate, Jackie helped herself to a couple off his. "What was she like?"

"It wasn't fair of me to marry her."

His second apology in one lunch. Dennis must want something really badly.

"Now answer my question. What's Chris Boyd like?"

"Decent guy." Dennis speared some onions with his fork and offered them to her. They were caramelized. Even better than the chowder. Without being asked, he gave her the rest. "Shark in the boardroom and a personal life so dull it's pathetic. But give the guy credit for taking his name back."

"I didn't know he'd lost it."

"Chris was nine when it happened. His stepfather died in a car accident that fall and mom started hitting the sauce. Social services swooped in and placed him with a foster family. They adopted him and gave him their name. After that he was your typical overachiever. High school quarterback, merit scholar, the works. Turned down a year at Oxford to attend CU and was recruited by Frontier Banks. Junior Chamber of Commerce, Big Brothers, Young Presidents League—a résumé straight out of *Who's Who*."

"Sounds like your kinda guy. Or Kellogg & Kemp's."

Dennis gave her a fishy look.

"I mean," she said, "with all that effort to distance himself from his sister, why *did* he take the name Boyd back?"

"What do you have against Chris?"

"Other than the fact that he won't let Rachel get two words out of her mouth?"

"She ought to be grateful he took her in." Dennis paused to take a large bite of his burger, giving her time to protest. Jackie ate another spoonful of chowder. "You know what most cons receive when they get out? A roll of bus tokens and some Goodwill vouchers."

No leather suitcases, silk jackets or hand-tailored slacks. But nothing Dennis said erased Jackie's sense that Chris Boyd was relieved his sister was no longer under his roof.

"So your client's a prince among men. And Rachel is an ungrateful wretch. You still haven't said why he took back his name."

"You'll love this. Right after he got the offer from Frontier, he walked into the old CEO's office and told him about his past." Dennis saw her skepticism. "I got that from the CEO himself, not Chris. He never said anything about it till last week."

"So that's why he isn't worried about his job."

"I said he was a stand-up guy."

Jackie accepted the last bite of Dennis's burger.

"What about his personal life?"

"Aside from marrying the homecoming queen?"

The first mention of a wife.

"I take it that didn't last."

Dennis shrugged. "A year. Anyone can make a mistake." His own marriage. A quickie, Pilar had said.

"A guy that driven must have other outlets. What turns him on?"

"He's a gambler."

"Vegas?"

Dennis laughed. "Frontier may not care that its CEO is the brother of a murderess, but it'd raise a few eyebrows if he was seen shooting craps. No, darling, it's the art of the deal that turns Chris Boyd's crank."

Jackie couldn't help being disappointed. "Business?"

"He buys the piece of real estate no one else will touch. It pays off big and he buys an even worse one. His genius is identifying opportunities and seizing the moment." Dennis tried again. "I played golf with him once. Instead of using his five-iron to get up to the water hazard and then chipping with the nine, Chris takes his four-iron and goes for broke. Takes the shot over the water hazard to the green."

Bucking the odds. Was that why he'd brought his sister home, to thumb his nose at fate?

"And since he's such a stand-up guy with nothing to

hide, I assume you have no problem with my interviewing him?"

"Just say when—"

"Alone." She gave it a moment to sink in. "Without you."

Dennis's eyes narrowed. "That's Chris's call."

"Good. I'm sure he'll want to help his sister in every way."

"Look, there's something you should know." He hesitated. "Chris is free to do what he likes, but do you realize how far my ass is hanging out on this? What trouble I'd be in with my firm if they knew I had any participation in Rachel's defense?"

Jackie waited and Dennis shook his head.

"They'd just as soon see her cop a plea to make this go away fast. The managing partner even hinted I should use my influence with you to pressure your client to do just that."

"Your *influence*?"

He had the grace to look sheepish—as if half the lawyers in Denver didn't know they'd slept together for five damn years. There had to be more to it than that.

"That's all?" she said.

"'Tell her we'll protect her fee.'"

"I'll bet you can't wait to shower when you get home from work."

Dennis signaled the waiter and handed him a credit card. So this lunch was on Kellogg & Kemp after all. And she still hadn't asked the most important question.

"Why was Rachel tried as an adult?"

"You know how it goes," he said. "Prosecutors are politicians first. When the public is outraged, they jump to the front of the line. And nothing strikes fear in the public's heart like kids killing other kids. Especially thirty years ago in a rural area."

"But didn't her lawyer challenge the DA's decision?"

"According to Chris, the Boyds hired some local mutt who mainly did real estate work. He was a friend of the family. They didn't know any better until it was too late."

A familiar story. Was that all?

"Thirty years is an awfully long sentence," she said.

"Rachel was actually sentenced to an indeterminate term of years to life. She came up for parole several times."

"Why didn't they let her out?"

Dennis hesitated again. "According to Chris, they never felt she demonstrated sufficient remorse." He signed the credit slip and rose. "Speaking of Rachel," he said, "have you figured out your defense?"

"That'll cost you more than a burger and soup."

"You're on, but not tonight. I don't know how long my deposition will last. And if I were you, I wouldn't be so quick to dismiss the possibility of a plea."

"Plea?"

"Don't look at me like that. Chris is trying his damnedest to support his sister, but you have to deal with the fact that she may very well be guilty."

"How convenient for you both."

Dennis was undeterred.

"You know how toxic families can be. She did it before, and when adult siblings are under the same roof again they revert to old patterns. Unresolved rivalries, competition for power and space . . . I can cite a dozen cases where a brother or sister moved back home and—"

"Killed each other maybe, but not an innocent kid."

Thirteen

Grape hyacinths shot from the ground like rockets. Peach and maroon tulips and daffodils with frothy skirts soared above lavender rock cress. The magic of spring, before the weeds took root and the aphids and mildew attacked.

The girl on the porch next door watched the woman flick cigarette ash into a rosebush that had greened up miraculously after the snow.

"Who are you?" Lily said.

"I might ask the same of you."

"Why are you smoking in Jackie's yard?"

"I didn't want to stink up her house." The woman was wearing faded Levi's and a blue chambray shirt. From her breast pocket she withdrew a crumpled pack of Camels. "Want one?"

Lily ignored the question.

"What are you doing in Jackie's house?"

"Staying with her awhile." The woman flicked her ash again, which irritated Lily more. "Ashes are good for roses, didn't you know that?"

"Not as good as bonemeal."

The woman spat on her thumb and forefinger. She used them to mash out her butt, which she put in the pocket of her jeans.

"Doesn't that hurt?" Lily said.

"Not once you get used to it. Maybe I'll show you how."

Lily crossed into Jackie's yard. "Where did you—"

From the back a familiar voice rang out.

"Dishes are loaded, Rachel. It's your turn—" Jackie rounded the corner. Seeing Lily, she stopped. "When did you get home?"

Lily's and Rachel's eyes locked. When Lily turned to Jackie, her expression was studiously indifferent.

"My plane landed an hour ago."

"But school's not supposed to be out—" Jackie felt Rachel assessing the scene, saw Lily glance again at the older woman. How long had they been there?

"I'm an exception," Lily said.

"You got kicked out of boarding school?"

Lily shrugged. The gesture was meant to be defiant. Proud.

"But you were doing so well," Jackie heard herself blather. "Britt said you made a whole circle of friends. . . ."

Rachel was staring at Lily with undisguised interest.

"Why'd they throw you out?" Those were the first words Jackie heard her speak.

"We'll talk tomorrow, Lily," Jackie said. "It's late and you need to unpack."

Jackie saw Rachel slip something from her pocket and flip it into a rosebush. Then she followed Jackie into the house.

Fourteen

Fresh turds in your mailbox?" Pilar asked.

"Just the same old—"

"No need to be testy. You could change your number or have it unlisted, you know."

"I'm not getting into that," Jackie said. "Don't you have enough to do?"

The conference table was littered with crime scene photos and police reports.

It was the Monday after Lily had been expelled from boarding school, two weeks to the day since Jackie brought Rachel home. The reporters had dwindled to the occasional drive-by shooter but the feces on her front porch didn't belong to any of her neighbors' dogs, and the hang-up calls at midnight were enough to make her yank the phone from the wall.

"Since you asked, I do have one question. What's our strategy, boss?"

Jackie turned to the blackboard Pilar had wheeled in. Choosing a pink stick of chalk, she drew an ice cream cone at one end.

"Toody-Froody?" Pilar said.

At the other end Jackie drew a large square surrounded by green stalks.

"Celery?"

Halfway between the two, Jackie added a brown hump crowned by goalposts and a net. The total distance was the two miles between the ice cream shop and Christopher Boyd's house. "Doby's theory is Ben Sparks never made it back to the country club"—she pointed to the house with celery—"because Rachel killed him on the way home from Toody-Froody. We'll attack him on all three fronts."

"Ice cream, celery and a pile of dog shit?"

"Means, motive and opportunity."

"What're we shooting for, one out of three?"

Jackie ignored that.

"Rachel's access to Ben gave her opportunity. But depending on time of death, Cal Doby may not even have that."

"Back up," Pilar said. "How come nobody saw?"

"Saw what?"

"Rachel at Cheesman with Ben, or them on their way home?"

"Isn't there a statement in the file from a witness at the soccer field? At the bail hearing, Doby bragged about someone who saw them there."

While Pilar pawed through the reports, Jackie examined the aerial photo of Congress Park. The bramble was separated from the soccer field by a chain-link fence, with the bushes sloping sharply from the northern edge of the field. Could a player on the field identify a woman and a boy?

Pilar skimmed the report. "There's a witness statement, but nothing about a positive ID."

Dennis was right: if DA Duncan Pratt's right-hand man risked blowing his credibility with the judge by misstating evidence, he really wanted to win. Overplaying his hand was also uncharacteristically sloppy. Doby must have known she'd discover it. If he wanted the defense to chase rabbits, he had something else up his sleeve.

"Want me to interview that witness?" Pilar said.

Jackie shook her head.

"I'll have fun with him on cross. And who cares

whether anyone saw Rachel near Congress Park? She never denied being there with Ben." Returning to the blackboard, she walked two fingers from the ice cream cone over the hill and down the other side to the country club. "They had to pass the soccer fields on the way home. What intrigues me is why no one saw Ben back at Chris's. Or the body being dumped."

"Doesn't mean it didn't happen. You're the one who says never confuse reality with common sense."

"Doby's real weakness is motive. Why would Rachel kill a boy left in her care?"

"Why'd she kill that first kid, Freddie what's-his—"

"Gant. Freddie Gant. Greta Mueller will never let evidence of that in."

"You think Doby won't try?"

"Of course he will, it's his whole case. But that was thirty years ago. We'll preempt him with a motion to exclude on grounds that it's too prejudicial. I'll dictate it this afternoon so you can file it by the end of the week. Now let's talk about means. Is the autopsy report in?"

Pilar located it in the stack. "Official cause of death was a broken neck. Cleanly snapped, like Gant's."

"It's not so easy to snap a kid's neck. Particularly for a woman."

"But not impossible."

"Still, it'd be different if he was suffocated or strangled. When did Ben die?"

"At least forty hours before his body was found," Pilar read on. "Medical examiner bases his estimate on the fact that Ben was no longer stiff."

The first really bad news.

Muscles began to contract two to four hours after death. Within twelve hours rigor mortis was complete, but as the body decomposed the stiffness disappeared until forty-eight hours later, when it was gone. The problem with using that to determine time of death lay in the variables: temperature, location, the victim's clothing, even humidity played a role. And the longer a body lay undiscovered, the less precise the estimate was.

None of which boded well for Jackie's client.

Returning to the blackboard, she sketched a time line starting at 2 P.M. on Sunday at Toody-Froody, and ending at 4 P.M. Tuesday, when the boy's body was found. At midnight Sunday she drew a large red X. If the ME was right, that left a ten-hour window for the murder—ten hours during which Rachel had to account for every move. Jackie had expected a wide range and lots of fudging, but ten hours was ridiculous. She had to narrow it down.

"That snow Monday night really cooked us," Pilar said.

Cold weather slowed decomposition and snow made the estimated time of death even less accurate. Maybe they could exploit the lack of precision.

"Was the body frozen?"

"Nope, that ten inches of sludge acted as an insulating blanket. The snow was so heavy and the bushes so thick you couldn't even see Ben till it began to melt. That's why he wasn't found till Tuesday afternoon."

"What time did it start to snow?"

"About eight, Monday night."

"So he could've been killed anytime before then . . ."

"And dumped on the way home from Toody-Froody."

Jackie sighed. "Too bad we can't prove what time his body was left."

"What difference would that make?"

"If the body was kept somewhere before being dumped, that raises questions. Where it was kept, how it was transported. What else does the autopsy report say?"

Pilar skimmed it again.

"Just some dirt."

"Dirt?"

"In the cuff of Ben's pants."

"What kind of dirt?"

"I dunno. Just says garden dirt."

"I guess that makes sense." Harry Sparks was a gardener, and his son was snatched from Chris's backyard. "What about the ice cream?"

Pilar shuffled the reports once more.

"Sumbitch."

"What?"

"It ain't here."

"No stomach contents?" Something stank. "Make a written demand."

Pilar scribbled a note.

With a ten-hour swing, how far that ice cream made it down Ben Sparks's GI tract was vital. Would Doby stoop to burying part of an autopsy report? If it was important enough for the DA to conceal, the defense might need its own expert.

"What'd the witnesses at Toody-Froody say?" Jackie asked.

"The statements ain't here."

Doby's tricks were falling into a pattern: not just hide-the-autopsy-report, but pad the file with witnesses who saw nothing and leave out the ones who might actually have something to say.

"I'm always up for Rocky Road," Pilar said. "Want me to pay a visit?"

Jackie shook her head again.

"You've got enough on your plate with the old Freddie Gant case. And keep the pressure on Doby. We need the rest of that autopsy report."

Pilar looked at the blackboard. "What time did Rachel say she and Ben got home?"

"Around three." Jackie added that to the time line. "They were tired, so the two of them went inside to take a nap."

"Remind me not to have her watch my kids!"

Jackie let that pass.

Divorced three times before she was widowed, Pilar had just one child. Each night she lit a candle so her daughter wouldn't show up on her doorstep. Being saddled with four grandchildren would have cramped Pilar's style.

"She expected Chris and Ben's father back any moment," Jackie said. "And she thought the boy was taking a nap. By the time they arrived, he was gone. But that gets us back to the time of the murder."

"She told the cops Chris drove up twenty minutes later. That ain't enough time to murder a kid and hide his body."

"Right. Chris and Harry Sparks immediately started to search. Someone was with Rachel from then on."

"Says who?"

"Chris Boyd." They'd have to call him as a witness. For testimony as important as that, they couldn't count on the emotional testimony of a murdered child's father. Jackie looked up in time to see the cynicism on her investigator's face.

"Come on. Give her a chance."

"That's the jury's job," Pilar said, "not mine. I'm as committed to Rachel's defense as you are. Just don't ask me to like her."

Jackie erased the time line. "I have an idea. What're you doing Friday night?"

"Wanna go out?" When they weren't on a case, they

would grab dinner or go to the movies at least once a week. "There's a new Himalayan joint by the state capitol. We can take Lily—"

"I meant my place."

Pilar's eyes narrowed. "Oh?"

"Do it for me. If it's a bust I'll never ask again."

"What's on the menu, franks and beans? I hear that's the number one dish at—"

"Roast chicken with garlic mashed potatoes. And chocolate for dessert." Three for three. All Rachel had to do was deliver.

"We-ell . . ." Curiosity or Pilar's passion for garlic won out. "What can I bring?"

"Just your own sweet self. And a loaf of French bread."

Pilar stuffed the reports back in their folders. "How's Lily?"

"Not so good."

Jackie had heard the slammed doors, seen the girl's light on half the night in the bedroom across from hers. But Lily never missed the special signal she and Jackie had worked out years ago, tilting the slats of their blinds up forty-five degrees before bed. Their sign not to send the cavalry.

"She tell you what happened?" Pilar said.

"Not really."

Jackie's only real conversation with Lily since the girl had come home was the morning after Lily had met Rachel. She'd been waiting on Jackie's porch when the two of them returned from shopping.

"Who's she?" Lily had asked after Rachel carried a grocery sack into the house.

Jackie handed Lily another bag. "A friend down on her luck."

"What'd she do?"

Jackie hesitated. Lily was ten, just two years younger than Rachel when Freddie Gant was killed. But their lives were universes apart, and that was how she wanted them to remain. The less Lily knew about Rachel, the better.

"Sometimes people find themselves in trouble through no fault of their own."

"Oh, yeah?" Lily deposited the sack on Jackie's doorstep and went to the car for another. Jackie seized the moment.

"What happened at boarding school, honey?"

"Nothing."

The bravado rang false, and not just because boarding schools that charged as much as an Ivy League education were loath to offend parents. Lily had a history of being odd man out. And it wasn't because she was the only Chinese girl in Denver who wasn't small, cute and round-faced, or the only girl in her elementary school who refused to own a pink backpack.

"We talked about how cruel other kids can be. Did you get in a fight?"

"Hardly." Lily's attempt at scorn missed the mark and now she looked as if she might cry. "I'm a QB."

"Kewpie?"

"Queen . . . Bee." Jackie wondered if she'd been about to say another word. "We're the top girls in school. The QBs *rule*."

"So what happened?"

"I—"

The door opened and Rachel emerged. Nodding at Lily, she hoisted two grocery sacks. With her back to them, she shifted one of the bags to her hip and paused.

"Sometimes people find themselves in trouble

through no fault of their own," Lily said in a dead-on imitation of Jackie a moment before. . . .

That was a week ago. Pilar snapped her back to the present.

"—better keep Rachel and Lily apart. And that brother of hers is a real piece of work. Living example of the balance-sheet approach to life." In addition to the insurance adjuster, Pilar had dated an accountant. "If you take risks in business and always win, there's gotta be a compensating debit."

"If you mean his personal life, Chris Boyd apparently doesn't have one."

"Exactly!"

"Well, his balance comes in handy when it comes to his sister's expenses. Think we need to hire an expert to conduct a jury poll? With all the publicity Rachel's already received—"

"—not to mention dog turds—"

"—I'd hate to try this case in Denver."

Pilar flipped an autopsy photo across the table. It was a color close-up of Ben Sparks's lower abdomen. Three long scratches raked the pale flesh above the boy's groin.

"Where should Mueller move the trial?" Pilar said. "Alaska?"

She passed Jackie another photo, this time a black-and-white. Same three scratches, these not quite so deep. The edges seemed more ragged but there was no blood.

"After they cleaned Ben up?" Jackie said.

"Nope. It's Freddie Gant."

Jackie laid the photos side by side. The cuts were almost identical.

She sighed. "Thirty years ago insanity was easier to prove. You'd think her lawyer would at least have tried—"

"The real question is, why didn't he defend her at all?"

A tall man stood in the doorway. He wore dungarees and a corduroy jacket with leather shoulder patches. His pale eyes were bloodshot and his blond ponytail was streaked with gray.

"Who are you?" Jackie said.

He stuck out his hand.

"Lee Simms. Your ticket to winning Rachel Boyd's case."

Fifteen

EXCLUSIVE BY LEE SIMMS FOR
MODERN CRIMES—MAY 7, 1973

Saturday afternoon in early May, three weeks before the end of school. An arid wind fans the prairie grass as a quiet farm community tends to its chores before taking refuge from the sun. In the dark coolness of his living room on a modest street, a small boy switches off the TV. It is three o'clock, the hottest part of the day. But his cartoons are over and it is hours until supper.

"Mommy, can I go out and play?"

In the company of his eight-year-old brother Gregg and eleven-year-old sister Susan, he leaves for the park a half block away. He is wearing navy blue cotton trousers, a striped shirt and sandals. Just that morning his mother sewed new buttons on his pants. Navy blue to match the trousers, embossed with a bright red anchor. Freddie proudly fastened those buttons for the first time himself.

Debbie Gant stands at the window of her one-story white frame house at 60 State Street, watching her youngest toddle off after his adored older siblings, a shiny red truck clutched in his arms.

Freddie Gant has just celebrated his fourth birthday.

"Stay with Susie and Gregg!" the thirty-year-old brunette calls out. "Be home by six. We're having franks for supper." Freddie's favorite dish.

But Freddie Gant will not be home for supper that night. Or the next.

Vivian Memorial Park is located in the precise center of town. Three blocks to its north stands Vivian Elementary, where the popular and well-behaved Gant children attend class. Three blocks south lie the elevator operated by Vivian Milling & Grain and the Burlington Northern railroad tracks. Just beyond the tracks runs Highway 24, a four-lane bustling with tractor trailers like the one Freddie's father, Arthur Gant, drives. But the obedient little boy, who never went anywhere without permission, knew better than to venture from the safety of the park.

Shaded by elms as old as the town itself, the park has swings, a statue of General George Armstrong Custer and a small bandstand where the older children gather. On that afternoon the fountain is silent. Memorial Day is just weeks off, with summer and the end of school around the corner. Gregg joins a boy he knows by the bandstand. Susie sees two classmates and goes over to chat.

It is ten minutes past six when Gregg and Susie return home.

"Where's Freddie?" the attractive housewife asks.

And so Debbie Gant's nightmare began. Before it was over this quiet agricultural town would be shaken to its roots, a half dozen law enforcement agencies would join in the search, and Art Gant's employer, Western Freight, would offer a thousand-dollar reward for information as to Freddie's whereabouts.

Daylight was fading as the distraught mother went door-to-door asking if anyone had seen her son. With trembling fingers she dialed the Seward County Sheriff's Department, which dispatched a patrol unit within minutes. By 9:30 p.m. Deputy Peter Rice and Detective Sergeant Ryan Mitchell had questioned Debbie Gant and her children, Gregg and Susie, obtained a photograph and detailed description of the blond, blue-eyed toddler, and begun searching every backyard, shed and outbuilding in the four square blocks surrounding the park. When Art Gant returned home from a haul shortly before midnight, the exhausted father joined them. The only trace of Freddie was his red truck. It was found in the grass behind the swings.

One of the missing boy's neighbors, Wade Kunkel of 45 State Street, said he saw a small powder blue Volkswagen Bug in the vicinity of Vivian Memorial Park that afternoon. A couple of kids were talking to the driver, whom he could not identify. The incident stuck in his mind, Kunkel said, because he could not remember seeing a car of that description in Vivian before. Kunkel's account was confirmed by a friend of Gregg Gant's, who remembered seeing a young man with a slight build and pocked complexion in a Volkswagen by the bandstand. A three-county alert was issued for the driver.

By dawn on Sunday, it seemed clear this was not the case of a lost child, but something far more ominous. The Seward County Sheriff's Department was now joined by officers from agencies in Kit Carson, Washington and Cheyenne counties, who combed every drainage ditch and field in the surrounding area with the help of forty volunteers. Seward County Sheriff Wally Metz made a public appeal on radio and television for the safe return of the four-year-old boy.

"Whoever took this child abducted him for purposes I'm not at liberty to say," the sheriff privately confided. "I have no doubt he's in another county, or even another state. He could never have disappeared so quickly if he hadn't been abducted." He showed this reporter a snapshot of his own daughter. "I can only imagine what the Gants are feeling right now."

A break in the case appeared to come in early afternoon when officers located the owner of the Volkswagen in neighboring Washington County. The young man, whose name has not been released but who fits the description given by Gregg Gant's friend, said he drove to Vivian looking for someone he had met at a bar in Hoover. Unable to locate this acquaintance, he returned home. Although the young man has no previous record and his story seems to check out, further inquiries are being made.

A second flurry of activity came when a deputy from Kit Carson, searching a drainage ditch on the west side of Vivian, found a large towel with a stain that appeared to be blood. Authorities were preparing to send the towel to the FBI in Washington for analysis. Hopes that it might provide a clue to the fate of the missing child were quickly dashed, however, when the farmer in whose ditch the towel was found said one of his dogs had been hit by a car on Highway 24 two days earlier and he used the towel to staunch his wounds. When the dog died the farmer put the towel in a trash heap to be burned but it had apparently been retrieved by an animal and dragged to the ditch.

The second day of the search closed on a poignant note. A small figure knocked on the door of 60 State Street. It was a classmate of Susie Gant's, one of the girls who had been with Freddie's sister at the park that fateful Saturday afternoon.

"Is Freddie home?"

No one had the heart to answer.

Sixteen

"Can I help you, ma'am?"

Teenage boys were so easy.

Jackie could have done without the "ma'am," but she maintained her hundred-watt smile. She wondered why it never failed. Too shy to make eye contact with a grown woman unless she initiated it, then they couldn't be beaten off with a stick. Which was an advantage if you might have to subpoena them.

"Want a taste?" said the boy behind Toody-Froody's counter.

His voice remained in the lower register this time and she gave him another boost by affecting helplessness. The ice cream came in carnival colors and was studded with gems that would have done a mineral collector proud. Chocolate nubs, bits of toffee, pink and green splinters, and a conglomerate marbled like cookie dough. She pointed to something orchid-colored and he dished up a generous spoonful.

"Yum. Raspberries in white chocolate?" He nodded as proudly as if he'd whipped it up himself. His eyes strayed to her chest. "What's that green stuff with the nuts?"

"Pistachio." He gave her a taste without being asked, and Jackie rewarded him with another dazzling smile.

They had the ice cream parlor to themselves. It was Friday afternoon, too late not to risk spoiling dinner, too early for the dessert crowd. What Jackie didn't have was the Toody-Froody witness statement, which Doby had never turned over despite Pilar's written demands. Or any description of the kid who'd waited on Rachel.

Toody-Froody reminded her of kindergarten. Pastel colors, round tables too small to sit at, an enormous blackboard with selections listed in colored chalk. Even the waffle cones at the counter next to the doll-size sample spoons and mama, papa and baby bear cups made Jackie feel as if she'd walked into story hour. How different could it have been on a warm Sunday at the beginning of April?

"How long have you worked here?"

"Since spring break." He wanted her to think he was in college, but the baseball cap worn backward and the metal chain around his neck said otherwise. Still, this kid was running the place alone. He must be on the ball.

"You work weekends?"

"Best shifts." Unwilling to admit he had no say in the matter.

"Awful what happened to that kid in Congress Park." Such a small neighborhood.

"Yeah, he was here with that woman they busted."

"No kidding! You were on that day?"

"I'm the one who served them."

Bingo.

"That must've been something."

"Yeah, the cops asked a bunch of questions. I had to go down to headquarters." He shrugged as if it was no big deal. Jackie decided to see how suggestible he was.

"Busy as you must've been, I'll bet it was tough—"

"Actually, I remembered them real well."

"How come?"

"We weren't busy yet. It was only one in the afternoon, right after I started my shift."

Jackie hid her surprise. Hadn't Rachel said an hour later?

"You're sure of the time?"

"I went over that with the cops. Sundays we get real

busy by one-thirty, two o'clock. She was about your height but her hair was dark. Good-looking. The kid—"

Further questions about the time would only embed the memory deeper. And maybe it didn't matter. An earlier arrival left more of Rachel's activities on the back end unaccounted for, and her alibi and the estimated time of death were so loose there was no way for the prosecution to score on the discrepancy. But Jackie's antennae were humming. Was this why Cal Doby buried the witness statement?

"—came in, wasn't sure they were together."

Why did he think a six-year-old would be alone?

"Weren't they talking to each other?"

He shrugged. "There was a guy, I thought the kid was with him."

The door jangled and he turned to the new customer. A middle-aged man.

"What made you think that?" Jackie said.

"He was real friendly, made the kid laugh."

"Laugh?"

The customer was waiting, but an attractive woman was an irresistible force. And if she stopped now, there would be no way to pick up later without arousing suspicion.

"Guy had a puzzle. He was working it while he waited."

"Crossword?"

"A mindbender." He saw her confusion. "You know, two wires twisted like a pretzel. Trick is to find the weak spot in the link and take them apart. You can get them in any toy store. The kid couldn't take his eyes off it and the guy ended up giving it to him. I guess that's why I thought they were together."

"What did he look like?"

"The guy?" Another shrug. "Average, I guess."

"How was he dressed?"

"Like Sunday."

"Sunday sloppy, or Sunday neat?"

"He wasn't wearing a jacket, if that's what you mean."

"Was he blond?"

"Not really."

"Did the woman seem to know him?"

"Like I said, I didn't even think she knew the kid. She was kind of uptight, really."

Jackie let out her breath.

How like a teenage boy to be able to describe a couple of pieces of wire, but not the man who played with them! Of course his eye was keener for the opposite sex. More to the point, the man sounded nothing like Chris Boyd. He would have been at the bank then, anyway, but she was still relieved.

The other customer was shifting impatiently.

"You sure he gave the mindbender to the boy?" she said.

"Yeah, I remember that. He couldn't pull it apart and the kid wanted to try."

Nothing in the police reports about a metal puzzle being found with Ben's body. Maybe the man used it to establish rapport, to entice the boy so he would go with him later. Or maybe it was like so many other leads: a blind alley. She'd have to subpoena this kid for trial, but Jackie needed to know one more thing.

"Did you tell the police?"

One question too many: Jackie had reminded him of his mother. His eyes narrowed but her brilliant smile earned a final answer.

"They never asked."

The boy at the counter would never be able to identify the man he'd described, because he was a teenager who only saw breasts. But Jackie couldn't dismiss the possibility that someone had targeted Ben on his outing with Rachel and followed them home.

Rachel said she hadn't seen anyone at Toody-Froody. And if she had, then what? It would take an army of investigators to track down witnesses at Cheesman or Congress Park on a Sunday afternoon a month earlier. Unless they used Lee Simms . . . Turning into the alley behind her house, Jackie shook her head.

Pilar had done the background check.

Freddie Gant's murder had been Simms's entrée to mainstream journalism. Thirty years ago he'd had a lock on the case; when the story broke he was first at the scene, and he rode it until Rachel dropped. His stories were picked up by the wire services and the Denver papers vied for his byline. He'd done a short stint at the *Post* and an even shorter one at the *News*. After that he'd led a Hunter Thompson–like existence sans the money and glitz, living hand-to-mouth in Leadville and Silverton, working as a day laborer and occasionally penning puff pieces for the local rags. Jackie was under no illusions about why Lee Simms had resurfaced now. And the price he was asking was too much.

Access to Rachel and her defense in exchange for all he knew about Freddie Gant.

Jackie wouldn't have agreed if Simms had been awarded a Pulitzer.

Her first concerns were privilege and confidentiality. Doby could use anything Simms collected. There would be no lawyer-client privilege. Because Dennis wasn't part of the defense team, not even things Jackie told Dennis were protected. The press had stopped camping outside her office and neighborhood visits had dwindled to the occasional drive-by, but that only meant they were looking elsewhere for dirt.

Second, dealing with the media was a no-win game.

Talk, and you were accused of spinning; clam up, and you had something to hide. Background had a way of moving to front and center. The currency was information. Their job was to dig, hers was to keep a lid on the defense and stop matters from getting worse. No case was won in the press. Not by the defense.

And there was something about Simms that Jackie just didn't like. He'd crucified a twelve-year-old girl's reputation to make a name for himself and sell newspapers. But that wasn't it. Nor did the coke and booze that fueled his self-induced hibernation bother her. It was something else, something—

A car door slammed and stiletto heels clicked on concrete. Jackie turned in time to see a tornado in a designer pantsuit blow out of a Mercedes SL and up the adjacent driveway.

"Britt!"

"How dare you," Lily's mother said.

"How dare I what?"

"Isn't it enough that you represent criminals? That every pervert in Denver knows not just what you do, but where you live? Bringing that woman into this neighborhood, *onto our block*—"

"Britt, look—"

"We thought you cared about Lily. How could you expose her to that?"

She was panicked; if Jackie had a daughter, wouldn't she feel the same? But she and Britt had never seen eye to eye. For Lily's sake, Jackie counted to three.

"Rachel's no threat to anyone, Britt. If she was, the judge wouldn't release her on bond. What she might've done thirty years ago has nothing to do with who she is now."

"You're her lawyer, of course you'd say that!"

"Rachel Boyd was twelve years old, Britt. She paid her

price." Pilar's Rocky Road was softening in the bag, but Jackie stood her ground. "You know one child who's proved herself capable of change. Look how far Lily's come. Remember when she put Vaseline in her hair and told the other kids it was snakes? Or when she started a fashion riot by wearing that rhinestone dog collar to class?"

"And look at her now. Isn't it enough she's been expelled from school?"

So this wasn't just about Rachel. Jackie set down the melting ice cream.

"What happened, Britt? She was doing so well."

"They said she's a bad influence on her peers. Randy and I are at our wits' end. You're the only one that child talks to."

How that must rankle! But Lily shouldn't pay the price.

"I haven't really seen Lily yet," Jackie said. She'd been too wrapped up in this case.

"We're taking her to a psychiatrist Monday."

"Why?"

"Boarding school's not the answer. She's a problem child."

"Lily's not broken, Britt. She doesn't need to be fixed."

"What do you know? You've never been a mother!"

Jackie bit her tongue.

"I know you and Randy are frustrated, but the answer isn't to keep shipping her off. Control depends on fostering a healthy independence, not—"

"Lily thinks she has it rough? Why, when I was in junior high—"

The ice cream was dripping down the asphalt.

"—braces on my teeth, absolutely no sense of style. Talk about being ostracized. But did my parents coddle me? It wasn't till high school that I even saw a dermatologist!"

Not only clueless, but totally incapable of empathizing with her daughter.

"—think I climb that StairMaster at six every morning just for my health? Lily doesn't have it rough enough. Not by a long shot . . ."

Jackie patiently waited until Britt ran down.

"Can I come over later, after Lily's in bed?"

"There's nothing to discuss, Jackie. Randy and I forbade her to have any contact with you so long as that woman's staying here."

"What did you tell Lily?"

"That she murdered a child." Not only unfair, but the accusation was sure to whet Lily's interest. "Not that it did any good. I caught them in your front yard yesterday."

"And you think keeping Lily from Rachel is the answer?"

"I think keeping her from *you* is the answer!"

A calm voice interrupted.

"If I can't see Jackie, I'll run away."

"Lily!" Britt said.

"And you can forget those bullshit tests. If you want me to see that shrink, here's the deal. I won't see Rachel alone. Only if Jackie's there."

Jackie jumped in.

"And not just me, but at least one other adult. Okay, Britt?"

Britt had no choice.

As she grabbed her daughter's arm and propelled her into their house, Jackie pretended not to see the triumph on Lily's face.

Seventeen

Roast chicken perfumed the air as Jackie entered through her kitchen door.

Rachel was brushing the bird's skin with rosemary and olive oil. At the counter farthest from the stove Pilar whisked eggs into anchovies and raw garlic. Whipping was more like it. Her jerky motions were better suited to a cat-o'-nine-tails.

"Smells great," Jackie said, depositing the melted ice cream in the freezer. She looked at the macerated concoction in Pilar's bowl. "Your special Caesar?"

"Hmph."

Rachel straightened from the oven with a silver-wrapped lump the size of a tennis ball. She peeled back the foil and garlic filled the room. One whack with the flat of Jackie's butcher knife split open the head. The cloves fanned like petals.

"I told her it was too much," Pilar said. "Who puts a head of garlic in a coupla lousy spuds?"

Rachel popped the garlic from its papery shell. The cloves were the color of caramel. Her back to Pilar, she began mashing them into the potatoes with half a pound of butter and a cup of heavy cream.

"When's dinner?" Jackie said.

"Fifteen minutes," Rachel said over her shoulder.

Jackie peeked in the dining room. The table was set with her aunt's best china, an ivory and cobalt Scandinavian design. Her tulip-shaped wineglasses had been hand-washed until they sparkled but the napkins were new: a rose linen that made the cobalt leap off the plates. In the center sat a bowl of salmon-colored gerbera daisies.

Angry thwacks at the carving board drew Jackie back to the kitchen. Pilar was venting her frustrations on a baguette. Jackie hoped Rachel could turn whatever was usable into croutons. She went upstairs to change.

When she came down ten minutes later in Levi's and a cotton pullover, Rachel had finished carving the chicken and Pilar was pouring Merlot. Judging from the care with which they avoided contact in the stamp-size dining room, they seemed to have reached some sort of détente.

"To friendship," Jackie said, and Pilar downed her wine in one gulp.

The chicken was tender and juicy, the potatoes just lumpy enough to prove they were real. Rachel had strained the pan juices and basted the meat in them. Pilar reached for the gravy boat and doused her potatoes with what was left. Jackie poured them each a second glass of Merlot.

"What did you do today?" Jackie asked Rachel.

"The usual." Rachel avoided looking at Pilar. "Tidied up a bit, a little weeding in back. Another week and it'll be time to feed the roses."

"Where'd you learn that?" Pilar said.

"I wasn't in solitary, you know. We had a garden."

Pilar helped herself to more potatoes. "Quite the domestic, aren't you?"

Rachel smiled sweetly.

"I picked up a few things."

And missed so much more.

"Was it lonely in prison?" Jackie asked.

"Not really. It was like a family." Rachel cut a slice of breast. "What about you, were you raised by your aunt?"

"How did you know?"

"No pictures of parents around. Just one of a woman

who looks like you but is too old to be a sister and too young to be your mother. She's the one who gave you that ring, isn't she?" Rachel pointed to the star sapphire on Jackie's right hand. "Maybe it wasn't hers, but she kept it for you. Right?"

Jackie's fork stopped in midair.

"What happened to your folks?" Rachel said.

"Died in a car accident when I was little. And you're right, my father's sister raised me. The ring belonged to my mother."

"No brothers or sisters? You must've been lonely."

"Not really."

"Did you have many friends at school?"

"Some." But not in that school yard. Rachel's fascination with her private life was unnerving. "How about you? I mean, before . . ."

"One. Did you have a best friend?"

"Not until college."

"What about boys?"

"What's this," Jackie said lightly, "twenty questions?"

"Who was your first crush?"

"How about them Broncos?" Pilar muttered into her glass.

Rachel looked from one to the other without comprehension.

"You like sports?" she asked Jackie.

"Not directly."

Pilar giggled, and Jackie began to feel sorry for her guest.

"I mean, I'm not much into watching them. Why do you ask?"

"I didn't see any skis. Chris has three pairs. I thought everyone in Denver skied."

"Not Jackie," Pilar said. "You can't get her on a ladder or an airplane, much less a ski lift."

The one time she and Pilar went skiing had been a disaster. Jackie had been paralyzed from the moment the tow rammed into her backside and scooped her up like a forklift. Scuttling sideways like a crab, she reached the bottom of the beginners slope in a record two hours and forty minutes. But Pilar was wrong about airplanes. They didn't bother her at all. Unlike that schoolhouse roof, down was so far away it didn't look real.

"—goes double for flying insects," Pilar was saying. "You should of seen her when those yellow jackets came through her bedroom screen in March. They were big, but boy, were they slow. You would of thought—"

"They were *huge*," Jackie said. "Only the toughest ones make it through winter. The exterminator wasn't sure he got the whole nest."

"In the eaves outside your window?" Rachel said.

"He was afraid to seal it off." Jackie held out her glass and Rachel refilled it. "If yellow jackets get trapped, they eat through the walls."

"Hear about that hive in the attic on the other side of Cheesman Park?" Pilar said. "Couple gets home from work to find the whole damn ceiling collapsed on their bed! Seventy-five gallons of honey ate clear through the attic floor, ruined the furniture and drapes. Then there's that old cottonwood a couple blocks from here. Honeycomb the size of a fifty-gallon—"

"Could we talk about something else?" Jackie said. "Anything?"

"That first guy you kissed," Rachel said. "Who was he?"

The question was almost welcome.

"A jock, of course." The one who'd called a classmate who stuttered a moron. Was that when she began to fear her disability would be a life sentence?

"But you didn't fall in love."

Jackie looked to Pilar for help, but she was busy with her potatoes.

"Not once I realized what a jerk he was, no. What about you?"

"Crushes in reform school, but I've never been in love with a guy. Why do you collect rocks?"

Minerals will help you focus, her aunt had said, they'll clear your head so you can think. She'd given Jackie the Chinese fluorite with the ship inside, had taught her to read stories from the shapes in the crystals. Picture rocks would provide relief from the world of books, where Jackie would always be a stranger.

Pilar was pouring the last of the Merlot.

"Bet I know who gave you your first one," Rachel said.

"First what?"

"Mineral, of course."

She'd never guess. "Who?"

"The jerk."

He'd given her a pyrite, a fist-size chunk of metallic glitter. Fool's gold.

"Who told you?" Jackie said.

Rachel shrugged. "That means I get to ask another question. What've you got going with Dennis Ross?"

Pilar choked on her wine. "You mean *had*."

"He's very good-looking, Jackie, isn't he? How come you never married?"

"I—"

Rachel couldn't deliberately be trying to strike a nerve.

"The way he looks at you, I can tell he still cares." Rachel turned to Pilar. "But you've been married, haven't you?"

"More times than I care to admit." Pilar leaned back in her chair. Whether it was the Merlot or enough garlic to kill a legion of vampires, she was in an expansive mood. "None of them was worth a damn."

"How old were you the first time?"

"Sixteen. Two years and adios."

"Was that when you had a child?"

Pilar reached for her glass. "Who told you that?"

"Just a guess. You look like you'd be a good mother."

"I was." Feathers smoothed, Pilar took a final sip and Jackie let out her breath. Now that she needed a chaperone for Lily, it was all the more crucial that the two of them—

"Was the last one a cop?" Rachel said.

"An investigator for the DA's office. There's a difference."

"Did he hit you?"

"Look, kid. I don't know where you're getting your—"

"Why do you wear a bullet around your neck?"

"What?"

"If I'm not mistaken, that's a nine-millimeter slug. The one you plugged him with?"

Pilar sprang to her feet. Grabbing the pendant at her throat, she thrust it at Rachel. "This bullet was dug outta the hide of a creep in a case I worked when Jackie and I were at the PD's!"

But Jackie knew she was lying.

After Pilar was acquitted, she'd gotten a buddy on the force to give her access to the evidence carton. A jeweler in Larimer Square had turned the lead from her husband's spine into a pendant she claimed was a gift from a former boyfriend. Scratch Pilar chaperoning Rachel and Lily.

Jackie smiled blearily.

"Anyone for dessert?"

Eighteen

I arrived at the home of George and
Evelyn Boyd, 15 State Street, Vivian, at
2045 to interview the Boyds' twelve-year-
old daughter, a classmate of Susie Gant at
Vivian Elementary. The interview was a
follow-up on reports that Rachel Boyd
was seen at Memorial Park on May 5 talking to Freddie Gant the approximate time
he disappeared. Because the subject is a
minor, I went to the Boyd home at this
hour to ensure both parents would be
present during the interview.

The Boyd home is a white frame
ranch-style residence set back from the
street with a fenced yard and swing set.
The home is well maintained, one of the
few in town with a detached garage and
what looks like a workshop out back.
Mrs. Boyd came to the door and when I
asked could I speak to her daughter she
summoned her husband. Mr. Boyd
showed no hesitation in calling Rachel,
who was watching TV in the front room
with her younger brother Christopher
when I arrived. Christopher was told to

wait in his bedroom until the interview was over.

Rachel showed no curiosity why I was there. When I said I wanted to talk about the day Freddie Gant went missing, she smiled. I asked what she remembered of that day and she said it was a Saturday. Despite the late hour she was attentive and alert. The one time she hesitated was towards the end, when I asked about her clothes. With her parents' permission I taped the interview.

DSM: What else do you remember about that day?

RB: I went out to play.

DSM: Do you remember what time that was?

RB: No.

DSM: Who did you play with?

RB: My friends.

DSM: Let's start at the beginning. Do you remember what you did when you got up that morning?

RB: When I got up I brushed my teeth. Then I made my bed. After that I combed my hair. For breakfast—

DSM: What did you do after breakfast?

RB: Helped my mom around the house. Chris was out with my dad.

DSM: And then?

RB: Played with our dog. I threw him Chris's baseball. He chewed the cover off and the string got loose. I tried to get it away but it was too late, he swallowed it. The string, not the ball. Then I ate lunch. I think it was—

DSM: What did you do after lunch?

RB: Played.

DSM: Where?

RB: The backyard.

DSM: Were you alone or did a friend come over?

RB: I think I was alone. No, someone came over.

DSM: Who was that?

RB: Susie—No, it wasn't Susie. I guess I was alone.

DSM: When did you go to the park?

RB: I asked my mother and she said I could. Are you married?

DSM: I—What?

RB: You're not wearing a ring.

DSM: Do you remember what time it was that you went to the park?

RB: Afternoon.

DSM: Who else was at the park?

RB: I don't remember.

DSM: You don't remember anyone you talked to?

RB: No.

DSM: How about Susie Gant?

RB: She's in my class at school.

DSM: Did you see her there?

RB: Yes.

DSM: Did you know her brother Freddie?

RB: He's just a kid.

DSM: Did you like him?

RB: He's OK.

DSM: Did you talk to him that Saturday?

RB: Who told you that?

DSM: Now listen, Rachel, it's very important that you tell the truth. Did you see Freddie that day?

RB: Yes.

DSM: Why didn't you say so, then?

RB: You asked if I talked to him, not if I *saw* him.

DSM: What did you see?

RB: Freddie talking to a boy.

DSM: Did you know him?

RB: Who?

DSM: The boy. Had you seen him before?

RB: I don't think so.

DSM: Well, what did he look like?

RB: (Giggles.) He had pimples.

DSM: Do you know what he was talking to Freddie about?

RB: No. But next time I looked Freddie was gone.

(I don't know whether Rachel actually saw the boy with pimples. The lead was widely reported on radio and TV, and Rachel is extremely precocious. Throughout the interview I felt she was studying me and tailoring her responses to my reactions. I had to remind myself to watch what I say.)

DSM: Did you see anyone else play with or talk to Freddie?

RB: No.

DSM: You see Freddie again?

RB: I'll bet you're divorced.

DSM: That's not—

RB: Because you used to wear a ring. I can see the mark.

DSM: I—

RB: Is she the one who left?

DSM: (Silence.) When did you leave the park?

RB: Before supper. That night we had—

DSM: Where did you go?

RB: Home.

DSM: Did you go by the railroad tracks?

RB: (Giggles.) That's not the way home!

DSM: Were you near the tracks on Saturday?

RB: No.

DSM: How 'bout the grain elevator?

RB: We can't play there.

DSM: Did you?

RB: What?

DSM: Go to the grain elevator Saturday?

RB: No.

DSM: Have you ever been there?

RB: Well, once. But it was a long time ago.

DSM: What did you wear that day?

RB: What day?

DSM: Saturday.

RB: Well, when I woke up I was wearing pee-jays. My yellow and white ones. The ones with—

DSM: At the park.

RB: (Long silence.) My red shorts and tennies. It was hot.

DSM: Did you go to Freddie's house on Sunday?

RB: What for?

DSM: To ask if he was there.

RB: I don't remember.

DSM: His mom said it was you. Why'd you do that?

RB: On a dare.

DSM: Who dared you?

RB: Trina. Trina Maune.

Memo to file: If Rachel Boyd is charged, tell DA Floyd Garrett to hold something back at trial. Repeat offenders learn from their mistakes and this one could do it again.

Nineteen

"Round up the usual suspects," Jackie told Pilar. The rest of the autopsy photos had finally arrived.

"What about Lee Simms?"

Jackie shook her head. "Call Dennis for the name of that medical examiner he always used. I want him in the courtroom to keep Doby honest. And a retired detective, one of those posole-loving buddies of yours from the force."

"I know just the dick."

"Not someone you've had rack time with."

"Jackie!" Pilar pretended to be hurt. "I'd never jeopardize—"

"—a repeat performance in the sack."

"None of them was that good. By the way, I dug up Simms's stories on Freddie Gant. There was a whole series of them. Vignettes of the town, profiles of the Boyds. Must've had a helluva source."

"Hmm?"

"His stories were so detailed. He got in early and dug up stuff none of the other papers found."

"Like what?"

"What Freddie's mom made for supper that day. He even knew Art Gant got home from his haul at midnight and the little boy had new buttons on his pants."

"Tabloids pay for human interest. That's why they're dangerous. . . . Aren't you and Lily going to a matinee?"

Her investigator was dressed in a white pantsuit and a black fedora.

"We booked pedicures at Lalo's in Cherry Creek,"

Pilar said. "Think he can match this color?" Her nails were as red as the silk ribbon on her fedora.

"Don't let Lily paint hers black again."

"Why don't you come out and play? You could use a touch-up."

An afternoon at the beauty parlor with Lily and Pilar would be a relief from another evening at home with Rachel. And Pilar was right: she could use a touch-up. It wasn't just the gray. Spring always made her horny, almost made her miss Dennis.

"I've got work to do."

Ignoring Pilar's sigh, Jackie reached for the photos.

The bloody scratches on Ben Sparks's arms, neck and face dated those injuries to before or at the time of death. If his body had been kept elsewhere for twenty-four hours, they weren't from being dumped in the bramble. Her eyes dropped to the boy's stomach.

The cuts in Ben's lower abdomen were different from the scratches on his face. Evenly spaced but savage, frenzied—as if he'd been clawed. Sexual rage?

"Penetration?"

"Inconclusive," Pilar said. "Anus was dilated, but it's not uncommon for the sphincter to open after death. Like most muscles, it relaxes."

"No damage to the membranes?"

"Nope."

"Sperm?"

"Not in any orifices. Snow could of washed it away."

A color close-up of Ben's inner thigh showed two bruises. Violet in the center, they faded to a brownish yellow at the edge. One was in the shape of a circle and the other was a half-moon. Each was comprised of a series of smaller bruises linked like a strand of pearls. The flesh looked pinched but the marks seemed too small for fingernails.

"Like Freddie Gant," Pilar said. "Cuts but no conclusive evidence of rape. That's one reason they focused on Rachel."

"Doby still has to show motive." Sexual frenzy was tough to infer when the defendant was an adult woman and the victim a small boy. But that brought Jackie back to square one. Freddie Gant. Had Rachel killed him? And why?

Pilar had located eight-by-eleven black-and-white glossies of the first boy's autopsy. In the head shot Freddie's eyes were closed. His lashes were long and curly, so fine they were almost invisible. They made the crescent-shaped bruise on his cheek all the more cruel. Two distinctive marks in the center faded at the periphery—

"What's that gummy stuff on his eyelids?" Pilar said.

"Larvae," said a deep voice.

The reporter stood in their door.

"Look, Mr. Simms," Jackie said. "I told you—"

"Larvae?" Pilar said. "As in flies?"

Simms was wearing a clean shirt and this time his eyes weren't quite so bloodshot. He crossed the floor and reached for the photo.

"Different insects become attracted at each stage of decay. A necrophage—"

"Decay?" said another voice. "As in death?"

Lily was wearing red toreador pants and a black off-the-shoulder jersey. As she teetered into the office behind Simms on black wedgies and posed with one hand on her hip, Jackie saw she was beginning to develop curves. And she was wearing lipstick instead of gloss.

"Mr. Simms, I'm asking you politely to leave." Laying the photos facedown, Jackie pointed to the door. She turned to the girl. "Won't you and Pilar be late?"

Simms settled in the chair next to her desk and picked up a paper clip.

"As I was saying, necrophagous species feed on the body itself. Predators and parasites feed on the necrophages, and omnivores will eat anything. Those larvae were left by flies."

"Larvae?" Lily said. "Gross!"

Simms fiddled with the paper clip.

"Don't you like bugs?"

Lily was watching his hands. "Where'd you get that idea?"

He twisted the paper clip into a pair of rabbit ears.

"Young ladies aren't supposed to like bugs."

"Who says I'm a lady?"

Simms straightened the stack of photos, leaving them facedown, and took another paper clip. Gazing at Lily from the corner of his eye, he unbent the wire and folded it in half, securing the two strands with a firm twist.

"What makes you think it was flies?" Lily continued.

"They lay their eggs in orifices immediately after death. Lacking any shame, they've been doing it in daylight since the dawn of time." He flipped the ends of the wire up to form a dragonfly. He was enticing Lily. Like the man at the ice cream parlor with Ben Sparks? "Pretty neat, huh?"

"Mr. Simms!"

Ignoring Jackie, he handed the dragonfly to Lily.

"So you like insects. What's your favorite?"

Lily glanced at Pilar.

"Bees. Jackie has a huge hive, right here in her office. One day it'll explode."

"Doesn't surprise me. Unless you get the queen, the hive expands. But you shouldn't be afraid of bees. Proliferation is their nature. You like dinosaurs?"

"Sure!"

"I'm not joking, Simms." Jackie moved to the door. "Thirty seconds—"

"If you're not a fraidy-cat, there's something I might show you."

"When?" Lily said.

He looked at Jackie. "Some other time."

"Come on, pet," Pilar said. "Lalo will bump us if we're late."

"Where are you ladies going?"

"For a pedicure," Lily said.

Simms heaved a theatrical sigh. Having conquered Lily, he turned the full force of his charm on Pilar. "I have a weakness for painted toes. And fedoras."

With a giggle and a wave, Pilar and Lily left.

"Do you go after anything that walks?" Jackie said.

"Or flies."

Turning the autopsy photos faceup on the desk, Simms was suddenly all business. He reached for the close-up of the wounds in Freddie Gant's abdomen. They seemed shallower than Ben's, but more evenly spaced—a scoring so regular it could have been inflicted by a three-tined fork.

"Those lacerations—" Jackie began.

"Incisions." Simms gestured impatiently. "Lacerations are caused by blunt trauma that splits the skin and leaves a ragged edge. Incisions are a cut or a slash."

Rachel Boyd took a knife . . .

And it was sharp.

"They never found it?" Jackie said.

"Found what?"

"The knife."

"What makes you think that was the weapon?"

"I don't know. I guess I just—"

Simms shook his head in disgust. "Stab wounds are

produced by pointed instruments, the most common of which is a flat-bladed, single-edged kitchen or pocketknife. But fatal wounds have been inflicted with scissors and screwdrivers. Even pencils."

"You know a lot about wounds for a reporter. Why?"

"The mystery is, why does a defense lawyer know so little?"

"You didn't answer my question."

"I was a police reporter. Now answer mine."

"I told you. I'm not cutting you in on this case."

"Takes a certain arrogance to gamble with your client's life."

Jackie stood. "What part of no don't you understand?"

"The no that pretends there's no connection between two small boys whose necks were snapped and groins were slashed. And who were last seen with your client." His eyes bored into hers. "As I said, those cuts could've been made by any sharp-edged weapon, including glass, metal or paper."

"Paper?"

"The sharp edge is pressed into and drawn along the skin, producing a cut that's longer than deep. What's most significant is their lack of uniformity."

"They look the same to me."

"Two of them were hesitation marks. The first cut was here." He pointed to a three-inch slash just below Freddie's navel. The edges of the wound were smooth. "A test stroke. Barely scratched the skin. The one below is deeper, see? With the final cut they went all the way through."

Just above the boy's penis.

"They?"

"Two children switching off, or one slowly working up her nerve."

Her little friend begged for his life.

She'd risen to Simms's bait. If he knew so much about wounds, he owed her something in return. "What are those bruises on Ben's thigh?"

"Bruises?"

She passed him the color close-up of Ben's leg. The half-moon was about the size of the bruise on Freddie's cheek.

Simms sucked in every detail, then shrugged indifferently.

"Kids bruise more easily than adults."

Was that all?

"If it's any consolation," he continued, "it's impossible to say whether the same type knife was used on both boys. Too many variables: direction of the thrust, condition of the blade, how it was held as it entered the skin. Unless the tip broke off inside, the most you can tell from a wound is width, length and whether the blade was single- or double-edged. But practice makes perfect."

"Practice?"

"The scratches on Freddie Gant were child's play."

"Save that for the tabloids."

Simms's smile was patronizing.

"Ever watch a kitten with a mouse? Once she corners it, she'll bat it around, tease it by pinning it with her paw. She's experimenting. Testing the limits of her power. If the mouse is smart, it plays dead. Eventually the kitten gets bored and lets it go. The next time she catches a mouse, it might not be so lucky. And the third time . . . Well, by then she knows it's nothing more than prey. And with two little cats—"

"First insects, now cats. You're quite the animal behaviorist."

"Somebody better start thinking about who did this. And why."

"You're as full of it as Doby."

"So I noticed. His witness at Congress Park is useless, isn't he?"

If Simms wasn't one step ahead of Jackie, he was at least running even.

"Who told you that?"

"The DA's office is a sieve," he said. "Two reporters have already gotten leaks. They're just waiting for a chance to go to print."

"What leaks?"

"Wouldn't you like to know."

"What do you want?"

Simms laughed easily. "An interview with your client. Exclusive, of course."

"What's in it for her?"

"Aside from advance warning of Doby's tricks—"

"Which I couldn't care less about—"

"—and my brilliant investigatory assistance? A chance to tell her story."

"She gets that in court."

"To five million people?"

"Only twelve of them count. And it's such a better story if she's convicted. How do I know you're not trying to hang her?"

Simms rose.

"You don't."

Twenty

It was past six when Jackie left her office. The evening was warm, and she rolled down her window and tried to focus on the traffic. Lee Simms was getting under her skin.

His knowledge of knives and wounds was too encyclopedic for even the most dedicated police reporter. How many crimes had he really reported? She'd ask Pilar to dig a little deeper into his background—

Jackie looked up just as she missed the entrance to her alley. Now she had to circle her block. But a pickup truck double-parked in front of the house next door forced her to go another block before looping back to her alley.

Something else about that reporter. Maybe his talk about blades was meant to distract. Wasn't it curious that he showed so little interest in those boys' bruises? And what about those darker areas in the center of the discoloration? Could they have been punched by someone wearing a ring? Or maybe—

Damn. Now she'd gone right past the Botanic Gardens. Not the first time she'd been so distracted she got lost on her way home. She pulled into a side street that dead-ended at the no-man's-land north of Congress Park. She'd have to make a U-turn. . . . Through her open window she heard a shout.

"Goal!"

The soccer fields were directly above her. And the bushes where Ben had been found. Motive couldn't be the only hole in Doby's case.

Jackie parked at the foot of the steel staircase leading into the bramble.

The concrete retaining wall at the base of the incline was five feet high. Beyond the wall rose a chain-link fence topped by three strands of barbed wire. From there the hill sloped at forty-five degrees up to a second fence at the soccer fields' edge, covering twelve feet of elevation. Two flights of steps led from the street to the second fence. The stairway was painted playground colors. Teal treads, the railing rain-slicker yellow. Jackie put her foot on the first rung.

How much did a six-year-old boy weigh?

Six steps and a landing, then a sharp turn before continuing at a right angle. Twenty-two more steps to the top. Could a woman Rachel Boyd's size carry forty pounds of dead weight up those stairs?

Jackie looked at the three-story apartment complex at the base of the slope. The custodian was Russian; the weekend of Ben's murder she and her boyfriend had been out of town. The only potential witnesses were the tenants on the south side of the building, but Pilar had gotten zilch. Now Jackie understood why.

Another fence separated the bramble from the apartments. Each unit had a balcony, but a tree whose width spanned several units and whose crown soared above the roof obscured the view. The roof itself bristled with satellite dishes and cable antennae. The residents' priorities lay elsewhere than monitoring the bushes.

Jackie peered across the steep strip. Cars whizzed by two blocks away on the busy artery of Josephine, but the bramble itself was totally secluded. Below the dogwoods, tall grasses were already going to seed. Several varieties, all deep emerald from the late spring snow, tipped with patches of purple. Long ago someone had taken the trouble to plant them. This no-man's-land was an urban glen.

Jackie listened.

Cars on Josephine and far-off cries from the soccer fields. One sound was missing. No birds, though this time of day her garden was filled with them.

She turned to the bramble.

The dogwoods started just below the soccer fence. A dense stand of bushes six feet tall, stippled with tiny white blossoms. Continuing along their length she came to a break in the foliage invisible from the street. A scrap of yellow crime scene tape clung to the underbrush. Several branches were bowed but unbroken, as if something heavy had lain there. The wood was green but these twigs had no buds. Every spot but that one bore flowers.

If Ben wasn't killed on the way home from Toody-Froody, Doby's case against Rachel was much weaker. Even if a hundred-pound woman could have lugged forty pounds of dead weight up those narrow steps and a hundred yards through tall grass before heaving it up a forty-five-degree incline into bushes six feet tall, she would have needed a car to get there.

Rachel didn't drive.

Jackie counted off the paces to Josephine. Thirty-five yards. A chain strung two feet from the ground marked that entrance to the bramble. Petite as she was, she had no trouble stepping over it. There was parking on the street by the entrance; a private lot for the apartments stood directly to the north. If the killer waited for dark, it made sense to drive down Josephine, pull into the lot, step over the chain and dump the body at the break in the bushes. The snow would have been a bonus. She made a mental note to have Pilar photograph the site for trial.

Jackie would find out for herself why there were no buds in that one spot.

Twenty-One

Pilar downshifted and the Spider made the sharp left at the entrance to Boulder's Chautauqua Park. "Who's this Hart broad again?"

"A forensic botanist," Jackie said. They'd finally received the supplemental autopsy report on the contents of Ben Sparks's digestive tract.

"What's she got to do with cashews and coconut?"

"With a little luck, everything."

The rustic dining hall and auditorium atop the meadow overlooking the university town exuded a charm excessive even by Boulder standards. Had Pilar known it was founded at the turn of the preceding century by a bunch of visiting Texans, she would have liked it even less.

"How do you know her?" Pilar said.

"Flavia Hart was my biology professor."

"They made you take science in college?"

"Plants and Man was my favorite course."

Three one-syllable words. Was that why she'd chosen that class?

College was another experience she preferred to forget.

Jackie had missed orientation. Like her fellow freshmen, she'd received the packet; she just couldn't decipher the notice. Registration was a nightmare of forms, compounded by trying to figure out the required courses by their catalog numbers. This many hours of English, that much history . . . Could every one of the University of Colorado's twenty thousand students be tapping his foot in frustration in line behind her?

The next stop was the campus bookstore, where trying to match the cards on the shelves to her classes' texts almost overwhelmed her. Even the professors' names were incomprehensible. All around her, students were filling their shopping baskets with notebooks and pencils and bright plastic dividers. Jackie had never felt so alone.

When she entered the lecture hall on the first day of Intro to American History, the blackboard was so far away she couldn't read it if she'd tried. The screech of the microphone, the instructor's reedy voice bouncing off concrete walls and acoustic ceiling tile, the flickering fluorescent lights . . . and five hundred students unwrapping candy bars, shifting in their seats, metal squeaking as they lifted the arms of their chairs and snapped them into place before cracking open their notebooks. Jackie lasted until a teaching assistant handed out an eight-page single-spaced syllabus of reading assignments, with the dates of every test and quiz highlighted in bold.

That night she'd called her aunt.

"I can't do this."

"Yes, you can. You've never quit."

"But it's not like high school, it's—"

"Find the teachers who make it real."

Jackie dropped American History. Desperate for replacement credits, she returned to the bookstore and scanned the shelves. The biology texts were mostly pictures. Unlike language or history, biology was visual. Plants and Man sounded manageable and its text was the most lavishly illustrated. She could even pronounce the professor's name.

That afternoon Jackie slipped into Flavia Hart's class. A screen had been hung over the blackboard. The hall went dark and she took a deep breath. The first slide was a forest of giant kelp, with sunlight filtering through blue water and bathing the tips a brilliant green. The next slide showed red algae as delicately branched as lace. Professor Hart lectured without notes or a microphone; neither her voice nor her passion required amplification. At the end of the hour she said she'd forgotten to bring the syllabus, but not to worry because there would be no reading assignments for the first two weeks. Plants and Man was the only A in Jackie's academic career.

"How can this Hart broad help us?" Pilar said.

"By telling us precisely when Ben Sparks died."

The Spider crept past communal buildings and began a steeper ascent toward the Flatirons. A hundred cottages were tucked against the hillside, on rutted streets named Wild Rose and Morning Glory Lane.

"How will she do on the stand?" Pilar said.

"Flavia can handle anything."

It took a special kind of expert to communicate with jurors. To most academics, the culture shock was insurmountable. Designed to reveal truth, the laws of science had nothing to do with the rules of evidence. The ideal expert could give a crash course in forensics without boring the jury to tears or making them lose their lunch, and withstand a cross designed to expose him as a charlatan or a liar.

Flavia Hart no longer taught Plants and Man. In her retirement, she consulted gratis with law enforcement throughout the country. If Jackie's old professor was half as effective in court as she was in class, Cal Doby had better watch out.

Spotting a bungalow with an English garden of larkspur, roses and cosmos and a woman with a bird's nest of hair, Jackie tugged Pilar's sleeve.

"There she is!"

"What makes you think she'll remember you?" Pilar said.

Flavia Hart waved from the porch.

"Flowers?" she boomed. "That you?"

Of the hundred students in Plants and Man, perhaps it was Jackie's name that endeared her to the botanist. Or was it because for her term paper on the vanilla bean, Jackie submitted the report her aunt typed on sheets soaked in eighty-proof vanilla extract? Whatever the reason, Flavia Hart was more than happy to receive a former student. Particularly one who offered her a chance to apply her expertise to a gory crime.

It was cool inside the stone cottage and Flavia offered refreshments. Scanning the materials Jackie had brought, the retired professor cut to the chase.

"Where's the poo print?"

Pilar's herbal tea sloshed in her cup.

"I take it your friend here skipped freshman biology?" Flavia said. "You, on the other hand—"

An old saying popped into Jackie's head.

The work of the digestion is done in the small intestine.

"—can explain to her why I hold plant cell walls in such reverence."

"They're eternal," Jackie said.

"Yes!" Beaming, Flavia fixed on Pilar. "The living part of a plant cell is enclosed in a sac of cellulose so tough that termites are the only ones who can digest it. We still identify plant cells in mummies, bog people and woolly mammoths; even when they're excreted we can tell what they were. Remember what your mother said about chewing each bite ten times? Luckily, we don't chew enough—especially teenagers—so things pass through virtually intact."

Pilar bit into a muffin. "What's in this, pumpkin seeds?"

Flavia winked.

"Plant cells are very distinctive. Some have spines or hair."

"You don't say," Pilar said.

"Pineapple has crystals like needles. Okra's the easiest to identify; I just wish more people ate it. Do you enjoy Chinese food, my dear?"

"It's okay."

"Next time you bite into a water chestnut, remember you're just eating a piece of wood. Now olives, on the other hand, have enormous globules of fat—"

Pilar stopped in midbite.

"—but pulp all looks pretty much the same. You understand how digestion works? The mouth breaks plants into smaller pieces mixed with saliva, and the stomach bathes everything in acid. A healthy gut's pumping and churning breaks up the clumps."

Pilar set down her muffin.

"The pyloric valve is the gateway to the small intestine. Unlike the anal sphincter, it stays shut when you die and doesn't relax until decomposition advances. I remember one case with chilies, black beans, onions and— Are you all right, my dear?"

Pilar wiped her mouth on a napkin. "Just peachy."

"As I was saying, the contents of a victim's last meal can show where he ate, who he ate with and the time of death. Why, I had one case where the victims ate pizza. The stomach contents were so fresh, the tomato sauce was still red and you could smell the oregano!"

"Uh . . ."

"Vomit also provides a rich source of plant materials, but I prefer poo. Feces can be complex to analyze, of course, depending on the victim's eating and bowel habits. A single sample can contain material from more than one meal— You're sure you're all right?"

Pilar nodded.

"Good. Now, some forensic botanists stop at the pyloric sphincter—"

"They don't do doo-doo."

Flavia looked at Pilar with new respect.

"They don't know what they're missing. Fecal material never disintegrates, especially in the dryness of Colorado. And poo prints can be as distinctive as fingerprints."

"Poo prints?"

"Perfect poo matches are not uncommon in burglary scenes; it starts with the adrenaline rush during the first robbery and becomes a pattern. You rehydrate the material to mount it on a slide." She turned to Jackie. "Which I did not see in your packet."

"That's because the ice cream Ben Sparks ate never left his stomach."

"Yes, I noticed that was his last meal. Coconut and cashews, I believe?"

"Can you tell how soon afterwards he died?"

"Within two hours."

A two-hour swing was tighter than ten, but Flavia's verdict made the discrepancy between Rachel's story and the Toody-Froody clerk's even more crucial. If they arrived at the ice cream parlor at one that afternoon, instead of two as Rachel claimed, and Ben was killed by three, Rachel Boyd wasn't just the prime suspect. She was the *only* suspect. And she had time to hide his body. But if the clerk was wrong—

"—sorry I can't be more helpful. Is there anything else in the autopsy pertaining to plant material?"

"Dirt in the cuff of the kid's trousers," Pilar said.

"What sort of dirt?"

"Garden dirt."

"Philistines. Was the body transported in a vehicle?"

"It must have been," Jackie said. "Why?"

"A car can be linked to a crime scene, if police collect the proper material. They tend to overlook seams in the pedals, under the windshield wipers, the wheel wells."

Flavia led them to the door.

"Do come again, perhaps for dinner?" She gave Pilar a sly look. "I promise not to serve pineapple or okra."

As they walked to the car, Jackie noticed bushes flowering along the sheltered side of the cottage.

"Dogwoods?" she asked.

"They survived the late snow," Flavia said. "Lovely, aren't they?"

Before the April storm the lilacs in Jackie's own garden had been about to bloom. "You'd think the snow would kill the buds."

"Not at all. A heavy snowfall insulates against a rapid drop in temperature."

"And if the place where a body lay never bloomed—"

"—you know the body was left shortly before or after the snow began to fall."

They were back in the game.

Regardless of when Rachel and Ben left the ice cream parlor, the snow proved his body wasn't dumped until around eight o'clock Monday night. If Doby staked his case on the boy being killed and his body left in the bramble on the way home from Toody-Froody on Sunday afternoon, Rachel would walk.

"Will you testify for the defense?"

"I assume you don't want a report," Flavia crisply replied.

Jackie's old professor had been around the block

enough times to know expert witness statements had to be disclosed to the other side. But if she wanted Flavia to testify, she still had to give Doby her name.

"The DA will send someone to interview you," she told Flavia. "It's up to you whether to talk to his investigator or not."

Jackie's old professor brightened.

"I have a splendid recipe for okra."

Twenty-Two

TRANSCRIPT OF INTERVIEW OF TRINA MAUNE
CONDUCTED BY DETECTIVE SERGEANT RYAN
MITCHELL ON MAY 11, 1973

> At 1725 this date I interviewed Trina
> Maune at the Maune home at 60 Bell
> Street, Vivian. It is a more modest resi-
> dence than the Boyds, with a tarpaper
> roof and no garage. Trina is thirteen years
> old. She is the oldest of six children of
> Harold and Lucy Maune. Her mother was
> present during the interview, which was
> taped.

DSM: Trina, are you friends with Rachel Boyd?

TM: Um, we're in the same class. She's my best
friend.

DSM: Were you with Rachel a week ago Saturday?

TM: Where did you hear that?

DSM: Were you?

TM: Was I what?

DSM: With Rachel Boyd last Saturday?

TM: Uh-huh.

DSM: You remember what you girls did?

TM: Not really.

DSM: Try.

TM: Uh, I think I went to her house. Or maybe she
came here.

DSM: Was that in the morning?

TM: I think so.

DSM: Or afternoon?

TM: Could of been.

DSM: Did you go to the park?

TM: Yeah.

DSM: Who else did you see?

TM: I don't remember.

DSM: Was it Susie?

TM: Susie?

DSM: Susie Gant.

TM: Yeah. I used to be in her class.

DSM: Did you know Susie's little brother Freddie?

TM: We used to babysit him. Susie's mom gave us each a quarter.

DSM: Were you babysitting Freddie that day?

TM: No, silly. The quarters were always new.

DSM: Shiny?

TM: With eagles on the back.

DSM: Did you see Freddie at the park that day?

TM: He had a truck. I think.

DSM: Did you play with him?

TM: It was a red truck.

DSM: You like shiny things, don't you, Trina?

TM: Rachel does too. Susie said he got that truck for—

DSM: Did you talk to Freddie?

TM: We told him to go away.

DSM: Who?

TM: Me and Rachel. He was always following us around.

DSM: Did you see Freddie with anyone else?

TM: No. Unless . . .

DSM: Unless what?

TM: Nothing.

DSM: Was there a stranger at the park that afternoon, anyone you didn't know?

TM: Unh-uh.

DSM: What time did you leave?

TM: I had to help my mom fix supper.

DSM: Did Rachel go with you?

TM: Why would she? I mean, it was *my* mom.

DSM: Remember what you girls were wearing that day?

TM: I—my blue shorts and a bandanna shirt.

DSM: How 'bout Rachel?

TM: (Hesitates.) I think it was a dress.

DSM: A dress?

TM: Yeah.

DSM: On Saturday?

TM: The one with pink checks. It has this real pretty sash, it ties—

DSM: Do you remember what Freddie was wearing?

TM: Freddie? Why would I remember that?

DSM: You remember Rachel's clothes.

TM: I told you, I never saw him up close.

DSM: Have you ever been to the grain elevator?

TM: No.

DSM: But your dad works there, doesn't he?

TM: So?

DSM: You must have gone there.

TM: Where?

DSM: The grain elevator, Trina.

TM: He took me there maybe once.

DSM: Were you girls at the elevator or the railroad tracks that day?

TM: We never! I didn't even—

DSM: Didn't what?

TM: (Hesitates.) See Freddie after. (Long silence.)

DSM: After what?

TM: You know.

DSM: No, I don't. Why don't you tell me, Trina?

TM: Rachel said—

DSM: Not to talk?

TM: I can't say if I don't know.

DSM: But you can tell me what Rachel says.

TM: Who said she told me anything?

DSM: You did, Trina. Just now.

TM: You know what happens to rats.

DSM: Did she threaten you?

TM: (Laughs.) Dear me!

DSM: Beg pardon?

TM: Rachel never tells me what to say.

DSM: The kids at school, what do they think?

TM: About what?

DSM: What happened to Freddie.

TM: We don't talk.

DSM: Sure you do. I mean, you must have some ideas.

TM: About what?

DSM: Who could have hurt Freddie.

TM: There was a man.

DSM: What man?

TM: I don't know.

DSM: Does he live in town?

TM: He hung around Freddie. I don't know.

DSM: You don't know his name, or you don't know whether he hurt Freddie?

TM: Why would the man hurt Freddie?

DSM: You tell *me*, Trina. You're the one who said there was a man.

TM: I don't—

DSM: Do you know a man who wanted to hurt him?

TM: (Long silence.) Maybe.

DSM: You know what, Trina? I don't think there was a man.

TM: Um.

DSM: I think it was a girl.

TM: A girl?

DSM: Maybe more than one girl. We know you were there, Trina.

TM: How?

DSM: Because Rachel was there.

TM: Where?

DSM: At the elevator, by the tracks. What we need to know is whether it was planned. Was Rachel mad at Freddie?

TM: He had a red truck.

DSM: Did Rachel want the truck? Is that what happened?

TM: (No answer.)

DSM: He had shiny new buttons on his pants, didn't he? Is that what she wanted?

TM: Buttons?

DSM: Special buttons. What made them so special, Trina?

TM: They were blue, with a pretty red anchor. (She stops.)

DSM: Did Rachel take you to Freddie? After?

TM: (Long silence.) How did he look?

DSM: Who? Say his name, Trina.

TM: (No answer.)

DSM: Did you tell Rachel to go to Freddie's house on Sunday?

TM: Sunday?

DSM: To ask Freddie's mom if they found him yet?

TM: It was Rachel's idea.

DSM: Why?

TM: I don't know. Ask her.

DSM: Why would I do that?

TM: Rachel always knows.

During the interview Trina kept looking at her mother. She was nervous but I got the idea she enjoyed the attention. She was clearly at the scene of the crime. I think she would have said more if her mother wasn't there.

Twenty-Three

The sconce at the entrance to the restaurant hinted at adventure. The foyer had stuffed chairs and a velvet love seat, the bar sat eight and the maître d' had rings in both ears. As Jackie scanned the dining room for her dinner date, she wondered why he'd so carefully set the scene.

It wasn't as if she and Dennis had no history in places like this. He'd chosen this restaurant because the location had turned over so many times and after each inaugural meal they'd ended up in the sack.

This time Jackie intended to do the pumping.

The waiters wore black trousers and sapphire shirts, and the swirled plaster walls evoked Tuscany. The tables were set with sprigs of narcissus and votives in tin holders. The menu would be written in a florid hand.

Just order the special. This was on Dennis's dime.

"There you are!" He stooped to kiss her cheek, this time ending at the edge of her mouth. He'd shaved before leaving the office and his skin was smooth and cool. "I was afraid I'd be late."

"Another deposition?"

He smiled.

"Something more up your alley."

The maître d' showed them to a table at the picture window overlooking the street. In winter the trees on the sidewalk would be festooned with tiny white lights. Pedestrians strolling arm in arm to the corner cinema were so close you could touch them if not for the glass. Dennis ordered martinis.

"I didn't know Kellogg & Kemp represented rapists and thieves," she said.

"Not in a manner of speaking, no." He sounded disappointed. "An embezzler."

Embezzlers were Jackie's least favorite clients. Crime was in their bones; even their lawyers were fair game. At least that was the reason she gave for turning those referrals down. In truth, she had more in common with garden-variety frauds than the street criminals who were the meat and potatoes of her practice.

It wasn't as if she'd deliberately concealed her disability. In fact, Dennis had been warned.

Because he was on the hiring committee at the Public Defender's Office, he knew Jackie had graduated from law school with the lowest passing GPA. When she told him she flunked Criminal Procedure, he'd laughed. And when she argued her motions without notes, he held her up as an example to the other rookies. *Watch how Flowers does it. She uses that legal pad as a prop, not a crutch!* She always wondered whether he knew how close to the truth that was. How could someone as astute as Dennis be so blind?

"—could really use you in this case," he was saying as the waiter handed them menus embossed with rose petals. The paper was like cloth and the pen strokes utterly illegible. "You'd love this guy, Jackie, he'd sell his own grandmother for a cup of coffee—"

When she left the PD, Jackie had been so desperate for clients she'd agreed to defend the chief financial officer of a construction company who awarded himself an illegal bonus. He lied about everything from his date of birth to his mother's maiden name, but it was the nausea and fatigue from wading through the morass of paper that Jackie never forgot. As usual, she'd fared better in court.

Lamenting her lousy handwriting and lack of mathematical skills, she had the DA's witnesses perform the computations on the blackboard for the jury. When her client was acquitted she was so sick of the mess she didn't even chase him for her fee. Dennis had no idea what it was like. . . .

"—probably cop a plea."

She handed him her menu, slipping back into their comfortable routine.

"Order for me."

As Dennis read the menu, Jackie sipped her martini. The tables were close but low jazz encouraged conversation and the candy scent of the narcissus acted as a veil. The velvet curtains at the window and pedestrians walking by without looking in reinforced the sense of intimacy. She studied Dennis's reflection in the glass.

Rachel was right: he was good-looking. More than good-looking. His hair was graying faster than hers but it was still curly and thick. Unexpectedly soft to the touch. Like the hair on his chest. He was gazing at the menu with the same single-minded focus he gave a witness on the stand.

"I'll have the sweetbreads and the duck," he told the waiter. He frowned in concentration but knew Jackie's taste too well to stray. "The lady will have lobster risotto for her appetizer and scallops for the entrée." The waiter glided off and Dennis turned to her with brilliant eyes. "Where did we leave things?"

"Last time we talked, you wanted to know Rachel's defense."

"So much for soft lights and music." Did he switch to martinis when he joined the Seventeenth Street crowd? "If I were you, I wouldn't trust me either."

Because of attorney-client confidentiality, or something else?

Jackie raised her glass. "To the rules of engagement."

"What's it like, having a client stay with you? The most I've done is let a guy sleep it off on my couch."

"Rachel's the ideal houseguest. Did you ever represent someone who asks for nothing? Makes you want to do that much more."

"I know the feeling."

"She's quiet as a mouse. Gets up with the birds and is in bed with lights out by nine. I don't know what she does during the day, but my house has never been so clean and that fountain out back is actually running. I should be paying *her.*"

"No flak from the press?"

"We had a come-to-Jesus the first time they set foot in the yard. They probably think they'll get more out of Doby."

And they would. After the hint the prosecutor had dropped at the bail hearing, the *News* had printed a nasty story about Rachel's personal relationships in Cañon City—based on unattributed sources. Doby's coziness with the local press made it all the more imperative to get the trial transferred out of Denver.

"The avuncular executioner," Dennis said. "Don't turn your back on him for one minute."

"Me trust a DA!"

"Lots of defense lawyers have made the mistake of underestimating Cal Doby, Jackie. That buffoonery is a screen."

"For what? Serious incompetence?"

The table was so small the butter was stacked on the napkin-draped bread. Dennis tore off a piece and buttered it before handing it to her. "He still manages to score points. But every DA has the same Achilles' heel."

"They follow the recipe on the cereal box." Dennis had taught her that more years ago than she could remember. Especially under the influence of what had turned into a second martini. "The only challenge is figuring out whether Doby had Cheerios or cornflakes and skip three steps ahead."

"So what's the breakfast of champions today?"

"Kix and Dirty Trix."

Dennis had no trouble reading that recipe. "Guilt by association. Pound Rachel on the Freddie Gant conviction—"

"—play hide-the-autopsy-report, and make me chase every rabbit down the hole."

"It's not a game to Doby," he warned. "Duncan Pratt's office is really hurting. You've had too many high-profile wins for their taste."

"My last big trial was in Boulder," she said.

"Doesn't matter. Pratt's still smarting from your client walking in that decapitation case out in Castle Pines two years ago. It's a miracle he won his last election. He even counts the misdemeanor plea on your I-25 case as a loss. At the City and County Building they're making book on who takes you down."

"Well, it ain't gonna be Doby."

The waiter brought their appetizers and poured wine Jackie hadn't heard Dennis order. Her eyes slid to the painting on the wall behind his head. It was tinted with a waxy substance that caught the light and made it glow like honey. Her risotto had morels and something tender and perfumed. She began to appreciate the languid pace.

"So how are you going to defend Chris's sister?" Dennis asked.

"That depends on what Doby throws at us."

"Come on, Jackie. You can trust me. . . ."

Could she? He was Chris Boyd's lawyer. She kept it vague.

"Attack the weaknesses in the prosecution's case. Means, opportunity—"

"What about motive?"

"Rachel has to be either incredibly stupid or nuts to commit a carbon-copy murder months after being released from prison. Her IQ's off the charts and I don't plan on entering an insanity plea."

"Any motions in the works?"

A matter of public record. Or they would be soon enough.

"Our hearing on change of venue is set for a month from now. Next week I'm arguing a Rule 404 motion to exclude evidence of the Freddie Gant case. Maybe I'm blind, but I just don't see the similarities."

"Aside from the victims' ages and their broken necks?"

Not to mention those claw marks. And what about the bruises?

"Greta Mueller's no pushover," Jackie replied. "To let the jury hear about a thirty-year-old murder, Doby has to show more than a superficial resemblance."

Dennis nodded. "He'll have to produce evidence of the same MO or intent."

Back to the slashes on Freddie Gant's abdomen. And the real reason Jackie had agreed to this dinner. "Speaking of which, didn't you represent an abused boy once?"

"Once?" Dennis snorted. "Darling, ninety percent of guys charged with crimes were abused. Who do you mean?"

"That kid who terrorized his classmates. The one with the strange weapon."

He topped off their wineglasses before replying.

"Ice pick. Same tool his mother's boyfriend used on him before he started cutting boys two grades below him at school. My kid was pricked so many times in the back it looked like he had smallpox. Just deep enough to inflict pain—they always remember the pain. His way of controlling the boy so he'd submit. Not to mention marking his territory."

"What was your defense?"

"What else? We put on a shrink. He talked about abused kids acting out against pets or smaller children the rage they experience against their own aggressors. They master their abuse by exercising the control they didn't have before. The wounds my client inflicted on his victims were the same ones he'd received."

Doby would argue Rachel had been molested and acted it out against a child who was even more defenseless. Was that the story Lee Simms hinted at? Even if Doby couldn't give the jury evidence or a name, he'd find some way to sneak it in. But child abuse cut both ways. Could Rachel use it as a defense?

"You've handled more than one of those cases," she said. "What do you look for?"

"Old fractures, scars from belts. Bite marks are pretty common."

"Bite marks?"

"On the back and face, sometimes the abdomen and buttocks. They tend to be associated with caretakers. Usually female."

The bruises on Freddie's face and Ben's thigh.

"Can you tell the biter's age?"

"From a bite mark? You'd need a forensic odontologist."

"Know a good one?"

"Most dentists are to the right of Attila the Hun. But there's always Gordy Spitz . . . What's this about?"

Female caretakers. If an adult bit Freddie, there went half of Doby's case. So long as they couldn't match the mark on Ben's thigh to Rachel.

"Nothing. Did Chris say anything about Freddie Gant?"

His eyes shifted. "Nothing you don't already know. What does Rachel say?"

"You heard her. She did her time and you can't turn the clock back."

Dennis reached across the table for Jackie's hand. His touch was warm and sympathetic. "You've got two choices, darlin'. Same two you always have. Take your chances on what Doby might not know, or get Rachel to trust you."

Like most savvy defense lawyers, Dennis belonged to the first school. Show the client the police report *before* you got his side of the story. That wasn't exactly inviting the client to lie, but the problem was you could never be sure of the truth. Jackie was ambitious enough to believe she could work with any set of facts so long as they bore a passing resemblance to what actually occurred. But could she believe Rachel?

"There's one other source," she said.

"Who?"

"Lee Simms."

"You're kidding! He's a maggot, Jackie. You wouldn't believe the things—"

"I know what he wrote. He obviously had good sources."

"The worst tabloid trash. He hounded the Boyds, even tried to get to Chris."

"When?"

"Then *and* now. How'd you like to be a nine-year-old who can't take a leak without some reporter in your face? Asking your playmates the most intimate questions about your sister and parents? Even when you finally get placed in a foster home and your new family has to move you out of state—" Dennis lowered his voice. "There's two kinds of reporters, dear. For most of them, contacting the victim's family is the worst part of the job. Simms took up residence. Did he tell you why he got fired from the *News*?"

Pilar hadn't mentioned that.

"He took a swing at his editor," Dennis continued.

"So?" Jackie was strangely relieved. "I remember a couple of news-hounds you wanted to deck, even a judge or two."

If there was more to the story, Dennis wasn't about to say. But his antipathy for Lee Simms seemed overblown. Did the reporter pose a risk to Chris Boyd? The only alternative was equally unthinkable. Dennis couldn't be jealous. No, it had to be the martinis. And it was warm in the restaurant; Jackie didn't envy his coat and tie. As she slipped off her own jacket down to her lace-trimmed camisole, the waiter arrived with their entrées. Dennis began carving his duck.

"Want a taste?"

She smiled. "I was afraid to ask."

Her scallops were dusted with fennel pollen and too rich to eat more than one. For the rest of the meal she watched Dennis, and listened absently to the antics of big-firm litigators who did anything to avoid trying cases. She told him about the hive in the chimney and the one-step-forward, two-steps-back remodeling of her office. Mostly she watched his hands, the confidence with which he maneuvered his knife and fork. By dessert the cinema had let out and its patrons were heading for the sushi bar up the street. It was past ten. Rachel would be in bed.

"I can't eat another bite," Jackie said. Her cheeks were hot and she knew it wasn't just the wine. She should hit the ladies' room, freshen her lipstick and see if she was still wearing powder. But she didn't trust her knees.

"Where did you park?"

"Pilar dropped me off." She waited for a knowing grin, but Dennis didn't blink.

"Want a lift?"

"Let me out and I'll unlock the door," Jackie said.

They'd pulled up in front of her house. The windows were safely dark.

"Okay to park in your driveway?"

"Drop me off and I'll let you in the back. We'll have to be quiet. . . ."

Dennis rounded the corner with his lights off and pulled into the alley. He cut the wheel just before the hedge and made the ninety-degree turn onto the asphalt leading to Jackie's garage. His car practically guided itself, it seemed like just yesterday—

"Where's Jackie?" a voice said.

As Dennis's eyes adjusted to the dark, he saw a small figure in black leggings behind the hedge. Hadn't Jackie mentioned some kid next door?

Slipping through a break in the bushes, the girl planted herself in front of Jackie's gate. The turtleneck came past her chin and a red silk sash was knotted at her forehead.

He smiled. "What are you, a ninja?"

"Why are you in Jackie's driveway?"

"She invited me in for coffee." He congratulated himself for not mentioning the hour. "Care to join us?"

He tried to step past, but she barred his way. Her eyes were like a cat's.

"You're Dennis Ross."

"And who might you be?"

"I know all about you."

"Oh, really?"

"Rachel says you and Jackie aren't lovers anymore."

Not a bandit—a brat. He reached past her for the gate.

"Then you shouldn't care what Jackie and I do after your bedtime."

A light blinked on upstairs and the curtains fluttered. At the same moment Jackie called softly from her back porch, "Dennis?"

The ninja stared at him with an expression bordering on contempt. He'd played poker long enough to recognize a bluff.

"Dennis?" Jackie's voice was a little louder.

A light came on next door. The ninja held her ground. This was one hand Dennis couldn't win.

"I guess we'll call it a night."

Twenty-Four

Gordon Spitz's waiting room was furnished in walnut with red and blue upholstery. A crocheted replica of the original Stars and Stripes hung on one paneled wall. Beside it was an oil painting of the *Bonhomme Richard* under attack by a British frigate. All that was missing were the Founding Fathers.

Jackie wondered if she'd gotten the name wrong.

When she'd made this appointment, she told the dentist's receptionist she was a friend of Dennis Ross's. The woman asked no questions before scheduling Jackie for Spitz's next opening. Judging from his waiting room, he maintained an active practice in addition to his forensic work.

Jackie paged through the magazines. Instead of *Time* or *Newsweek*, Spitz had copies of *American Home* and *Colonial Collectibles*. It was hard to imagine him and Dennis hitting it off.

"Doctor will see you now . . ."

Spitz kept his antiques in the waiting room. His taste in dental assistants was considerably more modern. This one led Jackie to a room with a dentist's chair.

"So you're Dennis's friend."

If not racquetball, Gordy Spitz looked as if he spent his lunch hour in some other athletic pursuit. Hadn't Dennis said something years ago about never dating dentists' ex-wives? He started washing his hands in the sink.

"Actually, I'm a professional colleague," she said.

Spitz snapped on a latex glove. He had a brush-cut mustache and small teeth.

"So much the better."

He pulled on the other glove. She had to stop this now.

"I should've explained over the phone. I want to consult with you on a case. Not necessarily to testify, just—"

"So you're a defense attorney."

Disappointment. Did he like having lawyers in the chair?

"Is that a problem?"

"Anything for good old Dennis. What've you got?"

Jackie reached into her briefcase for the file.

"Maybe a bite mark."

She handed Spitz the photo of Freddie Gant's cheek. He took off his gloves and tacked the photo to his light box.

"Hmm . . ."

"It *is* a bite mark, isn't it?"

"Swabbed for DNA?"

Did they even have DNA thirty years ago?

"No."

Spitz shook his head disparagingly. "A dentist could get DNA off a bite in a piece of cheese."

Score one for forensic dentistry.

He took down Freddie's photo. "How old is this?"

"What difference does that make?"

"It's not good enough to make a determination. The nose works as an anatomical landmark, but the resolution's poor and there's no formal scale of any kind. Hate to disappoint you, Counselor."

"Can you give me your best guess?"

"That's not very professional."

Score two.

"What *can* you tell me?"

"Off the record?"

"Yes."

"The bruise on the cheek is probably a bite mark."

"Child's or adult's?"

"You get some sense of scale from the nose, but not enough to measure the biter's arch. If you really pushed me, I'd guess it was another kid."

Don't go there.

"What else?" she said.

"The bite was made at or immediately before the time of death."

So much for earlier abuse in the Gant home.

"How can you tell?"

"The bruise. And there's no elevations."

"Elevations?"

"Indentations in the skin. If it doesn't break the skin, a bite on a living person usually disappears within an hour. Your victim was alive. The biter wanted to inflict pain."

"Pain?"

Spitz was enjoying her discomfort. "Teeth are our most primitive weapon, Ms. Flowers. Biting is sadistic and barbaric. I've seen bar fights where the victim's nose and ears were bitten off. But this is probably a case of child abuse."

"Why?"

Spitz shrugged. "Suck marks are common in sexual assaults. They leave a sunburst pattern in the center. Because the biter takes his time, the resolution's often excellent. But with battered children the bites are more rapid and random. They tend to leave poor detail, like this one."

"Why would an adult bite a child?"

"Interpretation of wound patterns is beyond my expertise."

Score three. But Spitz had to have some ideas.

"Off the record, Doctor."

"Punishment. Rage. To force the victim to comply. Even if you can't match it to a suspect, it shows a violent struggle before death."

Jackie handed him the photo of Ben Sparks's thigh.

"Good news for you here," he said.

"Oh?"

He pointed at the violet strand of pearls. "This is definitely a bite—"

How could Doby have missed that?

"—by an adult."

Shit.

"Male or female?" she said.

"No way to tell, no matter how detailed the mark is."

"If you had a suspect, could you make a positive ID?"

"Only on TV, or if the biter has distinctive teeth. Chipped or crooked uppers, a lateral or cuspid sticking out. And two bites by the same person can look very different, depending on whether it was a nibble or a full arch, and if the victim was moving or wore clothing. But your biter's uppers are straight."

Like Rachel's. And probably half the adult population.

"No swab on this one either?" Spitz said. If they had, Doby would have demanded a DNA sample from Rachel. "DNA's more reliable than the mark, but you need techs at the scene who know what they're doing."

Thank God for incompetence. A match would have buried Jackie's client. She didn't want to go there, didn't want to think her client was guilty.

"How long after the fact can they swab a bite?" she said.

Spitz shrugged again. "DNA deteriorates if it's exposed to UV light. It can be washed away, or cross-contaminated by other body fluids. Remember the O.J.

case? Unless they swabbed the wound at the scene and properly preserved it, forget it."

Maybe Jackie wasn't the only one who should be relieved.

They'd missed the bite on Freddie's cheek thirty years ago. What did a bite on Ben's thigh do to Doby's theory that it was the same killer?

Spitz winked.

"No report. Right, Counselor?"

Twenty-Five

C al Doby paced the well of the court.
"—admissible *not* to prove Rachel Boyd's character
to show she acted in conformity therewith, as it were, her
propensity to commit this crime—"

Jackie tried to focus on the prosecutor's tortured
syntax.

She'd misplaced her keys that morning and almost
been late for court. Luckily Pilar swung by in time to give
her a lift. She could have sworn she'd left those keys on
the kitchen counter when she went to bed. She was careful about things like that, especially the night before a
hearing where she had to function at her peak.

"—but rather, a distinctive factor in *the methods
used.*"

As Doby's voice dropped to a whisper, Jackie winced.

Venetian blinds cut blue sky and bright sun, casting
shadows like bars in the window wells of Courtroom 12.
On this Friday morning at the end of May the frieze
behind Mueller's bench looked less like a shrine than a
gilded cage. It was too early in the day for a migraine
but the sourness in Jackie's stomach reached clear to her
ears. She was certain she'd left those keys on the
counter but they'd turned up in the earthenware bowl
where she kept coupons and receipts. By then Pilar had
arrived.

"—also admissible as proof of motive, *opportunity,*
intent—"

Along with his lumbering gait, Doby's erratic emphasis made Jackie feel even more out of synch. He'd spent

twenty minutes on the history of Rule 404, which deter-
mined the admissibility of a defendant's prior bad acts.
After reviewing its placement in the pantheon of jurispru-
dence, he'd glossed over a dozen cases construing it,
touching only briefly on the actual wording of the rule.
The Honorable Greta Mueller had absorbed his wisdom
without comment, nodding once as he acknowledged that
evidence of Freddie Gant's murder three decades earlier
would normally be inadmissible and again when he con-
ceded her discretion to weigh its similarities and dissimi-
larities with that in Ben Sparks's death.

Rachel sat at the defense table with her hands folded.
In an old linen pantsuit of Jackie's that she'd expertly
altered, she might have been a lawyer herself. The lemon
yellow was more becoming on her than it ever was on
Jackie. And a better fit.

"—preparation, plan, knowledge, *identity*—"

Doby's voice had risen in a dramatic crescendo, and
Rachel sighed. Nothing seemed to surprise her. Hearing
shuffling in the front row, Jackie resisted the impulse to
turn. The courtroom was packed with reporters and any
reaction would find its way into print. She forced her
attention back to her adversary.

"—or absence of mistake *or* accident."

A fly lit on the prosecution table.

"—review for the Court the myriad of similarities
which compel the admission of the *he*nious murder of
young Freddie Gant. First and foremost are these children's tender years—"

The fly wiped its leg on Doby's motion.

Focus, Jackie willed herself, *focus*. What she really
needed was an antacid. Reaching in her pocket, she felt
for the moss agate shard she always brought to court. Her
fingers closed around the silken sliver. Block out every-

thing but those feathery inclusions. As she caressed the cool surface with her thumb, the fog began to clear.

"—separated as they may be by the sands of time, they both—"

"Mr. Doby," Mueller said, "do you intend to finish by Memorial Day?"

"Why, yes, Your Honor. I simply thought it might be instructive for this Court—"

"Because I would also like to hear from the defense."

"Yes, ma'am. In a matter of such grave—"

"Two minutes."

"Uh—" Returning to the prosecution table, Doby wrested his motion from the fly and resumed. "Freddie Gant was four years old and the Sparks boy was six. The cause of death in both cases was a broken neck. Both bodies lay undiscovered for days, Freddie stuffed between storage bins at a grain elevator and Ben in a thicket of snow. As to each child, Rachel Boyd occupied a position of trust."

A caretaker, typically female . . . Jackie jumped to her feet.

"Trust? My client—"

"—was the last person seen with them. And, most significantly—"

"Yes, Mr. Doby. The scratches." Mueller waved. "You may be seated."

"But, Your Honor, I haven't—"

"Ms. Flowers?"

Jackie took the lectern.

"Freddie Gant's neck was broken in a fall; Ben Sparks's was snapped. One child was a neighborhood kid, the other accompanied his father to work. The first killing was of a younger boy, allegedly—"

"Allegedly? Your Honor, her client was *convicted*—"

"—by an older child," Jackie said. "The accused is an adult. Ms. Boyd made no effort whatsoever to hide the fact that she took Ben to an ice cream parlor and the park the afternoon he disappeared. His scratches could've been caused by those bushes where he was left. But even more tellingly, the district attorney has presented absolutely no evidence of motive—"

"Those boys were sexually molested!"

"There's no evidence of that, Your Honor." Doby either hadn't identified those bite marks or he was afraid they'd backfire. And Mueller was with her now, she could feel it. "Molestation is in the eye of the beholder. In this case, the mind of Calvin Doby."

"What other explanation could there be for those marks on their groins? Half an inch lower and their little weenies—"

"*Mr. Doby.*"

The courtroom fell silent and Mueller continued.

"If that's all you have, I'm inclined to agree with Ms. Flowers. Scratches do not a motive make. Much less do they amount to sexual molestation. And absent a sufficiently distinctive factor in the methods used in both crimes, I'm forced to rule inadmissible—"

"One more thing, Your Honor," Doby said.

Hand on gavel, Mueller paused.

"If luring young boys to a secluded spot and mutilating their groins before snapping their necks doesn't suggest a sexual motive or a distinctive MO, then ponder this. Why did the killer cut buttons off both victims' pants?"

"Buttons?" Jackie said.

Doby had sandbagged her again. Turning, she saw Rachel looking over her shoulder. Lee Simms was directly behind them. He coolly met her client's gaze.

"—supplemental autopsy report," Doby was saying.

The chamber was so quiet Jackie could hear the pages of a dozen notepads flip. "In each case, the top button of their trousers was sliced off. That's how she pulled their pants down around their hips. That never came out at the first trial. Only the killer knew." He handed Jackie a paper she knew her office had never received. No time to decipher it.

Jackie advanced on the bench.

"Your Honor, this is outrageous! This is the first notice—"

"Check your mail," Mueller said. "It's in the Court's record." She located the report in her file and peered at it with a fascination Jackie knew enough to dread. "I see what you mean, Mr. Doby."

Mueller rapped twice.

"Evidence in the murder of Freddie Gant will be admissible to establish similar intent or modus operandi. Court adjourned."

Distrust him or not, they needed Lee Simms.

Twenty-Six

EXCLUSIVE BY LEE SIMMS FOR
MODERN CRIMES—MAY 12, 1973

A brick building with a bell tower. Two stories tall and square. For the bewildered residents of this quiet agricultural community, Vivian Elementary School is their source of pride. How can this be? said the shock on the faces of teachers walking the beloved halls a week before summer recess. Just one month earlier they'd celebrated Pioneer Day by dedicating the annex it took five years to build. Is it possible their school nurtured the killer in the most heinous murder in the history of Colorado's Eastern Plains?

It is a tragedy that has pitted neighbor against neighbor in this humble prairie town. From the moment Freddie Gant's body was found wedged between storage bins at the base of the grain elevator from which he was apparently pushed, attention has focused on the institution that has produced generations of law-abiding citizens. For Vivian Elementary is also the school attended by Rachel Boyd, the child suspected in the attack. On a quiet weekday afternoon, a startling portrait of a deeply disturbed girl emerged.

Millicent Trent, Principal of Vivian Elementary since 1947, calls each graduate by first name. She still sees many of them every day. At bake sales for the softball team and fundraisers for the school annex, or when they return for Pioneer Day. At the local diner after school, Mrs. Trent shared a cup of coffee and a slice of cherry pie with her close friend and colleague, sixth-grade teacher Althea Robey, and certain observations about their students.

"Freddie Gant was a lovely boy," Mrs. Trent begins. "His sister Susie is one of our most popular girls, and brother Gregg is quite the scholar. Their parents are so devoted. Our hearts go out to the entire family."

What does she think about the suspicion focused on one of Susie Gant's classmates? Mrs. Trent and Althea Robey exchange a glance. Miss Robey is their teacher.

"Rachel Boyd is quite bright. There have been minor disciplinary problems in the past. She's best friends with Trina Maune." At a nod from her principal, she continues. "Trina's her only friend. One week before Freddie died, Trina picked a fight during recess with another girl. That was so out of character for Trina we knew Rachel had egged her on. We wanted to discipline Rachel—"

Mrs. Trent completes her colleague's thought.

"—but how could we when it was Trina who bloodied the child's nose? And that's not the only incident. Rachel is a rock thrown into a pond. In all my years teaching, I've never seen anything quite like it."

No one will say the words. But aren't they talking about a bad seed?

"Any group of children has its leaders and followers," Althea Robey says. "The leaders tend to be the more attractive ones, of course. But the hold Rachel has over Trina . . ."

"They feed off each other," says Mrs. Trent. "Rachel just looks at her and Trina knows what to do without being told. If she doesn't, Rachel has ways of getting even. And she lies."

Lies? About what?

"Dear me! About things that are obviously untrue, or don't even matter. Althea caught her with her hand in Janet Nye's purse and Rachel just looked at her with those big dark eyes. 'I don't know what you mean,' she said, innocent as can be. Then she spread the most scurrilous rumors about poor Janet. A certain amount of fibbing is normal, but Rachel would lie about the time of day if you asked her. We started to notice that in fifth grade, the year Trina was forced to repeat in Rachel's class. That's when it began."

"Rachel wouldn't be half so bad if it wasn't for Trina," Miss Robey chimes in.

"And Trina would be no problem at all if she were alone."

This pattern of one girl egging the other on has led to more serious escapades. Each March, Althea Robey's sixth-grade class takes a bus trip to Denver, where they tour the State Capitol and the United States Mint. In Mrs. Trent's early tenure as principal, a highlight of the trip had traditionally been a visit to the Daniels and Fisher Tower, once the tallest building in downtown Denver, but closed for many years since the adjacent department store was torn down. When Miss Robey's class gathered for a final head count before boarding the bus back, Rachel and Trina were missing. While the two women frantically searched, the girls had somehow broken into the Tower, scampered up an abandoned ladder to the third floor, and taken the stairs to the old observation deck on the twentieth floor.

"They acted like it was a joke," Mrs. Trent recalled. "When Althea took Trina aside and asked why she did it, she said it was on a dare. They were fortunate they weren't arrested for trespassing, or worse. We wrote it off as a prank. But now I'm not so sure."

Was luring a classmate to the top of the highest building in Denver a dry run for enticing a four-year-old boy to climb to a forbidden catwalk scarcely a month later? Maybe Trina Maune was the lucky one.

The women also have a theory about one of the more curious aspects of the case. On May 7, two days after Freddie Gant went missing, Vivian Elementary was broken into. The vandalism was minor but authorities have questioned whether writing left on the blackboard of the sixth-grade classroom provides a clue.

"Obviously fake," Miss Robey says. "'Will get you—yore next.' Such atrocious spelling. No one in my class! I'd say whoever did it was trying to make hay of what happened to poor Freddie Gant."

Another piece of the puzzle is offered by Janet Nye, Rachel's fifth-grade teacher. Miss Nye remembers Rachel as a loner but quite protective of her brother, whom she walked to school. Reminded of the incident with her purse, she flushes and then laughs.

"My goodness, that story does go round! As I recall, Rachel was looking for a comb. If you were looking for a comb and were accused of stealing money, wouldn't you deny it too? Perhaps that's why she's so angry."

Were there problems in the Boyd home? Janet Nye bristles.

"George Boyd never misses a parent-teacher conference."

A final word is offered by Carla Miller,

the classmate whose nose was bloodied by Trina Maune's fists.

"I don't like either one of them. Rachel's mean. Sometimes Trina tries to say something, and Rachel gives her that look. It's spooky. Susie Gant hates them both, but I think Rachel's the leader."

Twenty-Seven

B a-*long*, ba-*long* . . .

The six-foot-long minute hand of the clock at the Daniels and Fisher Tower joined its mate at the twelve. With its blond brick and terra-cotta facade, and its cameo medallions surrounding the gold work at the loggia, Jackie could imagine this tower's attraction for a pair of school-girls from the Eastern Plains.

Lee Simms slid onto the bench. "So you changed your mind after all?"

"That depends on you," she said.

He'd dispensed with the pretext of a jacket, and his blue oxford shirt was frayed but clean. Jackie doubted it had ever hosted a tie.

"I audition better on a full stomach."

"I'm not a ten-year-old girl. Save your charm."

"Lily's a knockout. And I'm buying."

For the price of a meal . . . But lunch actually sounded good. Jackie's appetite had been off for days and Pilar blamed it on Rachel's cooking. What had she put on the fish the other night? Cumin, she'd said. And the greens had tasted bitter, almost metallic. It couldn't possibly have been coriander.

"You're in the habit of paying your sources?" she asked.

Simms laughed easily. "It's not my problem where the information comes from, so long as it's true. Speaking of money, why'd you take this case?"

"It happens to be what I do."

"For Chris Boyd's fee, or to become a superstar?"

Jackie kept her cool. "I don't work for free. And I've had my share of high-profile cases."

"Not a jockstrap sniffer, are you?" He made a peace sign. "Come on, you've got to eat sometime. How about a hot dog?"

The steam from the cart made her stomach rumble. "No, thanks—"

"Two Polish."

The man in the apron handed Jackie one and she paid for it before Simms could get his wallet out. He sprang for the Diet Cokes. They crossed the street and sat on the steps leading down to the sunken plaza behind the D&F Tower.

Skyline Plaza's grassy berms, fake boulders and vertical-slab waterfalls were designed to give office workers a respite from city life. The plaza had been sunk and the sidewalk torn out to insulate patrons from traffic and noise. But mall rats and hobos displaced from their habitat on the banks of Cherry Creek had driven the workers out, and the plaza was slated for renovation. The tower itself had paid the heaviest price. After a near-fatal encounter with urban renewal to construct this three-block cement canyon, its backside was scarred a ruddier brick.

"What do you want?" Jackie said.

"I told you. An exclusive with your client."

"Whom you railroaded thirty years ago. Painting Rachel Boyd as the bad seed—it took the jury all of two hours to convict her."

Wiping his lips with his mustard-smeared napkin, Simms lobbed it at the trash.

"They deliberated over lunch. Verdict would've been quicker if the food wasn't free. But why blame me? Rachel's lawyer screwed her. He's the one who wouldn't let her take a polygraph."

"Didn't you care about the rights of a twelve-year-old girl?"

"I cared about the mother of a dead four-year-old who had the right to know *why*." He jerked the tab of his soda can back and forth until it snapped. "If the press has a piece of the puzzle, we have to print it. Now I want to help your client."

"By tipping Doby to our defense?"

"What?"

"That story in the *News*."

"What story?"

"About Rachel's life in the women's detention unit in Cañon City. It wasn't you who leaked those embarrassing details about her domestic arrangements in maximum security, was it?"

This time Simms's outrage seemed genuine. "I never tip off competitors!"

"Then maybe you'd like to help by making this trial even more of a circus than the last."

He bristled again.

"A story like Rachel Boyd's feeds on itself. It's my job to be suspicious; when you say 'no comment' we dig harder. A smart lawyer tries to get ahead of the story."

"Come off it." Jackie set her untouched Polish on the cement step. "If you care so much about helping, why didn't you warn me about those buttons on the boys' pants?"

"Rachel didn't seem surprised. And cultivating sources is a two-way street."

"She won't talk to you even if I recommend it. Which I won't. What do you really want?"

Simms picked up her hot dog and began to munch.

"Police reports on Ben Sparks."

"Why?"

"Not convinced they got it right the first time."

"Little late, isn't it?" Jackie was tired of fencing. "Who were your sources?"

"Besides the ones I quoted? I'm a reporter, Ms. Flowers, not a magician."

"You had someone on the inside."

"What makes you think that?"

"You quoted sources close to the investigation. Responsible journalists don't fabricate attributions. How'd you know so much about the Gants?"

"Responsible journalists win their subjects' trust."

Jackie rose. "You're wasting my time. You don't know a damn—"

"What if Freddie's body was moved?"

She freed her arm from his grasp. "Who cares?"

"You ought to care about every detail of that murder. If Doby retries the Gant case, Rachel's freedom rises or falls on how similar those crimes were."

"I can get that from the police reports—assuming Doby gives them to me. He's too smart to pull the same stunt twice. In Mueller's court, two strikes and you're out."

Simms nodded in resignation. Would he finally show his hand?

"Not everything was in the Gant file," he said. "Want to know what was left out?"

Those bite marks, she hoped. "What I really want to know is why I should trust you."

Simms sighed. "I was twenty-two, fresh out of journalism school and itching to make my name. Stringing for the *Seward County Call*, covering cattle auctions and county fairs and the occasional bust for joyriding with a six-pack. Strictly the agricultural beat. Didn't even have a byline till Freddie Gant fell in my lap. Like lots of folks, I guess I was looking for someone to blame."

"Blame?" It was hard to work up sympathy for a guy who saw the murder of a child as his ticket out of a dead-end career. "Sounds like you should've been grateful."

"You know what I mean."

"Well, you certainly found an easy target."

"My features were picked up and the offers poured in. But after Rachel was convicted, I couldn't let go. On the fifth anniversary of Freddie's death I went back to Vivian for another look. Hardly Pulitzer material, I admit, but it raised questions about the way the investigation was handled. *Post* wouldn't print it, so I shopped it to the *News*. They hired me and sliced the guts out of my story. I took a swing at the managing editor and got canned. No other paper would touch me, so I left Denver. Worked ski lifts, swabbed toilets in the off-season, got into some crazy shit . . ."

If he'd been around that long, it was strange she'd never heard of him. And Pilar had said Simms reported on just that one crime. Why was he so obsessed with Freddie Gant?

"I really feel for you, Simms. But I still don't see why Rachel should—"

"The tenth anniversary, after she was transferred to Cañon City, I did a retrospective on Freddie Gant's murder. Her stepfather was long dead and Chris was living with a foster family out of state, but I talked to Evelyn Boyd and got five minutes with Rachel. No problem selling my story—bad seed behind bars, that kind of stuff. But I reconnected with Ryan Mitchell, the chief investigator."

"So?"

"Most cops who worked the case were straight out of *Mayberry, R.F.D.* Mitchell was different. He graduated from a police academy. Rachel never confessed to killing Freddie, but she never really denied it either."

"Mitchell's still in Vivian?"

Simms shook his head. "Died a few years back—heavy smoker. Rachel gave him the willies, but later on he was less convinced she did it. Or if she did, that she acted alone. That's why he gave me the file."

"Did you copy it?"

"Better than that. Mitchell said he thought Freddie was moved."

"Why?"

"Livor mortis." Discoloration of the skin after death. Blood pooled when oxygen stopped circulating. "It can be misinterpreted as a bruise, but it tells us if a body's been moved."

"And?"

"Lividity gets fixed eight to ten hours after death; it can't be shifted by moving the body. If it's on the back of a corpse found facedown, you know he was on his back when he died and someone moved him later."

"What's that got to do with Freddie Gant?"

"You saw his face. Remember a bruise on his right cheek?"

Jackie held her breath.

"There was also one on his right forearm and wrist," Simms continued. She remembered them from the autopsy photos; those discolorations were larger than the bite mark on the cheek, and the shape was wrong. "He was found on his back, but he was lying on his right side shortly after he died. Somebody went back to that grain elevator and turned him over. The question is why?"

"What do you think?"

"Either to finish what was started, or retrieve something that was lost."

"What's it got to do with Rachel?"

"She knows what that was. Or she's covering for someone else."

Jackie still wasn't buying. "If you thought Rachel was railroaded, why wait so long?"

"Until Ben was killed, what could I do? The day that story broke in April, I headed for Denver."

"You said Mitchell doubted she acted alone. Who'd he think the other person was?"

"Trina Maune."

She'd seen the name in his stories. "Her friend? But why—"

"Trina wasn't the only person Rachel covered for."

"Who else?"

"Someone both girls feared. Whoever cut Freddie Gant."

Twenty-Eight

**TRANSCRIPT OF INTERVIEW OF RACHEL BOYD
CONDUCTED BY DETECTIVE SERGEANT RYAN
MITCHELL ON MAY 14, 1973**

> Rachel Boyd arrived at HQ at 1530 with
> her mother Evelyn. The interview was
> taped with Mrs. Boyd's consent.

DSM: Now, Rachel, do you remember the last time
we talked?

RB: Yes.

DSM: You remember what we talked about?

RB: Yes.

DSM: I have a few more questions. OK?

RB: OK.

DSM: Last time we talked, you said you went to the
park alone. Did you forget Trina Maune was
there?

RB: Is that what she said?

DSM: Is it true?

RB: I guess so.

DSM: Is Trina your best friend?

RB: Not really.

DSM: But you girls do lots of things together.

RB: If Trina says so.

DSM: You also said you didn't talk to Freddie Gant. Is
that the way you remember it now?

RB: We might of said hi.

DSM: We?

RB: Trina and me.

DSM: I bet Freddie liked to tag along with you girls.

RB: And I bet you cough because you smoke.

DSM: What?

RB: My mother says it's not ladylike to smoke.

DSM: She does, does she?

RB: Is that why your wife left? Or was it because—

DSM: Did Freddie like to tag along?

RB: Susie was always telling him to go away.

DSM: Little boys can be a pain in the butt, huh?

RB: (No answer.)

DSM: Was Freddie being a pain in the butt that Saturday?

RB: I saw him with one of Gregg's friends.

DSM: His brother Gregg?

RB: That's who he left the park with.

DSM: What's Gregg's friend's name?

RB: I don't know.

DSM: Last time, you said you saw Freddie talking to a boy with pimples.

RB: That was after.

DSM: After he left the park with Gregg's friend?

RB: I meant *before*.

DSM: Do you remember what Freddie was wearing?

RB: Shorts. A blue shirt. I told you we weren't with him.

DSM: Do you remember telling me you wore red shorts that Saturday?

RB: It could of been a dress. What difference does that make?

DSM: That the way you remember it now?

RB: (Inaudible.)

DSM: Have you been talking to Trina?

RB: (Giggles.) You're the one who says she's my best friend.

DSM: About Freddie Gant.

RB: We don't know anything. We told you that!

DSM: Then you won't mind showing me the shorts you wore that day.

EB: Rachel doesn't wear—

DSM: Mrs. Boyd, please.

RB: It was a dress.

The interview was ended by Evelyn Boyd, who turned the tape recorder off. Mrs. Boyd said it was dinnertime and she and Rachel had to go home. On the way out she told me her daughter tended to "tell tales" and it was best not to believe anything she said.

Twenty-Nine

Chris Boyd's mansion near the Denver Country Club was built for a governor. It had once been part of a family compound with the house on the adjoining lot, but blood had thinned and a twelve-foot wall now separated the two. Even at half its original size, the property was impressive.

Jackie pulled into the double-wide entry and parked in front of the cement urns. The driveway was empty and the neighborhood so quiet it might have been quarantined. When she'd called Chris's office his secretary said he'd left for the afternoon.

Banker's hours. Or did he skip town for the weekend?

A wrought-iron fence surrounded the stone Tudor, leaving a setback deep enough for the swimming pool and tennis court Rachel had described. Not that the country club set displayed such amenities on their front lawns. They were out back, along with the terraced garden, lily pond and groundskeeper's digs.

Jackie looked up at the gabled roof and leaded windows, the arched entryway for cars. It was easy to imagine its owner inviting his sister to stay; this mausoleum could host a dozen guests without any of them bumping into one another. She walked around back. Ben Sparks's disappearance from this tree-lined Eden wasn't hard to picture. The tougher sell was Rachel and Chris puttering around with rosebushes and compost. What was a groundsman for?

"Ms. Flowers?"

He'd come up behind her.

"Chris!" She fumbled with the photo album in her

hands. "I wanted to return this personally. I know how precious your memories must be."

And how vital his sister's alibi would be.

Chris Boyd was dressed in chinos and a faded polo shirt, the kind without the logo. His hair was damp and his feet were bare. He looked as if he'd just stepped out of the shower. If he was surprised to see her he didn't show it.

"Thanks. What's going on with the case?"

Surely he read the papers. "Hasn't Rachel told you?" she said.

"Dennis said to keep my distance." Chris tucked his shirt neatly into his trousers. Buttoned-down even when he should have been slumming it. "It's not easy, but he's concerned about the bank."

"And you."

"Maybe a little too concerned."

"Dennis is a good lawyer."

"That's what he says about you. And he's a helluva friend . . . I haven't spoken to Shelly in days. How's she holding up?"

"As well as can be expected."

"She was always the strong one."

A hint of resentment? Jackie waited.

"On the outside I was an apple polisher, but I pulled my share of pranks. You know, kid's stuff." Jackie tried to imagine Chris Boyd as a child. A playful boy with a nose for soft spots. "Sticking a mouse in the teacher's desk, hiding another guy's homework . . ."

"That's the worst you did?"

"I could regale you with frat stories—but that's not what you're interested in. Here I am, running off at the mouth."

"What *am* I interested in?"

"Why, Shelly, of course!"

But suddenly Jackie wasn't. She was more interested in what Christopher Boyd wanted her to think. "Why do you call your sister Shelly?"

"Our stepdad's pet name for her."

"What was yours?"

"'Boy.' George thought that was pretty funny, once he gave us his last name. Boy Boyd." Chris raked his hair back from his forehead. "It's awfully warm. Want a beer, some lemonade?"

The patio overlooked a lily pond. The fountain tinkled like wind chimes and the water shimmered in the late-day sun. Was this where he and Rachel had read the Sunday papers the day Ben disappeared? Jackie followed Chris inside.

"Take the grand tour, look anywhere you like. I'll show you the outbuildings later."

French doors opened onto a breakfast nook that led to a hotel-size kitchen. Through a doorway Jackie saw a paneled dining room with a fieldstone fireplace. The mahogany table seated two dozen.

"Cozy . . ."

Chris mixed lemonade from tap water and frozen concentrate and served it to Jackie in a tall glass with ice. Popping the cap off a bottle of ale, he took a long drink before answering.

"Built in the days when there was live-in staff. Eleven bedrooms and fourteen baths. Six suites for servants."

"Cook, maid, chauffeur . . ."

". . . nursemaid, laundress, handyman. Most of the upstairs is closed off." He shook his head. "I always wanted a house like this. Of course, I didn't plan on living in it alone."

"Why do you?"

"Where's the wife and kids? The corporate ladder's steep. She bailed out on the second rung."

No bitterness, just that same self-deprecating candor that was so easy on the ears. But hadn't Dennis described a bank's power structure as a pyramid? Promotion required not just ambition but skill at cultivating relationships. Chris was being far too modest.

"Every CEO needs a castle for entertaining," she said.

"Exactly why I keep it. If Mom could see me now . . ."

He laughed again, and Jackie found herself joining in. Beneath it all Chris Boyd was lonely; no wonder he'd wanted his sister here. And without half trying he was winning her over. What was he like when he had a real prize in his sights? Fetching the lemonade pitcher and another bottle of ale, he led her outside.

"Speaking of parents, how did yours find the guy who represented Rachel?"

Chris winced. "He was a business associate of George's, some guy who did property foreclosures. If they'd gotten a criminal lawyer—"

"—the result might have been the same. Entering a not-guilty plea and going to trial can net a stiffer sentence than pleading guilty. The real mistake was letting your sister be tried as an adult."

"Who decides that?"

"When they enter the system, kids are slotted into four categories: mad, bad, sad or can't add. If you can't add, they put you in special education. If you're sad or crazy-mad, it's a mental institution. Just plain bad gets you a one-way ticket to the state pen via reform school. Being tried as an adult eliminates two of the three. What was Rachel's lawyer's strategy?"

"None."

"He refused to let her take a lie detector test. . . ."

"My parents wanted it over fast. Thank God, Shelly has a real lawyer this time."

Beyond the lily pond lay a manicured lawn with terraced beds. At the far corner a shed faced a thick stand of aspens. Jackie caught a glimpse of a tennis net and what might have been a swimming pool. Keeping a six-year-old boy in sight would have been the miracle, not losing him. Chris whistled and two tawny creatures bounded across the grass. The larger one leaped at Chris, knocking back his chair.

"Down!" Chris was laughing.

The dog licked his face twice before settling at his feet. Its mate rolled over beside him. Golden retrievers.

Not collies. And no leashes.

Jackie leaned down and scratched the female between the ears. She looked up with liquid eyes and moaned.

"How long have you had them?"

"Since they were pups."

"Good watchdogs?"

"You kidding?" The male tried to jump back in his lap and Chris wrestled him away. His shirt pulled free and Jackie caught a glimpse of pale skin before he tucked it in again. "They're bred to hunt ducks, but all these two do is lie around and eat. If anyone tried to break in they'd lick him to death. Their idea of fun is riding in a car."

"Have you taken them to the mountains?"

"Most of my trips are business. When I go to Las Vegas, I fly."

"I hear you're a shark at the tables," she said.

"Dennis tell you that? He's not bad himself."

Jackie was too surprised to respond.

"He never mentioned our trips to Vegas?" Chris said.

So it wasn't just golf.

"I didn't realize that was the kind—"

Chris's amused expression confirmed there was a side to Dennis she knew nothing about. "I should learn to keep my mouth shut."

"No, tell me," she said. "Dennis plays blackjack?"

"Well . . ."

"The slots?"

Chris was suddenly uncomfortable. "I've said enough."

"Come on, I won't tell."

"You don't think that's all there is in Vegas?"

Jackie flushed.

A personal life so dull it was pathetic? Chris Boyd evidently liked his women just a tad on the trashy side. She could hardly blame Dennis for misleading her about his client's social skills, or what he himself did in his free time. But he'd lied about Chris going to Vegas. Maybe they went with that dentist, good old Gordy Spitz—

"So," Chris said, "what's going on with the case?"

How do you like them Broncos? The change of subject was welcome, even if there was nothing but bad news to report. "Frankly, Mueller's last ruling was a blow. Not only do we have to deal with the afternoon Ben disappeared, but now I need to learn everything I can about Freddie Gant. What can you tell me?"

Chris leaned back in his chair. "It was a Saturday, I remember that."

"Did you know Freddie?"

"Just another kid."

"What else?"

"George was looking for Shelly. He wanted to take her on one of his trips."

"Trips?"

"You know how some people collect antiques? Well,

my stepdad was a nut for farm tools. He drove all over the county looking at property for sale or in foreclosure. Most of the stuff he picked up was useless to the folks buying the land, but it was an adventure finding it. Drove my mom crazy."

"And he wanted to take you and Rachel with him that day."

"That's why Shelly sneaked off to the park. I thought the tools were pretty neat but she didn't like them. I talked him into going without her."

Two kids on a sled. This time the little brother had looked out for his older sis.

"Was Rachel there when you got home?"

"I don't remember. Wish I could be more help."

"Did the police interview you?"

"Not really. But the press sure tried." His face tightened. "My parents shipped me off to Nebraska because of that hack."

"Hack?"

"That reporter."

"Lee Simms?"

"He was digging up whatever dirt he could. Not that I had anything to tell him."

"Vivian must have been swarming with reporters from out of town. Did any of the others—"

"What makes you think Simms was an outsider?"

He'd said he was fresh from journalism school, working as a stringer.

"I guess I assumed that."

"Look, Jackie. I threw him out of my office last week. If he starts hounding my sister—"

"I told him to take a hike. But did he live in Vivian before the murder?"

"He hung around the school. I saw him waiting outside with Freddie and other little boys lots of times. Claimed to be covering that annex they were building." Chris finished his ale. "You ask me, he's the guy they should've been looking at."

Was that why Simms played up the bad seed? And why hadn't he said he knew Freddie Gant? "Did anyone—"

"Those cops? No way. They had their suspect and made sure she hanged."

"Did you know Trina Maune?"

"Shelly felt sorry for her, I remember that." His eyes narrowed. With distaste, or the effort to recall? With the mention of Simms, something had changed. "Shelly was tenderhearted. Had a soft spot for kids no one else could stand."

"You think she had anything to do with Freddie Gant's death?"

"Trina? No way."

Chris seemed increasingly distracted. Any moment he'd look at his watch and say he had to be somewhere else. She had to keep him talking, learn all she could before Dennis got wind of it and shut down any further attempt to interview him alone. Chris was a control freak, a take-charge kind of guy. Maybe she could appeal to his need to be on top.

"What do you think happened to Ben? You must have a theory."

"I've thought about it. Ben was a handful, even for a six-year-old." Just what Pilar had said. "And that morning he was in a real snit. I think he wanted to teach his dad a lesson by running away. He waited till Shelly fell asleep and then he took off. After that, he either got lost or was picked up by someone driving by. The mood he was in, he would've been an easy target for the wrong guy—"

Maybe. Or did blaming Ben absolve Chris? After all, the child had gone missing from his home. After a day at the park with his paroled sister.

"—should have been relieved."

"Relieved?" Jackie said.

"Hell, he got to go with a pretty lady for ice cream, instead of being cooped up with his dad at a bank."

"But that's not how it ended, is it?"

"No." Chris dropped his head in his hands. When he looked up again he met Jackie's gaze. "You think I'm pretty callous, don't you?"

"Doesn't matter what I think."

"Yeah, it does. You know what it's like trying to explain this to Harry Sparks? He left his son in *my* care, and I blew it. I told him Ben would be OK. And he wasn't, he—"

So his compassion wasn't just for his sister; he'd felt something for the boy too. But like Rachel, he wasn't asking to be comforted or let off the hook. Taking responsibility kept Chris in control.

"Let's go back to your scenario," Jackie said. "It makes sense, except for one thing. If a stranger picked Ben up because he was an easy target, how do you explain the similarities between his murder and Freddie Gant's?"

"Who said it was a stranger?"

Now she was lost. "You think it was someone Ben knew?"

"Of course not."

"Then who?"

"It had to be a copycat. People knew Shelly was paroled. They knew she was living here, and they tried to make her life hell. We kept getting calls."

"Calls?"

"Hang-up calls. All hours of the night."

Rachel had never mentioned those.

"Did you report them?"

"To who, the police?" Chris laughed. "And give them another crack at my sister?"

"And you didn't try to trace them."

"God, how I wish."

"So you think whoever was making those calls—"

"—kept his eye out and seized the moment. Ben was a good-looking kid."

She'd ask Pilar to see if the phone company kept records, but Jackie knew even a slight chance to identify the caller had probably been lost.

"Go back to that day," she said. "What time did you return from the bank?"

"Around three."

"Did you drive there with Ben's father?"

"I took my SUV and Harry followed in his truck. He had the sprinkler equipment."

"What happened when you got home?"

"Shelly was taking a nap. I woke her and asked where Ben was. She said she'd put him to bed in the guest room down the hall. I checked, but he wasn't there. Harry drove up about fifteen or twenty minutes later. We looked in the shed and the garage. Then we canvassed the neighborhood."

"Was Rachel with you?"

"The whole time. We didn't even split up to knock on doors. Harry thought Ben was mad because he wanted a video game and he wouldn't buy it for him. We came back here and reported him missing. The cops searched the house."

"Anyone hear the dogs bark?"

"Dogs?" Chris's eyes lit. "You're right. If a stranger entered the yard, they would've raised a ruckus. Ben *must* have run—"

Despite his claim about the hang-up calls and all his theorizing about a copycat, had he doubted his sister's story, too?

"Where were you the rest of that evening?"

"Shelly and I drove around together looking. I have a Land Rover and a Mercedes SUV and we could've taken both cars, but she wanted—"

"Rachel drives?"

Chris looked confused. "Well, sure."

"Since when?"

"George let her take the wheel on county roads. She's never had a license but I gave her the keys to my Land Rover. . . . As I was saying, I was with her the entire time. We finally gave up at two in the morning. Came home and crashed."

So Rachel could drive. And she'd had access to a vehicle. They had to stop before Chris realized how significant that was. On top of the hang-up calls and his catting around with Dennis, Jackie had learned enough for one day.

"Sorry to put you through this, Chris," she said, rising. "And it won't be the last time. We'll be calling you as a witness at trial."

His laugh was weary.

"You know the hardest part of the past thirty years? Not being at Shelly's side. At her trial in Vivian, while she was in that juvenile facility and all those terrible years in Cañon City. That's why I invited her here. And look how that turned out! I know Dennis means well—"

"He's only trying to protect you." Not to mention those trips to Vegas.

"—but I'm sick of being treated like the one who needs to be saved. I wasn't there for my sister thirty years ago, but I'm damn well here for her now."

Thirty

The sun was setting as Jackie drove home.

She hadn't known what to make of Chris Boyd before, but now he seemed like a man with nothing to hide. Hell, he even showed her his garage. Dennis, on the other hand . . . She shook her head. It had been years since they'd had any sort of relationship and she had no claim on him now. He was free, attractive and over twenty-one. So what if he slummed with a client in Vegas? Pilar would applaud him and suggest she and Jackie do the same.

She was more worried that Rachel could drive.

What did her client say at their first meeting? If she hadn't actually lied when asked why she didn't drive to Toody-Froody, she'd certainly allowed Jackie to be misled. And she'd said nothing about hang-up calls.

Did her silence have a reason? Or was it the wariness of an ex-con?

As Jackie neared Congress Park, the beacon on the transmission tower south of the soccer fields winked. The overhead lights and parked cars meant a game was being played. She tried to picture the slope at the edge of the field. Even if Rachel had driven Ben there, was it possible for a woman her size to haul a boy's body up a steep hill and hurl it into the bramble?

She pulled over at the entrance to the apartment building on Josephine. Parking in the lot, she stepped over the chain that fenced off the bramble from the street. She walked along the ravine at the base of the slope for a few yards and stopped.

Ch-ch-chhh . . .

A dry sound, like sticks rubbing together.

Did it come from the apartments? All she could hear from that direction was water running in a sink and the hum of a TV set. A muffled shout from the soccer field; someone had scored a goal. Jackie held her breath and focused.

No birds.

Crickets. Unidentified bugs.

Chhch. Chchch . . .

This time the rustling was louder.

Shielded by the tree that spanned the apartments, Jackie crouched against the fence. She stared up at the halogen lamps that marked the edge of the soccer field and illuminated the crowns of the dogwoods. As her eyes adjusted she saw movement. A man was digging through the branches. He straightened and the light caught his hair. The blue glow gave it an eerie gleam.

Chris?

He couldn't have beat her— No, this man was taller. Stoop-shouldered.

Lee Simms.

He felt along the top of a bush, then shook the upper branches. He dropped back down on his knees and felt along the ground.

Simms was looking for something small.

He crept along the bramble, seemingly oblivious to the futility of his task. The foliage was dense—the branches were leafed and in full flower. He repeated each step, running his fingers over the dirt like a blind man searching for a key.

Something the killer dropped?

A-yay!

The shout was followed by the whump of rubber against chain link.

"Got it!"

A man in a striped jersey slammed into the fence and grabbed the ball. Standing, he held it over his head and stood framed by the light. He was looking down.

Simms crouched in the bushes, ducking his head. In dark clothing and sneakers he was almost invisible. After a moment, the man turned and ran back to the field. Simms got to his feet. As he turned in her direction Jackie shrank against the tree. He hurried to the far entrance to the bramble, where she'd parked on her last visit. In the failing light a yellow Corvette revved up and quickly drove away.

Jackie stood. She didn't need crime scene tape to recognize the portion of the bramble Simms had been searching. Whatever he was looking for, he hadn't found.

Cool grass tickled her legs. Even the crickets were silent.

What if he returned?

She continued up the hill, to the precise spot where the dogwoods refused to flower. Two feet from where Simms had stopped searching, bare branches poked up like bony fingers. The lamp from the soccer field shone almost directly down on this bush. Was that why Simms had shied away?

She felt along the crown, stabbing her palms on twigs that had never greened. Like Simms she ran her hands under them to catch whatever fell. With one ear cocked for his return she moved to the next clump.

As she jostled a branch, she felt something cold. It landed with a soft thunk.

Two pieces of wire, twisted together—a puzzle no boy could resist?

Heedless of sharp twigs and her linen trousers, Jackie

crawled into the foliage. A branch snapped back and hit her in the eye. Pushing it aside, she probed the roots. Her fingers touched something solid.

A flat piece of metal, small and heavy for its size.

She held it to the light.

Four inches long and a quarter of an inch thick. One end was jagged, as if it had broken from a larger piece. The other tapered into a sharp hook.

Jackie turned it over. Flecks of paint gave the pebbled surface a dull gleam.

A scrap from when the soccer field was built. Nothing to do with Ben Sparks. She was about to toss it back in the brush.

Then why did Lee Simms care?

Pocketing the shard, Jackie ran to her car.

Thirty-One

CONFIDENTIAL MEMORANDUM

TO: DA Floyd Garrett
FROM: Detective Sergeant Ryan
Mitchell
DATE: May 17, 1973
RE: Homicide of Freddie Gant

State crime lab has completed its
analysis of the threads at the
waistband of Freddie Gant's trousers.
They now believe the top button to
his fly was cut off with a sharp
instrument. (See Report of State
Crime Lab dated 5/16/73.) The button has not been found, but this is
important for several reasons.

First, Rachel Boyd lied in her
interview about what Freddie was
wearing that day. Witnesses have
placed her with Freddie that afternoon. She admitted wearing the
red shorts we know she wore, then
she tried to deny it. (Rachel also
lied about playing with her dog
that morning. George Boyd had a
dog, but it ran off two days earlier.) We also know she spent part
of that time with her friend Trina

Maune. In her interview Trina let it slip that she saw Freddie's body. More importantly, Trina was able to describe the buttons on Freddie's trousers, which were distinctive. That confirms both girls were at the scene. If Trina was not directly involved in the murder, I believe Rachel took her there later that afternoon, or the day after.

Second, we know some type of weapon was used to make the cut marks on the boy's groin. In all likelihood, the same weapon was used to slice off the button. Like the button, the weapon has not been found. I believe the fact that the button was cut off confirms that the crime was committed by a child and not an adult.

It is very difficult to unbutton somebody else's pants. It's even harder for a child to do than it is for an adult. An adult would have unbuttoned Freddie's pants or, if he was acting in a sexual rage, forced them down or torn them off. A child wouldn't have the strength or manual dexterity to do either, especially a girl. I think Freddie refused to pull his pants down so Rachel had to cut the button off.

The case against Rachel Boyd is very strong. In addition to witnesses placing her at the scene and her deceptiveness in interviews, there is of course the red cotton thread from her shorts which was found on Freddie's shirt. (See Report of State Crime Lab dated 5/14/73.) Her real mistake was not realizing what cutting off that button tells us. To my mind, this evidence clinches the case.

In the course of this investigation I have spent a good deal of time in Rachel Boyd's presence. I think I know what makes her tick. I can say without exaggeration that she's the most cold-blooded killer I've ever met. She is also a very clever child. She grasps things very quickly. She clearly has the ability to learn from her mistakes. In my interviews with her, I could almost see the wheels turn.

We know even the most hardened criminals learn from the forensic evidence presented at trial. If not from the evidence itself, then from the reasoning tying the defendant to the crime. That's why it's good to hold something back.

Children who commit these sorts

of crimes against defenseless playmates are rarely capable of rehabilitation. No matter how long she's put away for, one day Rachel will be out. And when she does get out she may very well kill again.

I don't know what attracted her to Freddie that day. Maybe she wanted his truck, maybe it was those shiny buttons. Or maybe it was because he was small and help-less. But our evidence is strong enough that there's no need to put any special emphasis on the fact that the button was cut instead of torn off. I'm not suggesting with-holding anything from the defense, just not making an issue of it in front of Rachel before or during the trial. If she ever does get out and repeat her act, it may trip her up again.

Mitchell playing Sherlock again with that police academy crap. Cutting or tearing—talk about chasing a rabbit down a hole. Could just as easily have been an adult, which is why I will deep-six it. Time for another chat with Wally Metz about keeping those Keystone Kops of his in line. FG

Thirty-Two

By eight-thirty Saturday morning, the Cherry Creek Farmers Market parking lot was jammed. Yuppies in jogging briefs and air-jet sneakers, dogs with bandannas, an entire family in desert headgear who looked as if they'd lost their way out of the Sahara . . . Pulling free of Jackie's hand, Lily made a beeline for the herbal facials with Rachel at her heels.

"Not up for a makeover?" Dennis said as Jackie struggled to keep Lily's glossy black hair in sight. "Don't worry about her, she's tough as steel."

Jackie had taken pains to ensure that Rachel and Lily were kept apart. She'd made it clear to each of them that she intended to honor her promise to Britt. Rachel had nodded, accepting without question where Britt was coming from. Lily was another matter. Why did she have to obey? Hadn't Jackie always said you were entitled to a second chance? Your mother loves you, Jackie told her. She's doing what she thinks is best. As a reward, she'd promised to take them to the farmers' market. All they needed was a chaperone.

The problem was, after that disastrous dinner weeks earlier, Pilar wanted nothing to do with Jackie's houseguest. When Jackie asked Dennis to accompany them he'd agreed with surprising grace. In his Volvo on the way over, Lily had stationed herself as far from him as physically possible.

"Don't feel bad," Jackie said as Lily and Rachel ran off. "Girls her age don't know what to make of men. One minute you're a hero, the next you're a jerk."

If Dennis noticed the emphasis on that final word, he didn't react.

"If she were on my client's jury, I'd break out the hemlock. Or her neck."

"Just give her a chance. Once she gets to know you . . ."

A farmer was unloading stock, snapdragons and baby's breath from the back of his truck. Handing him a dollar, Dennis plucked a hot-pink gerbera daisy from a galvanized bucket and slipped the stem inside the waistband of Jackie's shorts. From twenty yards away Lily gave him a look that would have turned a lesser man to stone.

"Do I need her permission for a date?"

"She's ten years old. She has no idea what to make of our relationship."

"She's not the only one." He softened it with a peck on the cheek. "Know what I find particularly amusing? That you invited me to chaperone Lily, when she's digging the moat around *you*."

"Who said anything about chaperones? Rachel's never been to a farmers' market and look how wonderful she and Lily are together. . . ."

Thirty years in prison had made it tough for Rachel to know how to act in normal society, much less the carnival atmosphere of an urban farmers' market. She was a rabbit with nowhere to hide.

"What'd you expect?" he said. "She's never shopped at a Super Kmart. Half the products she used, they don't even sell anymore. She's never been on the Internet or withdrawn money from an ATM."

Neither had Jackie.

"But Rachel worked at a restaurant and lived in a halfway house," she said. "Not to mention three months with boring old Chris. You know, the guy with no personal life? And speaking of Chris—"

"Those environments are as artificial as they come. She's never had to pay rent or a phone bill. And you plunk her in this circus and expect her to take it in stride . . ."

Rachel was an island.

At first she'd hunkered down in the center of the parade, arms close to her sides. Shoppers cut a wide swath and Jackie couldn't help feeling sorry for her. Rachel slowly turned, taking in the endless array of offerings, each more enticing than the last, through opaque eyes. Then Lily grabbed her hand and the two of them were off.

Taking note of the location of the booth where Lily and Rachel were trying out sunscreen made from beeswax, Jackie turned back to Dennis. She was curious about Rachel's relationship with Chris. Rachel never talked about her feelings, and she didn't like to talk about her brother. She hadn't even mentioned him since that first night at Jackie's house; when Jackie brought up his name she changed the subject. Was it painful for her?

"Did Chris visit her in Cañon City?" she said.

"She wouldn't let him. He tried a few times but she turned him away."

"Why?"

"She didn't want him to see her like that."

They were at a tent with kitchen gadgets.

"Ergonomic," Dennis said. "What's ergonomic about a corkscrew?"

Plastic and aluminum utensils and older tools were on display. Jackie remembered the shard she'd found in the bramble. The closest she could find was something with a flat handle that ended in a closed hook.

"What's that?" she asked.

"A bottle opener. Don't you ever drink beer?"

She reached for a heavier tool that might have been a

paint scraper. Like the shard, it was cold and awkward in her grasp.

"What's this made of?" she asked the man at the booth.

"Cast iron. Pioneer stuff."

"Hardly ergonomic," Dennis said.

"Exactly the point. They don't make iron tools anymore because—"

A group of women in sandals and Bermuda shorts descended. With their straw handbags and wide-brimmed hats they looked as if they were on a gardening tour. They swept Jackie into their midst and carried her to the vegetable stand next door. The smart blonde in the sun visor pointed to a bin of hairy tubers.

"Now, some people think there's no justification for calling beets a vegetable. But they make excellent low-fat dishes."

"I thought you ate beets in winter?" said a die-hard Martha Stewart fan.

"Where's *she* been hiding?" Rachel was at Jackie's elbow. "In a cabbage patch?"

Lily giggled.

"Shh," Jackie said. "It's a cooking class. And don't stare."

"Why?"

"It's rude," Jackie said.

The instructor had segued into zucchini. "Know how you pay two-fifty a pound in winter? Well, now it's dirt cheap."

"Don't talk about zucchini," a woman groaned. "You can do *everything* with zucchini."

Her friend snickered. "Gives new meaning to 'home entertainment.'"

Pretending not to hear, the blonde began pointing out

the differences between wilted and fresh while her charges nodded like Kewpie dolls. "Now, girls, be careful to wash things when you get home. It may say organic, but—"

Dennis was waving from the pasta tent, where there was a run on Szechuan linguine. Were they buying because others were grabbing it or because spicy was always a draw? Jackie bought a pound of jalapeño angel hair for Pilar and was about to ask Dennis what he liked when she realized Lily had disappeared.

"Where are they?"

"Last I saw, at the vegetable stand."

"Some chaperone you are!"

"Now, don't panic . . ." Grabbing Jackie's hand, he shouldered his way through shoppers lined three deep. "Is that them?"

Rachel and Lily were at the other side of the tent, standing behind two twenty-somethings in jogging shorts oohing and aahing over fruit-flavored pasta.

"It's so *pretty*," said the one in yellow trunks. The macaroni was shaped like seashells and came in rainbow colors.

"Great with yogurt dressing," the proprietor said. "Main dish or dessert."

Jackie slowly exhaled. Everything was all right.

"Lily—" She stopped when she saw the look on Rachel's face. She was staring at the joggers as if they were a two-headed dog.

"—could have Brian over," yellow trunks was saying.

"Well, if you want." The other shrugged. She was much plainer than her friend, with pudgy cheeks and moles on her throat. "It's your dinner party. I'm just bringing the croissants."

"I thought you liked him . . ."

"Better than that cooking class," Rachel whispered to Lily. "Watch that girl. She's a pro."

"Which girl?" Lily said.

"The one with the moles. Watch how she does it."

"Does what?"

"Plays up her own weakness to make the other strong . . ."

"But who should we invite?" Yellow trunks sounded uncertain.

"Whoever you want," moles said. "You're the one with the address book—"

"See how it works?" Rachel said to Lily.

"How *what* works?"

"Control. Power. It takes two."

"Why?"

"Unless one's weak, how can the other be strong?"

"—right," yellow trunks said. "Pasta is kind of out."

"I'm sure Brian would enjoy it—if you want him to come. But wouldn't we be better off with steak?" Moles poked her friend. "Meat. Isn't that what guys really want?"

"I guess so." With one last wistful look at the pasta, yellow trunks turned away. She didn't know it yet but the dinner party was no longer hers. "I'm sure glad you came."

"Who, me? I'm just bringing the croissants."

Thirty-Three

EXCLUSIVE BY LEE SIMMS FOR
MODERN CRIMES—MAY 31, 1973

A patch of grass and a blue Schwinn tricycle lying on its side. Blinds drawn against hot sun and prying eyes. Neighbors suddenly strangers. And a hardworking couple with no answers why.

No one wants to understand more than Harold and Lucy Maune. Their thirteen-year-old daughter Trina was the last person with Rachel Boyd, taken into custody May 18 for what authorities are describing as the thrill murder of four-year-old Freddie Gant in the quiet farming town of Vivian. In the wake of these shocking events, the Maunes and their daughter spoke of that fateful day and the girl who used to be Trina's closest chum.

"I don't know why she did it," Trina says. Her soft eyes fill with tears. "We liked Freddie, we really did. I have two little brothers myself."

Harold Maune's callused hands twist in his lap. This father of six and foreman at Vivian Feed & Grain was one of the first to join in the search for the missing toddler. Little did he know how close to home the tragedy would strike.

"Soon's we heard he was missing, I started beating the bushes. Them kids know to stay away from the tracks. If I ever thought—"

He breaks off and his wife Lucy pats his arm comfortingly. She doesn't have to remind him of the obvious: that by the time little Freddie Gant was known to be missing he was already lying dead at the very place where Harold Maune works.

From the front door of the Maunes' modest one-story home at 60 Bell Street, you can see the tall white elevator with VIVIAN GRAIN emblazoned in red. It and the water tower, which also bears the name of the town, are the tallest structures for miles around. The sun glints off the storage bins where young Freddie's body was found and Harold Maune looks away.

Tell us about Rachel, the reporter asks.

The girl's eyes well and her mother strokes her back. This seems to give Trina strength and when she answers her gaze is steady and her voice firm. Willing or not, she has come to understand her role in this drama and is eager to provide whatever answers she can.

"She was lots of fun. I didn't have too many friends before."

Trina is sturdy and well built for her age but her doe-like eyes bespeak a habit of doing what she is told. The eldest of the Maune children, this thirteen-year-old dresses her younger siblings, prepares their lunch and walks them to school. Lucy Maune, who bakes pies for the local diner to make ends meet, confides that Trina is such a help around the house she was held back a grade. That's how she was befriended by Rachel Boyd, who is a year younger. Her mother shakes her head as she recalls how pleased she was that Trina had made a special friend.

"The Boyds are good people," Harold Maune says. "George Boyd has appraised darn near every piece of land in this county. Lots of folks hereabouts owe him their livelihood. And he's been more than a father to Evvie's two kids."

Harold Maune himself is respected for his generosity. Modest as the Maune domicile is, he has been known to let men down on their luck stay in the small shed out back of the house. Sometimes they hire on at Vivian Feed & Grain, other times they move on. His charity perhaps explains why his daughter was drawn to a younger girl who apparently lacked direction. For isn't this story as much Trina's as it is Rachel's? One wonders what made them so close.

You know how girls are, Lucy Maune says, but her daughter excitedly cuts in.

"We had secrets. I have one of my own. It's important not to tell. . . . We talked about running away." Recalling times when Rachel's plans must have sounded like a lark, Trina's eyes brighten and the weight of that dreadful day seems to lift from her shoulders. "That's all we ever talked about. She wanted people to remember her."

Is that why she left the notes on the blackboard?

Trina looks puzzled, and then the awful realization of what Rachel's scribbled messages meant must have dawned on her.

"I don't know why she did that," she says, slowly shaking her head.

Thirty-Four

I thought you wanted nothing to do with Simms," Pilar said.

"Just curious where he's staying." After seeing him at the bramble Jackie had tried to find his address, but directory assistance had no record. "He mention it to you?"

"One of those places named after the dead guys they make you read in high school. Mark Frost and Robert Twain, Louisa May what's-her-name . . ."

Poets Row. The reporter had rented a room in a Depression-era apartment building in a run-down district south of the state capitol. Luckily he drove a distinctive car. Reasoning that Sunday morning was the best time to find his Corvette out front, Jackie went there alone the day after the trip to the farmers' market.

Simms's neighborhood was a study in faded pretension. A Moorish complex evoked Hollywood in the twenties while smaller rooming houses looked to Gotham of the same era. Poets Row itself was strictly art deco with an emphasis on black, chrome and glass. Rental agents tried to appeal to bohemians by describing the accommodations as studio apartments, but bike racks and crooked Venetian blinds identified the tenants as students and waiters.

Street parking was tight and there was no Corvette. Jackie circled the block on foot, finally locating Simms's car in an assigned slot on the side of a building with a rounded marquee and faux-marble glass bricks. The foyer was smaller than a Denver County Jail cell and the intercom had no names. A Sunday *Post* was scattered across the floor. She pushed the button for the unit corresponding to the lettered space where the Corvette was parked.

No answer.

The carpet was damp and the walls stank of mold. She rang again.

A glass door barred access to a staircase and the ground-floor units. It was locked. The only light came from a fluorescent tube in the hallway. Jackie was about to ring a third time when a man with a stud in his lower lip entered from the street. Stooping to pick up the *Post*, she let a couple of sections slip to the floor.

He held the door for her.

Waiting as he clattered up the stairs, Jackie carried the paper down the hall and set it on the carpet near Simms's unit at the rear of the ground floor. She knocked.

No answer. Maybe he was doing laundry.

She knocked again, then peered down the hall. Where would a laundry room be?

No elevator, no stairway leading to a basement. The hall smelled of dirty sneakers and the door next to Simms's was marked EXIT. Jackie twisted that knob. It was locked. Turning back to his unit, she knocked louder.

Still nothing.

She tried the knob. It turned.

Maybe he was in the john.

Feeling a little foolish, she knocked harder. This time she called his name.

"Simms?"

He could have gone out for coffee. She opened the door a crack.

"Lee?"

One furnished room with a breakfast bar. A half-open ɔor led to the john and another looked like a closet.

No sign of Simms.

The shard lay in her pocket like lead.

What harm would it do to look? If he caught her she'd say it was payback for his showing up at her office unannounced.

Closing the door behind her, Jackie looked around the room. It was dark and musty, sparsely furnished with a hard sofa and a scarred chest of drawers. A half-empty coffeepot sat on a hot plate at the breakfast bar. The bathroom sink had a razor and a crusted tube of shaving cream. The basin was still wet. Simms's sole luxuries seemed to be a twenty-four-inch TV and a VCR on the wall opposite the closet. A stack of videocassettes stood next to the VCR. Where did he sleep? She went to the closet.

The door pulled out instead of opening in.

Jackie leaped back just in time. An unmade Murphy bed crashed down, narrowly missing her head.

Get a grip, she told herself.

Turning, she saw a card table in the corner of the room. On it sat a laptop computer and a mouse, beside them a pile of opened bills. She started with the bills.

The first was for a credit card in Simms's name. The second was for his cell phone. No long-distance charges. The third was a utility bill. A sizable balance was due; more than you'd expect for a month's service in late spring. Jackie took a closer look. The balance was past due from March and it was for this address.

He'd said Rachel's arrest brought him to Denver.

Ben was murdered in April. He'd been here in March.

What other lies had Simms told?

Jackie stuffed the utility bill in her pocket and opened

the computer. The screen was blank and she couldn't get it to work. As she turned away, she jostled the mouse.

The computer sprang to life.

At first she didn't recognize what she was seeing. Muscular but pale, two rounded lobes . . . The screen pulsed and the image sharpened. Suddenly she was staring at an enormous disembodied pair of buttocks. They floated seductively and then bent over, issuing an obscene invitation. Without warning the screen went blank.

Jackie closed the computer and turned to Simms's dresser. The top drawer held underwear and socks and an unopened box of condoms. Ultraribbed. Shirts and trousers were in the next, a couple of sweaters—as she ran her hands through the third drawer she touched something solid. A cardboard box.

Long nails, a screwdriver with a filed tip, a glass or linoleum cutter. A length of wire. Guy toys. The sort of junk you'd expect to find in a garage or tool chest. Or the trunk of a car. At the bottom lay something heavy.

A four-inch scrap of iron with a jagged end.

In the dim light she saw flecks of blue paint. She reached in her pocket and took out the shard. The two pieces matched—

Footsteps outside the door.

Jackie froze.

Movement blocked the light under the door. She heard shuffling.

He was picking up the *Post*.

Could she brazen it out?

Jackie shoved the box back in the drawer and slammed it shut. Scrambling over the Murphy bed, she dove into the open closet.

The front door opened and Lee Simms entered his

room. He dropped the *Post* on the bed and unbuckled his belt.

Jackie shrank against the back wall, certain he could hear her heart pound. The closet was roomier than she'd thought. Instead of shelves, a clothes rod hung across the back. She crouched behind a tweed jacket.

Whistling, Simms headed for the john. He left the door open and paused. After an agonizing moment he began to urinate.

Did she have enough time to climb back over the bed and dash out the front? If only he'd shut the door to the john . . . The toilet flushed and water ran. The back wall was blessedly cool. Leaning against it, Jackie tried to calm herself by breathing through her nose. Any minute he would emerge and— The wall shifted under her weight.

She pushed harder and it gave a little more.

Running her fingers over the surface, she found a seam. It was a door. That meant there had to be—a bolt. It slid back.

The rear wall of the Murphy bed closet opened into a cubicle behind the exit door in the hallway. The barred emergency door behind that opened onto the street.

A moment later Jackie stood in the alley behind Simms's building. His Corvette was parked in the last space, one slot from the door. Two industrial-size Dumpsters shielded the emergency exit from view.

She looked across the alley. Simms's apartment faced the back of a broadcasting station. It had satellite dishes but no windows or public access from that side. A large cool closet with a private exit, no witnesses—

What better place to hide a body until it snowed?

She'd unlatched the closet door from the inside. If

Simms didn't know someone broke in, he'd soon find out.

Jackie rounded the building and hurried to her car. As she turned the key in the ignition, she patted her pocket.

Simms's utility bill was there.

Her iron shard was gone.

Thirty-Five

S urely Ms. Flowers doesn't mean Your Honor can't manage the trial to avoid unfair prejudice?"

Doby's suit was a notch above his normal attire, but the dandruff on the collar confirmed his common touch. If only shabbiness could save Jackie! In Greta Mueller's court fighting for a change of venue that Monday morning, she was on the verge of losing more than her composure.

If Simms went to the bramble, maybe he went just looking for the iron hook. That wire puzzle had never been found. Was he Toody-Froody's mystery man? But when Jackie returned from his apartment Sunday afternoon and asked Rachel if Simms was at the ice cream parlor the day Ben disappeared, her client recalled nothing.

"You're sure?" Jackie said. "The kid at the counter—"

"I don't remember."

"Why would he say a man talked to Ben if it never happened?"

"Don't you trust me?"

"It's not a matter of— Is that cologne?"

There was a cloying scent in her front hallway.

"I don't know what you mean. Of course I'd remember Simms if I saw him."

"What is it, rose oil?"

"I don't smell anything."

"Was someone here?"

"You think I have people over while you're gone?"

Jackie was suddenly on the defensive.

"You're welcome to, you know. It's just that—"

"Where were you this morning, anyway?" Rachel said.

"I went to the store." Rachel eyed Jackie's empty hands. "For thread."

"Thread? On Sunday?"

"Gold thread, to replace a button on a blouse."

"Buttons? My, my . . . Between you and Cal Doby, you'd think buttons—"

"They didn't have the right color."

And Jackie didn't even own a gold blouse.

As she heard herself dissemble, a wave of confusion had washed over her. Under the best of circumstances she was a poor liar. If nothing else, the constant need to focus kept her honest. One lifelong cover-up was enough!

First breaking into Simms's apartment, then thinking someone had been in her house, now lying to Rachel . . . She was starting to lose it, something kept throwing her off her game. A trial lawyer's worst nightmare was getting distracted; it was a risk you faced each time you entered the courtroom. For Jackie, even on a good day the risk was multiplied a thousandfold. She was starting to feel it happening now. In fact, each time she had an important hearing—

Focus on the case. Simms was in it up to his neck and probably feeding information to Doby. She had to get Rachel's trial moved out of Denver. Maybe to Trinidad, the southernmost part of the state.

Jackie had gone upstairs to lay out her clothes for court.

Monday morning her alarm didn't go off. Then she couldn't find the right blouse.

"Did you see it?" she asked Rachel.

"If you mean your cream silk, I took it to replace that button. Wasn't it the one you were talking about yesterday?"

The cream blouse wasn't missing a button. And Rachel knew it wasn't gold.

"Could I have it back, please?"

"I was looking for the right thread."

"Rachel, we have to be in court—"

"Pink looks better with your blue gabardine anyway."

In court listening to Doby thirty minutes later, Jackie was still trying to claw her way out of the fog.

"—extensive pretrial publicity does not, *in and of itself*, preclude fairness and justify a change of venue—"

Venue motions were an uphill battle for the defense.

Jackie had to prove that the public perception of Rachel's guilt was so great she couldn't get a fair trial in Denver. If Mueller ruled a fair trial was impossible she'd be admitting she couldn't control her own court. And because the ruling was discretionary, her knuckles were unlikely to be rapped on appeal. But Jackie was tired of being hometowned by Doby with the local press.

At least Simms wasn't in court.

Focus.

"—preferred practice is to conduct a careful and searching voir dire of each prospective juror to determine whether such juror is capable of being fair and—"

Jackie had more than one reason for wanting the case transferred to Trinidad, if not Timbuktu. The Gant murder had made Rachel Colorado's own bad seed, but she was Denver's problem now because of Ben. What twelve local citizens hadn't seen her face, then and now, in every newspaper and on every network? Move the trial across the Continental Divide to the Western Slope and rural chauvinists would consider it a Denver affair.

And Doby's leaks made it personal. She had to knock him off his home turf.

Rachel was staring coolly at their opponent. Her insistence that Simms wasn't at Toody-Froody made Jackie feel even more confused about breaking into his apartment. Not confused, but angry. No, not angry . . . *furious.* How could she have lost the only solid clue in a case where the weapon had never been found?

Who but Simms poked around bushes where bodies were dumped? Who else lied about when he had blown into town, and who else had a closet big enough to hide a kid . . . and kept a cardboard box filled with broken cutting tools in his dresser? She still hadn't told Pilar.

And why hadn't she told Pilar? Pilar wasn't just her investigator, she was her closest friend! Jackie reached into the pocket of her blue gabardine suit. Her fingers scrambled for the moss agate.

It was gone.

The light above Mueller's bench started to flicker. The courtroom began to spin.

Rachel was looking at her strangely.

Focus, *focus.* Not on Rachel, but on Doby . . .

"—large metropolitan community with superior resources and availability of an extensive jury *pool.*"

Never mind his crazy emphasis. The words, listen to the *words.*

"In addition, the court facilities in Denver are well suited—"

—to a prosecution team with the local press and law enforcement in its pocket, and a place where citizens who voted on the judge's retention lived. Not to mention Doby's boss, who'd put a price on Jackie's head. Suddenly she could breathe again. Shuffling back to the prosecution table, Doby pretended to search for a document in plain view on top of a folder.

"In deference to this Court's overriding *concern* for fairness, however, the People have commissioned an opinion survey conducted by Stanford Price, a qualified expert who has opined as to the results of such surveys on numerous occasions. If this Court would care—"

"This Court does indeed. Get him up here."

Stanford Price took the stand. A dapper squirt in a three-piece suit that cost twice Doby's entire wardrobe, he seemed congenial enough. Until he smiled.

"Dr. Price," Doby said, "your firm was recently retained by the Office of the District Attorney of the City and County of Denver, was it not?"

"Yes, it was." Price's shirt was so white his teeth looked stained.

"And you were asked to conduct a survey of a statistically significant sample—"

"Cut to the chase," Mueller said. "Results?"

"My interviewers polled four hundred and six Denver residents aged twenty-one years or older. Each of the respondents was either registered to vote in the city and county, and/or owned a vehicle licensed in Denver. The goal was to test their ability to be fair and impartial jurors."

"What questions did they ask?" Doby said.

"You were concerned with the effect of media coverage, so the first question was whether they recognized the name Rachel Boyd."

"And?"

"Seventy-two percent did. Several thought she was a line of cosmetics." Price poured himself a glass of water to give the titters a chance to die down. "Testing visual frame of reference, we then asked the subset of respondents who correctly identified Ms. Boyd if they would recognize her if they encountered her on the street. Forty-eight percent said they would. We asked *those* respondents if what they'd heard, read or otherwise seen regarding Ms. Boyd would have any effect on their ability to be impartial if they were selected to hear her case."

Four hundred and six citizens aged twenty-one or over, seventy-two percent of whom . . . or was it forty-eight? What percentage of what Rachel told her was a lie? Doby was nodding for Price to continue.

"Only twenty-one percent felt their prior knowledge of Ms. Boyd might taint their impartiality. Twenty-one percent of forty-eight percent of seventy-two—"

"—means seven and a quarter percent of your respondents," Mueller cut in, "or fewer than twenty-nine and one-half of the persons you polled, were adversely affected by pretrial publicity." She'd kept the books for her father's farm. "That's all?"

Doby shuffled his feet. "Yes, ma'am."

"Ms. Flowers?"

Something was rotten and it wasn't sugar beets.

Jackie slowly rose. Visual . . . something visual. Reference, reference, who's got the reference? The numbers were spinning. Forget the numbers.

Think, Jackie, think.

Pictures. Think about *pictures.*

"You say you tested their visual reference frame. Does that mean you showed them photographs?"

"We used a head shot of Ms. Boyd taken when she was released from Cañon City." Price anticipated her next question. "Nothing indicated she was or had been in custody."

"And that was the *only* photo—"

Doby sprang to his feet.

"I resent counsel's implication! If we used a booking photo, Ms. Flowers would complain that the very act of polling prospective jurors tainted them."

Taint, photo, poll . . . None of the switches worked.

Fly, Jackie, fly!

"The media has demonized Rachel Boyd," Jackie heard herself prattle. She was running on autopilot. "Should we ignore the clips of her in shackles and orange scrubs? The continuous running of thirty-year-old footage is even worse. That same footage has played on every TV newscast of the Sparks case. It's run every five years on the anniversary of Freddie Gant's death for the past—"

"I've read your report on news media analysis, Ms. Flowers," Mueller said. "And I'm quite aware of Mr. Doby's office's leaks. But humans aren't lab rats and bias is difficult to prove. Absent any indication that the polling was conducted in such a way as to prejudice the respondents or otherwise skew the results, I simply cannot dismiss Dr. Price's survey."

"But, Your Honor—"

Mueller showed her teeth. Unlike Price's, they gleamed.

"You're not suggesting I can't ferret out prejudice in my own courtroom?"

Jackie's autopilot crashed.

"Defense motion for change of venue is denied. Trial will commence six weeks from now in this court."

Thirty-Six

G et a load of her!" Pilar pointed at the TV.

It was noon and they were taking a break from reviewing witness statements. Since Jackie had lost the venue motion, Doby had seized the momentum. He was whipping the press into a frenzy and bombarding the defense with trivia. Dozens of statements regarding the search of the country club for Ben Sparks, countless motions.

"Get one of your friends on the force to tap into that national database," Jackie said. They'd struck out with the phone company on the hang-up calls. "Look for similar crimes over the last thirty years. Boys with necks snapped, groins slashed, buttons—"

"Bite marks?"

"Stay away from those for now."

Pilar's eyes were on the TV. "Some dames will do anything to get in front of a camera." They'd ordered sandwiches from a deli that catered to the Seventeenth Street crowd. Pilar slid her chips across the table to Jackie. "Tired of French cuisine?"

"What makes you say that?"

The woman at the microphone on TV was short and blocky. Oversized glasses made her eyes bulge like a Chihuahua's.

"The way you're wolfing down that sandwich. Either you're not eating at home or you ain't getting laid."

"How perceptive."

It wasn't just the case Jackie felt she was losing.

All of her perceptions were askew. The morning coffee

had been tinny and Rachel said it was chicory; the ground pepper in her eggs had tasted like grit. The moss agate had shown up in Jackie's jewelry box and her silk blouse was returned with the button replaced, but she'd spent ten minutes searching for her favorite pumps and never found the earrings she'd wanted to wear. Some disorientation could be attributed to the stress of the upcoming trial, some to sharing her home with a guest. . . .

She could hardly blame Rachel for the venue fiasco; that was her own fault. In fact, Rachel hadn't mentioned it at all. But Jackie felt her client watching her. Was she waiting for Jackie to lose it again? Or was it something more?

Jackie visualized Rachel picking up her key ring and hefting it. How would it feel for Rachel to have a ring of keys, an office to go to, a home of her own? Or a closet filled with silk blouses and designer suits? To *be* Jackie . . .

"Well, which is it?" Pilar said.

"The chow remains first-class, as you'd know if you accepted any of my many invitations—"

"I had such high hopes for you and Dennis this time around."

"Given this case, I don't think it's a good idea."

"Why?"

"I have to watch what I say about Rachel. He represents her brother. Besides, Dennis is the one who stepped on the brakes."

"Maybe your new roommate has something to do with that. Not every guy likes to perform for an audience."

"He's a trial lawyer, for God's sake!"

"The well of the court ain't exactly the sack. . . . Je-*sus*."

The TV woman's outfit was even more bizarre. Calf-length black skirt and lace-up boots despite the midday heat, an oversize blouse with a multicolored rayon scarf at her throat. Topping it off was a straw cowboy hat with a black ribbon around the brim.

The camera zoomed in. A large pair of earrings dangled below the rim of the hat and her lip liner was a shade too dark. Too much lipstick, too much rouge.

"Who's she?" Jackie said.

"Maybe an audition for Jerry Springer."

The camera drew back and Jackie saw a movie theater with a stained marquee. "Colfax. A neighborhood activist, they're always trying to clean up the block."

"Nut is more like it."

The woman stepped closer to the mikes. Why the live coverage?

"—my duty to talk."

"Have you been contacted by the DA's office?" a reporter said.

"Noo."

"What about the police?"

"They don't know the facts." Her voice was high-pitched, the enunciation childlike. "What really happened to Freddie Gant never came out."

"Oh, jeez," Pilar said. "Not another . . ."

Rachel's case had brought a torrent of squirrels out of the woodwork.

Talk shows were inundated with callers insisting they had vital details about the Gant murder, from the man who claimed to be the brother of a cop who'd worked the case to a psychic who knew where the "real" Freddie was hiding. Pilar had followed up on some of the leads, including the cop's brother, who turned out to be a second cousin of the part-time janitor in the Seward County Sheriff's Department. He swore someone broke into the evidence room years earlier in a cover-up that reached all the way to the governor's office. Jackie had told Pilar to quit wasting her time.

"—only two people alive know. It's time the true story was told."

"Are you saying Rachel Boyd isn't responsible—"

He was out-shouted by another reporter.

"Do you know who killed these boys, Miss Maune?"

Maune?

Jackie and Pilar leaped to turn up the sound on the remote.

"I never talked in public before. I'm here for one thing."

With the timing of a pro, Trina Maune waited until she had their full attention.

"To save my old friend, Rachel Boyd."

Thirty-Seven

EXCLUSIVE BY LEE SIMMS FOR
MODERN CRIMES—JULY 9, 1973

There was no need to summon spectators for the trial of the twelve-year-old girl accused of murdering her four-year-old playmate. Every seat in the Seward County Courthouse was taken and a line stretched out the door.

In an apple green and white gingham frock with a Puritan collar and satin sash, the accused sat with shoulders squared and hands neatly folded on the witness stand. Her black tresses were drawn back from her forehead with a white plastic band. One would never suspect she had been confined since her arrest for murder to a juvenile hall a hundred miles away. Rachel Boyd was as fresh and alert as if she had spent the last seven weeks with her family at home.

The jury could not see the telephone book on which this child, so small even for her age, perched. But the witness stand was two steps up from the oak floor and all eyes could see one black patent leather shoe and a lace-trimmed sock relentlessly swing against the leg of that stand.

Seasoned courtroom observers noted

the unusual events taking place in this trial. In a traditional criminal proceeding the prosecutor has no power to call the defendant as a witness. There is, however, nothing ordinary about a charge of murder leveled against a twelve-year-old girl. Rachel Boyd's counsel, Howard Gore, revealed his strategy after court adjourned.

"My client is a child. The most effective defense is for her to tell the jury in her own words what happened the day Freddie Gant disappeared. Her parents have made that quite clear. Rather than put her on the stand myself and make her say it twice, it's less traumatic for Rachel and her family to let the prosecution put her on."

District Attorney Floyd Garrett fixed the girl with his steely gaze. The tapping stopped.

"Rachel, tell us what happened that Saturday."

There was a palpable hush as the last person to see Freddie Gant alive prepared to speak.

"That morning I woke up." She patiently awaited the next question.

DA Garrett was only too happy to oblige. What did she do after that?

"Got out of bed and brushed my teeth."

And so it went for the better part of the morning, as the tiny girl fenced with the veteran of hundreds of trials over the precise time she left her house for Vivian Memorial Park and whether she picked dandelions or clover along the way. Before calling midmorning recess an exasperated Judge Francis X. Horan asked whether the testimony could be speeded along.

"That is entirely up to Miss Boyd," DA Garrett said. "I am simply following her lead. We must have the fullest and most complete answers."

The message was not lost. What could be more instructive for the jury than a firsthand view of this pint-sized defendant's extraordinary intelligence and control? If spectators expected to see a frightened child, they were disappointed.

When the examination resumed promptly at ten forty-five Rachel stuck to her story.

No, she hadn't played with Freddie Gant that day. She was forbidden to play at the grain elevator or go anywhere near the railroad tracks. She went home directly from the park. Her increasingly long-winded answers and the relentless tapping of her foot made more than one juror shuffle in his seat. When the noon recess was called there was a collective sigh of relief.

Court reconvened and DA Garrett tried a different tack.

"Now, Rachel, you were in this courtroom yesterday, weren't you?"

She nodded her glossy head.

"And you heard your friend Trina say you didn't like Freddie Gant."

"That's not true."

"You don't like small children as a rule, isn't that right?"

"I like my brother."

For the first time Rachel looked past the District Attorney. Her eyes searched the courtroom and for a moment her mask of assurance slipped and she was a twelve-year-old girl seeking the comfort of a familiar face. Her parents, George and Evelyn Boyd, sat stiffly in the front row behind the defense table.

Over the last three days the only person with whom Rachel spoke was her lawyer, and on those occasions her impassive face came alive with interest. Even during recess her parents seem to hang back from her. Rachel's nine-year-old brother has not attended the trial. Except to testify, her little friend, Trina Maune, the only child in whom Rachel Boyd was said to have confided, has not appeared either.

"Rachel, do you know what evil is?"

For the second time her foot stopped tapping. In the sudden stillness a sound echoed through the courtroom like a rifle shot.

Rachel Boyd laughed.

In the shocked silence that followed, DA Floyd Garrett slowly took his seat.

"Nothing further, Your Honor."

Judge Francis X. Horan dismissed the witness but the silence lingered.

The jurors rose and slowly filed out. After six hours on the witness stand, the small figure in the gingham dress turned to the man in the black robe. A plaintive voice rang out.

"Now can I go home?"

Thirty-Eight

Chris Boyd showed up at Jackie's office the day after Trina's press conference.

"Why can't Shelly stay with me?"

"Judge Mueller knows what she's doing," Jackie assured him.

"I can protect my sister better than you. No judge can tell us where she can and can't live!"

"It's not a matter of protecting Rachel."

"They're pillorying her, just like before. That damned Simms—" He sank into a chair. "It's Shelly. I don't know how she's handling this."

"She's fine, Chris."

He'd taken Rachel to dinner a few times since she'd been staying with Jackie. Rachel primped for their outings but never talked about them afterward; she always seemed preoccupied. Still more concerned about protecting Chris than herself?

"Shelly never lets anything out. If you only knew what it was like . . ." He reached in his breast pocket for a three-pointed hanky and dabbed his forehead.

Jackie's air-conditioning was on the fritz. Her conference room faced south and opened onto a glass-enclosed porch, and the sun beating through the windows made it even more stifling. An advance party of bees had broken through the sealed fireplace only to die upon attaining their beachhead. Furry corpses lent the tile around the hearth the solemnity of a battlefield and a cloying sweetness seemed to emanate from that wall. Jackie signaled Pilar to make coffee.

"They simply won't leave me alone. At home, the bank. My staff spends half its time fending off reporters. Can't something be done?"

"Chris, we have to focus on the defense." She squeezed his arm but the flesh was as responsive as kapok. "The trial's just five weeks away."

"What do you want from me?"

"Everything you remember about Freddie Gant."

"I'm more concerned about what Trina Maune's doing in town!"

"You said she had nothing to do with his death. What about Lee Simms?"

Chris stared at the fireplace. Jackie tried again.

"If Freddie was molested, there must've been talk."

"Talk? About what?"

"Other suspects. Every town has weirdos."

"I remember some guy in the shack behind the Maunes' house. And the Gants weren't model parents either. Art was gone half the time and there was gossip about Freddie's mother letting the kids run wild."

"Was he a handyman?"

"Who?"

The smell of coffee from the butler's pantry cut the honey in the wall. "The man in the Maunes' shack."

"What does it matter?"

"If Rachel was railroaded, who killed Freddie?"

"I have no—" He stiffened. "Ask him."

Jackie turned and saw Lee Simms. What did he want? She blinked away the sudden image of a pair of naked buttocks.

"Ask me what?" Simms said.

"Now isn't the time." Jackie had to get rid of him.

"I disagree." Helping himself to coffee from Pilar's tray of brightly painted earthen mugs, he faced

Chris. "Maybe we'll get to the bottom of a whole bunch of stuff."

"I won't sit in the same room with this son of a bitch." Coffee sloshed in Chris's cup. "First he crucified Shelly. Now he wants to resurrect her!"

"I just want the truth."

"Truth?" Chris rose and Pilar stepped forward. Her sister had sent those mugs from Guadalajara. "That's why you dig through garbage cans?"

"At least I don't look in people's drawers."

Jackie winced, but Simms was staring at Chris.

"Isn't that where you find the good stuff?"

"Only if you put it there, pal."

Had he been in Simms's room, too?

"You think you're so smart?" Chris said. "I know what kind of music you like, the sick videos you watch, even what brand of—"

Jackie broke in.

"If we all want the truth, let's focus on who killed Freddie Gant."

"Chris knows damn well who was involved," Simms said. "Still hiding behind your sister?"

"You're the one who covered for Art!"

"Art Gant?" Jackie said.

Simms was suddenly defensive. "Art was one of the first people looking for his kid. He—"

"Where was he that afternoon?" Chris demanded.

"Driving his rig."

"When did he get home?"

"Right after Freddie left."

"That's not what you wrote thirty years ago."

"What I wrote—" Simms turned to Jackie. "What's he talking about?"

"I read and reread every word you wrote about my sister. According to you, Gant didn't get home till midnight. I wondered how you knew so much about his schedule. Why cover for him?"

"Cover?" Jackie said.

"He's just talking!" But Simms's laugh was forced. "No one questioned Art's devotion to his son. The only question was who Rachel covered for."

"What made you think someone else was involved?" Jackie asked Simms.

"The cops never worked the scene. They never found the knife."

"Knife?" Pilar said.

Not paper, metal, glass—or an iron hook. But Simms didn't miss a beat.

"The one they used to cut Freddie and rip the button off his pants."

"It'll only hurt Shelly to go into that now."

"Her, or *you*?" Simms turned from Chris in disgust. "He's not protecting his sister, he's protecting himself. His reputation if the rumors about Rachel come out."

"What rumors?" Pilar said.

"That she—"

"Shut your damn mouth!" Chris said.

Jackie stepped between them. "What does Trina Maune say?"

"She won't talk to me. *He* warned her not to." Simms turned back to Chris. "Put your money where your mouth is and launch an investigation into Freddie Gant. Or is that what you're afraid of?"

"I don't have to take this from the man who put the noose around Shelly's neck!"

Chris stormed out, slamming the door hard enough to

make two dead bees jump. Pilar rescued the tray and took it to the pantry.

"You provoked him," Jackie said. Simms calmly sipped his coffee. "Why'd you lie about Art Gant?"

"Who cares where he was that day? Freddie's parents had nothing to do with it."

"And you lied about why you came to Denver."

Not just why but *when*. Where had Simms really been for the past thirty years?

"Your client's the liar, or haven't you guessed?"

The rose oil no one but Jackie could smell. Not knowing how to drive—

"She's never lied to me."

"Didn't you ask the right questions?"

"We're talking about you. Not Rachel."

"I told you I came for this story."

"Before Ben Sparks was killed?"

Simms's smile turned cold.

"You followed her here, didn't you?" Jackie continued. "What if I did?"

"You knew Freddie Gant. And Chris."

He pushed back his chair and rounded the table.

"I knew lots of kids in Vivian. I lived there, remember?"

Simms was so close Jackie could feel his breath. Where was Pilar?

"Is that why Chris is afraid of you?"

"He was a coward then and he's a coward now. A stinking, little—"

"Get out of my office. And stay away from Rachel."

Simms threw up his hands in surrender, but his eyes held nothing but contempt.

"Ask your client how much she paid Trina Maune, Counselor."

"If you so much as blink at any witness in this case, I'll have you thrown in jail."

He turned from the door.

"Do that. And don't be surprised when another child gets killed."

Thirty-Nine

DIARY OF RACHEL BOYD DATED
AUGUST 8, 1973—MASON SCHOOL FOR GIRLS

Dear You,
I love this school. Its a special place for girls like me. Only four weeks and its like home!!!
They say if Im good Ill get out soon, maybe next birthday.

Miss me.

DIARY OF RACHEL BOYD
DATED SEPTEMBER 10, 1973—
MASON SCHOOL FOR GIRLS

Dear You,
English is my favorite class. We read books and write stories.
They ask us to make up a family. It was fun giving all the kids names.
I even put you in but didnt say who it was.
Im making friends. Its nice to talk!!

Miss you.

REPORT DATED OCTOBER 15, 1973—
CAROLINE DRISCOLL,
MASON SCHOOL FOR GIRLS

Rachel Boyd has now been with us for three months. While she has made certain superficial attempts to conform to our rules, little real improvement in her behavior is shown.

As the youngest child here, she continues to present the staff with many unique challenges. Rachel is very bright, extremely verbal, and quite the little mimic. She is more sophisticated than she lets on but continues to get into fistfights with older girls. It is difficult to say how often Rachel is the instigator; the others sense she has a short fuse and enjoy provoking her. When asked who starts the fights, she refuses to answer. Rachel does not like to be questioned. She is a very angry child who has significant problems with authority.

It was felt that encouraging her to keep a journal would provide an outlet for some of the emotions she is unable to release through other means. She has apparently kept a diary in the past. Upon reviewing her journal while she is away at class, however, it is quite apparent that the entries are written entirely for the benefit of the staff.

Rachel has a tremendous need for attention and approval. She clearly has the social skills to make friends but is wary of letting anyone close. If she were not the youngest child here (and so small for her age) she would probably have quite a following. Indeed, when she first arrived, the older girls fussed over her like a pet. The nature of her crime made them curious and Rachel was quick to oblige with details that had nothing to do with what actually occurred. What keeps them at a distance now is not so much her explosive anger but an intense neediness which is exhausting to everyone with whom she comes into contact. Some of the girls complain that she wants to know everything about their lives to the point of being a pest. She then "borrows" details of their history and tries to pass them off as her own.

Rachel is also adept at learning private information about the staff, which she squirrels away. She somehow discovered that Edith Marcus, the only counselor to whom she has grown moderately attached, had been undergoing marital difficulties. Edith insists she has never discussed private matters in the presence of any of our girls and was mortified when Rachel mentioned it in group. She apparently knows other details about Edith's personal life which Edith will not go into. Despite her embarrass-ment, Edith believes Rachel's be-havior represents an attempt to form a closer therapeutic bond. That would of course be a step for-ward.

In therapy Rachel continues to deny any knowledge of or responsi-bility for the crime she commit-ted. She also changes the subject when asked about her family.

The one time she displayed emo-tion was last Thursday, with Edith Marcus.

Rachel missed her session and Edith found her crying in her room. It was Rachel's brother's birthday. Rachel said she felt bad that she wasn't able to be with him for that occasion. "He's so lit-tle" were her precise words. Edith felt that Rachel's remorse was displaced guilt for her own acts against young Freddie Gant.

Rachel's mother, Evelyn Boyd, continues to visit every other week. On the off-weeks she sends Rachel packages of candy and fruit. Although the candies are quite expensive, Rachel never eats them. She doles out the fruit to children she favors and punishes others by denying them treats. The staff does not know what she does with the candy.

Evelyn Boyd is her only visitor, although Mrs. Boyd was told she could apply for and receive special permission for a short visit between Rachel and her brother. Yesterday Rachel asked Edith Marcus if she had to see her mother when she comes. Edith explained to Rachel that her mother loves her, and although it is undoubtedly painful to say goodbye when she leaves, the visits are quite beneficial to them both.

Forty

"Oh, joy!"

Dennis exited from the viaduct that spanned Denver's railroad yards.

They were on their way to Elitch Gardens, the amusement park.

"This'll be fun," Jackie said. In the backseat Rachel and Lily were transfixed.

Closer up the amusement park resembled an oil refinery. The Tower of Doom was as black as a smokestack and the world's highest free-fall swing was a swaying mass of cables. The conveyor belts, pipes and tubes that made up the other rides seemed more suited to transporting hydrocarbons than the high-disposable-income adolescents to which the park catered.

"Like getting gangbanged by the Mickey Mouse Club," Dennis muttered.

"Shush!"

They parked at a meter that didn't post rates under the apparent assumption that if you had to ask you couldn't afford them, and approached the park on foot. Xeriscaping and an artificial waterfall hinted at a Western theme, but plaster rocks and a gully of airbrushed cement were a far cry from the OK Corral. As they waited in the ticket line with a drove of junior high school kids, Jackie saw Lily covertly inspecting a group of girls.

Jackie remembered adolescence as a painful time, when each day another friend woke up with boobs and she didn't. But fashion had come a long way since then. These girls had the art of capitalizing on their best features down to a science. The ones with breasts made the most of them in skintight halters, and those without wore shorts too brief for a thong. If they had neither boobs nor legs they focused on makeup.

Lily didn't have a bosom, but she certainly had the face and the gams. Not to mention a world-class pedicure. In her crimson spandex tube top and black Lycra bicycle shorts she'd stretched into capris, she looked almost too sophisticated for this crowd.

"How many rides can we go on?" Rachel asked.

"As many as you can stand," Dennis said. "Point me to the beer."

In her lilac blouse and matching shorts, Rachel could have passed for a young matron shepherding toddlers were it not for the wary expression she couldn't seem to lose. In her own camisole and nylon expedition shorts Jackie felt overdressed. All around them girls were smearing on tanning lotion and sunscreen.

"What's a 'forty-eight'?" Lily asked. "That sign says forty-eight for the Mind Eraser and Tower of Doom."

"Inches," Dennis said. "You have to be at least forty-eight inches tall to go on those rides."

"The only ride a thirty-six can go on is the Carousel. That's for kids."

"'Free admission for guests under three and over seventy,'" he read aloud. "Makes sense. They can't ride anything; they'd fall overboard."

The teenagers ahead of them were paying with Visas and a Gold MasterCard. One tried to use an ATM card but was rebuffed. None of her friends offered to bail her out.

"Cruel world," Dennis said.

"She'll survive," Lily replied.

Over Jackie's protest Dennis paid for all four admissions. Rachel and Lily exchanged a knowing glance. It reminded Jackie of one of the few times her aunt had introduced her to a male friend, when she was Lily's age.

He'd taken them out to dinner and Jackie had hated everything about him, from his oxblood wing tips to his musty breath mints. The way he'd held the door for her aunt and then her chair at the restaurant. His solicitude when he told Jackie she could have anything on the menu, including a shrimp cocktail. She'd ordered the shrimp and, wanting at least one of them not to be indebted to him for anything more, limited herself to the appetizer.

Was Dennis that obvious?

They passed through the turnstile into an arcade with a sandwich franchise, popcorn wagon and shops selling fudge and saltwater taffy. Beyond the arcade was a mock-up of a Western town consisting of souvenir shops in Victorian storefronts labeled EMPORIUM and HABERDASHERY. The sun intensified the odors of sugar and hot grease. Quart buckets of fries the circumference of bread sticks confirmed size was all.

The rides were painted playground colors and looked as strong as plastic. The Ferris wheel was at least made of wood. Herded into line behind an overweight woman with sullen preschoolers, they were jostled by another matron with small children. Every two minutes a loudspeaker warned them not to jump the line. Spitting and throwing rocks or missiles were also grounds for ejection. The circular corrals in which they were queued made Jackie feel like a steer at a packing plant.

Rachel pointed at a green roller-coaster.

"Can we go on that one next?"

It rattled to a halt near the top of a monstrous track and plunged ten stories backward faster than Jackie could blink.

"The Mind Eraser?" Lily said.

"I believe *that*," Dennis said.

"No," said Rachel, "that's the turquoise and red one that goes through a roll. Can we really ride them all?"

"If they weren't free you couldn't get people to pay for half of them," Dennis said. The five-year-old in front of Jackie kicked through a puddle from hosing down the corral, splashing her shins with mud. Dennis leaned down to whisper in her ear, "Forget how obnoxious they are?" The boy's mother jerked him roughly. Just then a kid behind them whacked Jackie's arm with the swinging chain. "Best argument I've seen for birth control. Still want them?"

Jackie smiled, but her thoughts were as scrambled as the contents of her stomach. Dennis had been the one who wanted kids; did he really not know how she felt?

"Gonna get in, lady?"

They'd been inching forward to the gate. A boy too young to vote was looking at Jackie impatiently from the other side of the gondola. The cart swayed at what should have been a dead stop.

"I'm scared," she told Dennis.

"Can't imagine why, darling. Just think of an open elevator."

Before she could reply, he took her elbow and helped her in. Lily and Rachel stationed themselves opposite them. The gondola began to move. Dennis slipped his arm around her waist and Jackie closed her eyes.

"Rachel, what's that?" Lily said.

"An observation tower."

The gondola had stopped and Jackie opened her eyes a crack. The new football stadium lay to the west. It really did resemble a giant diaphragm— With a hideous screech, their car shuddered and took off. Suddenly they were dropping backward. Jackie opened her mouth but couldn't scream. The gondola slowed. Groaning, it gathered steam for another round.

"Get me out of here," she said to Dennis.

"What?"

Her nails dug into his palm.

"I mean it. Get me—"

"Honey, it's just a—"

"If you care at all, *g-et mee*—"

After the third cycle she lost count.

"That wasn't so bad, was it?" Dennis said as she staggered off at the end of the ride. Jackie wiped her forehead with his hanky. Her cheeks were aflame and sweat dripped from the curls at the nape of her neck.

"Dare you!" Rachel said to Lily, and they ran off in the direction of the Tower of Doom. The black cylinder was painted with flames and the smokestack had been transformed into a giant phallus.

"They'll be fine," Dennis said. "No motor, just gravity. Like a grain elevator."

A car crept up the side of the tower like a spider on a drainpipe. One of the riders wore Teva sandals. He swung his feet. When the car reached the top his sandals froze. For one horrid moment they hung there. With a whoosh the brake released and the passengers silently plunged two hundred feet.

"I don't want Lily on that," Jackie said.

"Darling, it's perfectly safe. And she's having the time of her life."

How many times had she seen Lily this carefree?

"But what if—"

He touched her lips.

"Don't give her your fears, Jackie. She already has enough of her own."

"What do you mean?"

Lily was heading back.

"Changed our minds," Rachel said. She had her arm around Lily's shoulders and was starting to lose that hunted look. Lily's gratitude at the reprieve was unmistakable. "Maybe later."

At the Demolition Derby, adults lined up to crouch behind the wheels of tiny bumper cars. The music started and within thirty seconds there was a pileup.

"Figures," Dennis said.

"What?" Lily said.

"Women are so aggressive."

Most of the drivers in the pileup were indeed women. Jackie turned to Rachel.

"I'll bet one of the things you missed most was learning to drive."

The black eyes turned to stone. "What makes you think that?"

"That you can't drive, or you missed it most?"

"Never said I couldn't." Seizing Lily's hand, she pointed to a giant swing whose riders were strapped in like mummies. "Race you!"

"What was that about?" Dennis said as they rushed off.

The chill in those eyes had told Jackie more than she wanted to know.

"Nothing," she said.

"How about a drink?" They were at a lemonade stand.

"I thought you wanted beer."

"That's before I started having fun."

Jackie's lemonade was half a lemon in sugar water. She drank greedily and when Dennis refilled her glass from a fountain she drained that too.

"Feeling better?" he said.

"More like a fool." They stopped at the ring-toss booth, where they could watch Lily and Rachel.

"For what?"

"Being such a sissy."

Rachel had gotten in line for the Swing but Lily hung back. Jackie was surprised at the number of girls attracted to this ride, which churned like an agitator in a washing machine. As they climbed on they smiled and waved like celebrities. The Swing swayed and there was a loud *oooh*. It gave a massive heave and the riders were suspended upside down. Now the screams sounded real.

"What attracts Rachel?" she said.

"Hmm?"

The Swing righted itself with a jolt. The girl next to Rachel looked terrified, but Rachel's head was thrown back and even at this distance Jackie could tell she was laughing. When the ride finally regurgitated its dazed passengers, they staggered off congratulating one another.

"These rides." Lily was shaking her head no and Rachel squeezed her hand before lining up for another round. "Whatever it is Rachel can't get enough of."

"The thrill's in the loss of control. Coming as close as possible to death."

Was it free fall Rachel craved, a sense of flight? And if it was flight—from what? "You'd think she'd want to stay away from that."

"After being locked up for thirty years? She'll never get enough."

And what about him?

"Does this bore you?" Jackie asked.

"What?"

"These rides."

He shrugged. "I prefer to be thrown off-balance."

The Swing rolled like a kid swinging a bucket over his head. Screams rose in a massive roar and as quickly died.

"You can't be any more off-balance than that."

Dennis shook his head. "A glorified ski lift. When you get flipped the identical way each time the thrill becomes predictable. With you, I never know what's coming next."

But Jackie did. It loomed like the Tower of Doom.

"We've never talked about it," she said.

"Your exquisite uptightness? It's actually a turn-on. Because I know just—"

"I'm serious."

"So am I. When will you learn to trust me?"

The agitator did another sickening roll.

"I do trust you. It's just that—"

"What are you trying to protect?"

The cries could have been pleasure or pain.

"Protect?"

A lifetime of hiding, of pretending she was like everybody else in order to survive? That she wasn't interested in kids when the truth was she was afraid they'd end up like her?

"I'm getting used to your hair," he said. "It's cute."

His eyes were bright. So warm and alive.

"I'm thinking of growing it in."

"What are you doing tonight?"

"After those two have tackled every ride in this place? Rachel's having dinner with Chris. Somewhere far away, in the foothills."

"And Mata Hari?"

"Lily's on curfew."

"How about dinner?"

"How about something else?"

They turned to face the ring toss. Dennis hoisted her onto the carpet covering the counter. She tilted her chin to meet his lips. Hers were cool from the lemonade but his burned. Soft and firm, salty and a little sweet—Dennis's taste. One of the players whistled and another began to applaud. Jackie broke it off and the next thing she knew Rachel and Lily were approaching.

They roamed the park, stopping as Lily and Rachel sampled the rides. Dennis bought foot-long hot dogs and one of those enormous buckets of fries and Jackie ate with an appetite she hadn't realized she had. Giggled and didn't know what she was laughing about. Relief from not having to go on another ride, she told herself. At last they ended up at the carousel under the Observation Tower.

"Care to get hitched?" Dennis said. "That stallion looks lonely."

The carousel moved at five miles an hour and not all the horses went up and down.

"You won't catch me dead on that," Lily said. "It's a thirty-six-er."

"Come on," Rachel said. Her cheeks were flushed with excitement. Lily had accompanied her on the spinning rides and a plunge over a waterfall, but to Jackie's relief Rachel had ridden the Mind Eraser and Tower of Doom alone. "It'll be fun."

"I'd rather watch. It's for kids." Lily looked at Dennis. "And old folks."

He lifted Jackie onto a horse and mounted the one beside it with a shiny pole.

"Does mine go up and down?" Jackie said.

"I thought you didn't—"

"Maybe it's time I tried it."

Jumping down, Dennis boosted her onto his horse and took one on the innermost circle. As the carousel slowly began to turn, he held out his hand. Jackie held on until his horse went up when hers went down and they had to let go. When they'd made one complete rotation she looked for Lily. Glimpsing a red tube top, she let out her breath and began to look forward to the evening. Once they dropped Rachel and her off . . .

"Where are they?" Dennis said over the music.

"What?"

"Lily."

Jackie stared at the spectators but there was no sign of her or Rachel. She tried not to panic. The carousel slowed and she jumped off her horse with Dennis behind her. Together they searched for a scrap of crimson.

It was Dennis who spotted them. In the elevator, halfway up the Observation Tower. Jackie's heart leaped to her throat.

"Don't worry." He held her tightly. "She's done nothing wrong."

"I should never have—"

"If she wanted to harm Lily, she's had plenty of chances."

"It's that tower, it just—"

"I know."

Jackie could feel Dennis's chest thumping. The elevator reached the top and a dark head emerged atop a speck of crimson. A lilac blur accompanied it. As she watched, the two figures moved to the edge. The smaller one seemed to be struggling. Was Rachel pulling her?

"Dennis, she—"

Lily stepped to the railing. She leaned over.

Dennis drew Jackie to him.

"Stop them!" she cried.

Suddenly his grip loosened.

"She's fine," he murmured. "She's fine."

Rachel was pulling Lily back from the edge. Was she embracing her?

The elevator descended and Jackie sagged against him.

"Nothing like Saturday at the amusement park," he said.

They had the house to themselves but tiptoed up the stairs.

At the top he lifted her in his arms and began kissing her throat. The hair on his head was silky but his beard scratched and Jackie's laughter came out in gasps. That moment with Lily had brought her to the edge and she hadn't come back.

As Dennis carried her into her bedroom she caressed his face. He set her on the edge of the bed and slowly unbuttoned her camisole. She freed his shirt from his trousers and started unbuckling his belt. He slipped his other hand up the inner seam of her shorts—

"What's that?" she said. It had sounded like creaking on the stairs.

"Shh . . ." His mouth was warm and moist and his tongue on her—

"Wait."

Jackie pulled off her camisole and unhooked her bra, dropping them to the floor at the side of her bed. Half dressed, she walked to the door and closed it. Rachel had a key but she wouldn't be back for hours. The upstairs lights were out and she reached for the switch to the overhead fan. Unzipping her shorts, she let them drop and joined Dennis in the moonlight that streamed through her window.

Five years, but nothing important had changed.

As she rubbed her cheek against the wiry hair on his chest, Jackie lost herself in his familiar scent. The heat of his skin, the dried sweat from the afternoon at Elitch's, the salty taste as she licked his nipples until they were pebbly and hard. He pressed against her and she dropped her hands from his chest to his buttocks, cupping them tightly to draw him closer. He pushed her back on the bed, falling to one side, and began stroking her as she ran her fingertips across the skin on the inside of his thigh.

The only sound was the lapping of the fan. Through the transom the hallway was dark. Dennis's mouth had moved from her breasts to her stomach.

If she let go would he see what she was hiding? And what about the next morning? Did he think they could just pick up where they'd left off, as if nothing had changed? What if he wanted more?

He stopped.

"What?" she said.

"How come we only make love in the dark?"

Loss of control. That moment of panic when Lily leaned over the railing—

"You know what I look like. We've done it a thousand times."

"The light. I want to see you."

Climbing over him, Jackie switched on the bedside lamp.

"Satisfied?"

He smiled. "Not yet."

Eyes locked, she climbed onto him and wrapped her legs around his waist. He lifted her and carried her to the wall by the window. She looked one last time at the transom above her door. As Dennis entered her with a hard thrust all other thoughts fled.

"Jesus H. Christ!"

Jackie's eyes flew open.

A small white face stared at them from the opposite window.

"Who the fuck is that?" he said.

Lily.

The blinds. Had she forgotten to tilt them up?

"Dennis—"

He was pulling on his trousers. Not an easy task, given the fact that at least one part of his anatomy didn't want to leave.

"What the hell was I thinking? Why can't anything with you be normal?"

"You're the one who wanted the lights on."

"I don't screw for an audience." Dennis yanked his polo shirt down over his head. "I'm getting awfully sick of your domestic arrangements."

"What do you expect me to do, throw them out?" His briefs were still on the floor but it wasn't necessary to remind him of that. Worse yet, she was struggling not to laugh. If she did that he'd never speak to her again. "You don't have to go."

"What, shall we wait until Rachel gets home and play to a full house?"

"Dennis—"

But the unpardonable laughter was bubbling from her throat.

Shoes untied, he stomped out the door.

Forty-One

Dear You,
    *Today we strung up red and green lights.
Made me miss you even more.*
    *Tomorrow will have a party and open pre-
sents. Did you send anything?*
    *Am doing quite well in group. (So I am
told!!!)*

Rachel Boyd continues to make
progress in fits and starts. Un-
fortunately her pattern is one
step forward, two steps back.

Write-ups for infractions continue. Large or small, the nature
of the violation doesn't seem to
matter. One gets the impression
Rachel disobeys simply to establish that she can.

Although well aware of the

rules and certainly intelligent enough to follow them, she cannot resist breaking them. Attempts at controlling her are as likely to be met with outbursts of rage or a sullen silence which presages a repetition of the very behavior for which she is being disciplined. She continues to hoard items and information, and to use the food her mother brings to punish or reward her peers. The counselor in her wing reports that no one has seen Rachel eat any of it herself. Strides in therapy mirror her general pattern of behavior.

When Rachel was informed in late October that her father, George Boyd, had died in an automobile accident, she took the news calmly. The staff was quite impressed with the maturity and compassion she displayed. According to Edith Marcus, Rachel's reaction was, "It's best. This was very hard on them." Evidently Rachel is accepting some responsibility for the heartache she brought upon her family.

Edith Marcus also became quite excited at what she believed was a breakthrough in their counseling sessions. At a group meeting in mid-November, Rachel admitted for the first time that she had been

present at the scene of Freddie
Gant's death. When pressed for
further details, all she would say
was "I was there." At the following
session she said the young boy
slipped: "It was an accident." She
then burst into tears and had to be
excused. Edith wondered at that
time whether the unprocessed grief
Rachel must have been experiencing
at the loss of her father had
opened the floodgates to acknowledging her guilt in the Gant
child's death.

In private counseling two days
later, Rachel told Edith that the
day Freddie Gant was killed, "I
was angry." When Edith asked what
she was angry about, Rachel refused to say. She also said "It
wasn't me" but would not elaborate
on what she meant. Edith believes
rage at some unnamed person or
event was the motive, but that
Rachel's comment regarding the
presence or participation of an
imaginary "other" was an attempt
to displace her own guilt.

Since that day, Edith's repeated efforts to draw Rachel out
as to a motive for her crime have
met with little success. Indeed,
in last week's session, Rachel
abruptly retracted her confession

and insisted she wasn't there at all and had made up what she'd said. Edith continues to believe that Rachel's confession and remorse were genuine and that she is on the verge of providing meaningful details of what actually occurred.

The staff concurs in my assessment that Edith has been "played." Rachel is clearly manipulating her rapport with her counselor in order to please her in exchange for the attention she so desperately craves. Rachel's deviousness has been remarked upon many times by staff members who are in a position to be more objective than Edith. Overidentification with a subject, particularly one as challenging and compelling as Rachel, is of course not uncommon and is no reflection on Edith's integrity or skills.

Edith will be rotated off Rachel's case at the end of this month and a new counselor assigned.

Forty-Two

H is milk was sour.

His bread had grown a beard, and his blue cheese had the wrong kind of mold.

If Dennis liked his women just a tad on the trashy side he obviously didn't bring them home. Satisfied that he'd been celibate for at least the recent past, Jackie hit the third button on his speed dial to order pizza.

As she walked naked to the nook where his bed was located in the spacious loft in a renovated saddle factory in LoDo, she wondered where the paralegal had kept her things. The floor plan certainly wasn't conducive to having kids.

"What are the first two numbers?"

"Numbers?" he said.

"On your speed dial."

"My office."

"And?" A toots from Vegas? Or the ex?

"Remember when I bought this place?"

"I thought you were nuts. This floor-to-ceiling glass is a fishbowl."

"That's why you wouldn't move in?"

"And there are no closets."

"We could find a place for your clothes. Unless you prefer your current roommate. What's that been like?"

"Living with Rachel?" Jackie absently stroked his leg. The sheets had been fresh when she'd come over to return his underwear after the fiasco the night before. Now they were all sweaty. "To tell you the truth, it's a little weird."

"Like, how?"

"I'm used to living alone." Strange tastes, smells . . . Her bedroom blinds. The suspicion that Rachel had not only been in her closet, but had gone through her drawers. And that disaster at the venue hearing. Dennis would say she was imagining the rest, or that he'd warned her it would be difficult. "Guess I underestimated the adjustment."

"Change can be good."

Her fingers moved higher, where the skin was hairless and smooth. "What changes did you have in mind?"

"Something along the lines of what you're doing right now . . ."

"What did that wife of yours think?"

"About what?"

"Your lack of closets."

"Do we have to talk about her?"

Jackie converted the caress to a pat on the knee. "Not if you don't want to."

He moved her hand back.

"She wasn't around long enough to tell me."

"Poor baby." She pinched his inner thigh. "Was the breakup very painful?"

"Not nearly as painful as what I'm about to do to you." Dennis nipped her on the neck and continued down her torso. Despite herself, Jackie began to feel aroused.

"How many frequent flier miles do you get for Vegas?"

"Vegas?" He looked up. "Who said anything about Vegas?"

"I'll tell you if you tell me. What's the second number on your speed dial?"

His head dipped again. "Try it and see."

"Pizza's coming . . ."

"It's always late," he said from the vicinity of her lower abdomen. "And I know something better—"

"What do you think of Lee Simms?"

Dennis looked up again.

"What?"

"You think he had anything to do with Freddie Gant's death?"

"Look, darling, I know the trial's just a month off, but even the greats need a little R & R. You can't go in front of a jury all tense and—"

"You never celebrated till afterwards."

"Call this a celebration?" Dennis reached for his trousers, only to remember he'd quit smoking. "Simms is bad news. He's using Rachel to replay his fifteen minutes of fame."

Maybe that was it.

"At least he's trying to find out what Trina Maune knows. And speaking of which"—she slapped away the hand that crept beneath the covers—"why'd your client put a lid on her?"

"What client?"

"Chris Boyd. Did he pay Trina to keep her mouth shut?"

"What makes you think that?"

"She directs all her calls to him, she won't even speak to Pilar. And Doby listed her as a prosecution witness."

"If you want to know what Trina has to say, why not subpoena her?"

"And run the risk of that loose cannon going off on the stand? No thanks." Jackie snuggled into the crook of his arm and rested her head on his chest. He began stroking her hair. "Can't you talk to Chris?"

"I thought you wanted to keep me out of this."

"Just a thought." She slid down on the bed.

"Well, it's not a very good— What are you doing?"

"What does it feel like?"

"I thought you wanted pizza."

"If Simms can't be trusted, why does he want to reopen Freddie Gant?"

"That old case?" Dennis was breathing harder now. "Like it or not, Jackie, Rachel said she was responsible. . . . Can we talk later?"

"They never found the weapon. It must've been sharp, to slice off his button."

"Jackie . . ."

"How do I get to Trina Maune?"

"Flush her—out."

"You're the master strategist. How?"

"Rachel as bait." He was gasping.

"I guess I can wait for the details later." She slid her head back under the sheet.

When the pizza man buzzed they didn't even hear.

When Dennis dropped Jackie off four hours later, Lily was waiting by the hedge.

He tapped his watch. "Got her home before curfew, ma'am."

"That's not funny."

"A sense of humor's an awful thing not to have."

She perched on the Volvo's hood. "I don't have much to laugh about these days."

"I guess not." He opened the passenger door. "Get in."

"I know what you're doing."

"Then you're old enough to recognize Jackie's free to date whomever she wants."

"Date?" Lily snorted. "Is that what you call it?"

"And you're certainly old enough for a Frappuccino or a granulated latte or whatever the hell they call it. Shall we walk or drive?"

Minutes later they were at the coffee shop three blocks away. Lily's drink was as thick as a malted and she'd dumped enough cinnamon and chocolate sprinkles on top to kill whatever caffeine it once had. She spooned it with her straw.

"So why'd you get kicked out of school?" Dennis said.

"Are you and Jackie getting married?"

"If I couldn't talk her into that five years ago, why would she do it now?"

"You haven't answered my question."

"Nor you mine." He took a long sip of iced coffee. "I can outwait you."

"What makes you think that?"

"Practice."

Lily took a few nibbles before answering.

"Want the whole story? The one not even my shrink knows?"

"I'm in no hurry."

"I got caught on the roof."

"Roof?"

"At school. Kids aren't allowed there. Don't tell Jackie, she'd kill me."

"Why?"

"Didn't you notice? She's weird about heights."

"Still sounds more like a misdemeanor than a felony. Want to go back?"

"Not unless they beg me."

"There's some value to finishing what you start." Dennis frowned. "Sneaking up to the roof. That's all it was?"

"Well, we were also smoking."

"Pot?"

"Cigarettes."

He decided not to push. "Who's 'we'?"

"Just the coolest girls in the entire school." And Lily was proud of it. "The QBs. We do anything on a dare."

"Still doesn't sound like an indictable offense. So the whole bunch of you were expelled . . ."

"Just me."

"Why?"

"I wouldn't rat on the others."

"And your buddies left you to shoulder the blame."

For the first time, Lily met his eyes. "There's more. But you can't tell Jackie."

"My lips are sealed."

"I wasn't even *on* the roof. They found the butts and figured it was me."

At least it wasn't crack.

"Why else don't you want Jackie to know?"

Lily took another bite. "I chickened out."

"How come?"

"I don't like heights either. You think I'm a schmuck, don't you?"

"Better than a rat." Dennis set down his cup. "Listen, Lily. There's only one type of criminal I refuse to defend. Know who that is?"

She stared.

"An informant. You know why? Because it doesn't end there. Someone who rats out a friend will sell his own mother. But let me tell you something about dares."

"What?"

"Friends don't have to prove themselves to each other. And speaking of friends, don't you think it's time you gave Jackie a break?" Lily's eyes narrowed. "Don't take that tough-girl routine too far, okay?"

"What do I get in exchange?"

"I'll plead your case to the court of appeals."

Forty-Three

N ervous?" Jackie asked Rachel.
"Trina's very good at what she does. She always was."

Jackie had used the only Swiss pastry shop in Denver as bait. Gabriel's was a slice of Zurich, a crumbly tart with apricot glaze and a pouf of whipped cream.

She'd chosen Gabriel's not for its confections, but for its obscurity and its patrons. They were a cadre of northern European retirees whose social life revolved around coffee and pastry. The males were aristocratically thin and bent at the waist. The women were blond and as wrinkled as crepe, with dark sunglasses and small hairpieces covering pink scalps. Everyone except the waitresses spoke in a German accent. At the end of the fashionably late lunch hour on a weekday afternoon, the place was half empty and most of the customers were more than a little deaf.

Butter cream and almond wafted over antiseptic coolant. A refrigerator held frozen quiches and pie crusts; Pilar would have loved the prefab meringue shells. The display cases were a fairyland of pink napoleons and marzipan bumblebees with chocolate wings and stripes, rum bars with pineapple and maraschino cherries stuck in the glaze. Here, there was no such thing as cake; everything was a *kuchen* or a *torte*.

The door opened, heralding a blast of warm air with a musky scent. The clerk at the counter had been filling a box from a tray of petits fours. In the finest Swiss tradition, she stopped just long enough to wrinkle her nose before resuming her methodical count.

Rose oil. The perfume Jackie had smelled in her own front hall the day she'd gone to Lee Simms's apartment. Struggling not to react, she stared at the woman in the doorway.

Trina Maune was a triumph of flair over physique. Sashes and scarves suggested a neck and waist, her flowing skirt and high-laced boots a coquettish leg. Beneath it all she was round as a cream puff. Now the cowboy hat she'd worn at her press conference made sense. It had covered a nest of dreadlocks more colors than Jackie could count. Behind oversize glasses with black plastic frames, her eyes roved like a raptor's.

"Rachel!" Trina tripped forward and flung out her arms as if they hadn't seen each other in thirty years. Rachel endured the embrace before disengaging. "They said you were in trouble. I had to come."

How long had she really been in town?

They followed the hostess past pennants with crossed swords and bears on hind legs to a table under an enormous pair of brass cowbells. How closely would Rachel and Trina stick to a script? Jackie's usual concerns about pairing client with witness before trial seemed ridiculous now; how Rachel must have laughed when she'd cautioned her not to talk to Trina about the case! And how she must resent Jackie forcing her to play her role.

"Whatever happened to Althea Robey?" You had to admire Trina for pretending this were nothing more than a meeting of chums who hadn't seen each other since grade school. The girl other kids couldn't stand, Chris had said. The ones Rachel always had a soft spot for. But underneath her chatter lay a coiled wariness. "And that bitch Millicent Trent?"

The questions were purely for Jackie's benefit.

According to Pilar, Trina had never married or moved out of Vivian. She made her living waitressing at the same café her mother had baked pies for. Her outrageous costumes and peripheral role in Freddie Gant's murder made her the town eccentric.

Dumping four packets of sugar into her coffee, Trina chose a raspberry square with extra whipped cream. Jackie's iced tea came with a lemon wedge in an aluminum press on its own plate. The rest of the world used lemon to freshen their hands; the Swiss didn't even want to touch it.

"Who's that gal we both hated?" Trina continued. "The crybaby who—"

Rachel shrugged indifferently. "Carla Miller."

"Dear me! You sure don't forget." Trina's tone was ironic. She traced the rim of the plate that held Jackie's lemon press. Her hands were as soft and plump as a child's but the fingers were surprisingly nimble. "Where would we be without friends?"

"And Susie Gant. She still in Vivian?"

Fork halfway to her lips, Trina paused. Was this a deviation from the script? "How's your mother?"

Let's get right down to it.

Rachel's eyes flickered. "She died while I was in prison."

"Pity about your stepdad. Never know when your ticket's up."

Rachel smiled enigmatically.

Watching them was like being in a fun house with distorting mirrors. Trina stretched the image like taffy; Rachel compressed it to an impenetrable glob. Jackie couldn't tell who was calling the shots. But she was getting tired of playing dummy.

"Speaking of your brother," Trina said, though they

hadn't, "I'll bet you're grateful. Denver's so pricey, 'specially if you stay somewheres nice."

Did she mean Chris taking Rachel in after prison? Or was he footing Trina's bill?

Enough.

"Where are you staying?" Jackie asked Trina.

"A motel on Colfax."

So Cal Doby hadn't paid her way; even the Denver DA's office could afford better than that. Did Doby list her just to throw off the defense?

"But you've spoken with the DA."

"What makes you think that?" Trina replied.

"He endorsed you as a witness."

"I guess."

Whose pocket was Trina in?

"Why did you come?" Jackie said.

"Today? Anything for my old friend Rachel—"

"To Denver."

"I told you, I'm here to help."

"You know something about Ben Sparks?"

"No."

"Or what happened to Freddie Gant?"

"Dear me!" That was the second time Trina had used those words; out of the corner of her eye, Jackie saw Rachel frown. Was it some kind of code? "You got the wrong gal. Right, Shelly?"

So now she was Shelly.

"Shelly's looking real good," Trina continued. "The years have been kind to us both."

Jackie reached for the sugar but the packets had all vanished.

"Course, I could do better," Trina went on. "We both could."

Blackmail?

Rachel's fork sliced into her napoleon, breaking it cleanly in two. "Or you could be doing a lot worse," she said.

Before Jackie could digest what was happening, the waitress came by with a fresh assortment of pastries. Hand hovering over the tray as if it were a Ouija board, Trina squinted at a marzipan bumblebee, then moved to the petits fours with elaborate knobs of icing on top. She closed her eyes.

"Button, button, who's got the button . . ."

Rachel blanched.

Trina's fingers stopped at a rum bar. "And little Chris has become quite the success," she continued. "Who'd ever think he'd be president of a bank! Why, the last time I saw him—"

"When was that?" Jackie said.

"Sneaking in to watch Shelly's trial."

So he hadn't kept away after all.

"Of course, Chris always had more backbone than people thought," Trina rattled on. "Why, I remember that day he set George's collie free just like it was yesterday. . . . Make new friends but keep the old, that's what my mom used to say. One is silver, the other's gold. We're gold 'cause we remember, good times and bad."

Maybe it wasn't Chris who brought her here. Or Doby. Maybe it was—

"Anyone jogged your memory recently?" Jackie asked.

"Like who?" Trina said.

"Lee Simms."

"That reporter? He don't take no for an answer, does he, Shelly? Wonder what makes a fella like him tick? Not that he and I actually *talked*. That wouldn't be—"

Rachel calmly set down her fork. "Know what I always

wondered, Trina? Whatever happened to that guy who lived in your shack?"

"Shack?"

"The toolshed behind your house." Her tone was clipped. Any pity she'd felt for Trina was history.

"—isn't every family needs a shed." Trina's voice trembled. "That's the thing about a town like Vivian. No such thing as secrets."

The lemon press had disappeared along with every pastry on the tray.

Rachel's gaze devoured her former friend.

"You'd better hope there are."

Forty-Four

INTERNATIONAL INQUIRER EXCLUSIVE
BY LEE SIMMS—MAY 5, 1983

<u>Where Is She Now?</u>

The first week in May. The time millions of Americans start fiddling with the sprinkler system and drag the lawn mower out of the garage. But to a small farming community on Colorado's Eastern Plains, May 5 is a painful reminder of wounds that will not heal and questions that won't go away.

A four-year-old boy goes missing from the local park. Two days later his abused body is found at the base of a grain elevator, almost within sight of his anguished parents' home. Who killed little Freddie Gant? A drifter passing through town? An adult the toddler knew and trusted?

A twelve-year-old girl who laughed when asked if she understood the meaning of evil.

The brutal murder of Freddie Gant by his playmate Rachel Boyd rocked the quiet agricultural town forever. It was the kind of place where everybody knew each other—or thought they did. On the tenth anniversary of that crime, perhaps it is time to travel into the mind of a child-killer who at the time of her crime was a child herself. Only then can we answer some of the questions that have made this case so unforgettable.

"For every psychopath . . ."

"For every psychopath who comes from an abusive home, a dozen others grew up in a warm and caring environment like yours or mine."

So says Dr. Lyman Morse, nationally recognized expert on those children we call bad seeds. "Luckily, age is the great reformer. Most of them grow out of it. Of course, for the ones who don't, years of incarceration only make it fester."

Has Rachel Boyd outgrown her evil act? And were there warning signs?

Until that sunny Saturday in May, 1973, Rachel seemed a perfectly normal twelve-year-old girl. She was raised in a stable and loving family. Her father, George Boyd, was one of the most highly respected businessmen in Vivian. She had a younger brother who never got into trouble. By all accounts, both parents were attentive and involved with her life. On a warm afternoon, not unlike that fateful day, Evelyn Boyd recently shared memories of her daughter.

"All I can say is, Rachel liked to tell tales."

Evelyn Boyd sips tea from a china cup.

Her blond hair has been touched up but she still wears it in the same stylish perm. Always in fragile health, she suffered a breakdown following the death of her husband in an automobile accident months after the murder of Freddie Gant. She now resides in a town a hundred miles from Vivian. Her circumstances are comfortable but bleak.

"I lost everything. My children are all I live for, and they're both gone."

The past decade has not been kind to Evelyn Boyd. Despite her careful grooming, her face is careworn and she looks older than her forty-three years. Like her son, who was raised in another state after the tragic events of 1973, she has changed her last name. But not her love for her daughter.

"Rachel broke my heart. I've tried to see her, but she turns me away. I don't know why."

Is the reason guilt? Or shame?

Rachel's guilt in the murder of Freddie Gant has never been in doubt.

"I never had any doubt"

Detective Sergeant Ryan Mitchell of the Seward County Sheriff's Office has less hair than he did in 1973, and a greater proportion of what remains is gray. But with the gray has come a contemplative tone that marks a change from the gung-ho cop of a decade earlier.

"I knew Rachel did it the minute I laid eyes on her," says the chief investigator in the Freddie Gant case. "I never had any doubt."

What gave the twelve-year-old girl away?

"Rachel was very clever. Amazing powers of deduction—she would have made a hell of a detective. Had to keep reminding myself to watch what I said around her, because she picked things up so fast. But she had trouble keeping her story straight. First she said she hadn't talked to Freddie that afternoon, then she admitted she did. I always wondered . . ." He pauses. "She had a friend with her that day at the park, a girl a year older but not nearly so sharp. If that friend hadn't filled in some of the blanks it might have taken us longer, but we would still have got her. There was no way to argue around the fiber on the boy's shirt."

You might say the case against Rachel Boyd hung on a thread. Certainly no evidence was more damning than the red cotton fiber found on Freddie Gant's shirt. A thread that happened to be an exact match for the red shorts Rachel was wearing the day the boy disappeared.

"Rachel at first told the truth about what she was wearing," Mitchell says. "It was her friend who tried to lie for her." He shrugs his broad shoulders. "That's kids for you. They'll protect each other without

knowing why. But I always wondered . . ."
Again that nagging doubt. And this time
Detective Sergeant Ryan Mitchell com-
pletes his thought.

"I knew Rachel did it but you have to
consider all the possibilities. She was
small for her age, but how strong do you
have to be to push a four-year-old boy off
a catwalk? And if someone was with her,
why didn't she say so?"

Those aren't the only questions that
rob the detective of sleep.

"I'm not at liberty to reveal all the evidence we had, and there were certain
things we didn't go into at trial. But that
button was the key."

Mitchell is referring to one of the most
disturbing aspects of the crime, the only
real clue to the troubled girl's motive.
Freddie Gant was found with his trousers
pulled down around the hips, the top button of the fly missing, and the third button
inserted in the second hole. His mother
had replaced those buttons the day her son
disappeared. When he left the house that
afternoon they were securely attached and
the toddler took pride in fastening them
properly. But one final question bedevils
the Detective Sergeant.

"Why did she scratch him on the belly?
There was so little blood. Never did find
the weapon, just some useless old iron
scrap."

And herein lies the strangest piece of

the puzzle. The autopsy revealed Freddie died of a broken neck, but his body was found spread-eagled and faceup. His shirt was bunched up and there were three parallel scratches across his lower abdomen. Although they were first thought to have been caused by the fall from the catwalk, given the position in which he apparently landed that could not have been the case. Although the Detective Sergeant is too discreet to say it, the position of those cuts suggests the killer attempted to mutilate the little boy.

Only one person knows the answers.

"They're different from you and me"

After she was convicted of first-degree murder in the death of Freddie Gant, Rachel Boyd was sentenced to an indeterminate term. Parole is possible but she could spend the rest of her life behind bars.

Because of her tender age at the time of the crime, Rachel spent the first six years of her sentence at the Mason School for Girls, a custodial institution for juvenile offenders. On her eighteenth birthday she was transferred to the Women's Detention Unit at the Colorado State Penitentiary in Cañon City.

This reporter followed her there.

Cinder-block walls and the smell of disinfectant and paint. Barred doors and windows too narrow for a head to squeeze through. Cold metal bunks, hard pillows and thin wool blankets that scratch.

Quite a change from the comforts George Boyd worked so hard to provide for his children. Welcome to Rachel Boyd's new home.

"They're different from you and me," says Captain Marty Reed. "They have a little black spot on their brains. If you could cut out that spot and apply all that energy and street smarts to something productive, you'd have another Howard Hughes."

Captain Reed also sees differences between male and female inmates.

"The guys have problems with authority figures, especially women. For men it's about power. The gals are more confrontational. You never want to get between two of them in a fight. They'll tear off an ear or take an eye out. Even their crimes are emotional. They murder out of love or hate."

Was Rachel driven by hate? Or a twisted kind of love?

"And they're real domesticated," Captain Reed says. "Soon's a gal lands inside, she joins a family. She might become the grandma, the uncle or a kid brother regardless of her age. You're nothing without family in here."

The prison staff declines to talk about the adjustment Rachel has made, other than to say that when she first arrived she had her share of write-ups. Six years in juvenile detention clearly taught her the ropes. Rachel Boyd lives by an old code: she has never been known to snitch on another inmate. A lesson learned at the Mason School—or earlier?

Her booking photograph shows a girl with unruly hair that dips over round black eyes, a starched white shirt and cheap cotton jacket on her sloping shoulders. The tough urchin bears little resemblance to the doll with razor-straight bangs who showed such poise on the witness stand. When she left the Mason School, Rachel Boyd looked more like an adolescent boy than a girl on the brink of adulthood.

Who is she now?

"A terrible mistake"

Rachel never speaks of the day Freddie Gant was killed, or of the circumstances leading to his tragic death. She would like us to forget.

"It was a terrible mistake," says the petite young woman with neatly bobbed hair.

She tilts her head slightly to the left and her lips curve in detached bemusement. Along with her feminine side, Rachel Boyd seems to have discovered a new serenity. "That's all I can say."

During her time at the Colorado State Penitentiary, her only visitor has been her mother. At Rachel's request those visits stopped six months after her arrival.

"I have a new life here," she explains.

But what of the one she destroyed?

"More than one life ended that day," she says.

An extraordinary admission from one who, when her own liberty was at stake, refused to concede she was even present when Freddie Gant was killed. Perhaps Dr. Morse is right; maybe time is the great reformer. But has Rachel Boyd truly changed?

To answer that question, two others must be asked. First and foremost, on that day ten years ago, did this genteel creature act alone?

"Whether someone is with us or not, we're never really alone."

A facile answer, suggestive of a religious conversion. But true penitence requires offering up one's accomplice if indeed she had one. Rachel's toe swings against the metal leg of her chair, and one is reminded of a small foot in a patent leather shoe tapping the wooden leg of a witness stand. Her smile broadens and the ghost of a laugh hovers in the airless visitors' room. But perhaps she will indulge another question.

After Freddie Gant was killed, did she go back to the body?

Rachel's lips tighten, a reminder that she can end this talk at any time. We turn to another subject.

How does she spend her days?

She smiles prettily.

"I keep a journal."

Does she think about being released?

The round eyes blink. The pupils are so large her eyes at first seem black, but they are indeed a startling blue. For the first time during this interview an unguarded emotion crosses Rachel Boyd's face.

It is surprise.

"In prison I feel safe."

She signals the guard and the interview is over.

Forty-Five

C aw ... caaw ... caaww ...
On the utility pole in front of Jackie's house a crow lit and began a raucous chant.

Jackie opened one eye. The day had dawned hot and clear. She pulled the covers back over her head.

It was the Fourth of July, but no holiday. Rachel's trial began in three weeks. Pilar had invited Lily and her to Central City, but Lily was still in the doghouse and Jackie didn't want to leave Rachel. Dennis was wrapping up a monthlong fraud case that was going to the jury next week. And Rachel's defense was finally taking shape.

The prosecution's first problem was motive. Jurors always wanted to know *why*.

Mueller had made it clear molestation wouldn't fly unless Doby showed something more. But sex abuse never occurred in a vacuum. Unless he was prepared to go into Rachel's childhood history and name her abuser, Doby would have a tough time making even innuendo stick. And unless he planned to argue Ben Sparks's murder was opportunistic or the product of an irresistible impulse, there had been no time for Rachel to premeditate.

The DA's next stumbling block was physics: the physical improbability that Rachel had transported the boy's body to the dump site and flung it straight up into the bushes during a blizzard. Then came timing. Immediately after Ben went missing, Chris's house had been thoroughly searched and he would testify he'd been with his sister every minute after he arrived home. Flavia Hart said Ben died two hours after leaving Toody-Froody, but his body wasn't dumped until it began snowing the next evening. Where could Rachel have kept it?

Then there was Mr. X: the man with the wire puzzle at the ice cream parlor. Was it so far-fetched that a guy who enticed a child with a toy could have followed him home and snatched him when no one was looking? Jackie wasn't prepared to accuse Lee Simms; she didn't have to. So long as the kid behind the counter stuck to his story, the jury could point the finger at whomever they liked.

Even Trina Maune had fizzled out. Her last public appearance had been tea at Gabriel's. Until Pilar found her motel, Jackie had thought she'd left town.

"Jackie?"

Rachel stood in her doorway with a tray.

"What's this," Jackie said, "Queen for the Day?"

The tray held a bud vase and a pot of coffee. This time it smelled like the real thing. Rachel poured them each a cup and settled at the foot of the bed.

"I got up early," she said.

"How come?"

"To deadhead your zinnias and snapdragons so they'll bloom again. And your roses."

"Fixing breakfast, mending my clothes . . . Rachel, you don't need to do any of this. Your brother's paying me."

"But you didn't have to take my case." She watched Jackie over the rim of her cup. "Or take me in. I know the hassles it's caused."

"Lily's parents? Once the trial's over—"

"Not just them. The crank calls, the stuff in your mailbox. Do you really think I stand a chance?"

If Dennis were trying this case, he'd put Doby to his proof and rest without calling any witnesses. But Rachel was the key to the defense. If she took the stand, her performance would either send her back to prison or set her free. Jackie had to start building her self-confidence.

"Doby's case is Freddie Gant, not Ben Sparks. I'll hold his feet to the fire."

"But Chris—"

"Rachel." Setting down her cup, Jackie took one small hand in her own. "You have to stop caring what people say. Not Chris or the press or anyone else."

Rachel shook her head, but her eyes never left Jackie's.

"You know what that's like."

"What?"

"Being an outsider. You've been one since the other children learned to read."

"What makes you think I can't read?"

"There are no books in your house."

Jackie didn't blink. "Neither of us are girls anymore, Rachel. If you've told the truth, you have nothing to fear."

Her client looked away.

"There's nothing I should know," Jackie said, "is there?"

"Like what?"

"The guy in the ice cream shop."

"I said I didn't see him."

"Or Trina Maune."

Rachel disengaged her hand. "You heard her. She doesn't know a thing."

"About Freddie—"

"*Or* Ben. I told you, I had nothing to do with his death."

Jackie banished that rose oil.

"And I believe you." She jumped out of bed. "Dibs on the Weedwacker . . ."

The morning passed quickly. They cut back the annuals, broke for lemonade, then cleaned the yard. It was almost lunchtime when they finally tackled the roses. As

Jackie stooped to open the bucket of rose food, something feathery brushed her face. Startled, she drew back.

"What's wrong?" Rachel said.

Now the wasp hovered at her sleeve, its nipped waist no wider than a hair. It lit on her forearm.

"Oh, right. You're scared of wasps."

Jackie stood very still as it probed her with one spidery leg.

"They can smell when you're afraid. But look how slow it is . . ."

The wasp floated at eye level before gliding off.

Jackie reached into her pocket for a bandanna and wiped the cold sweat from her forehead. Rachel's laugh was sympathetic.

"Know what we used to do when we were kids?" She waved her pruning shears. "Snip 'em in half. Whoever got the most—"

"Ugh!"

"They're not interested in you. Outdoors they've got better things to do."

"So do we." Jackie pulled back her hair and tied it with the bandanna. Rachel looked at her curiously.

"That's why you wear bangs."

"Hmm?"

"That scar. How'd you get it?"

On Trail Ridge Road the year before.

"A car accident."

"I noticed you don't drive."

"Only when I have to."

"Were you behind the wheel?"

"Yeah. Look, why don't we—"

"In the mountains, wasn't it?" Rachel said. "When was the first time you were up so high you were afraid to come down?"

Buck, buck, bu-uck . . .

"What makes you think I was afraid?"

"You said you were scared of heights, remember? What was the first time?"

Fly, Jackie, fly!

"In grade school. Some classmates and I snuck up on a roof."

"What did they say to get you up there?"

What about you, Jackie? Not scared, are you?

"What difference does that make?" she replied.

"I'd like to know."

They were standing toe to toe.

"But you don't like to be questioned."

"So take your shot."

Off-balance, Jackie asked the first thing that popped into her head.

"That scar on your temple. What's it from?"

Rachel's fingers rose to the pale crescent but her eyes remained on Jackie's.

"The playground. Vivian Elementary."

"And?"

"I was on a seesaw and the other kid jumped off."

Not with Chris on the sled. Or was she lying?

"Who?"

"Trina."

"Why? She must've known you'd fall."

Rachel knelt to score the ground at the base of a rose-bush. "Why does Trina do anything she does?"

"You tell me."

Her trowel cut into the roots. "If I'm not my brother's keeper, I'm hardly Trina Maune's."

"You didn't want to meet with her the other day, did you?"

"You got what you wanted."

"Not really. Who lived in Trina's toolshed?"

Rachel's laugh was short. "A disgusting old man, with yellow teeth and bad breath. Is that what you want to hear?"

"Why didn't you tell me Trina came to my house?"

"Because she didn't."

"When are you going to trust me, Rachel?"

"When you start trusting *me*."

She started to turn, but Jackie seized her arm.

"Afraid I'll be like Trina and jump off the seesaw, too? Abandon you when you need me most?"

Rachel was silent for the longest time.

"No," she said softly. "I think you're the only real friend I've ever had."

"I meant what I said, Rachel. You're not the little girl you were."

"You really think so?"

Her face was naked with longing.

"I *know* it," Jackie said. "You were weak then. Now you're strong."

They fed the roses and it was past noon before they went inside. The thermostat in the upstairs hallway was stuck at eighty.

"I can't believe you don't have a swamp cooler," Rachel said. "Chris could get you a deal."

"They put in an attic fan when I insulated the house a couple years back. That was supposed to do the trick."

"I haven't heard it all week." On tiptoes, Rachel peered at the ceiling grate in the hallway. "Something's stuck in the blade. Where's your ladder?"

"Ladder?"

"How do you get to the attic?"

"Trapdoor in the laundry room. I'll call a heating guy tomorrow."

"What do we need him for? Looks like a scrap of—"

"No, it's fine. Let me call him."

"All we need is a ladder. And a screwdriver."

"No!"

Rachel shook her head in amusement. "How long have you owned this place?"

"Five—six years."

"You've never been in your own attic, have you?"

"Never had a reason to."

"Then don't come up. Is the ladder in the garage?"

"I'm not afraid—"

"Just show me where it is."

They brought in the ladder and positioned it under the trapdoor.

"Don't come up with me," Rachel said. "I can do it myself."

The ladder was aluminum with a plastic cap. The sides were painted green and the rungs were silver. How many steps—six?

"It's not tall enough," Jackie said.

"Sure it is." Rachel was already on the fourth tread. She reached for the rope attached to the trapdoor and pulled. The door swung down and fluff wafted from a cavernous hole.

"What's that?"

"Insulation." Rachel brushed it from her hair. She stood on the top rung, grabbed the sides of the opening and hoisted herself up. "Wait there."

"You sure?"

"The way you feel about heights, we'll both be safer."

Jackie grasped the ladder with both hands. Before she could change her mind, she clambered up and with an assist from Rachel tumbled through the hole.

Forty-Six

The attic was ten degrees hotter than the second floor. "Watch your head," Rachel said just in time. The roof was steeply pitched and nails protruded. Crouching, Jackie crab-walked to the center of the planked floor. She turned and slowly stood.

Sunlight streamed through chinks in the rafters, suspending thousands of particles of dust. Insulation was crammed into boards and beams and wrapped around heating ducts. It lay in gray snowdrifts and was strewn like loosened hay in bales across the floor. The hush reminded Jackie of a church.

"Who insulated this place?" Rachel said.

"A former client." The dust was making Jackie's face itch. It clung to her sweat and worked its way under the back of her collar.

Whoomph.

The furnace kicked on with a smell like burnt toast. The air crackled.

"It's connected to your humidifier," Rachel said. Squatting by a metal box in the floor, she pulled a large screwdriver from the waistband of her shorts.

Over the thump of the furnace Jackie heard a hiss. A movement on the south wall caught her eye. Rachel spoke without looking up.

"That's where the nest was, isn't it?"

"Nest?"

"Those yellow jackets Pilar was talking about. Think they got 'em all?"

Jackie tore her eyes from the wall above her bedroom window.

"Of course they did. Can we fix that fan?"

Rachel pointed to the yellow sticker on the metal box. "It says not to open it."

"Great. Let's go down."

But Rachel was already prying off the lid. "Not gonna let a little warning scare you, are you?" She set the lid upside down with its sharp edges protruding, and peered into the fan. "I see what's wrong."

Looking over Rachel's shoulder, all Jackie saw was a nest of wires.

"I really don't think it's safe—"

"Don't be silly." She poked at one of the wires with her screwdriver. "This'll take just a minute . . . It was my turn, anyway."

"Your turn?"

"To ask a question. Have you ever really loved someone?"

Jackie struggled to switch gears.

"Loved?" she said. "Lots of people. My aunt, Pilar—"

"Not a relative or someone you have to love. I mean totally, with all your heart."

Jackie hesitated.

"Lily?" Rachel said.

She nodded. "How about you?"

"I . . ." Rachel set down the screwdriver. Jackie had expected her to say Chris, but she seemed to be struggling for words. Stumbling under a burden of guilt? For exposing Chris to their stepfather's brutality to that collie—or what she'd done to Freddie Gant? "Aren't you afraid?"

"Of what?"

"Loving too much. That something will happen, that you yourself might—"

"Hurt her? You can't be afraid."

"I think one day I—" Rachel was interrupted by a shrill sound.

The telephone.

"I'll answer it." Rachel jumped up as if reprieved.

"Let it ring."

But Rachel's head was disappearing down the hole. "Be right back," Jackie heard her say. The next moment the trapdoor swung up and the latch clicked.

"Hey!"

She pounded on the door with her shoe. With the trap closed, the attic seemed stuffier. She stared up at the rafters, felt the enormity of that cavernous maw. Not a church. She'd been swallowed by a whale.

But Rachel would be back any minute.

As she settled on the floor, Jackie thought back over their conversation. Was it any wonder Rachel was afraid? Look how many people had betrayed her. Her parents, Trina, that real estate lawyer the Boyds hired who didn't know his ass from third base. And what about the other people in her life, before Freddie Gant? The teachers who knew something was wrong but did nothing—

Zzzz.

Not a hiss like before, but an irritated sound. From the south dormer.

Was that a speck on the glass?

Jackie started to bang on the trapdoor, then hesitated. It was her own attic, for God's sake. Her house. Her closet, her clothes, her keys . . . The bedroom blinds she knew she'd closed. Rachel knew how little it took to derail her.

When they asked what she had done,
She said, "I did it all for fun!"

Jackie looked at the window again. Nothing was there.

Of course Rachel feared intimacy. Her inquisitiveness, the intrusiveness of her questions, the need to explore every facet of Jackie's life—weren't they all a defense? A way of keeping people at a distance instead of allowing them to get closer? Wasn't it natural to go two steps forward and one back, that whenever someone got close she pushed them away? The fact that Rachel was opening up to her at all—

ZZzzzzz.

Outside or in? *They can smell when you're afraid. . . .*

Jackie closed her eyes. Something brushed her forearm like a hair dragging across skin.

Outdoors they've got better things to do.

"Rachel!"

The name rang from the rafters.

How long did it take to answer a phone?

Jackie opened her eyes. There was nothing on the window.

Get a grip.

Rachel knew so much about her, she must know how she felt about enclosed spaces. And she certainly knew how afraid she was of wasps. Ex-cons were different, Dennis had warned. Thirty years in the can, charged twice with the same crime, and you expected her to take it in stride? Her first lawyer hadn't even tried to defend her and the second roped her into meeting the friend who'd betrayed her.

Of course Rachel was pissed. Was she trying to teach Jackie a lesson, establish who was boss? What in God's name had happened to her to make her this way in the first place? Jackie was tired of shooting at phantoms, tired of—

BZZzzzzz . . .

Wings beat against the south dormer, on the inside of the glass.

Jackie hammered at the trapdoor.

It took every ounce of self-control to stop.

Rachel would be back any moment. Unless she wasn't coming at all.

Unless the phone call was planned.

Rose oil. Trina Maune. Which version was true—the seesaw or the sled? Or were both of them lies? In prison the truth only bought trouble. After thirty years in the can, maybe truth was too much to expect.

Jackie took a deep breath and in the heat of the attic she smelled tar.

Buck, buck, bu-uck.

Her mouth went from dry to wet. Her bandanna was sodden and all she could smell was the rank odor of her own sweat.

You have never been safer.

This is *your* house. You can always break a window.

Believe Rachel—

But what about the other lies? Letting her think she couldn't drive. And the man with the wire puzzle. Was Jackie supposed to think the kid at the ice cream parlor made him up? All the little things that went wrong before each important hearing, the misplaced keys and earrings and shoes. Was Rachel trying to throw her off her game to keep her from the truth? Was she trying to sabotage her own defense? Jackie pounded the trapdoor again and suddenly the very air she was breathing seemed to come alive.

Tiny shapes danced across the south dormer, jigging

and jogging and swarming across the glass. Her pounding must have agitated them; they were trapped in here with no way out either. Soon they would—

Something brushed Jackie's face. She batted it away.

Just your imagination, running away—

Wings touched her face again and Jackie saw stripes.

Yellow and black. And didn't it have reason to hate her?

A fat one, the granddaddy of the yellow jackets that had succumbed to the poison sprayed into their hive. It hovered before flying off to rejoin its friends. Biding their time. Unable to get out through the eaves above her window, they'd bored through the wall. Sweat poured from Jackie's skin.

She started counting backward.

Ten, nine, eight . . .

You are not in this attic.

Seven, six, five . . .

You are at a party, in a crowded room. There are sofas and chairs and couples standing around with drinks. Your destination is the dormer on the east wall. Not the south, the east wall.

Four, three, two . . .

Eyes straight ahead, you will walk slowly across the floor, one foot in front of the other, careful not to make any extra motion or bump into the nails sticking out of the rafters. And when you get there—

As Jackie took a final step backward the heel of her sandal struck something round and hard. Skidding on the screwdriver, her feet went out from under her. She threw out her hands to brace her fall and landed on something sharp. White heat seared her knee. It began to throb, an excruciating pain that pulsed from her toes to the tips of her ears. Warm and wet, blood gushed from a gash in her leg. Just then something soft brushed her face. She heard herself scream—

Brilliant eyes peered up from the hole in the floor.

"Oh, there you are! I thought you followed me down."

Jackie stumbled to her feet. Blind to the agony in her knee and the blood pouring down her leg, she thrust herself through the opening in the laundry room ceiling, flew down the ladder and didn't look back.

Forty-Seven

I've got something that'll break this case wide open. But I want cash."

Despite the July heat, Trina's fringed shawl, black skirt and boots attracted little attention at the doughnut shop on Colfax. She looked almost as desperate as Jackie felt.

It had taken twenty-five stitches to close the gash in her knee in the ER yesterday, not to mention a tetanus shot. Falling on the lid of the fan box, Jackie had narrowly missed severing a tendon that would have left her with permanent damage. She didn't believe for one moment that Trina had anything to sell. And she was in no mood to screw around.

"I'm not in the habit of buying evidence."

"Then maybe Cal Doby will."

The blackmail at the pastry shop. But Jackie smelled a bluff.

"I couldn't give you money if I wanted to, Trina. You're a witness in the case."

"I gotta get out of town."

If Rachel's trial hadn't been three weeks off, a hundred bucks not to see Trina Maune again might have been a heck of a deal. But obstruction of justice had never been Jackie's favorite charge and Doby would like nothing better than to get her disbarred for it.

"Why come to Denver in the first place?"

"Like I said. To help Rachel."

"Oh, yeah—your best friend. That's why Doby subpoenaed you?"

"I can't stay at that motel."

"Sorry, Hotel Flowers is booked. You've been there, you should know."

Trina stared. "I don't—"

"Did Rachel call you that Sunday morning, after I left?"

"Look." Trina seized Jackie's hand and Jackie tried not to feel sorry for her. She'd had clients like Trina. Histrionic and marginally stable, more dangerous to themselves than anyone else. How many people had Trina conned into taking care of her? Was her client just the latest, or did Trina really have something Rachel wanted? "You're the only one I can trust."

"What about Chris?"

"He doesn't know I'm talking to you."

"Why not? Hasn't he been paying—"

"You don't get it."

Don't let her call your bluff.

"So tell me."

"I've got something Doby would kill for."

"Then go to him."

"This is heavier than you think."

"It doesn't get heavier than first-degree murder, Trina. If you know anything that can hurt Rachel, tell me now."

"I'm scared."

Jackie stood. "Know what scares me, Trina? The thought of my client—*your best friend*—being sent up for the next thirty years for a crime she didn't commit. If you're not willing—"

"Will you pay me if I talk?"

"I can't do that."

Trina's voice was steady but her hands trembled.

"Then it doesn't matter who subpoenas me. I won't live to testify."

"If you've been threatened, maybe I can arrange for protection. But I have to know who and why. And what you know about Ben Sparks's death."

"Not him. Freddie."

Jackie sat down again. "Were you there?"

"Not then. Later."

"How much later?"

"Next day. Shelly took me to see him."

When the body was moved.

"What did he look like?"

"Dead."

"How was he lying?"

No hesitation. "On his back."

The killer had already returned. For what?

"What did Rachel tell you?" Jackie said.

A shy pride crossed Trina's face.

The girl Rachel had a soft spot for. The one no one else could stand.

"She wished I'd been there."

"Why?" Jackie said.

"I made her strong."

They were going in circles.

"It was an accident, then?"

"No."

End of mystery.

"Why'd she kill him, Trina?"

Trina's fingers tightened on her cup. "There was a man."

"Who?"

"We were afraid. It was too late for her."

Wasn't that where Doby's theory inevitably led? That Rachel had been molested and lashed out against an even more defenseless child? But what hold could her molester have over either woman now? Jackie had had just about enough.

"That was thirty years ago, Trina. You can't possibly still—"

"Nothing changes the past."

"Exactly. What's past is past. Whoever he is, he can't hurt anyone anymore. Right?"

Trina stared at the scarred Formica.

"Was he after Freddie?"

"Ask Simms," she said. "He knows."

"Yeah, I heard. He was in Vivian back then. So what?"

Trina's laugh stopped just short of hysteria.

"Shelly's no schoolgirl, Miss Flowers."

Jackie dropped a couple of bucks on the table. "Thanks for wasting my time."

Trina grabbed her arm and Jackie looked into her eyes.

They were remarkably sane.

"You're being set up," Trina said.

"Sounds like I'll have to talk to Simms."

"No!"

"Why not?"

"It was him or us."

"Us or *who*?"

"If he didn't get Freddie, he would of gotten us."

"But you said it was too late for Rachel."

"You don't get how it was. Then or now!"

Jackie silently counted to three.

"Look, Trina. I understand you kids covering for someone thirty years ago, especially if you were threatened. But why keep doing it?" Trina had closed her eyes. "Know what? I think this is one sweet scam."

Still no response.

"Who brought you to Denver? Simms?"

"Don't tell," she whispered.

"Makes a helluva better story that way, doesn't it?

'Witness in Freddie Gant murder comes clean.' That what you promised Doby? No wonder Simms wanted an exclusive. Quite the little hustler, aren't you?"

"I never should of left. In Vivian I was safe."

"Hell, if Rachel didn't recognize you, I'd wonder if you even were Trina Maune!"

"Cash," she said. "I need cash."

"I told you—"

Trina rose.

"If you won't help me, go ask Freddie Gant."

Forty-Eight

The Spider zipped through the industrial northeast side of town, sped past Quonset-hut bars where cars were still parked from Friday night, flew over the railroad tracks and landed smack on I-70 heading east before Jackie downed her first cup of coffee. Eyes thankfully on the road, Pilar held out her mug for a refill.

"Who asked for sugar and cream?" she growled.

In no mood to be reminded she herself had brewed it.

Traffic was light on the truck route from Denver to Kansas City, and as Pilar wove through dump trucks and construction equipment Jackie clutched the thermos with one hand and her door handle with the other. South of the airport, produce warehouses and technology parks with runty trees gave way to faux châteaux catering to passengers on layover.

"Nouveau cheese," Pilar rated the architecture. "What McDonald's is to filet mignon . . . Thank God," she said as the limit jumped to seventy-five. They were bound for Seward County, at the eastern border of the state. For her, the sooner this trip to Rachel's past was over, the better.

"It was no act, Pilar. Trina's scared witless—"

"Wouldn't take much."

"—and whatever she's afraid of is in Vivian. She's covering for someone and I want to know who."

"Trina's a flake trying to make a splash. A Squeaky Fromme. Just after another fifteen seconds of fame." Steadying the wheel with her knees, Pilar reached for a chocolate croissant. "I still don't see why we have to go all the way to East Bumblefuck for answers your client could give if she'd open her pretty little mouth."

"They have a pact."

"Pact? From what you described, there's no love lost between those two."

"Rachel was abused."

"Oh, come *on*."

To the west the mountains were obscured by haze, either a brush fire in the foothills or dust from Mongolia that had blanketed the area for days. To the east lay a mobile home park with a Tuff Shed on every lot. Entering the high plains, where nomadic tribes had chased bison, the highest structure for miles around was the sign on a Tomahawk truck stop.

"Why are you so hard on her?" Jackie said.

"Cookie, you've been had. You're the one she locked in the attic with killer bees and a lethal ceiling fan!"

"That was my fault." The exterminator had found nothing and her knee was halfway back to normal size. "You and I haven't always agreed on clients, but—"

"What about those bite marks? When you gonna face the fact that your client made them?"

"Kids act out what's done to them."

"Rachel Boyd doesn't know the meaning of abuse."

"What's your problem? That her brother lives near the country club?"

"Now *there's* a tragic figure. Him I could really get behind." Pilar cut off a tractor trailer. Its horn bellowed like a dozen elephants breaking wind. "The little boy who never grew up."

"I thought you liked older men."

"Only when I've been naughty . . . Gotta admit, there's something about Chris Boyd that makes me want to do the spanking. Now, Lee Simms is kinda cute. In a slovenly, obsessive sort of way."

A screen saver with swaying buttocks and a box of sharpened blades. Were Ben and Freddie the only boys whose necks had been snapped and groins clawed? Even without the bite marks to complicate matters, Pilar's sources had found no matches. But Jackie still wasn't convinced.

"You did that background check," she said.

"On Simms. So?"

"Were there any gaps?"

"Gaps?"

"Years he can't account for."

"There's nothing wrong with Lee Simms!"

"Trina doesn't think he's so attractive."

"Oh, yeah? Didn't stop her from taking his money."

"She never actually said—"

Pilar flipped off a driver who had the nerve to try to pass her. Coffee sloshed, narrowly missing her duck trousers. She tapped the brake and the Spider slowed a mite. "Who else would pay her to slither out of the woodwork? Cal Doby?"

"Not his style," Jackie said.

"And isn't a molester in the toolshed a little convenient? Can't remember the last time I found a weenie-wagger in mine."

"He could've used one or both girls to lure Freddie Gant."

"Why cover for him?"

"Shame," Jackie said. "At being abused themselves. Or their real role in Freddie's death."

"But if they'd already been molested, why lure another kid? And why not tell us who the creep is now? It's been thirty damn years!"

Clouds hovered over the roadway like buffaloes frozen in midstride. Farther east the horizon flattened, with promontories shading into buttes. The terrain was harsh, not meant for habitation; spring came late and in summer the sun baked the soil.

"We'll hit Vivian for lunch." Having consumed most of a king-size thermos of coffee and an entire bag of pastries, Pilar was fully awake. Preening in the rearview mirror, she adjusted the silk scarf at her throat. "Enough time to nose around before heading back."

"You don't have a date tonight, do you?"

"Why?"

"We didn't come all this way to turn around. How many witnesses did you find?"

"Freddie's dad disappeared and his mom moved to Nebraska. No leads on Susie or Gregg Gant."

"Carla Miller?"

"Better luck there. She owns a hair salon in town— the Touch 'n Blow." Pilar rolled her eyes.

"Did you find Rachel's teachers?"

"After Althea Robey died, Millicent Trent moved to Oklahoma to live with her daughter. Some improvement..." A gust rocked the Spider. The roadside was spotless; the eighty-mile-an-hour breeze took care of trash. "But Janet Nye's still around. At least Simms identifies his sources."

With Rachel refusing to give names, Pilar had been forced to comb the reporter's stories for witnesses. That reminded Jackie she'd yet to come clean on burglarizing his room. "I've never been clear on what a hotdog like him was doing in Vivian that summer," she said. "Seward County wasn't exactly ground zero for breaking news."

"He's no child molester, Jackie."

"Chris said he hung around boys. Especially Freddie Gant."

"So?"

"How come he never married?"

"Happy reporters are the ones who drink themselves to death."

"Dennis doesn't trust him either."

"I'm telling you, Lee Simms is a red-blooded heterosexual male!"

Jackie glanced at her investigator. Pilar's ducks were new and her lipstick was a bolder shade, a mulberry that made her eyes jet. "Sounds like you know him better than I do." Pilar just smiled. "Isn't he a little—"

"Speaking of Dennis, how's he getting along with Lily?"

"The ice is thawing. At least, she doesn't seem to despise him quite so much."

"Smart kid."

"Not that we've been seeing a lot of each other. We both have trials coming up."

"And having a houseguest must cramp your style."

"Rachel's quite self-contained. And nothing's going on with Dennis anyhow."

"At your place, you mean. I assume home delivery's a little more varied in LoDo. . . ."

The main traffic headed south, to the fertile Arkansas Valley or Oklahoma and Texas. Towns were heralded by water towers on stilts with the name painted in tall letters on the tank. They started to see grain bins. Squat and round, the color of pewter. Always clustered. Stubby bullets three stories high.

"What makes you think the Miller broad will talk?" Pilar said.

"She hates Rachel."

"And Janet Nye?"

"Only one with a sympathetic word. Between the two, we may actually learn something."

The first grain elevator rose from nowhere.

The surrounding structures were single-story and looked deserted; the town was an appendage, soon to disappear from the map. But Jackie could feel the elevator's allure. White and stark as a Greek temple, it dominated the landscape for miles. In this flat terrain, wouldn't anything that let you see beyond the next field be irresistible?

The elevators became more numerous. Seven, eight, ten stories tall. Some painted, others steel, each crowned with a steeple and buttressed by gigantic bins. Like extraterrestrial invaders they dwarfed even the water towers. Circle, triangle, square—the lack of adornment and purity of form reminded Jackie of otherworldly cathedrals.

Just before the Vivian exit, they came upon a haunting sight.

"Pull over."

Pilar turned into the rest stop. The sky was overcast. Wind rocked the sports car and whipped the flags overhead to confetti. Across the road stood a grain elevator. The only one for miles around. The place where Freddie Gant had died?

Steel drums thirty feet tall flanked an edifice twice as high. From this distance Jackie couldn't tell whether it was wood or concrete, but as she watched, the sun broke through the clouds and bathed the elevator and its peaked roof in a dazzling light. Glinting off the bands on the massive bins and up the steel stabilizing ropes to the mighty tower, it framed an arrow against the gunmetal sky. Like a rocket ship on a launching pad, the entire apparatus seemed primed to take off.

"Know what that looks like to me?" Pilar said.

"Hmm?"

"What every cowboy wishes he was packing."

Forty-Nine

V ivian commanded two exits off the interstate.

Pilar took the one marked BUSINESS DISTRICT with a smaller sign proclaiming it HOME OF AN ASTRONAUT. It was also home to two Conoco stations, a Napa Auto Parts, a Pizza Hut, an Arby's, a Taco Bell and a John Deere dealership. Jackie saw several boarded-up storefronts and motels along the main drag. One particularly seedy motel was topped by a black Sputnik with yellow and red spikes.

"Hell of a lot of hair in Vivian," she said as they passed the fourth beauty salon.

"What else can a gal do after high school, in a town with only one bank?"

The buildings were single-story, including the aforesaid bank. The Farmers Equity Co-op windows were hand-painted with a cowboy on a hobbyhorse and an invitation to "Giddy Up and Go to the Fair." Pickups nosed out American-made sedans, and shingle-sided houses jockeyed with factory-builts and Quonset huts. The fancier yards were planted with gravel instead of weeds. Gals as hefty as their menfolk wore unisex T-shirts, Levi's and farm caps.

"Out here a liberal believes in gummint-financed highways," Pilar said. "A blond chick and a Mexican in a red foreign car should be the talk of the town."

The Farm Insurance Bureau showed the most activity.

"They may want to go back on the gold standard," Jackie said, "but they sure don't mind federal programs." Sun pounded the Spider's roof and she fanned herself with the file that held Carla Miller's address. "Can't we stop and ask?"

Pilar turned onto a dirt road that looped back toward the highway, and soon they were driving parallel to the railroad tracks. This part of town was older. Homes were shingled with asphalt or were trailers with add-ons, and garages had turned into carports. The wind was strong enough to wag a spruce and even the church was for sale. At the end of a wide empty street, Jackie glimpsed a sturdy building with a mansard roof and a bell tower. A newer brick addition was tacked to one side.

Vivian Elementary School.

"Too bad it's Saturday," Pilar said. "Not to mention the middle of summer."

"That must be the park." A grassy stretch with an old bandstand and a statue of a soldier with a drooping mustache and a cavalry hat. "Where's all the kids?"

"At the picture show four exits down." Pilar made a U-turn in the deserted square. She parked and looked at the file. "Touch 'n Blow should be just north . . ."

Straight ahead lay the grain elevator.

Jackie stepped out of the Spider. The wind was a furnace blast, but from three blocks away the tower beckoned. She started walking.

After a hundred yards the pavement ended and the road turned to gravel. The only sound was their own footsteps. To the right lay a field dense with purple flowers. The breeze carried a musky scent, basil or thyme. They passed a rusted trailer with a chicken-wire hutch.

"Rabbit coops," Pilar said. "Don't get all dewy-eyed. They raise 'em for food."

The smell of tar heralded the tracks. A pickup truck and a boxcar of sand, a yellow and green John Deere . . . Jackie looked straight up.

The elevator was massive.

Ducts and chutes, an inverted cone, suspension wires strung from the ground to the top of thirty-foot corrugated steel drums. The tower itself was so high she couldn't see the top. A catwalk clung two-thirds of the way up, with a wooden platform jutting out over the storage bins. The crevasse between the drums was shadowed and the dirt was littered inches deep with rusty scraps.

"He was carried," Jackie said.

"Who?"

"Freddie Gant. After he was dead."

"Yeah?"

"That's when he was cut and how the weapon was lost." Pilar was skeptical. "You read the police report. They found his body between those bins."

"Yeah, so?"

"See for yourself. If he was pushed or thrown from the catwalk he'd land where we're standing. Not in the shade."

"And?"

"Unless he got up and walked, someone carried him there. Probably an adult."

"Why bother?"

"Privacy. He wanted to take his time and didn't want to be seen. If he dropped his weapon or the button, no wonder he couldn't find them."

"She could of dragged him—"

"—through this debris? Not without leaving tracks. You couldn't miss them."

"A twelve-year-old—"

Jackie shook her head.

"If Rachel was here, she wasn't alone."

Fifty

The Touch 'n Blow's pasteboard sign was a guy with an Elvis haircut.

"Got an appointment?"

The woman at the manicurist's table wore spiked mules and a butterfly-strewn thigh-length rayon kimono. Her eyebrows were shaped like scimitars, and her lashes were black widow spiders.

Jackie gave her a friendly smile.

"We're looking for Carla Miller. Know where we can find her?"

"That depends."

Carla's hair was too black and her skin was varnished like an egg-washed brioche. You could see why Vivian had room for more than one beauty shop.

"I understand she was a classmate of Rachel Boyd's," Jackie said. Pilar wandered to the beehive dryer and peered under the hood.

"You're her lawyer. She must really be in trouble."

Jackie dropped all pretense. "You and Rachel weren't the best of friends."

"That would be correct."

"Was there any particular—"

"Besides getting Trina Maune to break my nose?"

"That's what happened?"

Carla picked up an emery board and began sharpening her fingernails.

"Trina's a real piece of work." She moved down her hand. "Pretending to be slow. Everyone wanted to protect her. They felt so *sorry* for her. That's why they hired her at the café. Freddie Gant's murder was the only attention she ever got."

"I heard Rachel called the shots," Jackie said.

"Maybe Trina gave Rachel the push."

Not half so bad if not for Trina . . .

"Was there talk about a child molester in Vivian?"

"That poor old drunk in the Maune shed?" Carla laughed. "If some creep was bugging kids thirty years ago, there would of been more than talk. Not hushed up like . . ."

"Like what?" Pilar said.

"Why go there now? She paid the price."

"Who?"

"Debbie Gant. She was banging some guy the afternoon her kid wandered off. Hubby's always the last to know." Carla's sigh was as phony as her lashes. "Susie and Gregg sure did. That's what busted up the Gants, not what happened to Freddie."

Jackie wondered how many times she'd told that story.

"What about the Boyds?"

"Kept to themselves. Except Trina, the only one Rachel hung out with was her kid brother. Then their stepdad packed it in—"

"George Boyd killed himself?" Pilar said.

"One-car accident on a road he knew like the back of his hand. You tell me."

"Anyone else who might talk to us?"

"If you found me, you know about Janet Nye. But don't waste your time. That bat couldn't tell her ass from her elbow thirty years ago."

Jackie thanked her.

"It's a slow day." Carla winked at Pilar. "Come back tomorrow and I'll give you a special on waxing."

In the Spider, Pilar kept looking at her face in the rearview mirror.

"What's the matter?" Jackie said.

"Is it that obvious?"

"For God's sake, she was trying to get a rise out of you!" The sky was darkening and thunderstorms on the Eastern Plains were no joke. "You know I'd tell you. Let's find our Miss Brooks before it pours."

Janet Nye was in her backyard, a patch of cultivated grass on a dirt road that dead-ended in prairie. More a hummingbird than a bat, she was trimming a rosebush with clippers the size of nail scissors.

"Miss Nye?" Jackie said.

"Do I know you?"

"I was hoping to speak with you about a former student. Rachel Boyd."

Janet Nye stripped off her gardening gloves. Her eyes were surprisingly sharp for a senile old broad.

"Dreadful thing. Not that I couldn't have predicted it." Jackie's heart sank. "I always felt so sorry for her. . . ."

When they refused tea, she poured herself a glass from a pitcher in her refrigerator.

"What was it about Rachel?" Jackie said.

"Such a sad little girl. Her brother received all the attention. When her acting-out became more flagrant, some of my colleagues tried to 'protect' Christopher from her. Encouraging him in activities that excluded Rachel, trumped-up after-school conferences, that sort of nonsense."

"Was she a good student?"

"Smart as a whip. And so observant! If anything, she saw too much. That's why they were afraid of her. Of course, with a mother like that . . ." Like Carla Miller, she broke off in a way that invited pursuit. This time

Jackie waited her out. "Evvie Boyd was histrionic, what we used to call a hysteric. Sometimes she would pick up her children and other times she wouldn't. Youngsters need consistency."

"What was George like?"

"Never missed a parent-teacher conference." The same words she'd used when Lee Simms interviewed her thirty years earlier. She took another sip. The tea was strangely colorless. "If you want to know the Boyds, talk to Roy Switzer. They ran that appraisal business together."

Pilar jotted down the name.

"Sounds like George was more involved in the children's lives than Evelyn," Jackie said.

"I wondered if she beat her."

Janet Nye said it so softly Jackie wasn't sure she'd heard correctly.

"Beg pardon?"

"Just a suspicion. Anger and depression are closely allied, you know." Like gin and tonic. Or was the old schoolteacher drinking vodka? "But every family is a constellation of unique circumstances. You can never see into another's heart."

"How well do you remember Freddie Gant?"

"Such a sweet boy."

"Was there talk of a child molester in the area?"

"Such nonsense!" Her gesture made the liquid in her glass slosh. Janet Nye teetered on the brink of sobriety. One push and she'd clam up or burst. "The only gossip was about Debbie Gant."

"We heard about Freddie's mother."

"Ah, but did you hear who?"

"Miss Nye, I really don't—"

"Not that you could blame him. He had no idea what he was walking into."

Pilar couldn't control herself. "Who?"

"Why, that young reporter, of course! You thought it was a coincidence he knew so much about the Gants?"

"Lee Simms?" Jackie said.

"Shameful, really. The way he used that to advance his career . . . Are you sure you wouldn't like some tea?"

Fifty-One

Switzer Realty was closing when they arrived. The girl at the desk said her boss was out of town.

"When do you expect him back?" Jackie said.

"Sunday."

Pilar sighed. It was now official: they would spend Saturday night in Vivian.

"One of those Bob Wahr trips," the girl said as if they should know Switzer's clients. She made up for it by giving them his home address and the time she thought he'd return.

"Can you recommend a motel?"

She tittered. "Only one don't rent by the month or week . . ."

The Sputnik on the main drag.

"Twin beds?" the manager asked primly.

"Just one more reason to remember that blond chick and the Mexican in the foreign car," Pilar muttered on their way to the room. Her ducks were grimy from the grain elevator and her mood was increasingly foul. Sprawling across one of the beds while Jackie headed for the shower, she opened a copy of the *Seward County Call*.

"You think what Nye said is true?" Jackie said through the bathroom door. "It could explain a lot. Like why Simms stuck with the story all these years. And why he hung around Freddie—"

"I don't wanna talk about it."

"At least this trip hasn't been a total waste. And you never know what Roy Switzer will say after he gets back from his jaunt with Bob."

"Go soak yer head."

Jackie knew she was in trouble when she couldn't tell which faucet was hot. Not being able to figure out which way they turned was worse, and when she pulled the lever for the shower and freezing water gushed into the tub it was definitely time to get out.

"Great shower," she said. "Want one before dinner?"

"I'd rather sleep in these clothes than put them on again after I wash."

"We'll send Chris your cleaning bill. And I'll make it up to you. A steak dinner with the man of your dreams."

"I said there's nothing between me and Simms! Think we've got cable?" All but three of the channels had static, and the good ones were local. Pilar flung down the remote. "You take this bed. It's lumpier."

"Guess I owe you that much."

As Jackie combed her hair, Pilar opened the *Call* to the women's page.

"'I keep hearing about sushi,'" she read aloud. "'Can you tell me what it is?' Jeez! I'm telling you, Jackie, I don't know how much more I can take."

"This case finally getting to you?"

"It's that Nye woman. What if she's right?"

"About Simms? At least it explains—"

"I don't give a rat's ass about that jerk. But what if Rachel really was abused?"

"By the drunk in the Maunes' shack? Not even Janet Nye believes that."

"But it fits. She's right about anger being the flip side of depression. And isn't it funny the way everyone dismisses that molester?"

Not three hours ago, Pilar had dismissed him herself.

"The only one who thinks he could've been real is Chris," Jackie said.

"And who's in a better position to know? You're the one who said a molester could have used Rachel and Trina to lure Freddie."

"Why would they do it?"

"To save themselves or another child."

"Who?"

"Miller and Nye both said how attached Rachel was to her baby brother. Is it such a stretch?"

"I have an idea." Jackie pulled on her socks. "When we get home, you can ask Rachel yourself. I'm sure she'll be glad to fill you in on the details. Or maybe Trina—"

Jackie ducked as Pilar threw a shoe.

"Taco Bell or Pizza Hut?"

Fifty-Two

Roy Switzer lived in the newer part of town. A Ford van was parked on the white rocks that were the front lawn of his ranch-style home. Before Jackie could knock, a man came barreling out from around back.

"He'p you, ma'am?"

Despite the booming voice, Switzer was in his seventies. Five feet tall, he wore a buff-colored Stetson with his bolo tie, pressed Levi's and a silver belt buckle the size of a hubcap. A key ring almost as big as the buckle was clipped to his jeans.

Jackie explained why they were there.

"George Boyd was salt of the earth," Switzer said. "He worshiped Evvie and those kids. Took them two everywhere with him. He was 'specially fond of Shelly."

"I understand you were partners."

"Boyd and Switzer—biggest farm and ranch appraiser in the county. Nothing worse than having to foreclose on some old boy's farm, but it happens. 'Specially after seven years of drought. Notice all them shops closed on Main?"

Jackie recalled a boarded hardware store and a soda fountain for rent. Was Bob Wahr one of the casualties?

"Hunnerd percent of Vivian's economy is tied to agriculture. It ain't growing and it don't take too many bad years to put it on the ropes. Dry-land farmers depend on rain. With the wheat harvest down fifty percent, it's cheaper to sell yer cow for ninety cents a pound than feed her alfalfa and corn and risk 'er not producing a calf."

"So a bum year for Ol' MacDonald is a bumper year for you," Pilar said.

Switzer took no offense. "Between fed'ral insurance, disaster relief and crop subsidies, he might squeak by. Depreciating equipment helps. But two bad years in a row spell the big B."

"And that's where you come in."

"George and I had a fine relationship with the bank."

Before Pilar could launch into a defense of the Grange, Jackie jumped in.

"What happened to Freddie Gant must have devastated the Boyds."

"You would of liked George, he was a real down-home kind of guy. Loved all kinds of music, 'specially folk songs—Kingston Trio was his favorite. Died right after Shelly went away." Switzer's jowls wagged. "Helluva thing."

The accident, or his stepdaughter being sent up for murder?

"We heard," Jackie said.

"Yep, freak of an accident. Wheel come off and his car went into a barrow pit at the side of the road. Snapped his neck and that was the end of it. Never seen nothing like it, not before and not since."

Suicide. Because he'd lost the target of his abuse?

Switzer seemed to think the better of it.

"Course, George was so distraught over what happened with Shelly, he prob'ly forgot to tighten his lug bolts last time he had a flat. That's how farm accidents happen all the time, some guy not thinking about what he's doing . . ." Another wag of the jowls signaled the topic closed. "If you really want to understand George, you have to know what he cared most about. Can I show you something? It's in the shed out back."

Jackie and Pilar exchanged a glance. Jackie shrugged, and they followed Switzer to his backyard. Unclipping his keys, he inserted one in the padlock and rolled up the aluminum door.

"Ladies, meet George Boyd's passion." He gestured grandly. *"Bob Wahr."*

The shed's walls were covered with wooden display cases. A hundred more stood in a rack at the back. Hung by baling wire to burlap and suede was the strangest assortment of instruments Jackie had ever seen.

"Took him ten years to figure how to mount them," Switzer said.

"What the heck are they?" Pilar said.

"Largest collection of barbed wire tools in the world. George drove all over the county collecting 'em."

Those trips Chris had mentioned. Where Chris himself was, the day Freddie disappeared.

"One of the perks to being an appraiser, you might say," Switzer said. "Evvie hated his hobby but he tried to interest the kids. Been pickin' up dust since George died—a darn shame. He left the whole shebang to me."

The cases nearest the door held strands of wire. Each specimen was about eighteen inches long, with three thorns spaced at regular intervals along the twist. Their colors ranged from carbon to rust to the dappled amber of a wild pony.

"Rope that tamed the West. If Custer waited a couple years, there wouldn't of been a Little Big Horn. It's all about territory. Control." No stopping Switzer now. "Hunnerd years ago this prairie was desert—nothing but buffalo and Indians. Then millions of settlers poured in. The land was too arid to raise crops, and without trees to build fences, there was no way for ranchers to pen livestock or farmers to mark their land. When barbed wire went up, bison couldn't roam and Indians were fenced out."

Some of the barbs were as elaborate as sailors' knots. Through the palomino strands of one slender coil, two sharpened wires twined. The four barbs each pointed in a different direction, like an arabesque.

"Pretty, ain't it?" Switzer said.

"What makes the colors?" Pilar said.

"In a high and dry climate like Colorada, old wire can be black as new. It's red in Texas 'cause it rusts."

A twisted strip with lance points and a reinforcing core floated across the suede. Fins hugging the graceful curve reminded Jackie of a shark. A galvanized steel ribbon clamped with saber-sharp tips was more deadly. Through a double strand of wire on a third specimen, sheet-metal barbs zigzagged like broken teeth.

"—earlier forms was vicious. Tore up cattle pretty bad till they learned to keep their distance. No one ever called a steer stupid; most of 'em gave it one try and stayed clear after that. But that's why church folk named barbed wire the devil's rope. Now, wire wasn't George's real passion."

Switzer moved to another display case. The picks, stretchers and clamps belonged on a dentist's tray in the days before Novocain. And, judging from their rust, before anyone knew the cause of lockjaw.

"Like most of us, George started out collecting wire. The sameness of it got to him and he switched to tools." Switzer pointed to a sodbuster's version of a Swiss army knife. "Hammer, screwdriver, leather punch, pliers— even a nutcracker, all in one. That notch is for cutting wire. Them old boys sure knew which end was up. . . ."

The notch looked sharp.

"The shiny ones ain't worth a damn. Best tools are the ones that are patched."

"How come?" Pilar said.

"Take that one." He pointed to an implement with a seam that gleamed like a scar. "Cast iron's brittle, it shatters when it's run over by a wagon or dropped. Some old boy liked this tool so much he broke it in half. Mended it with a farmer's weld of lead and flux."

Others had been painted a rust-resistant red, yellow or green. The robin's egg blue of one smaller tool made it stand out. It was eight inches long and tapered. Flat, with a hook at the narrow end.

"What's this?" Jackie said.

"A clincher. Most collectors nowadays wouldn't even recognize it."

The enamel made the pebbled surface glimmer. Without touching it, she knew it would be cold.

"How was it used?"

"To string wire on a fence. Twists the nail running through the picket, making a loop for the wire to run through." Switzer unfastened the tool from the baling wire that held it in place and handed it to her. "Course, it ain't quite as heavy as the original . . ."

Indeed it wasn't.

"That's because it's a facsimile," he said.

"A fake?" Pilar said. Because Jackie had never showed it to her, she hadn't recognized the hook end as the shard from the bramble.

"Not a fake, a *facsimile*. Them old boys made 'em for collectors 'cause an original was too rare to find. George had one but he lost it."

"When?" Jackie said.

"Last time this collection went on display."

"Where was that?"

"Vivian Elementary. Pioneer Day, when they dedicated that annex to the school."

"Pioneer Day?"

"The *Call* did a heckuva story on it."

"How long ago was that?"

"Right before Freddie Gant got killed."

Fifty-Three

I warned you to stay away from Vivian."

Jackie had called Rachel on Pilar's cell phone.

"Did you give your stepdad Freddie so he wouldn't go after Chris?"

"I was weak instead of being strong."

"Give me a break!" Jackie tried to control herself. "In two weeks you're going on trial for murder. Doby's whole case is that if you killed one kid thirty years ago, you'd do it again today. We both know what happened to Freddie was more complicated than what came out at trial. Who else was there?"

"Whether I was with someone or alone, whether Freddie fell or he was pushed . . . Aren't I just as guilty?"

"Not if I was defending you."

"I've told the truth about Ben."

"If you have nothing to hide, who were you with?"

Silence.

"Why did you do it?"

"I guess I couldn't take it anymore."

"You *guess*? Did he threaten you, tell you if you didn't bring Freddie—"

Rachel's laugh chilled Jackie to the core.

"You know nothing."

Enough to stay away from those bite marks.

Caretakers biting on the face. Kids acting out the abuse they'd endured. She'd heard two versions of how Rachel got that scar on her temple. Was there a third? But one mention could destroy whatever trust was left between them. And that was damn little.

Jackie backed up.

"I know Freddie was cut with a tool from your stepfather's collection. George lost it at the grain elevator. Is that why he made you go back?"

Nothing.

"You took Trina with you to cement the pact. So she wouldn't squeal?"

Silence.

"I know Trina was at my house. What's she holding over you?"

"Nothing. I told you—"

"Why are you lying to me?"

"I—"

"If Ben had nothing to do with Freddie, why were they cut the same way?"

"You'd be the first person I'd tell."

"Don't bullshit me, Rachel. Give me names. There must be someone in Vivian—"

"All dead. Or might as well be."

"Who are they?"

"I've already lost everything, Jackie."

"And you're about to lose it all over again. Why are you sabotaging your own defense? Do you want to go back to prison?"

"At least I was safe."

The phone clicked in Jackie's ear. Pilar pulled out of the lot behind the Farmers Equity Co-op and headed north. As they drove down the main street that Sunday afternoon, FOR SALE signs leaped out. Rachel was right; a few more years of drought and Vivian would be a ghost town.

"I should have listened to you," Jackie said. "Never taken this case."

"Because Rachel did it?"

"Because she won't defend herself."

"Maybe that's because she's guilty." Pilar turned onto the state road to avoid the interstate. The last thing either of them wanted to see was another grain elevator.

"She said she didn't do it."

"Since when do you take what a client says at face value?"

"I did with you."

They cut through prairie on a course so straight and flat that arrows alerted drivers to curves to stop them from sailing off the edge. Clouds were so low their shadows leaped across the road, blackening patches of range. The sun broke through and the asphalt became a silver ribbon.

"You're being too hard on Rachel," Pilar said. "Can't you see why she doesn't trust you?"

"I've never violated a confidence."

"Not you. But burned once, twice shy."

"So you *do* think she was betrayed. Which gets back to who she's covering for."

"Maybe her pact is with herself."

"She has nothing to fear from me, Pilar. You know that better than anyone."

Pilar's hands tightened on the wheel. "Do I?"

East of Joes, more cattle and hay. Towns were a gas station or a Knights of Columbus lodge; at Lindon they didn't even tell you to slow down. Russian thistles shorn at the roots somersaulted through the fields, some as big as a full-grown chow or a bale of hay.

"Secrets let you live with yourself," Pilar said. "Why's it so important to confess?"

"Telling your lawyer the truth is hardly a public confession. It's tough to convince a jury if I'm flailing in the dark."

"There's such a thing as knowing too much. You say you want the facts, but do you really?"

"I asked her about that tool—"

"But not the bite marks."

"Rachel knows it's not my job to judge."

"But you couldn't help feeling different about her if you knew what she did."

"I know so damn little now, the truth could only help."

Yucca and prickly pear erupted like pimples west of Last Chance. Cottonwoods and chokecherries marked the draws, and a trio of tumbleweeds pirouetted across the blacktop. Lightning flashed in the distance toward Denver, atmospheric forces colliding as mountain met plain.

"You act like nothing a client says affects you." Pilar's voice was thick. She fingered the silver bullet at her throat.

"Come on."

"How well does any of us know anyone?"

"I know you pretty well."

"What if I shot my husband in the back? What would you think of me then?"

It had happened six months after Jackie joined the PD.

Pilar was one of the secretaries and her husband had been an investigator for the DA's office. Cats and dogs, they joked, until Jackie got the call from the county jail. It was her first solo murder case, her first big acquittal all on her own. Afterward she and Dennis had gone out and—

"Exactly what I think now," she said. "You were a battered wife and Mike came home in a drunken rage. You shot him as he turned to reach for his gun."

She'd seen Pilar's bruises, interviewed the ER docs, reviewed the X-rays. Even the cops at the scene knew Mike's reputation for brutality . . .

"A little tough to load—"

She didn't want to hear any more. "Pilar—"

"—when you're passed out on the bed. I did it to him before he did it to me."

"Did he threaten you?"

"Not that night." Pilar stared through the windshield. "Too drunk when he got home. Said he was going to sleep and I'd better have a steak ready when he woke up. That he'd eat first and then decide whether to bang me or beat me."

Hadn't she suspected as much?

"Know what the scariest part was?" Pilar's mouth twisted. "Not so much what that bastard did. It was the terror—"

"Pilar."

"—when he was sleeping and not knowing what would happen when he woke."

"What did you do with the sheets?" Details. Bury Pilar's pain in the details.

"Stuck 'em in the washing machine. I burned them later."

"Did the cops know?"

"They suggested I caught him 'on the spin.'"

Pilar had always gotten along with the boys in blue. And she'd paid them back every Easter and Christmas with her trays of tamales, her vats of posole—

"Did Dennis know?"

"Not in so many words."

"That's why you've been so hard on Rachel. It's yourself you can't—"

"What would you have done if I'd told you the truth?"

Jackie chose her words carefully.

"Justice recognizes the human breaking point. No less for you than it should have for Rachel."

Not good enough for Pilar.

"You entered my plea of self-defense. Would you have done that if you knew what really happened?"

"Self-defense is a matter of timing."

"Would you have lied for me?"

"If the law doesn't provide for justice, it's my job—"

"Would you lie for me now?"

Jackie had no answer.

"Or for Rachel?"

"Pilar . . ."

"Then get ready to flail in the dark."

Fifty-Four

DIARY OF RACHEL BOYD
DATED DECEMBER 31, 2003

Dear me,

Last step before freedom. I never thought the day would come.

Did you?

I've been to the classes. How to catch a bus, budget my time, dress for an interview. Reintegrate, they call it. Learn to cope. Patience is the key, they say. Don't expect it all to happen right away. Slow down because life outside moves fast. Don't give in to urges. You don't want to end up back inside.

Mind your own business. Keep your nose clean. Be grateful for any rope that's tossed. Expect nothing because you've earned nothing.

Be prepared for doors to slam. Roll with the punches. Never lie in an interview. Tell them you're a felon. They'll ask what was it, how long did you do. When did you get out. If they won't hire you or rent you a room don't get mad. They have rights. You don't.

You are not the person you were. If you're lucky, you will never be that person again. You have learned who she was and have chosen to change. You make that choice yourself. Every morning when you wake up you get to make that choice all over again.

One foot in front of the other. One step at a time. Tell the truth.

Don't be afraid to be scared.

You think everyone's looking at you but they're not. It's not like you have child-killer written on your forehead. No one needs to know unless you tell them.

Unless they ask.

Choose your friends wisely. Stay away from everybody else, including all the people you've known the past thirty years.

There's only one thing I want to do. I can wait however long it takes.

And aren't I the lucky one?

Chris invited me to stay with him till I "get on my feet." Like I'd been on a ship or in a hospital instead of behind bars. How strange it will be to sleep under my little brother's roof. A real family again!

By being weak I made you strong. Damn you.

Fifty-Five

The bell at the Daniels and Fisher Tower struck noon.

"I'll give Chris Boyd one thing," Pilar said. "He sure is a quick pay."

Pilar never let a check go stale or cash grow cold.

"Let's hope he continues to keep his nose out of the defense," Jackie said.

It was the day after they returned from Vivian, and she'd gone with Pilar to deposit the balance of Rachel's retainer. She also wanted to pick up a few pairs of panty hose dark enough to cover the scar on her knee.

"What defense?" Pilar said.

Jackie ignored that. "And that Trina leaves town. Did you reach Simms?"

"No answer at his number. Been trying since last night. Come to think of it, I've never—"

Yaaah!

They were directly across from the tower when they heard the muffled shout.

Skateboarders in the fountain at Skyline Park, Jackie thought. Glancing up, she saw a head lean out a window overlooking the plaza.

"—don't think he gave me a phony number on purpose, do you?"

Aargh!

The hot dog man turned from his customers. A woman rose from a bench.

"What the hell?" someone said.

A third scream and everything froze. Then sound and motion blurred. Shoppers pushing past, heading in the direction of the park. Horns bleated as pedestrians crossed against the light.

A siren wailed.

Pilar grabbed Jackie's arm.

"Let's go!"

A fire truck and an ambulance pulled up at the far end of Skyline Park.

Paramedics unloaded a stretcher as diners on the patio of Denver's most expensive steak house watched. Shouldering their way through brown baggers clustered between the fountain and the tower's base, they set the gurney next to a clutch of dark cloth. Someone had thrown a jacket over its head.

Crimson seeped from the fabric and ran between the paving stones. Splatters had already stained the steps a darker pink. A dank smell, like a decaying rose, issued from the cement. Jackie turned away so she wouldn't gag.

Then she looked again. A leg protruded from the long black skirt.

Like a barb on a twist of wire, it bent back on itself.

And ended in a boot on a dainty foot.

Fifty-Six

S uicide." Pilar dropped the mail on Jackie's desk.

Jackie wasn't so sure, but Pilar's police contacts ran wide and deep.

"How'd Rachel react?" Pilar continued.

"Cool as ever." Yesterday had been chaos. And Jackie's client wasn't just cool. She was unsurprised. "What'd you expect?"

"Oh, I dunno. 'Gee, I'm gonna miss her. Trina sure was a great friend. . . .'"

"Hypocrisy's one thing you can't lay at Rachel's door. What makes them think suicide?"

"Gal made an appointment for noon with a lawyer who has offices in the D & F Tower. The elevator's card-operated, with a phone for visitors. They buzzed her up. She rode past his office to the last floor and took the stairs to the old observation deck. That's where she jumped."

"What name did she give?"

"Tawny Moon. They thought she was a stripper."

Swaying buttocks . . . No reason to suspect Lee Simms. It was Trina's style to use a name like that. Even as a kid, people had felt sorry for her. Rachel was her only friend. "Anybody see her go up?"

"Nope."

"She leave a note?"

"No, but she was clutching something in her hand. They had to pry her fingers open to get it loose."

"Oh?"

"Some cheap piece of plastic. A flaky good luck charm."

Jackie stopped flipping through her mail.

"What'd it look like?"

Pilar shrugged. "Dark blue . . ."

The button from Freddie Gant's pants?

". . . some kind of design on it, but it was worn off."

Block out the fear and sanity in Trina's eyes at that donut shop.

"How do they know it didn't come from an attacker?"

"It was old and cracked. Trina was a magpie, probably had it since she was a kid."

"Well, she certainly went out with a splash." Jackie tried to return to the mail. It was a large stack, some of it having arrived before the Vivian trip. "At least they're not trying to pin it on Rachel. Not that that isn't what Trina intended."

"Come again?"

"You said it yourself, Trina was a flake. Anything for another fifteen seconds of fame."

"But you thought she was scared."

"What she wanted was money. Someone lured her to Denver with the promise that she'd be in the spotlight. When Doby bit, she knew she couldn't deliver. That's when she tried to hit me up for cash to get out of town."

"Who paid her way out here?"

"Lee Simms. Or Chris Boyd."

"Why Chris?"

"Maybe he thought Trina could help his sister. It could be why he hasn't been bugging us about the defense." Jackie shrugged. "My bet is Simms. Trina surfacing before Rachel's trial made it a hotter story."

"Even if she had nothing to say?"

"Just her presence— What's this?"

The manila envelope at the bottom of the stack had Jackie's name on it and nothing else.

"Someone left it this morning."

"Who?"

"It was there when the receptionist arrived."

The envelope was stuffed with signed papers, with a yellow sticky with a smiley face on top. As Jackie passed the papers to Pilar, an object the size of a quarter slipped from the middle of the stack. It was translucent and weightless in her hand. She held it to the light.

"What's that?" Pilar said.

The honeyed glow encased a tiny winged form.

"Is there a note?" Jackie said.

"'I'm sure you'll know what to do with these,'" Pilar read. "'The bee is for the little queen. LS.'"

Jackie tossed the fossilized amber onto her desk.

"The less Lily has to do with Simms, the better. What are those documents?"

Pilar was racing through the stack.

"Two dozen affidavits from potential jurors Doby's expert polled . . . *Jay*-zus!"

"What?"

"Good ol' Stanford Price played it a little too cute at the venue hearing. Forgot to tell Mueller he threw in one more question when he asked if they'd made up their minds. And it's a whopper."

"Will you just—"

"'If both young boys were sexually molested, would that affect your opinion?'"

Doby's expert had invalidated his own poll and tainted the jury pool.

Of the thousand ways to avoid jury service, Denverites knew them all. Since only their bus fare was paid, Jackie could hardly blame them. High-profile trials were the exception; in Rachel Boyd's case, every registered voter would be clamoring to serve. And there was nothing worse for a defendant than twelve eager men.

This was Rachel's ticket out of a trial in Denver. But no gift was free.

"Who collected these affidavits?" Jackie said.

"The final one's from Simms. He swears he personally conducted his own random sampling of the folks Price contacted and that each affidavit was independently witnessed. Not only that—"

"Get Simms on the phone."

"—he also says Doby promised him an exclusive on a certain smoking gun the prosecution intends to produce at trial. Evidence that George Boyd abused Rachel, creating a motive for both crimes. . . ." Pilar's smile faded. "What's wrong?"

"This stinks to high heaven."

"Well, of course it does. No DA can get away with—"

"A hundred bucks says you can't get Simms."

Pilar reached for Jackie's phone and punched in a number.

She waited, then tried again.

"You think he's setting Rachel up?" she said.

Jackie eyed the amber. A bee embalmed in its own honey.

"Simms lied about Freddie. Who knows what else is up his sleeve?"

"What're we gonna do?" Pilar said.

It was payback time.

"Call Mueller's clerk."

Fifty-Seven

Courtroom 16 was packed.

Greta Mueller had wasted no time acting on Jackie's demand to reconsider her motion to change venue. Scanning the gallery as she waited for the judge to take the bench, Jackie spotted a reporter from *USA Today* along with the stringer from Reuters and two sketch artists she'd never seen before. Doby must have tipped them off. Instead of laying his blunder on his subordinates, he evidently planned to brazen this one out.

Mueller wasn't about to make that easy.

"Is there any reason why I shouldn't hold you in contempt?"

Doby affected a perplexed look.

"Why, Your Honor—"

Mueller's cheeks had dime-size splotches of pink.

"Don't try me, Mr. Doby. You misrepresented the contents of your expert's opinion poll to this court."

"He didn't mean—"

"He? I'm speaking in the royal *you*, Mr. Doby. Not only did your expert lie by omission on the stand, he skewed the results of that poll by introducing facts not in evidence."

"What facts?"

She waved the affidavits. "Are you challenging the veracity of these statements?"

"I— No."

"Then what evidence do you have that those boys were molested?"

"It was posed as a hypothetical."

The dimes grew to quarters.

"Hypothetically speaking, how would you like ten days in the poky?"

"It was done for the best—"

"As would jailing you be."

"She cut open their flies and came within an inch of slicing off their little—"

"Must I explain to you the distinction between motivation and act?"

"Come again?"

"Mr. Doby." Mueller's face was now the color of pickled beets. "Those facts might indicate a sexual motivation. They are not, however, evidence that either boy was molested."

"She couldn't molest Freddie Gant because she was twelve years old. That doesn't mean she didn't try—"

"Mr. Doby." The courtroom was silent. With visible effort, Greta Mueller restrained herself. "Unless you are prepared to offer conclusive proof of the latter at trial, your expert has both misstated the true nature of his survey and actually or potentially tainted the pool of jurors available to try this case in Denver. Nor am I—"

Taint. Pool. Denver.

Music to a defense lawyer's ears.

The only problem was Simms. What was in it for him?

"—inclined to give the district attorney's office the benefit of the doubt. And while we're on the subject of your abysmal judgment, do you recall my warning not to try this case in the press?"

Doby's shoulders jerked.

"Yes'm."

"What on earth possessed you to leak to a member of the press your intention to impugn the reputation of a pillar of the Vivian community? A man no longer alive to

defend himself against the scurrilous and totally unsub-
stantiated rumor that he molested his stepdaughter?"

"But that's our evidence of motive!"

Motive. The gaping hole in the prosecution's case. If
the only reason Rachel hadn't molested Freddie was
because as a child she lacked the maturity, why would she
hold back with Ben now that she was an adult? And if
Simms was the one who had tipped Doby to George
Boyd's possibly being a molester, as Jackie suspected, why
would he pull the plug on Doby's plan to expose Boyd
now? Maybe Simms wanted the trial moved so he could
have a total lock on the story.

Mueller allowed herself a rare smile. "You're going to
like Montrose."

Over the rumble in the gallery Jackie heard Pilar
whistle.

"Montrose?" Doby gasped.

"Surely you've been to the Western Slope?" The DA
sagged like a hundred-pound sack of potatoes. "Why, it's
the loveliest part of our state."

You could take the gal out of the country, but not the
country out of the gal.

Within yodeling distance of the Utah border,
Montrose was the quintessential you-can't-get-there-
from-here kind of place, Grand Junction or Salt Lake City
being the somewhere-else-first half of that equation.
Unable to transfer the trial to her native Eastern Plains
for obvious reasons, Greta Mueller had made the next
best choice.

"—courthouse old but perfectly serviceable, and I've
already checked on the availability of space. Chief Judge
Gruder is a dear friend who'd be delighted to host us. And
parking won't be a problem."

"But I have witnesses, evidence, an entire staff—"

"Of course you do! If I recall correctly, Montrose's *gem* of an airport has commuter flights, so your entourage won't even have to drive eight hours over those mountain passes." She cut Doby off with a wag of her finger. "The Montrose County DA may be a Democrat, but like all your brethren he's a true professional. I'm sure he'll do nothing to interfere with your case. If you're polite he might even give you tips about a country jury. They tend to distrust city folk, you know. Especially politicians."

"But logistics alone will take months to organize!"

"Ten days is more than adequate."

"Your Honor, *please.*"

"Why, postponing the trial would allow you to profit from your own misdeed. You don't hear Ms. Flowers asking for a continuance, now do you?"

Nor would she.

Having moved for the change of venue, Jackie was trapped. And regardless of Simms's motive in procuring the affidavits, transferring the case caused Doby more pain than it did her. His protests were increasingly feeble.

"But—"

"Mr. Doby, you've given me no choice. This case has had more than its share of pretrial coverage and we can't risk prejudicial publicity during the main event." Mueller shook her head in a show of regret. "I might have considered Grand Junction, but it has local stations with national affiliates. Not to mention a much bigger airport with commercial flights. You'll be better off with country folk. They don't pay attention to TV and newspapers. They're too busy earning a living."

"Your Honor—"

Greta Mueller reached for her gavel.

"Best of all, I'm going with you."

Fifty-Eight

J ackie handed Pilar an armload of files.

"They'll never fit in the Spider," Pilar said. Lily sat on the floor next to her, assembling cartons. "With two passengers it's already a tight squeeze."

"Can't I go with you?" Lily begged.

It was the Thursday before trial. Jackie and Rachel were supposed to leave with Pilar the next morning, arrive late Friday and have the weekend to settle in Montrose before jury selection began on Monday.

"Your parents wouldn't go for that," Jackie said.

"They don't have to know. They're at that conference in Durango."

Britt, who owned a real estate brokerage, was bidding on a piece of the action on resort condos in the southwest corner of the state. Randy made his deals on the links, but they'd be spending most of the weekend networking with developers on a raft in the white waters of the Dolores River. They would have taken Lily with them if not for her Friday appointment with the shrink.

"What about Dr. Embry?" Jackie said.

"He smells bad." Lily reached for another carton. "Not like Dennis."

Pilar looked at her with new interest.

"How do you know how he smells, pet?"

Lily gave a one-shouldered shrug. "Just an impression."

"I thought you couldn't stand Dennis," Jackie said.

"I didn't say I could *stand* him. But he obviously has a certain appeal . . . And Embryo couldn't care less if I cancel. He gets paid either way."

"Your parents care. Embry's the best in town."

"Well, if he has a magic wanger he hasn't twanged it at me yet."

"And you're supposed to be staying with Mrs. Gordon." The widow at the end of the block. "Isn't her granddaughter visiting?"

"She plays with dolls!"

Jackie tried not to laugh.

"Honey, it's nothing but a long, boring car ride. And you heard Pilar. There's barely enough room in the Spider for Rachel and us. Besides, what would you do once we got to Montrose?"

"Watch the trial and hang out with Pilar." Hearing no opposition from her henchman, Lily plunged ahead. "How will I know if I want to be a lawyer if I never see you in action?"

"Two weeks is out of the ques—"

"Then send me home Monday. If Montrose has an airport I can fly."

Shaking her head sympathetically, Pilar left to fetch more boxes.

"Lily, look. Even if there was room in the car, Britt and Randy would never go for it. And we can't even reach them to ask. When they're not rafting they'll be touring development sites."

The intercom buzzed and Pilar sang out. "The aromatic one for Jackie on line two . . ."

Locating her phone behind a stack of police reports, Jackie picked up.

"Have you heard?" Dennis said.

"What?"

"Autopsy—" He was on his cell phone and she could barely hear. "—Maune."

"What?"

"Only—minute." Dennis completely cut out. When he came on again the reception was clearer. "I'm at the City and County Building. Court's in recess, I've only got a minute. A deputy told me this on the QT. There's an APB out on Simms."

Jackie turned from Lily's curious eyes. "Why?"

"They think he killed Trina."

"What?"

"The coroner found deep bruises on her wrists. They reinterviewed the girl at the lawyer's office where Trina made the appointment, and now she thinks it could've been a man who set it up and not a woman. All she really remembered was 'Tawny Moon.'"

There had to be more.

"Why Simms?" Jackie said.

"Cops went to Trina's motel. Manager said a guy visited and she heard shouting. Trina told her she was afraid—"

She'd known all along who Rachel's abuser was.

"—picked him out of a photo array."

"But why—" Drawn by the urgency in Jackie's voice, Lily had edged closer.

There was a burst of static.

What if Simms's target thirty years ago wasn't the boy's mother, but Freddie Gant? Maybe Debbie Gant was a way to get close to her son. And if Simms liked little boys, why stop with one?

Lee Simms was more than a sweet talker: Lily was a tough sell and look how quickly he'd penetrated her defenses. Thirty years ago Trina Maune had been malleable enough to be intimidated, but Rachel was another story. To protect himself, Simms had railroaded her in the press, and to save Chris from his grasp Rachel had gone along. Prison—*at least I was safe*, Rachel said. Now Jackie understood why.

Once Rachel was released it would have been easy to set her up again. It also explained why Simms didn't react when Doby announced in court that Freddie's button had been cut off—and why he hadn't thought it necessary to bring that fact to Jackie's attention when he delivered his tutorial on knives. When Chris vowed to defend Rachel, Simms had wormed his way in, eliminated Trina, ensured the trial would be moved to the most isolated—

"The bailiff just—" The rest of what Dennis said was unintelligible.

"Dennis, wait." Jackie stared at Lily. Simms had made a play for her once. Was he desperate enough to set Rachel up a third time? "Can you take Lily this weekend?"

"Lily?"

"She likes you."

"Right. But—"

"Her parents are out of town till Monday." With Lily there, she couldn't say more. And she certainly couldn't leave her in the hands of a seventy-year-old grandmother.

"Darling, I'm in the middle of a two-day hearing. I have a major trial starting next week and I'm stacked up all weekend. Have to meet with the client, witnesses—"

"What should I do?"

"Take her with you."

"There's no room in the Spider."

"Chris has that SUV. I'll ask him to drive."

"I thought you didn't want him near the trial."

"And he's been a basket case because of it. This'll give him something constructive to do. Put Lily on a plane home Sunday night, and I'll pick her up at the airport and deliver her to her folks Monday morning. I assume she eats pizza."

"But I can't even reach Randy or Britt—"

"Believe me, they'll thank you. And if they raise a fuss, I'm very persuasive with authority figures. . . . Gotta run. Call me every night, okay?"

Fifty-Nine

Denver's skyline shrank in Chris Boyd's rearview mirror. Jackie settled back in the passenger seat of the Mercedes SUV and tried to relax.

Out of the corner of her eye she watched for a yellow Corvette.

They'd be in Montrose before dark. She'd called Mrs. Gordon and told her she'd be taking Lily for the weekend, and Lily and Rachel were buckled in safely behind her. Chris kept his eyes straight ahead and stayed within a mile of the speed limit. The Spider accelerated and Pilar waved as she passed on the left. The Mercedes was so smooth it felt as if they were standing still.

To the east the new football stadium tilted and swooped like a roller coaster at Elitch's. Rachel and Lily were glued to the windows. Rachel had never been to the mountains, and Lily's only experience was on a bus of would-be ballerinas the previous summer bound for camp in Steamboat Springs.

Who would ride with whom had been unexpectedly painless.

Lily wanted to go in the Spider, but changed her mind when Rachel wouldn't fit. Jackie had promised Britt two adult chaperones and the Spider was too small to comfortably seat four. That's what she'd told Lily; her real reason for vetoing the Spider was that a sports car loaded with women was a sitting target. Chris's SUV, on the other hand, was as sleek as a missile and as solid as a tank. Pilar's acquiescence to Lily's riding with Rachel had been the surprise.

"That Nye broad was right," she told Jackie. "You can never see into another person's heart. I've been too hard on Rachel."

The sheer capacity of Chris's SUV silenced any further objections. It was more than large enough to haul them, their bags and the case files Pilar was unable to fit in her trunk. They set out in a caravan of two, with Pilar promising to remain in visual contact at all times.

"If you see any sign of Simms or his Corvette—" Jackie said.

"He'll rue the day."

Then they were off.

On the approach to the Continental Divide the highway cut through stone, scarring the mountainside pink. Houses sprouted from granite high above the roadbed. Rock glistened with hidden springs; one good rain would trigger a landslide. Pickups bounced past the SUV, eating the Spider's dust.

No sign of a Corvette.

What was that game her aunt had played to pass the time, on that car trip to California when Jackie was nine? "A Hundred Bottles of Beer on the Wall" had grown stale and they'd sung every folk song they knew. Not name-the-state-by-the-license-plate—the letters fled too quickly for Jackie to grasp.

Colors. The first to spot five yellow Corvettes—

"So," Chris said, "how do you feel about the defense?"

"Stronger and stronger."

Barring a last-minute disaster.

Jackie had two choices: sit back and lob grenades at the prosecution's case, or present a theory of her own. With no proof that Rachel had been framed, they were lucky Doby's case had so many holes.

Doby would claim Ben's murder was a carbon copy of

Freddie Gant's, inviting Jackie to stake her defense on the inconsistencies. But the prosecution's real weakness was the similarities. Maybe a twelve-year-old girl lacked the maturity to molest a four-year-old boy, but what prevented a forty-two-year-old woman from doing so? And if the same impulse drove the same person to kill both boys, wouldn't her methods change in three decades? But relying on Doby to stumble carried its own risks. As a child, Rachel had been convicted of murdering Freddie, and Jackie couldn't discount the primeval fears that case still evoked.

"—seems awfully confident," Chris said. "Is that unusual for a prosecutor?"

"Doby? I've got a few surprises up my sleeve."

"Such as?"

"A forensic botanist to blow his autopsy report out of the water. Flavia Hart has some interesting opinions about the insulating effect of snow. Not to mention the physical impossibility of a hundred-pound woman lugging forty pounds up a forty-five-degree slope before flinging it six feet in the air. But I'll save that for when I cross-examine Doby's honchos."

"Who do you think did it?"

Jackie couldn't answer, not with Lily in the backseat.

But the bite on Freddie's cheek clinched it.

Freddie's father was a truck driver. Weren't they away from home for days and weeks at a time? Simms's affair with the boy's mother gave him an excuse to hang around. With Art Gant out of the picture, he'd probably acted like an uncle. It wasn't such a stretch to call him Freddie's caretaker. His mistake had been involving Rachel. His leverage with her had been his threat to hurt her little brother.

How hard would it have been for Simms to pocket that

cast-iron hook on Pioneer Day? He'd covered the dedication of the Vivian Elementary annex for the *Seward County Call.* If he needed a fall guy, who better than George Boyd? All he had to do was use George's tool to molest Freddie.

The hook had broken when Freddie plunged from the catwalk. Simms went back for it later and turned over the body. That was his second mistake. His third was thinking he had to use the same tool on Ben. If Jackie hadn't seen him beating the bramble for it . . . She glanced in the rearview mirror.

Yellow car gaining . . . Not a Corvette. Back to zero.

"How do you rate your chances?" Chris said.

"I never bet against a client. Or myself."

"Dennis says you're a tiger on cross. But there must be more—"

"I'm bored," Lily said.

Chris's hands tensed on the wheel.

"With scenery like this?" Jackie said.

Pinnacles jutted over the roadway, frozen in cosmic upheaval. Desecrating eons of geologic splendor, steel netting had been slung across a two-hundred-foot outcrop to prevent massive boulders from hurtling at their heads. Jackie saw a red slick and a smear of fur on the asphalt. She switched Chris's CD player on to distract Lily. A raunchy tune about picking up a woman in a bar filled the air.

> *Rhythm and rouge?*
> *What a smooth combination . . .*

"What's a kiss-me pump?" Lily said.

Jackie glanced at Chris. Barry Manilow or Burt Bacharach—she'd expected something low-key, respectable. But Jerry Jeff Walker?

Eyes still on the road, he reached for the power button.

"Don't turn it off!" Lily said.

"Garth Brooks too tame for you?" Jackie asked.

Chris smiled sheepishly. "Oil and gas clients are the worst. You wouldn't believe some of the guys who've been in this car."

Vegas. It wasn't just Jerry Jeff who liked his women a tad on the trashy side.

Jackie flicked off the player and fished in Chris's glove compartment for another CD. *My Fair Lady,* an unopened selection of arias, more country with an edge . . .

"You'll love this one," she told Lily.

The Mercedes entered the Eisenhower Tunnel. As they bored through the Continental Divide under millions of tons of granite, the music began to play.

> *Well let me tell you of the story*
> *of a man named Char-lie*
> *On a tragic and fateful day . . .*

"What's that?" Lily said.

"The Kingston Trio," Rachel said.

Jackie hadn't heard them since college. Even then, they were a little dated. This song was about a guy who boarded a commuter train in Boston and was never allowed off.

"They were big when I was a kid," Rachel continued. "Remember those car trips, Chris? George played that tape so often it drove us nuts."

The tune played endlessly, echoing poor Charlie's plight.

"What happened?" Lily said.

"To ol' Charlie?" Chris yawned and flexed his fingers. "They raised the fare while he was on board. He couldn't afford the increase, so they wouldn't let him off."

"But he had ten cents!"

"I guess freedom cost too much. What it's really about is being at the mercy of an all-powerful machine. In this case, politics."

"You sure you work for a bank?" Jackie said.

"Under every pin-striped suit—" he began.

"—lurks a pair of FDIC-insured BVDs," Rachel finished.

Chris wasn't the only one who was unbending. In the few short months Jackie had known her, Rachel had transformed from a self-effacing creature into a woman unafraid to poke fun at her overbearing brother. Maybe she could hold her own on the stand.

They picked up speed coming out of the tunnel and Jackie spotted the comforting wink of Pilar's taillights. The SUV slowly dropped into a valley—not like being in the mountains at all. She leaned back in her seat. Two yellow cars so far but no Corvettes. Should she change the rules and award herself half a point for each?

At Gypsum the cliffs turned to chalk and the trees became scrub. Without warning, the SUV descended into a gorge and the rock went from gray to brown to a rich sedimentary red. Clouds stained the canyon walls, making them dark and cold. Stone cathedrals hundreds of feet tall abutted the roadbed, and as the gorge narrowed one side of the highway folded under the other. Plunging yet another geologic period, the massive slabs reverted to a dull gray. The road grew even narrower. As asphalt hugged rock, Jackie's stomach lurched.

"Are we stopping soon?"

"Glenwood Springs," Chris said. "I told Pilar we'd catch up with her for gas. You okay?"

"Just a tad on the queasy side."

The mountains always did that to her. The only thing

worse than being on the bottom looking up was the reverse.

"Want to pull over?" As if there were room for that.

"No, no. I'm fine."

"We'll be there soon."

Pilar was waiting for them at the Conoco in Glenwood.

"What took you so long?"

"The speed limit," Jackie said. "It's refreshing to drive with someone who respects it."

"Is McClure open?" Chris asked the gas jockey. The pass over the mountains going south to Montrose.

Jackie scanned the road. One car, two car. Red car, blue car . . .

"Sometimes it is, sometimes it ain't. Last I heard they were blasting up there. Where you headed?"

"Montrose."

"You'd be smarter going west to Grand Junction, then double back south. Thirty, forty miles out of your way, but even if McClure was open you'd only lose a half hour." He glanced at the women. "Wouldn't want to be stuck in a car, waiting three or four hours in this heat. Play it safe."

Sixty

West of Glenwood Springs the landscape exploded with color.

The mountains were maroon, coral and rust. War paint, mascara—rouge. The valley opened onto a fertile plain, sage green with a chartreuse scrim highlighting the contours of the hills. Rachel and Lily had fortified themselves with pop, and Chris turned the music back on.

Was there a bounty on yellow cars? Jackie hadn't seen one since the Eisenhower Tunnel. Or a Corvette. Of course, if *she* were Simms—

"You must have something up your sleeve besides physics and snow," Chris said.

"It's not what the defense has. It's what Doby lacks."

"Which is?"

"Motive." Mindful of Lily, she kept it abstract. "A motive that made sense in the case of a kid is simply not credible for a forty-two-year-old."

"But I thought—"

"Doby doesn't have to prove motive. But no jury will convict if he doesn't."

"You still have an uphill battle. Isn't there any other suspect?"

Dennis said molesters marked their territory, that victims remembered the pain.

If Simms had persuaded Rachel to lure Freddie because she wanted to save her brother, Chris's hostility toward the reporter was even more understandable. And Jackie was all the more grateful he was at the wheel. "We'll see." She turned up the volume.

Hang down your head, Tom Dooley . . .

Lily listened, entranced.

"He sure loved that song," Rachel said.

"Who?"

"My stepdad. George." Rachel was watching Chris in the rearview mirror. The song was about a man who killed his lover. It had a haunting refrain.

> *Hang down your head, Tom Dooley . . .*
> *Poor boy, you're bound to die.*

"Who's Tom Dooley?" Lily said.

"An innocent man," Chris said.

"But he stabbed her with his knife. He said so himself!"

"Just because someone says they did something doesn't necessarily mean it's true. Right, Shelly?" His eyes flickered uncertainly as they met Rachel's. Was he responding to his sister's newfound assertiveness?

"But why confess to something you didn't do?" Lily said.

Chris smiled and Jackie marveled at his patience. Lily was playing the Kingston Trio for the third time, and she was starting to feel like Charlie stuck on that train.

"Maybe a friend got him to do it. Like on a dare." Chris was looking at Lily now. "You ever do things on a dare, Lily?"

"I'm not scared of anything."

"Really? Everybody has things that go bump in the night. Even me."

"Oh, yeah?" Rachel said. "What're you afraid of?"

"Like any kid brother"—Chris laughed—"my big sister."

Hang down your head, Tom Dooley . . .

The next verse had Tom lamenting the fact that because he was caught by someone named Grayson, he couldn't escape to Tennessee.

"Who's Grayson?" Lily said.

"Beats me," Rachel said. "But this sure brings it all back. Doesn't it, Chris?"

He was concentrating on the road.

"I think Tom killed her," Lily said.

"Not killed," Chris said. "Sacrificed."

"Why?" Lily was more confused than ever.

"To save her from Grayson. He was going to ruin her."

Jackie had always found "Tom Dooley" hopelessly enigmatic. And wasn't Grayson the sheriff? But Chris's interpretation captivated Lily.

"Who *was* Grayson?" she asked.

"The devil. That's why he hangs Tom with his rope."

"What's so special about Tennessee?"

"Could've been anywhere, Lily. But Tennessee has mountains like Colorado." He flicked off the CD. "Tom could have lived there in peace. Instead he got dragged back against his will."

"Spoken like a true defense lawyer!" Jackie said.

Chris grinned.

"Shelly's a thousand times better off in your hands than mine."

At Palisade the mountain was sliding onto the road. Channels marked where rivulets had flowed, the rock was gray and sodden as a hippopotamus hide, and boulders stopped midway down the slope. Jackie had to pee. She closed her eyes and when she opened them again, lush orchards had replaced the mountains. Fruit stands dotted the roadside. Cherries, peaches, tomatoes, corn . . . No yellow cars at all. A pickup that had tailed them since Glenwood pulled up to the passenger side.

If Simms were on the lam, would he drive a yellow Corvette?

Jackie stared hard at the driver. He gave her a lazy salute and kept going.

They passed another orchard. The trees were as small and shapely as dancers, with branches flung out in ecstasy or supplication. They reminded Jackie of the gate to Elitch's. She had to call Dennis tonight. Would he be home by the time they got to the motel?

"How far to Montrose?" she said.

"Not long now."

They'd left the mountains, and the clouds on the horizon were as flat and dark-topped as the mesa.

"Where's Pilar?" Lily said.

"Passed us twenty minutes ago." Bracing his hands against the wheel, Chris stretched. Jackie knew people who claimed to enjoy driving, but he actually seemed to be energized by it. "With the time she's making, it's a good thing we agreed on a motel."

Delta brought the first grain elevator, and with it three small bins that huddled together like schoolgirls. Rain pelted the windshield. It was Lily who spotted the sign for Montrose.

"'Home of the Black Canyon,'" she read. "Can we go?"

"Not today, honey," Jackie said. The pickup was long gone. In its place was a red Camaro. "Chris is tired."

"But when will I be here again?"

"At some point in your lifetime—"

"I think it's a good idea," Chris cut in. "What is it? Five, ten miles? Lily may return, but who knows when Shelly will get the chance?"

That lingered in the air.

"What about Pilar?" Jackie said.

"So we'll be a half hour later. She knows where we're staying."

In the distance lay more mountains. Clouds rose from their peaks like wisps of smoke.

"But it's raining . . ."

Just then it stopped.

"Fate." Chris winked at Lily. "Like ol' Charlie on that train."

Sixty-One

The SUV climbed from the valley on a winding two-lane blacktop. The grade grew steeper. When a sign warned of a double hairpin, Jackie flicked the button on her door to make sure it was locked. The mesa was forested with juniper and piñon pine and cows grazed in tall grass. They couldn't be very high; wouldn't the milk curdle? Patches of burnt trees stood on a rise to the left. The earth underneath was pink and shiny as a newborn's gums.

Just before the guard shack a sign warned visitors to unload firearms.

"Why?" Lily said.

"We're on federal land," Chris said.

As they stopped to pay the entrance fee, cars streamed down the opposite side of the road. Lightning split the sky straight ahead.

The ranger seemed distracted. When Chris opened his billfold, he held up his hand to wait.

"Maybe the park's closed," Jackie whispered.

"Sorry about that, folks." The ranger turned down his radio and exchanged their money for a tourist brochure. "Fire on the north rim. Reports of smoke just coming in. Prob'ly a lightning strike."

"It doesn't sound like a good idea—" Jackie said.

"This road leads to the south rim, miss. Just follow the rules and you'll be fine."

The first lookout point was the visitors' center. Jackie jumped from the SUV and ran to the log-sided facilities. The john had a normal seat, and when she peered in, she thought she saw water. But like a puddle shimmering on hot asphalt, it was a mirage.

Blackness yawned.

A crazy giggle rose in her throat. She clasped her hands together to keep her fingers from twisting. With all her might, Jackie fought the urge to toss her mother's sapphire ring into that bottomless pit.

She hurried back to join the others.

"We have to turn around. It's almost four, Pilar will be worrying."

"But we just got here!" Lily dragged her to the fenced platform jutting over the canyon. "Jackie, look!"

The silence was breathtaking, but the sight brought Jackie physically to her knees. Despite her existential experience with the toilet, there had been no real warning the earth was about to crack open a half mile under her feet.

Fly, Jackie, fly!

"I'm getting out of here."

Chris put his arm around Jackie's shoulders.

"Shelly told me how you feel about heights," he said in her ear. What else had Rachel said about her? But just as quickly her irritation disappeared. His embrace was firm but gentle, his sheer solidity comforting. And for once in her life she didn't have to pretend. "You've really got it bad. I'll get you to the car. . . ."

They drove on to Pulpit Rock.

"Can we stop?" Lily said.

The rest area had cold pop and souvenirs, but Chris said it was too crowded. He studied the map from the visitors' center.

"Not far to Chasm View." He looked at his watch. "Last tour starts at four."

"Always gotta go that extra mile. Don't you, Chris?"

There was an edge to Rachel's voice. Was she creeped out by the climb, too?

Chris shrugged.

"No sense being in the game unless you play to win."

A handful of tourists in T-shirts and shorts were waiting at the trailhead. Jackie rolled down her window. A pair of swifts swooped in the brush and rain perfumed the air. Lily and Rachel went on ahead.

Jackie didn't want to go.

"The trick is not to look down," Chris said. "Just take the tour and listen."

He helped her from the SUV and took her hand.

Prickly pear and tiny daisies flanked the gravel path. Those gave way to gnarled piñon pines, Gambel oak and serviceberry bushes with clusters of bright red fruit. They joined the tour halfway through the ranger's spiel.

"—steepest, deepest, narrowest canyon in the world." The ranger was a young blonde in forest green trousers and clodhopper boots. World War II navy surplus binoculars hung from her neck and a water bottle was cradled in the webbing of her backpack. "Forty feet wide at the narrowest point at the bottom. Its depth is twenty-four hundred feet. Carved by the Gunnison River—"

Jackie hung back, enveloped by the heady aroma of wild sage. She plucked the fuzzy tendril of a mountain mahogany pod. In one direction the plume was feather soft. The other had teeth to clutch the earth and ensure its seeds took root.

Teeth. Our most primitive weapon.

"—Black Canyon because of the color of the rock. Originating below sea level and formed by tectonic pressure and heat, this basement rock is the oldest exposed rock on the planet. Sixty million years ago a big block of it pushed up, forming an anthill called the Gunnison Uplift—"

The others clustered around the ranger at the threshold to the observation point. Jackie stayed at the rear. The fence had three flat foot-wide rails with enough space for an adult to slip through. It wasn't meant to contain, but to mark the edge. Across the canyon the wall was pink and marbled like fat in a slab of raw meat. She heard a rushing sound, like crows circling overhead.

"—San Juans erupted and spewed lava over the harder rock. The Gunnison River cut through the ash and volcanic debris, and became trapped by the basement rock. It's been trying to escape ever since." The ranger smiled at Lily. "Which do you think is stronger, water or rock?"

So much for scissors, paper . . . Before she realized what she was doing, Jackie reached for her sunglasses and yanked them from her face.

Fly, Jackie, fly!

The white noise was grabbing her and pulling her in.

"Rock."

"Wrong. Water always wins. The river's still carving that canyon at the rate of one human hair per year."

Jackie stopped herself from flinging her glasses over the rail just in time.

She reached for a boulder to still the pounding in her ears. Orange lichen crumbled under her fingertips, giving way to chartreuse scales, furry patches of green and a gray moss that looked like mold.

"—sure to see the Painted Wall. Steepest cliff in the United States. If you put the Empire State Building at the bottom, it'd reach only halfway to the top." A light rain had begun to fall, and Jackie's fellow tourists were wandering back to their cars. The tour was at an end. "Best view's just ahead at Dragon Point."

Jackie sagged against the rock, this time with relief.

"Want to go there, Lily?" Chris said. "It's awfully late."

Lily looked up at Jackie with enormous eyes.

"Jackie, *please* . . ."

She'd been to the edge of the earth. But she'd survived, hadn't she? She could never say no to Lily. And this time she would wait in the car.

"Okay."

Mountain mahogany and Gambel oak hid the sign for Dragon Point. The only warning that they'd arrived was a slight widening of the road, a few parking stripes and a bicycle rack. None of the tourists from Chasm View had followed them and Jackie hadn't even seen the red Camaro since Montrose.

Chris pulled to the gravel at the trailhead and Lily jumped from the car.

"Coming?" she said.

"I think I'll stay here."

The three of them tripped down the path.

Leaning back in her seat, Jackie took one deep breath and then another. Chris was right; the trick was not to look down. From the safety of his SUV she felt more than a little foolish. How Pilar would hoot when she told her she'd almost tossed her mother's star sapphire down the john! And that crazy bit with her sunglasses . . .

She peered down the path. The three of them had disappeared. Any minute now they'd be back. The scent of sage enticed her and she opened the door and dangled her feet over the side of the SUV. A breeze tickled her legs, raising goose bumps and making the scar in her knee itch. Tall grass, sage. No sound but a distant rushing wind.

And not even a red Camaro on the road. Come to think of it, if she were Simms she'd be in California by now. Not this godforsaken place. If they had an APB out for him, they'd catch him soon enough. And nail him not just for Trina's murder, but Ben's too. The bite marks had to be the key.

But why Ben, why *now*?

Rachel getting out of prison must have been the catalyst. But after thirty years of silence, did Simms really think she'd incriminate him?

Sexual predators never changed. Simms had gotten away with it once. With Rachel out of the can, maybe he felt it was safe to attack another little boy. . . .

Those bite marks on Freddie's cheek and Ben's thigh.

Not suck marks, as in a sexual assault. Those biters savored their act. They wanted to prolong it. These bites were rapid and random, with poor detail.

Child abuse. The biter wanted to inflict punishment. Rage.

Why Ben?

Simms was Freddie's caretaker. He hadn't known Ben at all.

Kids acted out the abuse they suffered. . . . But finding the killer was Doby's problem. Not hers. She had to meet with Pilar tonight and talk about jury selection. And call Dennis. If the others didn't get back soon . . .

Jackie strained her ears. Still she heard nothing.

She stared at the clock on Chris's dashboard. The minutes were very long and the breeze was getting cooler. Jumping down, she circled the SUV and popped open the rear lid. She searched the luggage compartment for her sweater. It had slipped from a carton to the floor by the wheel well. She shook it out.

Fine dirt fell from one of the sleeves. It emitted a woodsy scent. Earthy, rich—

Compost.

The dirt in Ben's cuffs?

Lily.

Sixty-Two

Time and space compressed.

Jackie started to run.

The rushing had returned, accented by the *chip-chip-cheep* of swifts. Wings tucked, they swooped like bullets in the foliage. Serviceberries were apple green, ripe scarlet and a wizened black all on the same branch, as if their life cycle had condensed to a single instant. Ahead lay mountain mahogany and juniper, in the distance the broad mesa of the canyon's opposite rim. The path was wide and Jackie stuck to the center.

A slight rise in the grade and she could no longer see the trailhead. That meant she was now invisible from the road. The trail turned from gravel to pink crystal capstone. The wind was cold and the hairs at the nape of her neck rose. Beset by invisible gnats, she started to itch all over and her knee began to throb.

An ancient piñon threw up its arms and the trees seemed to writhe.

Leaning against the pine, Jackie closed her eyes and stroked the silver shaft. Its texture was satin and suede.

Rhythm and rouge? What a smooth . . .

She took a deep breath and focused on the scent of the wood.

You are in a room filled with furniture and people. Your destination is Lily.

Knees steadied, she continued down the path. As it

descended she caught a glimpse of the massive rampart across the gorge.

Pink granite and quartz ribbed the coarse-grained gneiss on the opposite side of the gorge, forming a tableau with the raw power of a cave painting. A panther with a dragon's head leaped across the sheer rock wall.

Over the hollow rumble Jackie heard voices.

"You wanna see it, don't you?"

Logs had been set into the trail to prevent it from washing out. Forming crude steps flanked by tall boulders on one side, they led to a semicircle eight feet wide and six feet deep. Rachel and Chris stood inside that clearing. At its outer edge smaller rocks formed a foot-high barrier. Beyond the rocks an outcrop jutted. Below the ledge the Gunnison River raged.

That ledge where Lily crouched.

"One more step . . ."

Standing on the third log and gripping a boulder with both hands, Jackie looked.

Rapids roiled over the rocks. Jade green and black, the river was moving so fast it appeared frozen. Trapped in a canyon of its own making, so deep that sunlight could never reach it, the Gunnison was an angry god.

She willed her eyes up.

The ledge jutted four feet out and was two feet wide. With her weight on her heels and her palms bracing against the stone, Lily was balanced at the end closest to the barrier. Rachel stood on the other side, Chris two feet away. He was reaching for Lily. Was he trying to save her from Rachel?

Kids acted out the abuse they suffered—at the hands of their own caretakers.

The weaker and the strong. But who was which?

Was it one of them, or *both*?

"What are you, scared?"

Chris's voice. Was that solicitude?

The rumbling in Jackie's ears became a roar. Lily was too far away for her to reach. Cry out and the girl would fall.

"Not gonna stop now, are you?"

Jackie heard derision.

She also heard luring and enticement, a reenactment of the taunting that had produced such helplessness and rage. Thirty years of rage, trapped like the river in an abyss of Chris Boyd's own making. And she heard fear. That the real truth behind Freddie Gant's death would come out? The monster hadn't lived in a shack, but in the finest house in Vivian. If Chris unbuttoned his shirt, would Jackie see claw marks like the ones on Freddie and Ben? And that scar on his lip—was it a bite mark like the one on Rachel's forehead? Those scavenging trips Rachel hid from, the folk music Chris kept to replay his childhood impotence. George Boyd's victim hadn't only been his stepdaughter. . . .

"What'd I tell you, Shelly?" Chris said. "She's a fraidy-cat. Too scared to go all the way."

Whether Rachel was in it with him or not, Chris had nothing to lose. If he was trying to incriminate his sister and Lily fell, he could say Rachel pushed her, his steadfast belief in his sister's innocence yielding at long last to the painful truth he now witnessed with his own eyes. Who would contradict him? Jackie was supposed to be cowering in the SUV. If she came upon the scene it would either be too late or he'd say it had all been a game. Rachel was the only one close enough to grab Lily. But would she?

Lily slowly rose.

"That's a good girl. One more step . . ."

Lily spread her arms as if she were about to dive.

Fly, Lily, fly!

Jackie pushed away from the rock and descended the final steps. The wind and roar of the river were so loud no one heard her, so intent were they on the drama on that ledge. Afraid to move closer lest she startle Lily, she stopped at the edge of the clearing.

She was about to gamble with Lily's life. Could she trust Rachel?

Could her client be redeemed?

In a clear voice she spoke.

"It's not too late, Rachel. You're not that little girl anymore."

Rachel stiffened but Chris was the one who turned.

"It's just Jackie. She won't come any closer. Look how scared she is."

Buck, buck, bu-uck.

Jackie took a step forward.

"Back then you had no choice," she said. "Now you do. Without you, he's nothing."

Chris edged closer to where Lily stood, whittling that six-foot gap to four. Rachel stood motionless, her back to them both. Chris's face twisted with contempt.

"Don't listen, Shelly. It's always been us. You and me. We've always been there for each other, haven't we?"

Jackie took another step toward the ledge. Lily had clamped her hands over her ears and squinted her eyes shut. She began to sway.

"You don't need him, Rachel."

"Doesn't need me?" Chris said. "I saved you from George, didn't I? He took me that day instead. It wasn't till later, when we got back—"

Rachel spoke for the first time.

"Don't talk, Chris. Not another word. We'll get through this like before."

She had to know he killed Freddie, she'd been at the

grain elevator with him. Did her lifelong loyalty make her powerless to defend herself, was she prepared to take the fall for him again? Or had they always been in it together? Jackie took a third step. Could she reach Lily? But Rachel was in the way and Chris was almost within arm's reach of the girl.

"What happened later, after you got back?" she said. "Did your stepfather make you get Freddie?"

Chris laughed. "George had me. He didn't need Freddie."

"But you did, didn't you, Chris? To show George you weren't his 'boy.'"

"That's why I set his collie free." He was talking to Rachel. "Used that damn clincher of his, didn't I? Trina was there—"

She'd found the button, must have known it was sliced off. If Trina saw Chris cut that dog's leash, maybe she'd put two and two together and come up with four for once in her life. And it got her killed. Chris was edging closer to Lily, but his entire focus was on his sister.

". . . furious at us, don't you remember? That's why he was looking for you that morning. He knew one of us stole that clincher and he wanted it back. Said if it wasn't returned, there'd be hell to pay and he'd start with you. I made him take me instead. When we got home I went looking for you."

"Chris—"

"I tried to warn you, but Freddie kept following us. He wanted to be a big boy, but he was such a weakling, such a sniveling little pest—"

So small and defenseless. And Chris had been so angry, so filled with hatred. For himself most of all. If Freddie resisted as Chris had been unable to resist with George, it must have enraged Chris all the more.

"—wouldn't pull them down, so I did what George did. Told him I'd cut it off—"

He must have gone back the next day for the clincher, but it was broken and he couldn't return it. Rachel had stepped closer to Lily. Jackie had to break the spell.

"George is dead. You didn't have to prove anything to him when you used that clincher again to cut Ben," she said. "Why another boy, why now?"

"Chris, don't—"

He was too far gone to heed his sister's warning.

"Why now? Because Shelly and I were finally together again, like we used to be. I had to remind her of all that binds us."

Chris Boyd no longer had to rely on a barbing hook; he was a businessman. His power was persuasion, his tools were his ability to identify opportunities and seize the moment. He'd arrived home twenty minutes before Harry Sparks, who'd stayed behind at the bank to finish fixing the sprinkler. What had he lured Ben with while Rachel napped, Nintendo? He kept the boy's body in the SUV until the snow began to fall the next day. The only thing he overlooked was that compost. . . .

"Remind her?" Jackie turned to Rachel. "You hear that? Chris doesn't care about you. You're nothing but a threat to him. He didn't kill Ben because he wanted it to be like old times: once you got out of prison, he was afraid you'd squeal. Each time you stood up to him you were a threat to his control. The stronger your defense became, the more desperate he felt."

"Desperate? Shelly, *she's* the one—"

"Now he's gone after Lily to make sure you'll never get out. But it's over, Rachel. You paid him for protecting you from George by taking the blame thirty years ago. Don't give up everything again."

"Don't listen to her, Shelly. I evened the score with George after they sent you away." So it wasn't an accident on that country road after all. "I *love* you."

Could Jackie push Chris aside and reach Lily? But Rachel was standing directly between them. She had one last chance.

"You know what love is, Rachel: look at Lily. It's devotion, not destruction. Don't make another child pay—"

"Do it, Shelly. One step forward and a little push. It's just a kid."

Rachel nodded. She turned to face Jackie.

"Prison taught me one thing: without family, you're nothing. I know what it's like in there. Chris couldn't survive a single day." As she accepted the inevitable, her eyes seemed to soften. "And you're wrong. We do still need each other."

Instead of reaching for Lily, Rachel turned and lunged at her brother.

Startled, Chris hesitated a fraction of a second.

Locking him in an iron embrace and using all her weight, Rachel pushed him away from the girl. The back of his knees struck the granite barrier and he tried to use that to arrest his momentum. His heel caught and he reached behind him. There was nothing there.

Tightening her arms around her brother's chest, Rachel stared straight into his eyes. At that instant he seemed to stop struggling. He sagged in his sister's embrace and let her weight carry them both over the edge. His cry echoed through the gorge as they fell.

Jackie sank to the ground. Frozen in shock, Lily was still facing the abyss. Then she began to tremble.

"Don't look down, baby." Jackie crawled toward her, heedless of rough stone tearing open the scar on her knee. "Come to me."

"I ca-can't."

On hands and knees, Jackie pulled herself to the edge.

"Yes, you can. I'm right here."

"I'm scared. . . ."

"But you can do it. I won't let anything happen to you."

Slowly Jackie stood.

She reached past the stone barrier and Lily collapsed into her arms.

Sixty-Three

W hatever happened to those bees at your office?"
It was two weeks later and Dennis and Jackie were
at a bar in Cherry Creek.

"Still in the chimney, between the brick and the flue,"
she said. "Not even killing the queen works; when one
colony's destroyed another moves in. Instead of shrinking,
the hive's expanding."

"What're you going to do?"

"Seal off the fireplaces. If we light them, the honey
will melt in the walls and incinerate the building if it
catches fire. But summer will be over soon and they'll
hibernate. Speaking of which—"

"Growing your hair?" Reaching out, he hooked a
strand behind her ear.

"I started to say, Lily's shrink thinks she belongs in
public school. Not an institution."

"Praise the Lord and pass the margaritas!" Pilar slid
into the booth.

"Not so fast," Jackie said. "Britt and Randy just got the
strangest letter from Miss Sullivant's in Vermont. They're
begging Lily to come back." She turned to Dennis, who
was smiling into his Guinness. "But you wouldn't know
anything about that."

"We civil lawyers like our clients to have an array of
alternatives."

"Lotta good that did Chris Boyd," Pilar said. "Heard
the latest? Witness saw him and Trina on the Sixteenth
Street Mall just before she took that header off the D and
F Tower."

"I thought she was afraid of Simms," Dennis said. "Weren't they arguing at her motel?"

"About Chris. When Rachel got busted for the Sparks kid, Chris looked Trina up and bankrolled her trip to Denver. Said he wanted her to save his sister by swearing Rachel had nothing to do with Freddie Gant's death. Trina knew Rachel had been molested by her stepfather and she knew someone had been with Rachel at the grain elevator, but she thought it was George Boyd. She never realized it was Chris. She found that button when Rachel took her to see the body the next day but never told anyone. It was supposed to be her insurance policy, but she was in way over her head."

"How do you know all this?" Dennis said.

"Trina spilled it to Simms that last day at her motel. But she wanted to hold Chris up for more money, so she told Doby she could nail Rachel. My guess is Chris lured her to the tower by promising her money to get out of town. When she showed him the button it was all over. Instead of a ticket out of town, she got an express ride twenty flights down."

"Charming. And where was Simms when the APB went out?"

"Vivian. Trying to track down some old iron scrap a cop gave him years ago."

"Scrap?" So Mitchell found the clincher's handle in the debris where Freddie's body was left. No wonder Simms was in the bramble looking for the hook.

It was Jackie's turn to peer into her drink.

Pilar shrugged. "He suspected Chris ever since he interviewed Rachel in Cañon City. That 'we are never alone' bit. Followed her to Denver, even to the ice cream parlor with Ben."

"Why didn't she tell me?" Jackie said.

Dennis sighed. "For fear that if she pushed him, he'd implicate Chris."

The loyalty that carried them over the edge.

Jackie turned to Pilar. "Join us for dinner?"

"I've got a date. In fact, here he is now. . . ."

Lee Simms had entered the bar.

Pilar gave a low whistle and the newsman sauntered over.

"Gotta love a man with rocks in his jock. I told you he had an eye for the broads. What do I want with some old guy who's circling the drain?" Pilar gave Simms a lusty smooch, which he reciprocated with a healthy pinch on her butt. Leaning close to Jackie, she slipped something in her hand. "Finally rid of that slug."

"What's that about?" Dennis asked after they left.

Jackie stared at the mashed bullet her investigator had worn almost as long as she'd known her. "I have no idea."

"Well, I promise you one thing. The DA's price on your head just doubled. How many more times are you going to make him look bad?" He plunked some bills on the table.

"Not a business expense this time?" she said.

"You could make it worth my while."

"How about my place?"

"Why, Jackie—it's broad daylight! What about your chaperone?"

"I have a feeling she won't mind."

Sixty-Four

DENVER *POST*—AUGUST 1, 2004

By Staff Reporter Leland Simms

Denver District Attorney Duncan Pratt today announced the reassignment of veteran prosecutor Calvin Doby to Juvenile Division. When asked if the transfer had anything to do with the prosecution of Rachel Boyd, who heroically lost her life saving another child when she was about to go on trial for the murder of six-year-old Benjamin Sparks, Pratt insisted the two events were unrelated.

Reached at his new office, where he is one of a dozen rookie prosecutors, Doby said he welcomed the change.

"I've always enjoyed working with children. Aren't they our hope for the future?"

AUTHOR'S NOTE

Skyline Park in downtown Denver was revitalized in 2004.

If you want to know the true story of Tom Dooley, read *Lift Up Your Head, Tom Dooley,* by John Foster West (Down Home Press, 1993).

All the clues point to Pocket Books for a good read…

Hoax
Robert K. Tanenbaum
All the bling in the world can't help New York City DA Butch Karp solve the murder of a rising rap star…

Maximum Security
Rose Connors
Should an attorney ever defend her lover's ex?

Blood Hollow
William Kent Krueger
A beautiful high school student has been murdered, and it will take a miracle to find her killer.

Blood Knot
S.W. Hubbard
Tough love escalates to murder at a school for troubled teens.

The Man Burns Tonight
Donn Cortez
Wild pandemonium is traditional at Nevada's famous Burning Man festival. But this year there's murder on the Playa…

12911

Dying for a good book?
Bestselling mysteries from
Pocket Books

Last Lullaby
An Eve Diamond Novel
Denise Hamilton
Eve Diamond puts her own life on the line to protect an orphaned girl,
the target of smugglers who trade in human life.

Havana
An Earl Swagger Novel
Stephen Hunter
Cuba, 1953. It's just 30 minutes from the United States, but it's a whole
new world of gambling, sex, drugs—and murder.

Remembering Sarah
A Thriller
Chris Mooney
Mike Sullivan's daughter Sarah is missing—and the only key to finding
her alive may lie in uncovering his family's troubled past.

Blue Mercy
A Thriller
Illona Haus
After her partner's death, homicide detective Kay Delaney's
determination to track the killer is more than a need for revenge—
it's a fight for her life.

Cold Case Squad
Edna Buchanan
A desperate woman claims she's been seeing her husband everywhere—
the same husband she saw die in an explosion twelve years earlier.

Available wherever books are sold.

Bestselling murder and mayhem from Pocket Books.

The Frumious Bandersnatch
A Novel of the 87th Precinct
Ed McBain

When a rising rap star is kidnapped, can the detectives of the 87th Precinct find her before her star is extinguished forever?

Vespers
A Novel of the 87th Precinct
Ed McBain

It will take more than a leap of faith for the cops of the 87th Precinct to solve a priest's vicious murder.

Something's Down There
Mickey Spillane

You're not retired until you're dead.

The Mesa Conspiracy
A Department Thirty Novel
David Kent

A dying woman's last words reveal a secret with the power to shatter lives and change the course of the United States government.

Available wherever books are sold.

The mystery never ends.

The biggest names in crime fiction from Pocket Books.

DENISE HAMILTON
Sugar Skull
With murders marked by intricate
Sugar Skulls, the Mexican Day of the Dead celebration
takes on a horrifying new significance.

MICHAEL MCCLELLAND
Oyster Blues
Shell' em. Shuck' em. Shoot' em.

S.W. HUBBARD
Swallow the Hook
In a small Adirondacks town, a big-time scam can be lethal.

ETHAN BLACK
Dead for Life
A tragic mistake from the past holds the key
to stopping a killer bent on revenge.

ERIN HART
Haunted Ground
The truth never rests in peace…

M.G. KINCAID
Last Seen in Aberdeen
In a Scottish village, murder is just the beginning.

Wherever books are sold.

www.simonsays.com

10416